MW01126215

The Reluctant Cowboy

A love story

E. A. Garcia

This book is a work of fiction. With the exception of recognized historical figures, the characters in this novel are fictional. Any resemblance to actual persons, living or dead, is purely coincidental.

Second Edition, 2014

Cover Art: Margarita Garcia
Editing: Lee Porche
Print Formatting: Lynn Hubbard

ISBN-10: 1495223388
ISBN-13: 978-1495223389

Dedication

This novel is dedicated to Lee Smith.
Rest in peace, Lee,
and know that you were loved.

Acknowledgements

With gratitude to My Girls, Margarita and Amber Garcia, who read this tale first as a short story and liked it, but I wasn't satisfied. I lengthened it into a novella—still no. I wrote it this way and that and must have rewritten it ten times before I told the story I was trying to tell. They patiently read it every time and helped me get it right. Thank you for the millions of words you continue to read on my behalf and for the constant love and support that holds me steady.

My daughter Margarita also designed the cover for this novel. She spends countless hours on my various book projects and I can't thank her enough. She makes me proud. My editor, Lee Porche, went through the manuscript with a fine-toothed comb until we banished the typos and corrected things that were confusing. It was a joy working with her, too. Many thanks to all of you!

Thank you to my sisters and friends who believe in me and encourage me to "just keep writing." Several people read this novel in its various stages, and not only gave me their thoughts, but their love and encouragement. You know who you are. I could never do it without my First Readers.

I love Balmorhea, Texas. I needed a tiny town and chose that one, but that part of this tale could have happened anywhere and does.

With gratitude and much love to my readers,

Beth Garcia
West Texas
September, 2013

Prologue

Abilene, Texas; September, 2005

My pop stood across the arena squinting towards the chute where I waited to mount a snorting, fire-breathing beast. He leaned into the fence with his big hands draped over it. When the rider hit the dirt he frowned, and then his focus landed on me again. Behind Pop were stands for spectators, but he didn't sit. He had to be close enough to feel the ground tremble, smell the sweat of fear, taste the danger in the dusty air. Mostly, he needed to see that I was doing things right, and not just by-the-book right but exactly the way he taught me.

The announcer was tongue-tied excited, yelling the stats on a bull named Death Wish, and the next rider up, Tommy Franklin.

Tommy was already in the chute. He was jumpy, checking his gear, and half-listening to last-minute advice and encouragement from teammates. Cowboys didn't need to hear the announcer enthuse about past performances, because that didn't matter when it came to this bull and this ride. And it didn't help a rider to be reminded that the bull was bad-tempered and outweighed him by two thousand pounds.

Tommy was nineteen, three years older than I was. He'd broken bones, and his face was a roadmap of bumps and scars. He rarely smiled, even if he made a high score, because he took his three fake front teeth out before every ride so he wouldn't choke on them. Tommy had lost those teeth by being thrown from bulls before he was old enough to shave. It was a wonder I still had mine.

When the gate slammed open, Death Wish leapt out. Before three or four seconds passed, the bull twisted one way and Tommy sailed off the other. Clowns shooed the animal to the other side of the arena while Tommy shook his head, hauled himself upright, and glanced around for his pride. He jerked up his hat, smacked at dirt clinging to his pants, and staggered back to his team. For a few seconds, the announcer commiserated at the top of his lungs. After that, static-filled loudspeakers blasted country-western tunes into the next hemisphere.

I was next.

The ton of fury in the chute with me was named Ripcord. If I could stay on him even one second I would be the first. In five previous rodeos he had never tolerated a rider that long. I had already ridden two bulls that day and made it to the finals. I was favored to take the event, which meant zip, especially when I pulled Ripcord's number. Surviving any time on him would score extra points, with 'survive' being the key word. He was already hammering his humongous head into the bars, fuming and flinging snot.

My father scowled as I powdered the glove then tested the rope. I gave it a hard tug. His earlier words echoed in my thoughts: *Get the feel of it, Son. Don't let them open that chute until the feel of it in your hand is perfect, not too tight and not too loose.* I tugged again. I was ready.

Before I called for the chute, I glanced up. Dust was still suspended in the air between Pop and me, but beyond him and beyond the arena, beyond everything, the sky was a deep and cloudless Texas blue.

I sucked in a breath, nodded to the teammate standing at the chute, and it banged opened. Ripcord didn't rush out. Instead, he reared in slow motion then dropped his front legs with the force of an anvil. My teeth rattled. When I bounced but didn't bounce off, he lunged forward bucking savagely. His head plunged and his hind legs kicked high. I held tight to the rope with my right hand, my father's voice in my head. *Stay up on that rope, Jed. Hold on with your feet!*

The roar from the crowd was deafening. I clung on through the leaps and twists until the ground flew up at me, three seconds before the buzzer sounded eight. Clowns distracted Ripcord while I scrambled for safety, sweeping up my hat before I escaped over the fence. My head spun and pounded and made my eyes burn, but I had to get out of the way.

A good cowboy won't let himself get hurt, Jed.

Right, Pop.

"Jed Petersen, ladies and gentlemen," blasted from the loudspeaker. I tried to focus when I heard my name. "What a gutsy ride by this young man! He's just rode Ripcord, and he sure showed us how that's done! Let's hear it for Jed, rodeo fans!"

The crowd screamed and stomped.

I'd been riding bulls since I was eight. Pop grudgingly admitted I showed promise, but claimed I was too stubborn to ever become a rodeo star. I wanted to tell him I couldn't be a champion and not be stubborn. What does he think keeps a rider on a bull? But you can't tell my pop anything.

He moved to the staging area where his friend, Mark Jones, came up to him. "That boy of yours is headed to the national circuit one day, Jeremiah. He's a champ."

"He's just lucky," my pop sneered. "You pull a good bull, and that's most of your score right there."

"Yeah, well, he stays on. That's the rest of it."

Three other young riders came up to me before Pop noticed I was there. They were teammates and friends, but sometimes didn't act like it.

"You got your new jeans dirty, Little Cowboy," Leroy taunted.

I swatted at the clinging dust. "Shut up! I stayed on that bull, didn't I?"

"Yeah, how'd ya do that?" Ray Bob wondered.

"I just stay on, that's all."

"Bullshit! You do somethin' to them bulls," insisted Leroy.

"He enchants them with his big blue eyes." Joe Neal batted his lashes.

"You're so little they don't notice you back there." Tony kicked at the dirt and watched dust swirl to avoid looking me in the eyes.

I shrugged and walked away. They could make fun all they wanted but I could stay on a bull. I had most likely won the event, and they hadn't come close.

"Hey, Jed." Connie Winston, a barrel rider my age, came up and hugged me. "That was some ride."

"Thanks, Connie."

"Are you goin' to the dance?"

"Prob'ly not, but I'm gonna ask."

"Good. I'll see you there if you get to go. I hope you do."

I wanted to say more, but my father blustered towards us. He took a dim view of talking to girls and everything else I wanted to do.

"Will you let me go to the dance, Pop?"

"No dancin', Jed; you know that. Dancin' is for the devil. Let's see what your score is, then we'll head home."

An old Willie tune, *Hello Walls,* was interrupted to announce noisily that Jed Petersen had won the event and five hundred dollars.

I showed the check to my father. "I really want to go to the dance. Everybody goes to the dance afterward."

"Not everybody, Jed. You ain't goin'."

"But I'm sixteen. And I won."

"One more word and you won't be eatin' supper, either."

That's how things went with my pop.

* * *

Midland, Texas; September, 2005

"Look at Jed Petersen on Big Trouble! He hasn't made a mistake yet today! Look at that boy ride! Folks, you're watchin' a winner!"

When the eight second buzzer sounded, I slid off the bull and landed on my feet. The announcer practically wet himself, but he could barely be heard above the thunder of the crowd. I bowed in their direction and threw my hat in the air.

I walked over to where my friends were congregated. A bunch of girls crowded around, talking all at once.

"We were just sayin'," Leroy said loudly, "how

you can't be a nice guy and a cowboy at the same time. Ain't that right Jed?"

"I never heard that."

"Well these girls were sayin' you was a gentleman and we said ain't no way that could be Jed. Bull riders are the worst."

"Don't listen to them," I told the girls. "They don't actually ride bulls. They spend more time on their butts in the dirt."

Everyone laughed at that.

My best friend Ron came up and I walked away with him to where the food and soft drinks were sold. Ron was a football player, not a rodeo man.

"You want a soda, Jed?"

"Sure. Thanks."

After he bought the drinks, we sat at a peeling red picnic table. "You scare me, Jed, riding those mean bulls."

I laughed. "I'm not afraid of them."

"Yeah, that's what scares me."

"It's no worse than bein' a linebacker."

He sighed. "We're both crazy, I guess." He was going to say more, but a group of girls came up and joined us.

"Are y'all comin' to the dance?"

"I can't go. My pop believes dancin' is a sin."

She shrugged. "Yeah, our church says that too. We just ignore it."

I wished my father would ignore one single thing our church said.

Ron told them his parents wouldn't let him go either for the same reason. Then he stood and said he had to leave. I hated that, since I rarely saw him anymore.

"I'll see you, Ron."

Francie sat next to me. "I wish you could come to the dance, Jed." She was the best of the barrel racers competing that day.

"Yeah, me too."

When Francie walked off, my buddies came up and sat at the table, their faces blank. I knew they were up to something.

"She's really aggravated with you, Jed."

"Oh yeah? Why's that?"

"She says you stay on her for eight seconds, jump off, and throw your hat in the air."

I laughed, but Francie didn't interest me.

* * *

San Angelo, Texas; September, 2005

"Look at that little Fort Stockton cowboy go!

We were at a bigger rodeo with larger stakes. The bull riding purse was one thousand dollars, a trophy, and a paid entry to the Amarillo Fall Rodeo.

I jumped sideways off the bull, scrambled towards the fence, and threw my hat into the air. I was pretty sure I'd just won.

A few moments later my score was announced. "Ninety-four points! He's got hisself a *ninety-four* point ride!" Ninety is considered excellent.

"Not bad, Jed." My friend Leroy met me as I stumbled out of the arena. "You're a risin' star, goin' up as fast and hard as a dick at a lap dance."

I laughed, but I was thinking how ninety-four points was great; I didn't care what my pop thought. That was damn good ridin' by the "little Fort Stockton cowboy." I still wouldn't get to go to the dance. Even if I scored one hundred it wouldn't be enough for my pop.

In the truck he started in on my hair. It wasn't that long, but it curled and made Pop crazy. He thought I looked like a girl.

"Cut it or I'll shave it off."

"I'm getting too old for that. There're no bull riders with shaved heads."

"You think that'll stop me?"

I knew it wouldn't.

"You're feelin' pretty proud of yourself, aren't you, Jed?"

"Well, yes sir, I won. I'm goin' to Amarillo!"

"Don't get a swollen-up head about it."

"I won't."

"Nobody likes a hot shot."

* * *

Del Rio, Texas; September, 2005

"He's taking the kind of ride that paychecks are made of!" yelled the announcer. Hey buckaroos! He's gettin' money time today! Look at him go!"

I took first place and won two thousand dollars.

"Come on, Pop. I did it again. Could I just go to the dance for half an hour?"

"What ya wanna go to a dance for? Some girl will just rub her titties up against you until you're half crazy. The next thing you know she'll be pregnant and you'll have to marry her and give up bull riding and get a shit-for-pay factory job."

My pop always made everything sound so romantic.

* * *

Amarillo, Texas; October, 2005.

I was in the chute on Rough Ride. He was furious, snorting and slamming his weight from side to side.

"Get a good hold, Jed," Leroy reminded me. "He's gonna come out blowin' hard."

When I gave the nod, Leroy screamed, "Let's go, boys!" and the chute slammed open. The bull went crazy.

Hold on, hold on. Eight seconds seems like forever on the back of a bull.

"Jed Petersen is the one to watch, folks. Look at the beating that boy is taking. Now this is bull riding, sports fans! The Fort Stockton cowboy makes it look easy. Watch for this young man on the national circuit next year!"

I didn't always do so well. I'd eaten arena dirt by the mouthful, or landed so hard on my butt I couldn't feel it for hours. My face had been busted open, scraped clean of flesh, and turned black and blue. I hadn't broken any bones, but as long as I was ridin' bulls, that was comin'. Sometimes I dreamed I jumped off a bull and my body just busted apart, exactly the way they do in cartoons.

On the Texas circuit, it was understood that I would be the next national bull riding champion from our state. Fans hounded me. Pop made me practice until I wanted to cry. One day I was ridin' high, flingin' my hat in the air, and the next thing I knew I was on my butt in the dirt. It wasn't a bull that threw me but my own father, who's a lot meaner.

It was about a week after the 2005 Amarillo fall

rodeo, but for you to understand how it happened, I have to take you back a couple of years.

CHAPTER 1

The day was bright, so dazzling it hurt. And hot for August, even in west Texas.

I was fourteen.

The lake was spring-fed with a smooth, sandy bottom, and stars skittering on the surface. I can still feel that water, cold against hot skin. It smelled slightly of the fish that darted in reeds near the bank and the slow, carefree days of summer.

To this day, that lake keeps a secret.

It was Saturday and there was a picnic with my folks and my best friend Ron's family. His parents and mine were close and attended the same church.

A wooden dock floated within easy swimming distance of the bank. My older sisters had escaped Ft. Stockton by marrying, so it was just Ron, his two sisters, and me horsing around out there.

I scrambled out of the water, dripping diamonds onto the slippery boards. The platform stood only two feet higher than the lake, but it felt like I was on top of the world. There would be no bull riding lessons this weekend. No rodeo, either.

"Yeeha!" I shouted and flung an imaginary hat towards the sun.

Behind me, Ron looked up and laughed. He'd been lying on his stomach with his sisters, peering through the slats, looking for fish.

"I saw a mermaid," Rhonda claimed.

"Did not!" squealed Carla.

Ron flashed a megawatt smile and returned his face to the slats. "You're wrong, Carla. I see them, too,

mermaids making mud pies." Both girls collapsed in giggles.

They called us in for lunch: crunchy fried chicken, pickle-speckled potato salad, sweet iced tea so cold it hurt our teeth, and for dessert, brownies.

After eating, our parents made us wait to go back in the water. Since my pop had time on his hands, he started in on me. Being a large man, it chapped him that I was small.

He rooted around in his arsenal of touchy subjects and brought out the touchiest one. "How tall are you now, Jed?"

I hated him for trying to ruin a perfect day.

"Jed!" he bellowed when I didn't answer or even look up. "Don't pretend you didn't hear me."

"I'm five-five." My voice was barely above a whisper.

"What's that? Speak up."

"Five feet, five inches." I upped the volume to overly loud. "Let's go, Ron."

Pop held up his hands. "Hold on there, boys."

"Honey," my mother warned in spite of the fact that he would smack her if her next words didn't suit him.

"You look even smaller standing next to Ron."

"Ron is fifteen."

"Ron looks like a man. You look like a girl."

"Ron is fifteen," I repeated stubbornly.

"Don't get smart with me, Boy."

"I'm tough Pop." I flexed my arms, unable to keep my body still or my mouth shut. "I'm a bull rider. Look at me. This is not the body of a girl."

Instead of hitting me, which would've been less painful, he turned to Ron, aiming to drag him into it. "How tall are you, Ron?"

My friend didn't want to be dragged into anything that would hurt me. He looked from me to my father and shrugged. "I don't know."

"Of course you do."

"I'm a hair under six feet," Ron admitted, his eyes downcast.

I hated for Ron to be ashamed of something that

I knew gave him pride. And I hated my pop double for causing him shame.

Meanwhile Pop circled in for the kill. "Don't you think a boy fourteen would look a lot less like a girl by now?"

Ron looked right at him, eyes blazing. "Jed doesn't look like a girl, Mr. Petersen. Girls chase him all the time."

Pop's eyes narrowed. "Is that so?"

Then Ron's mom picked up the gauntlet. "Jed is already so handsome I imagine the girls are falling at his feet."

"Well, I say Jed has girlie eyes." Pop couldn't let it go.

"He has beautiful eyes," countered Ron.

"Yes, he does," dared my mom.

Rhonda was not about to be left out. "He looks like a movie star."

"Yeah," chirped Carla, "he really does. We like 'im!"

I smiled at them.

"Girly eyes, looks like he's wearing mascara."

"Come on, Pop."

"Please, Honey," my mom laid her plea on top of mine.

"Your curly hair's hanging in your girly eyes, Jed." Pop was happiest when he was making life miserable for somebody.

Ron tried to defend me. "Girls swoon over Jed. You should hear what they say—"

"Bullshit," growled Pop. He looked like he was about to blow.

"What about bull riding, Pop? Girls don't ride bulls."

"Yeah," Ron agreed.

Ron's father stepped in to break the stand-off. "Run on and play now, boys."

Ron crooked his arm around my neck and yanked me from the combat zone before I was permanently maimed. We wandered off, past other picnic shelters, examining bugs, and talking about his band, bull riding, football, and horses. When I looked

back, the others were spreading towels under the trees. By the time an hour had passed, everyone had fallen asleep except Ron and me.

We chased each other back into the lake, *last one there is a rotten egg*. I arrived seconds before he did and bounced on the floating dock like a flea, re-soaking the slatted boards. When Ron gripped the ladder to come onboard with me, I reached out my hand to help him up. He grabbed it, but because the boards were slick I had no footing, and his weight dragged me back in. I crashed onto him and we wrestled, laughing and swallowing water; then we just bobbed there behind the floating dock looking at each other.

Ron took my arm gently, pulled me to him. His lips were chilled from the water and tasted like the lake.

On land our families stirred. The laughter of little girls skipped across the water, but that didn't stop us from kissing again.

"Jed," Ron whispered hoarsely, and his hand burned a path from my neck to my stomach.

I gasped.

Our families splashed towards us.

"What's the matter with you?" my father demanded to know.

"Nothin'," I said, furious, desperately aroused, and positive I was going to Hell.

"Did you have a disagreement?" My mother had never seen us so far apart in the lake or so quiet.

Ron came up behind us. "Everything is great. Isn't it, Buckaroo?" He crooked an arm around my neck and dragged me underwater before I could tell them different.

After that there was no touching or kissing. School started and I barely saw Ron. He was on our school's football team and I went to most of his games. He came to most of my rodeos, but we were estranged by the kissing as surely as we were drawn to each other.

* * *

One Sunday after an especially rousing sermon on the sin of homosexuality, Ron and I sat together awkwardly on a bench in the church garden while our

parents mingled with other narrow-minded people.

"Something is wrong with me, Jed, desperate wrong," Ron whispered.

"Are you sick?"

"Yes, to hear the preacher tell it."

"Ron, he wasn't talking about you."

"The hell he wasn't."

"What we did wasn't homosexual."

Thinking of what we did still caused unbearable desire and such conflicting feelings that my insides twisted. Still, I thought about it.

"It was, Jed. You need to grow up. I'm a pervert and you should keep away."

"You're no pervert!"

"Shh." He slid a hair closer.

There was a prolonged silence. Ron stared into space thinking who-knows-what. I thought about the kisses in the lake. If he was a pervert, so was I.

Ron's voice brought me back. "Don't be dense, I *am* a homo."

No way. The preacher said homosexuals were vile, perverted, living sinful lives that insulted God. They were dark and dirty, nothing like Ron.

"You're practically a brother to me. How will I stay away from you, Ron?"

"I don't know, but you better do it." He took a deep breath and swiped his palms against his denim-covered thighs. "I think about you, Jed," he whispered. "All the time—and not like a brother."

"Me, too," I whispered back. "I can't stop thinking about that day in the la—"

"You'd better stop thinking about that."

"I don't want to stop."

"You want to burn in Hell?"

"Do you really believe God puts people in Hell for loving?"

Ron's expression was grim. "He puts them in for having sex."

"Then everyone is going."

"You heard what the preacher said, Jed. You'd better get a girlfriend and promise God you won't ever touch another boy."

"Is that what you're going to do?"

"Hell, yes. That's what I'm going to do."

Neither one of us did either thing, but we stayed away from each other.

One day at school a group of gawking girls blurted that I had the *dreamiest* eyes. I kept telling myself that what happened between Ron and me was a fluke caused by raging hormones until I began to believe it. Almost.

I was busy with school, chores, unending bull riding practice, and rodeo. Illicit thoughts tugged at me, desires I hadn't acknowledged until that day in the lake. I wanted Ron to take it back but at the same time, I didn't.

* * *

Then came the late October day when Pop found out my secret. I was sixteen, Ron seventeen.

A brutal summer had given way to a cool fall. Ron and I were spending a rare afternoon together. We had lunch at my house then rode a couple of horses from our ranch to a nearby butte where the wind was the only sound, and Ft. Stockton seemed far away.

Ron barely talked. I was usually the quieter one, but I chattered about bull riding and other bullshit, nervous that he would touch me and frantic for him to do it. I was out of breath from looking at him and trying not to.

Ron has a dimple in his chin, shiny blond hair, brown eyes, and a tall, muscular body. There is a slender quarter-moon scar on one cheek from a football injury and it glows when he blushes. I had never paid so much attention to how he looked, and it was aggravating.

We never even got down from the horses.

On the way back we dawdled through a little copse of trees behind our horse barn. I struggled to make sense of the intensity of whatever it was between Ron and me, but it was like trying to look at the sun.

He pulled his horse close to mine. "Jed." When I turned, he leaned over and kissed me with such force it nearly knocked me off the saddle. A chute banged open inside me, and two years worth of lust and lonesomeness leaped out.

After a few minutes of desperate kissing, I crawled over to his horse and jammed myself into the saddle facing him.

"Oh, Jed."

I wanted to say something, but his lips stole my words. His hands crept under my jacket and pressed me to him until a sheet of paper wouldn't have fit between us.

That was when my pop showed up.

"Boys!" Pop opened his mouth and snapped it shut as if it was too awful for words. His face turned red and his eyes bugged. I thought he was having a stroke.

"Get the hell off my property," Pop growled at Ron, and he jumped down and ran. I couldn't get away because of Pop's vise-like grip on my arm. He dragged me from the saddle into the barn and beat me with his belt.

That was bad, but then came worse. "I want you out of here by tomorrow," he growled. His face was splotchy and scrunched-up with fury.

"But Pop—"

"Don't back talk me, Boy."

I tried to stay quiet.

"In good conscience I can't abide a homosexual under my roof. Man lying with man goes against God."

"But I'm your son and I'm not a—"

"Don't lie to me." He slapped me hard.

My horse, Indio, had followed me into the barn like an overgrown puppy. He tried to get between us. For that he got a vicious swat with the belt and cried out pitifully.

"Don't hit him," I screamed. "Beat me to death if you want, but don't hurt Indio."

"Don't you raise your voice to me, you little pervert."

I turned away from Pop to put Indio in his stall. While I had my back to him, he attacked me. The belt whipped around my neck and busted my cheek open. Blood spurted all over. Indio whimpered.

"You walk away from me again," Pop growled, "and it might be your last walk."

I didn't say a word. If I said what was on my mind he would try to kill me. If he did that, I'd have to defend myself. He was bigger, but I was younger and in better physical condition. Sometimes I wanted so bad to hurt him I could hardly stop myself, but he was my father.

He stormed off to the other side of the barn and began whaling on a stack of hay bales. I got the message and busied myself unsaddling Indio and putting tack away. If he ever beat me or my horse like he whipped that hay I would have to kill him.

After a while we both calmed down, and Pop came back. "I wish there was something I could do to make you understand, Jed."

"I don't see what the big deal is. It was only kissing."

"Boys kiss girls, not other boys."

Again, I tried to stay quiet.

"If I hadn't caught you, what would you two have done?"

That was a question I couldn't answer, but my silence condemned me.

"I knew no good could come of a boy who's pretty as a girl." He stepped back, as if I was contagious. That hurt worse than the belt.

Chapter 2

My mother freaked out when she saw all the blood and insisted I lie down with an ice bag on my face. She didn't say much because she'd learned not to rile Pop. I had given up hope with him. I was too pretty for a boy, end of story.

I didn't get supper that night, which was worse than being beaten. I could smell it cooking, and then heard them at the table. To get my mind off food, I started packing. I didn't see how I could take more than one suitcase which meant leaving my books and trophies and all the bull riding gear I had won.

Bull riding is not gay. I couldn't be gay. I was tough. I didn't want to be gay.

* * *

I had just changed into pajamas when my parents came into my room without knocking. My mother had been crying. My father seemed unnaturally calm but wouldn't look at me.

"I changed my mind."

That was so unlike him I nearly bolted.

"I don't want to send you away. I don't see how you could make it on your own."

My dream father would've hugged me and told me he was sorry, and that he loved me no matter who I kissed. But my real father cleared his throat. "Your mother and I are going to get you some help."

"Help for what?"

"Your homosexual tendencies."

My mother spoke not a word, but the look on her

face said this "help" would be seriously bad news for me.

"What are you talking about, Pop?"

"You're young and you can still be turned from the path of sin and degradation, Jed. If we start now, you can be changed."

"Are you talking about sending me to a psychiatrist or what?"

"It's more like a special school."

"So you're still sending me away?"

"Only for a few months." My mother jumped in, but she backed up my father as usual. She had gotten over defending me.

"There's nothin' wrong with me. What if I don't want to go?"

"Jed, it's a nice place." My father sat down at my desk. I had a real bad sinking feeling. "They even have horses."

It was double-bad if he thought he could still use my love of horses to lure me into something I didn't want to do. He'd been doing that since I was five.

"I have horses here."

"Please be reasonable, honey," my mother begged.

"I don't want to go to some mental institution."

"For the love of God, it's not anything like that." My father had already lost it with me. "You're going to go and that's the end of it."

"But Pop, I'm not homosexual."

He took a deep breath and let it out slowly. "You were kissing a boy. What would you call it?"

I wanted to say, "It was wonderful, you can't begin to understand, and nothing you or anyone else does to me will ever change my opinion about it, but instead, I lied. "It was a mistake, Pop, just one mistake."

"When I was your age I would have killed a boy who tried to kiss me."

"But it was *Ron.*"

"Well you're not going to speak to that pervert ever again."

"Okay, Pop."

"Are we clear on that?"

"Yes sir. Can I stay if I promise never to see Ron again?"

My mother brightened but looked to my father.

"I'll think about it tonight, and we'll talk tomorrow afternoon after you get home from school."

"You need my help around here, Pop, and what about bull riding?"

"Can you understand how being a homosexual will jeopardize everything you care about, Jed?"

"Yes sir."

"Well, you think on it and we'll talk tomorrow. It's late. Go to sleep." He turned out my light and shut the door.

Yeah, I love you, too.

* * *

I went to classes the next day as if it wasn't the last day of life as I knew it. When Ron and I passed in the hall, he pinned me with his eyes, then blushed and kept walking. I had to stop at the lockers to catch my breath.

I didn't see Ron again until the lunch break.

"He beat you up, didn't he?" Ron's hand came towards my face, but lowered again when he remembered where we were.

"My father wants to send me away for therapy, Ron."

He practically yanked me out of the cafeteria. We stood across the walkway from the double doors and tried to look casual.

"Have you told anyone?"

"Only you."

"Well, don't talk about it, okay?" Ron scanned our surroundings as if secret police lurked on campus. "It's better if nobody knows."

"Well, other kids might notice if I'm never seen again."

"That's not funny. Will your father tell people about us?"

"I don't know. I think he's too ashamed."

"Do you think he'll tell my dad?"

"I don't know, Ron. Maybe you should tell him

first."

"Jesus." He collapsed against the wall, hands jammed into jacket pockets. "I'm going to get thrown off the team."

"What about me? This isn't only about you. Pop doesn't want me to talk to you."

"Will you keep it down?" His voice was harsh, but his eyes were soft and full of the feelings that had led to this trouble. "I'm sorry. You know they aren't going to send you anywhere."

"Yes he will. He thinks I'm—" I hesitated to use the word. "He thinks you-know-what is the worst thing a person can be. He's never going to let up on me."

Ron glanced around and leaned towards me slightly. "Don't get all Patsy Cline on me, Jed, not at school." It was his way of saying I was being too emotional. Ron was crazy about Patsy and her heartrending songs, but he wouldn't have admitted it to the guys in school for anything in this world.

"Screw you, Ron." I walked away with my fists clenched.

* * *

At the end of last period our teacher, Mrs. Hume, stood in front of the room to make an announcement. "Jedediah, you're wanted in the front office."

My full name always caused a stir. When I complained about it, my father said it was a fine Biblical name, and I should be proud of it. It had been given to Solomon by God and means "beloved by Jehovah." To me it means fistfights and bloody noses.

My father was waiting in the office. Everyone there was so quiet and stared at me so hard I knew he had told them.

"Come in, Jed." Our principal, Mrs. Collins, invited me to have a seat.

I sat.

She studied me. "Jed, what happened to your face?"

"It was a bull riding accident," my father was quick to explain.

She turned to me. "Jed?"

"Yes ma'am, it's what he says."

She looked doubtful but changed the subject. "I've been trying to talk your father out of removing you from our school, but he's determined."

"Isn't there a law that I have to go to school?"

"Yes, but he's talking about a private alternative high school."

I turned to Pop. "We were going to talk about it."

"You're too young to make these kinds of decisions, Jed. I've made up my mind. One day you'll thank me for it."

* * *

When we got home, my mother was quiet and had been crying again. My father handed me a packing list of things I needed, which was next to nothing. The school provided nearly everything. They didn't allow preferred brands of cologne, aftershave, or deodorant—or even toothpaste or shampoo. There was no explanation; they just didn't allow it, and bags would be searched.

The school was called The Sunflower Project, with a logo so cheerfully bright and clean that it was as ominous as black clouds.

All underwear had to be white. I read that part over and over. Did they think colored skivvies caused boys' minds to wander; that we wouldn't have to waste most of a class period wondering what color the boy next to us was wearing? It would be white. Only. These people needed to get a clue. If I was going to think about the boy next to me, his underwear would never enter the picture.

* * *

I was packed and might have gone without much protest except for how falsely cheerful my parents were at supper. My mother was a half-breath from crying and I knew it. It put the fear of God into me.

They spent most of supper talking as if nothing was happening. About what, I couldn't say because I was planning complicated escapes from a place that, in my head, looked less appealing than Alcatraz.

After dinner my father said, "Turn in early, Jed. Tomorrow will be a long day."

"Please don't make me go, Pop. I swear I won't

kiss a boy again." It was hard to make that sound sincere when kissing a boy was all I could think about.

"Jed, you're going. You need help."

"Why do you want to change me?"

"I don't want to change you, except for the sinful part of you that would kiss a boy. Now go to bed."

I headed up the stairs, thinking that the sinful part of me that would kiss a boy was something I was going to hold onto no matter if they killed me.

* * *

I was lying in bed, staring at the ceiling, wondering how to get out of going. It was nearly midnight and cold. Suddenly there was a tap on my window. I jumped straight up to see Ron teetering on a ledge out there.

I opened the window and a blast of cold air came in along with my best friend. My anger towards him evaporated.

"How'd you get out there?" I whispered. "You're gonna kill yourself."

"I climbed over here from the stairs. Damn, it's cold."

"If Pop catches us we're dead."

"Shh, we're going to get out of here."

"But Ron—"

"Do you trust me, Jed?"

"Hell yes, I do."

"Pack some clothes and let's go. And dress warm. It's freezing."

My clothes were packed, except I added my best chaps, a few western shirts, and crammed in every piece of colorful underwear I owned. I also took "The Encyclopedia of Horses," my most treasured possession.

Ron and I crept out like a couple of bandidos and then ran like the devil was after us until we reached his truck.

We were headed away from my old life before Ron spoke. "Listen, I came for you because tomorrow your father is taking you to The Sunflower Project in Kansas."

"Kansas?"

"Yes, Toto, Kansas. Your old man came to see mine this afternoon."

"Did he tell him that he caught you and me—"

"He never mentioned me, but he told my parents he had proof that you're homosexual and he wants to turn that around before—before you become—uh—sexually active. Brother Herb told him about this place." Brother Herb was the preacher at our church.

"That's the best reason I can think of not to go there."

"No shit. Even my dad says it's a bad deal. They use electroconvulsive therapy to change your thinking, for one thing, and drugs for another, and a shitload of praying. Worse for you would be that they withhold food if you don't cooperate."

I groaned. "My father does that, too."

"You don't mean he shocks you?"

"No, he uses his fists and belt. I meant withholding food."

"Don't worry, I brought some."

"You brought food? That's great."

"I figured you'd be hungry. Dad said they've proved that no amount of therapy changes being homosexual. It's something you're born with. "

"So it's a birth defect."

"I would say it's a gift." He grinned. "But that's just my opinion, Buckaroo."

"Yeah, well... Where are we going, Ron?"

There was an ice-filled fog slinking through town and the heater in the truck was barely keeping the cold from freezing our feet solid.

"We're going to the Hilton, where else?"

He pulled into an abandoned gas station on a lonely stretch of road near town. "Sorry, this is the best I could do on short notice. Get out with your suitcase. I'm going to stash the truck up the road."

The station hadn't been open in so long I didn't remember it ever being open. A cracked plastic sign with a faded winged horse hung lopsidedly, held up by one rusty bolt. Dead wires dangled out of the back and clink-clacked in the cold wind.

It wasn't warm inside, either. Ron had swept a

pile of filth into a far corner. It had once been a party place, judging by the litter of bottles, beer cans, and condoms. If the weather had been warm it probably would've stank.

On the service counter were sleeping bags, blankets, and a couple of paper bags holding food. I grinned at Ron's Boy Scout preparedness.

The windows were mostly boarded, but in one place the plywood was ripped away, and I watched the fog dim the streetlights. Wind moaned through what was left of the eaves and tried to force itself in through the cracked windows.

I replaced blue jeans with long johns, two pairs of sweatpants, and then put on a sweatshirt and my jacket. I was lumpier than the doughboy but warm. I sat up on the counter to wait for my friend.

"Nice place you got here, Ron," I said, greeting him when he came in.

He shrugged. "You want me to take you back home?"

"Heck, no." I threw myself off the counter but stumbled.

He laughed and grabbed me by the shoulders. "Whoa there, Fat Boy. You think you got on enough clothes?"

"It's damn cold."

"Wanna eat or complain?"

That was no-contest. We sat on the edge of the counter and took turns eating steaming potato soup out of a thermos. It was so warm and tasty I forgot I was supposed to go to Kansas in white underwear to receive shock therapy.

Ron had also brought thick ham and cheese sandwiches, cookies, and even hot chocolate. There was no way I could eat all that, but I put a big dent in it.

"Go ahead, Jed, finish it. I already ate supper."

"I had supper, too, but it's been a long time since then, and yesterday they didn't let me eat any supper."

While I ate, Ron leaned against me and popped salted cashews into his mouth.

I wiped my face when I finished. "That was great, Ron. Thanks."

He jumped off the counter and swiped his palms down the sides of his jeans. He grinned when he saw me watching. "Salt."

"So," I said, and the moon on Ron's face rose and glowed.

In less than a second we were all over each other. Nobody showed up to stop us.

* * *

Later we were lying on top of a thick sleeping bag, with another one over us. I was so warm I might've been glowing. The icy fog seemed far away along with reality. Ron's arms were wound around me.

"What are you going to do?" he asked.

"About?"

"About your dad and a place to live, and a job."

"So this is as far as your plan goes?"

"Well, yeah, I just knew I couldn't let you go to that torture school. I bet kids come out of there slobberin' crazy."

The thought of it made me sick.

"I forgot to mention the ice baths. My dad says they put 'em in ice to calm their homosexual tendencies."

"Well, maybe that would cool us off."

He laughed. "Do you want to be cooled off?"

"No, I don't, and it isn't funny to be treated that way because you're different."

"I know it, Jed. That's why I came for you. I wish I could take you to my house to live, but you know why that's a bad idea."

"Yeah, it wouldn't take fifteen minutes for your parents to bust us—if they even let me in the door."

"If anybody at school figures out I'm gay they'll crucify me."

"You'll be thrown out of church." I don't know why I said that; it didn't matter to either of us.

"So? According to them I'm going to Hell anyway."

"That was a stupid thing to say. Anyhow, I don't believe anyone goes to Hell over loving someone."

"You don't?"

"Hell, no!" We laughed at that.

"I brought you some money because I figured you wouldn't have any."

"Thank you, Ron. I'll pay you back."

"Forget that, Jed. It's not much." He sighed. "I wish I could go away with you."

"I wish you could, too."

"I can't do that to my parents. I think if I told them the truth, they wouldn't hate me or send me away."

"Yeah, you have pretty good parents."

"I'm sorry you don't, Jed."

We began to kiss and touch again. In the back of my mind I could hear my pop ranting about eternal damnation, but for a sixteen-year-old, the threat of Hell can't compete with the promise of orgasm.

* * *

We got up later to finish off the rest of the food. We ate and laughed and didn't think about dawn or what it would bring.

"I'm going to have to leave here in the morning," I finally said.

"I figured you'd have to go."

"I guess I'll go to the Interstate, get a ride, and stop someplace and find a job."

"I wish you didn't have to do that. You won't know anybody."

"I know, but I don't have a choice, Ron. My pop will be looking for me, and it's a law I have to be in school. If I go to work here, he'll find me and send me away. I hate him for wanting to send me to that place."

"It seems sick to put a bunch of homos together and expect them to get over it. Wouldn't that make it worse?"

We climbed back onto the counter and lay down as if we always slept like that.

"I'm going to miss you," he whispered into my hair.

"I'll miss you too, Ron."

"I don't know if I can survive here without you."

"I can't stay. You understand that, don't you? My pop hates me, and I have to earn a living, and I never want to go to that Kansas place."

"Yeah, I know."

"What kind of father would send his son away to be hurt?"

"Not a good one," Ron said.

* * *

When I woke, traffic was moving on the highway. Ron was sitting on an overturned bucket, putting on his shoes and socks.

"I hope you won't have regrets about what we did." He said it without looking up.

"I don't, Ron. Do you?"

"No, I sure as hell don't."

"Are you going to school?"

"Yeah; I guess so."

I could hear sleet pinging against the windows. The day looked dim and dreary through the patch of uncovered glass.

"I wish you wouldn't go yet."

He looked up at me with a tender expression, and his eyes shone. Without taking them off mine, he rose slowly and came and stood beside me. He pulled my head against his stomach and we stayed like that a while, with his hands in my hair. There didn't seem to be any words worth saying.

Ron finally took off his hat, coat, and pants, and laid them at the end of the counter. Then he took out his cell phone and punched in a number.

"Mom? I left early for school because I have a hard test today." His face flushed with the lie and the scar on his cheek glowed.

"I packed a lunch. Thanks, Mom. I'll see you later." To me he said, "I hate lying." He came back, climbed up next to me, and dropped his shoes and socks to the floor.

"Thank you for coming for me, Ron."

"It was purely selfish, Jed."

"How so?"

"I don't want you to go to Kansas and get your brain rewired. Hell, their treatment might work, and where would I be then?"

We burst out laughing. It reminded me of when we were kids and spent nights together at my house or

his. We could never sleep for laughing, and either his father or mine would have to come settle us down.

Chapter 3

It was noon before we parted. I walked back towards town to a convenience store and spent over ten dollars trying to fill my stomach.

The sleet had turned to dismal rain. I stood inside the well-lit building watching the water running along the curb and thinking of Ron. It hadn't been thirty minutes since we said good-bye, and I already missed him.

A rancher I knew, Will Bradley, came in for coffee. We talked a while and I caught a ride with him to Interstate 10.

"Where are you going?" he asked, "and why aren't you in school?"

"I'm heading out." I didn't want to explain.

He studied my injured face. "Did you have a row with your father?"

"He threw me out."

"I reckon he'd take you back."

"I reckon he won't."

"I can take you as far as Balmorhea. I sure don't want to put you out by the side of the road in this weather."

"That'd be great." I had never been to Balmorhea, but as long as it wasn't Fort Stockton, I was into it. "Is it far?"

"It's about fifty-odd miles from here. 'Course I don't know what a boy alone will do." He sipped his coffee and peered through the windshield at the incessant rain.

I watched the road too, but my thoughts were

aggravating. I got goose bumps from the nature of them, but I couldn't get my head to quit.

There were mountains in the distance, only partly visible in the clouds. I wondered if Balmorhea was near them and liked the thought of living in a place with mountains. In Fort Stockton we had buttes and bumps, but nothing you could call a mountain even if you stretched your imagination all the way to where the land meets the sky.

"You did fine in that regional rodeo, Jed," said Mr. Bradley. "You made us proud."

"Thank you, sir."

"Most grown men can't ride bulls like you do."

"I've been ridin' all my life, seems like."

It had been my pop's dream to be a rodeo champion, but he hadn't made a go of it. I never heard the reason but if I had to guess, I'd say it was his attitude, especially his attitude towards animals. Bulls are athletes too, and deserve respect. They try as hard to buck us off as we try to stay on. If they didn't there would be no point to riding them. A cowboy without respect for animals is a sorry sort.

Mr. Bradley clicked on the radio. Garth Brooks was singing an old one, *The Thunder Rolls*, and his song about rain made me think of the sleet pinging against the front windows of that old gas station, which in my memory had already become a warm and golden place.

Hearing Garth made me think of Ron's exceptional voice. He could sing Garth Brooks better than Garth. Even when we were little he'd had the most amazing voice. He would stand on a stump in the copse of trees where we'd gotten ourselves busted and sing to whoever would listen or sing even if nobody listened, because singing was in his heart. Sometimes I sang with him, before I was old enough to be self-conscious about how bad I sounded.

"That was a good one," commented Mr. Bradley on Garth's big number one hit. "Who could forget it?"

"Yes sir," I agreed, but I was thinking of something entirely different.

* * *

"I like that big hat," Mr. Bradley said.

"Thanks. It was a gift."

"I bet your girlfriend gave it to you."

Ron insisted I take his Stetson, a gray felt beauty he'd worked hard to get. He had expensive tastes, but worked after school since eighth grade to buy what he wanted. I knew he'd paid three hundred dollars for it not counting the leather band with sterling silver inlays that was probably another three hundred or more. It was the most beautiful hat I'd ever seen, and he loved it. My thoughts instantly went back to that morning.

"I can't take your new hat, Ron," I'd told him.

"You'll need a good one," he said, and smacked it down onto my head. Of course it was too big. "You look like a real serious cowboy in my hat, like the rodeo champion you are."

We tiptoed around good-bye, neither of us wanting to say it.

"I'll miss you, Ron." I was near tears.

"Don't go all Patsy on me, Jed." He pulled me against him so hard it nearly knocked the breath out of me. We stood like that a long time.

"I tell you what, don't keep it." He stroked my cheek. "Bring it back to me soon."

"What if something happens to it?"

"Jed, you need a good hat. It looks perfect on you. Remember me when you wear it. It sure looks great with those big blue eyes of yours. I love your eyes."

CHAPTER 4

By the time we got to Balmorhea, the mountains were so shrouded by clouds we could no longer see them, and I had a hard-on from thinking about Ron.

"Thank you, Mr. Bradley." I was afraid to move. I pulled my suitcase out of the back seat and held it in front of me. "I appreciate the ride a lot."

"Anytime, Jed. Try to stay dry. The rain oughta let up by this afternoon, I reckon."

I waved at him and ducked into the convenience store, rain dripping off the brim of my hat. I nodded a greeting at the clerk and went to a snack table, put the suitcase on a chair, and took a deep breath. I had to stop thinking about Ron.

I leafed through a travel magazine, seeing nothing. The smell of hot dogs roasting on a spit made my mouth water. I needed to conserve my money until I saw how things would go. Ron had given me fifty dollars, but I could eat my way through that before the rain let up. After a while I bought coffee because it was only a dollar, and refills were free, but it didn't fool my stomach.

I figured the rain would let up soon, it being west Texas. Out of the corner of my eye I saw the clerk studying me. I hoped she wouldn't want to talk.

After watching me a while, she came over to eat lunch and invited herself to sit. I didn't see how I could tell her not to.

She smiled and handed me a plastic-wrapped burrito. "You look hungry enough to chew the legs off the table."

I laughed. "Thanks. I reckon I am."

I could barely keep myself from stuffing all of it in my mouth at once. I tried to be calm and eat civilized. It was meat cooked with green chili and was fiery hot and tasty. It brought tears to my eyes, but I didn't know if it was the chili or the kindness.

"Where you from, Cowboy?" Her eyes went to Ron's Stetson sitting on the table.

"What makes you think I'm a cowboy?"

"You look like one, I guess. Maybe it's that big hat and your boots. Are you going to tell me you're not a cowboy?"

"Well, no."

"So then you are one?"

"Not anymore."

"You're giving it up? What? You've had a movie offer?"

I laughed at that.

"Are you going to tell me where you're from?"

"I came here from Fort Stockton, but I don't live there anymore."

"So you're giving up the cowboy life and Fort Stockton—just like that?"

"Yes ma'am, just like that."

"Are you waiting on a ride?"

"I'm waitin' for the rain to let up so I can walk into town and look for work."

"It's three miles into town from here."

"I can walk three miles easy, but I'd prefer it not be rainin' when I do it."

"What kind of work do you do since giving up the cowboy life?"

"Anything I can find, I reckon."

"Shouldn't you be in school?"

"No ma'am, I quit school."

"You can't just quit. It's the law you have to go. You're not old enough to quit."

"Well, I quit."

She laughed and patted my arm. "I won't tell anybody." Her look turned serious. "Does quittin' school have anything to do with what happened to your face?"

"Nah."

"I was just wonderin' how it got all bunged up."

I was afraid if she knew the truth she would contact some government agency for my own good, and that was the last thing I needed. "I was hurt bull riding."

She seemed surprised. "Bull riding? As in rodeo?"

"Yes, ma'am, that's what I'm talkin' about."

"Are you givin' that up, too?"

"That's my plan."

"Are you any good at it?"

"Yes ma'am."

"Maybe you shouldn't be too quick to give it up."

I shrugged and she let it go.

She went to the bank of refrigerators, opened a door, and stood looking at the selection. "You want milk or juice?"

"I'd love some milk."

"White or chocolate?"

"White, please."

She set a quart in front of me. "Drink up. You look like you're still growin'."

"I'm hopin' to."

She laughed and told me to call her Sadie. I introduced myself. Then she took a plastic bag of oatmeal cookies out of her lunch sack and set them next to the milk. "I shouldn't eat these anyway. You eat them." I was more than happy to oblige.

We watched a trucker fill up at the diesel pump using a credit card. The canopy only partially sheltered him, and he turned his collar up against the rain, although I doubted it helped.

"I wonder if he'll come in." Sadie went to the register in case he did.

It took a long time to fill that big truck. I thought of asking him for a ride further up the Interstate to a larger place, but something held me back. He came in for coffee and cigarettes, spoke a few friendly words to Sadie, and ran back out into the rain.

A few others came and went but when the pumps were still and the parking lot empty, Sadie came back and sat with me. When I first came in I thought

she looked mean, but she was a little on the plain side, that was all. Maybe she had wondered what a boy was doing coming in carrying a suitcase between him and the world, but maybe she'd known what my problem was.

"I don't want you to take this wrong, but you have the most beautiful eyes I ever saw in my life."

"Thank you, ma'am."

"I guess people say that to you all the time, huh Cowboy?"

"Sometimes."

"And such curly black hair." She reached to push it back from my face, the way a mother would. "Your eyes are so big and blue. It looks like you're wearing mascara. Why are men the ones to get eyes like yours?"

I shrugged. I didn't know the answer, and as far as I was concerned it was a cruel joke. *Why are you the pretty one, Jed, when your sisters are so plain?* My father had accused me for something that wasn't my fault.

* * *

West Texas or not, the rain kept falling. Sadie said she would give me a ride into town when she got off work at three.

"It's no bother," she insisted, so I agreed.

She gave me a run-down on the few locals that came in and also told me about places where I might find work. Then a red Mustang pulled up.

"Uh-oh. Here comes a gal you need to meet—or not. She's a wild one." Sadie winked at me and went to the register.

A long-legged blonde in tight jeans came running into the store holding a flimsy plastic raincoat over her head. She glanced at me several times but pretended she wasn't looking. I could never understand the way girls act around boys.

"Hey, Sadie." She handed her a bill. She glanced over her shoulder at me then back to Sadie. "I'm puttin' in twenty. God, it's wet."

"Is that," Sadie agreed.

She ran back outside and started pumping gas.

"I thought you said I needed to meet her."

"I think she might be too wild for you."

"You should let me be the judge of that. For all you know I like 'em wild, and the wilder the better."

"You're much too nice for that one."

"You don't really know if I'm nice or not. I might be an axe murderer for all you know about me."

"You're sweet."

"You hope."

After a while a striking woman came in. Sadie wiggled her eyebrows. The newcomer was dressed like a person with money, but that wasn't why she was striking. Her smile was so bright it took the dreary out of the day. I can't tell you much about women's clothing, but she was stylish. Boots I do know, and hers were expensive. She was also blond and small, and even though I never paid much attention to women, I thought she was beautiful.

I heard her tell Sadie her tire was going flat and she was afraid to go home with it like that.

"I'm sorry, Kitty, but Abe isn't here today."

"Did his wife finally have that baby?"

"Yes, ma'am, there're over at the hospital in Fort Stockton."

"Well I don't know what to do."

I was already on my feet. "Ma'am, if it's just changing a tire, I can do that for you."

She turned to me and smiled. "Oh, would you? I'd be so grateful—and I'll pay you of course."

"That won't be necessary, I'm glad to do it." I handed Sadie my hat. "Will you hold onto this for me, please?"

"Sure." Sadie grinned and set it behind the counter. "Kitty, this is Jed."

I held out my hand. "I'm Jed Petersen."

"I'm Kathleen Worthington." Her smile made me want to smile on top of my smile.

"Where is your car, ma'am?"

"It's on the side of the building." She started to leave with me.

"Why don't you stay here, out of the rain? I can manage fine by myself if you trust me with your keys."

She handed them to me with a grin that made her seem more my age than hers. "If you've a mind to steal that ol' thing, help yourself. Maybe you would just give me a ride home first?"

I laughed and stepped outside.

She was driving an old blue Jeep Wrangler that looked like a late eighties model. It seemed to be in great condition other than the usual dents and scrapes of a hard-working vehicle. It had two fading bumper stickers: *Back off, city boy* and *Bull riders stay on longer!* My thoughts went x-rated and wouldn't let up.

Changing the tire was easy once I located the things I needed. The rain was the worst problem and I got soaked. Once I had the tire on, I pulled an old blanket out of the back, laid it across the seat, and drove the Jeep to the front.

When I went back into the store the women clapped and cheered. I bowed to them while water dripped on the floor.

"I can't thank you enough." Kathleen Worthington held out her hand. When I took it in my cold one, she pressed bills into it. I crammed them into my pocket, embarrassed to accept them, but at the same time, in desperate need of them. I thanked her, and she hugged me even though I was wetter than a newborn colt.

"You're the best." She caused me to blush hot.

I watched her go out the door and get into her Jeep. Then I fished the crumpled bills out of my pocket; it was fifty dollars. I bought food.

* * *

Some customers came in and Sadie was busy for a while. She came back to the table when she could.

"Listen. I called my husband, and he said it'd be okay if I brought you home for the night, since it's raining and so cold."

"That's real nice, Sadie. Thank you. I'd like that. I'll try not to be any trouble."

"I'll wash those wet clothes for you."

"I could do whatever chores you need done."

She smiled. "Sure, that'd be great. How old are you?"

"I'm eighteen," I lied.

"You look younger."

"How old are you?"

She blushed. "Men aren't supposed to ask ladies that question."

"Well that's not fair."

She laughed but still didn't tell me her age.

"What do you know about that woman?" I asked.

"Do you mean Kitty?"

"Yes."

"She's a rancher over near Fort Davis. Her husband died five years ago so she manages the place by herself."

"That's sad. How can she live in the middle of nowhere all by herself?"

"She has a large crew of cowboys working, so I reckon she's not alone."

Sadie went back to work and I tried to move my thoughts to rodeo. *There are no pussies riding bulls, Pop!* Thinking of it made me want to go back and argue with him. Stubborn? I would take a beating and come back just to show him. I was more bullheaded than boy-headed. The place in Kansas ended that train of thought.

"Do you think Kitty is over bein' sad about her husband?"

Sadie looked surprised. Sometimes my questions didn't even make sense to me.

"I don't know. You'd have to ask her."

"I'd never be able to talk to a woman like her, let alone say something like that."

"Why not? She's just a woman like the rest of us, 'cept a lot richer."

"Well, for one thing, I don't know the first thing about women."

"There's plenty of time for you to learn, Cowboy."

CHAPTER 5

The approach to Balmorhea was as forlorn as the day. Gigantic cottonwoods clung to their brown leaves as if they would never have a chance to grow more. There were abandoned buildings on property gone to weeds, deserted houses with rusted-out horse trailers in the yards, and faded, cracking business signs. A couple of bored-looking horses browsed a weedy pasture next to a tin shed.

Right away I saw it was a ranching community and thought I should've stayed up on the Interstate and moved on to a place where ranching was a foreign custom. But it was too late now and besides, where would I sleep in the freezing rain?

Balmorhea didn't seem pretty or prosperous, but it was a washed-out day. Maybe I was seeing the worst side of it. It seemed like it was too close to my parents and too far from Ron.

Do not think about Ron.

Sadie's house was set back from the highway a few hundred yards. She said she had a total of thirty acres that her parents had left her when they died. It was an older, wood-frame, ranch-style house that looked well-cared for except for needing paint.

After I carried in the groceries, she showed me to a guest bedroom that was plain, but neat and clean, like her.

"Make yourself at home, and let me know if you need anything."

"Thanks, Sadie."

I sat in an upholstered rocking chair and looked

out at the yard. The rain had stopped and a thick fog moved in. It made me think of the icy fog slinking around the streets last night. I reached to touch the Stetson. Like the memory, I touched it sometimes to see if it was real. I tried to make my head go to other things, but thoughts of Ron prevailed, for whatever hell that was going to bring me.

As the fog swirled and lifted, thickened and thinned, I saw a dilapidated wooden barn that came and went like something from a Harry Potter story. It was surrounded by standard livestock fencing that looked as if it had been there a long time.

Suddenly the phantom-like form of a horse floated into view. I stared, thinking it was my imagination. He waited, shifting his weight from side to side, and then crept out of the barn as if wild animals were waiting. He plodded to the fence, peered about, and finally picked at the weeds, there being no lions or tigers or bears.

The horse was a blue roan and probably had been a beauty. He needed brushing and hard to say what else from indoors, but I didn't need to see him close to understand that hang-dog look. He had been mistreated, poorly-trained, ignored, or had his heart broken in some other way.

After a few minutes I got up, went looking for Sadie, and found her in the kitchen.

"Have a seat right there at the table."

"I can do 'bout any chore you can think of."

"I'm sure that's true, but I don't need anything done right now. Just sit there and talk to me." She began to hum along with a tune on the radio. It was Brad Paisley singing *Waitin' on a Woman.* Again I thought of Ron and his mellow voice and his mile-wide shoulders, and I felt it in my stomach, then my thoughts went galloping to where I didn't want them going. Sadie was humming in her shiny-clean kitchen with her back to me while in my thoughts I was lying on a counter listening to Ron's heart beat, and nobody else was alive in the world to see what we were doing.

"You're a man of few words, aren't you, Cowboy?"

Her voice startled me. "I guess so."

"That's okay. I kinda like that about a man."

"What time does your husband come home?" I was desperate to change the nature of my thoughts.

"Depends on what he had to do today."

"What does he do for a living?"

"He works at the Triple R Ranch."

"So he's a cowboy?"

"Yep, I got a thing about cowboys, Cowboy." She had her back to me, but her neck flushed red.

"Seems like cowboys wouldn't be working on a day like today." I couldn't think what they would do in the rain all day and didn't really care, but I had to think about something besides Ron and the night we spent in each other's arms.

"He might be working in one of the barns." Sadie shrugged as if it wasn't anything to cause concern.

"Is that old barn yours?"

"Yep."

"And the horse?"

"He's mine, too."

"Could I go talk to him?"

"He used to be my dad's. He was a real good horse, but then my dad got sick and couldn't ride him, and he went back to bein' wild."

"Can I talk to him or not?"

"You talk to horses, Cowboy?"

"I listen mostly."

"Are you one of those horse whisperers?"

"I wouldn't call it that. I got my own way."

"Well, I imagine you do." She reddened so much I thought she meant something not about horses.

"Maybe I could feed him for you?"

"That'd be great. Then I won't have to."

"Doesn't your husband do it?"

"He won't take responsibility for him since he became so wild and mean."

I wondered what kind of cowboy her husband was and didn't think much of him. Then I felt guilty since I hadn't even met him.

"The feed's in the barn, along with fresh alfalfa. He won't let you get near him, so just put the feed in his stall—you'll see where—and he'll go in there after

you leave. Will you make sure he has water?"

"Sure. What's his name?"

"Hal."

"How old is he?"

"Maybe twenty-five, older than you anyway, so he won't pay you no mind."

"We'll see."

Hal looked up as I approached and moved down the way, as expected. I put my arms up on the fence and leaned there, watching the fog and feeling the cold creep in to make me shiver.

After a few minutes, I went into the barn, found a bucket, and put a little sweet feed in it. When I came out, Hal was at the far end of the corral. He glanced at me from time to time, and his nose worked the air. He knew what I had, but the distance between us was filled with distrust.

Horses are herd animals and don't like being alone. If they can't buddy up to other horses they'll buddy up to a human if the human doesn't frighten them. The cold made standing around impossible, so I walked to the middle of the corral and set the bucket down, then walked back to the doorway of the barn.

Hal's nose sniffed the air, and he snorted a few times. He looked from me to the bucket and back and forth, deciding. I shoved my hands into the pockets of my jacket and stood as still as I could. It took him a full five minutes. Step, look around, step, watch the human. Waiting on a horse can make a man crazy.

My pop would stomp up to that bucket and yell, "Look here, motherfucker, do you want this or not?" The horse would bolt. Pop would kick the bucket to the other end of the world and go inside. Sometimes I think I'm not even related to him.

When Hal finally reached the bucket, he made a half-hearted whinny. He dipped his head towards the feed, but his eyes never quit watching. When he rose, chewing and checking, we made eye contact. His eyes held mine longer than I expected. Hal was a lonely old man. When his head went back into the bucket, I turned slowly and went into the barn to complete the chores. On a warmer evening I would've waited.

I went back into the house, passed the kitchen, and went to look out the window in the bedroom. There was Hal standing at the fence watching the house.

I jumped when Sadie spoke from the doorway. "What do you think?"

"He's lonely, Sadie."

"Are you saying that's what's making him mean?"

"He's not mean. He's become anti-social from being alone all the time. Why aren't you riding him?"

She put her hands on her hips and gave me an exasperated look. "How can I ride? He won't let me near him."

"If I get him where he can be mounted, will you ride him?"

"How long will that take?"

"I don't know—it's up to Hal. I could come after work if you want me to retrain him."

"If you can get him back like he was, I'll ride him."

"Do you promise?"

"What are you, the horse police?"

"No. I just love them. If I was the horse police, there would be millions of people not allowed to have them."

* * *

"Can you peel potatoes, Cowboy?" We were back in Sadie's warm kitchen.

"Sure."

She put on an apron and turned to face me. "Would you like a beer?"

"Sure. I'd love one."

Sadie opened two beers and handed me one, then toasted me, gently knocking her bottle against mine. "Here's to you, Handsome Cowboy." She took a long drink and sighed.

"Thank you." I smiled at her. She blushed and went back to the sink. I'd never had a beer before, and it tasted nasty, but I drank it like a man.

"What about the potatoes?" I asked.

She handed me a bowl with three potatoes and a vegetable peeler. I looked at it. "I don't want to sound

wrong, but I can eat this many potatoes by myself. If you're making them mashed I can probably eat the whole sack."

She lifted the bag to the table. "Go for it. If you peel 'em, I'll mash 'em. I guess I'm not used to cooking for growing boys."

"I'm a man, not a boy."

"Excuse me. That's what I meant to say."

I laughed because I guessed she was right the first time. Maybe I was only a boy trying to be a man. The thing was if I was going to be on my own, I had to learn to be one and the sooner the better.

Sadie made fried chicken, mashed potatoes that were yellow with butter, green beans, and biscuits. If she cooked like that every night I could see why she was on the chunky side. She said we shouldn't wait for her husband; we should eat while it was hot. That would never've flown at my house. If we didn't wait on Pop, no matter how late he was, we'd be dead or wish we were.

I ate like a field hand while Sadie talked about living in Balmorhea. She said she was a nurse in Dallas, but returned to take care of her parents when they got sick. I paid attention, but I didn't say much. It's hard to talk and eat at the same time.

"Leave room for pie." She brought out a thick chocolate one piled high with meringue. "Everybody likes my pies."

I could always make room for pie and ate three pieces to prove it.

We washed the dishes together because I insisted on helping.

At one point she turned to face me. "Hal was waiting for you, wasn't he?"

"Yes, I think so."

"What did you say to him?"

"I didn't say anything. I let him know I mean him no harm. There's a lot of ways to communicate, Sadie, and talking is only one."

"Where did you get so much wisdom at your age?"

"I love animals, and I let them know it. I figured

out how to work with them when I was young."

"I hate to break it to you, Cowboy, but you're still young." She laughed and hip butted me.

I butted her back. "I mean when I was a little kid."

"I know what you meant. I just wanted to get a rise out of you."

I put my attention back on washing. She was drying and putting things away. When the dishes were finished, she asked if I wanted to watch television.

"Do you mind if I have a shower and go to bed?"

"Of course not."

"Will your husband get mad?"

"No, he won't care."

I took a hot shower and when I got out, Sadie's husband was still not home. I asked if we should look for him. That seemed to embarrass her, and it occurred to me that he was cheating on her and she knew. The thought made my heart heavy.

"Well, thank you for everything, Sadie. I'm going to turn in."

"Good night, Cowboy. Yell if you need anything."

I lay in the bed staring at the ceiling. Pretty soon there was a knock. When I yelled to come in, Sadie stepped into the room. "I saw the light was on."

She had taken a bath and her hair was wet. She was wearing a blue bathrobe tied at the waist. She looked so sad it took my thoughts away from my own sadness.

"Are you okay, Sadie?"

She walked over and sat on the edge of the bed. "I'm okay, just feeling lonely."

I honestly didn't know what to say about her lying, cheatin' dog of a husband. I wanted to kick his ass.

She studied her hands. "I feel guilty for lying to you about something."

"What's that?"

"I don't have a husband. I didn't think you'd come if I told you. I thought you'd think it improper to stay here without another man around. I just didn't think you'd do it, and I wanted you to have a place to

stay. It's so cold and—" Her voice trailed away and she began picking at the robe.

"What else, Sadie?" I had no experience with women, but I knew something was coming as sure as I knew the sun would shine again in West Texas.

"I wonder if you would hold me."

I sat up. "Listen, Sadie. That's a bad idea."

"Why? We're friends, aren't we?"

"That's just it. If I hold you in bed, well, it seems like—"

"You're thinking I'm too old for you."

"Sadie, I'm only thinking that I barely know you."

"I guess you have a pretty girlfriend back home."

"Well," I don't know where I was going to go, but Sadie saved me.

"It's all right, Jed, I understand."

"I've only been gone one day, and it seems wrong to be holdin' somebody else."

"You're more of a man than most men twice your age."

I smiled at her. "Thank you."

"I had a husband once, but he left me for another woman three years ago."

"I'm sorry, Sadie. He must be an idiot."

"Thank you for saying that, Jed. You really are a sweet cowboy."

When she finally left, I let out a long breath and collapsed onto the pillows. I had started to sweat.

Chapter 6

Sadie made breakfast and sat across the table watching me eat. She had a look in her eyes I was trying to avoid. She said she had to work at ten. I told her I was going to look for work. It was a toss-up which one of us was more nervous.

"I should apologize."

"Let's don't talk about it, Sadie."

"There's something about you that makes you seem older than eighteen."

I kept eating.

"I don't want to have this uncomfortable feeling between us. I'm much older than you, but I find you so attractive. I'm sorry if I was out of line."

"Thank you for the compliment. I hope I didn't hurt your feelings."

"Do you want to tell me about your girlfriend?"

"No, I'd rather not."

"I know you'll find something," she said regarding work, "and whether you do or not I want you to know you can stay here as long as you need to."

"Thank you, Sadie, but I reckon I need a place of my own."

"I wish you'd let me help you, Cowboy. No strings attached."

"I appreciate all you've done for me already."

"Look, I know you came here expecting things to be one way and—"

"Don't keep talking about it; there's no harm done."

"Will you consider staying here a while? I won't

come into your room again."

"I could pay rent as soon as I get a job. Until then I could pay you with work."

"It's a deal then. This is a big, empty house. You'll be doing me a favor."

"Not half as much as you're doin' for me. Where would I have slept if it hadn't been for you takin' pity on me?"

"There wasn't pity in it, Jed. I don't want to embarrass you, so that's all I'll say about it. If you help me with things around here, we'll be even."

"Okay, then we got a deal."

She served me more scrambled eggs. "Do you have family?"

"I do, but I displeased my father and he was going to send me away. I left before he had the chance."

"What about your mother?"

"My parents attend a church which teaches that a good wife supports her husband in everything and doesn't question him, so my father's word is law."

"What do you think?"

"I believe a woman should think for herself. If a man mistreats her, she should leave him and take her kids."

"How did you escape growing up to be like your father?"

"I don't want to be like him. I can't respect him, and I want to be a different sort of man. Anyhow, I've had enough of his meanness to last my whole life."

I finished up the meal and stood. "Look Sadie, I want you to leave a list of things you need done. If you don't, then I can't stay. I don't mean to sound bossy, but I'm not stayin' here for free."

"I'll leave a list on the table."

I tipped my hat to her. "See you later, Sadie."

"Happy trails, Cowboy."

* * *

Sadie offered to let me use the truck her former husband had left behind, but I wanted to walk to clear my head. She said it was about two miles from her house to the main part of town. It had quit raining but there was still a heavy cloud cover. It was cold, but I

was glad to get out of there. Sadie had put me in a position I'd never been in before and didn't want to be in again.

Right as I had that thought, the long-legged blond in the red Mustang screeched to a stop beside me and rolled down the window. "Get in, Blue Eyes."

"Excuse me?"

"Get in and I'll take you anywhere you want to go." That said, she turned as red as her car.

"Thank you, but I need to walk."

"So you're gonna make me beg? Is that your deal?"

She had on a denim skirt—the shortest skirt I'd ever seen, worn with pink tights, black boots, and a fuzzy pink jacket.

"I don't have a deal. I want to walk."

"Are you on a weight loss program or what?"

"I need to clear my head."

"Your head looks fine to me, not to mention the rest of you."

I opened my mouth but didn't know what to say.

"Please. The cold is coming in. I need to talk to you. Please."

I got in.

"Are you goin' to school?"

"No, I'm looking for work."

"So you already graduated?"

"Yes."

"I never saw you 'round here before yesterday."

"I just moved here."

"Nobody young and in their right mind would move here. How old are you?"

"I'm eighteen."

"So am I! So where do you live?"

"I'm renting a room up the road."

"At Sadie's?"

"How do you know that?"

"Truth is I saw you in her corral yesterday. I was looking for you 'cause somebody told me she gave you a ride, and I figured she'd take you to her place. Are you a relative of hers?"

"No, she's a friend I just met."

"Do you have a girlfriend?"

"No."

"You want one?" She burst out laughing. "Just kidding, don't look so scared. Everyone says I'm too forward, but I figure if I don't go for what I want, there's no possibility I'll ever have what I want."

I had started to sweat again.

"I'm not calling you a liar. Well, I sorta am, but I don't believe you don't have a girlfriend. There isn't anything wrong with you, is there? You don't have any terrible diseases or—oh my God!—or your private parts got damaged?

"No, nothing like that."

She took a relieved breath. "Anyway, aren't you the bull rider, Jed Petersen?"

"You know me?"

"I knew it! My older brother ropes, so we go to all the rodeos and I've seen you at most of them."

"I'm amazed you'd recognize me."

"You're kidding, right?" She banged her hands against the steering wheel and sped up to somewhere around double the speed limit. "Do you know how many girls—well, what I mean is a lot of girls are following your career. Hey, when is your next rodeo?"

"I don't know. I might give it up."

"What? You can't mean it. Why would you give it up?"

"It's a long story."

"Well, I have all day if I blow off school."

"That's not a good idea."

She squealed onto the Interstate, barely dodging an oncoming truck. We had passed through the town, and I hadn't even noticed for all the talk.

"Wait, I'm looking for work in Balmorhea."

"Yeah, don't get your jockeys in a wad. We're coming right back. Thousands of girls—well, about twenty from here—are big fans of yours—but probably thousands from all around. Everybody knows you. We think you're the best looking cowboy—but I hope you're not conceited. Are you? Please don't be, that would ruin everything. I hate conceited boys. They're such a drag."

I took a deep breath. "Are you making fun of

me?"

"Holy Moly!" She smacked her forehead so hard I thought it would hurt. "You must live on another planet."

She noticed me looking back over my shoulder. "I said don't worry, we'll go back—I just don't want to let you off until I know a few things."

"What is it you want to know?"

"For one thing, your real age, because I don't want to go to prison. And I recall that you're sixteen. That's what those goofy announcers always say about 'the Little Fort Stockton Cowboy' and by the way, you don't seem so little up close, either."

"You'd better talk slower or you're gonna choke. What's your name?"

"Oh. My. God! I'm Gina. I guess you think I'm rude. You didn't ever say your age."

"It's true that I'm sixteen."

"Shit!"

"What did you mean about going to prison?"

"A person eighteen can't have sex with a person sixteen because it's considered statutory rape."

"I haven't said a word about sex."

"I know that. I haven't even given you a chance, have I? Anyway, you'd have to swear you'd never tell anyone."

"Whoa, Gina."

"I don't usually wear this much make-up. I'm just experimenting, you know? Well, you probably don't. How much do you know about women anyway? Okay, listen, I have to get to school, but I'm available afterward if you want to get together."

She was wearing too much make-up, but it didn't hide the beauty of her face. I didn't know how to tell her she was chasing the wrong boy.

Gina did an illegal turn and flew across the grassy median of the Interstate. If we hadn't been moving so fast, we'd have gotten stuck in the mud, which sprayed out in all directions and splattered her shiny car.

"Do you like to dance? I really love to dance. I hope you don't drink a lot or smoke or do drugs. I don't

get it about drugs. I guess I'm high enough without them."

"I don't do any of that. I'm an athlete."

"Well, duh!" She smacked her head again. "What about dancing?"

"I think I'd like it, but I've never done it."

"You're shittin' me."

"No, actually I'm not."

"Am I gonna have to teach you *everything?* Oh. My. God. I bet you've never done it, have you?"

"Done what?"

"You know, *it.* Sex. No-no-no don't tell me. It's none of my business. My horoscope said I was going to get in trouble with my mouth today. Look, I'll find you at Sadie's, okay? I'll teach you to dance, for one thing."

"Wait a minute, Gina. I have to find work before I can—" I have no idea how I planned to finish that sentence, but she interrupted me.

"Can I let you off at school? I want the girls to see me with you."

"Sure, that'll be fine. About dancing—"

"You're an athlete. You'll be great at it! Don't worry about anything, okay?"

She pulled into the school parking lot spraying gravel. "Shit! Shit! Shit!"

"What is it?"

"I'm late and everyone's gone in."

"Do you want me to write you an excuse?"

"Hey! You made a joke! I bet you're a funny guy if I ever let you speak, huh?"

"Have a good day, Gina."

"I don't guess you want to kiss me good-bye? For old times' sake?"

I laughed. "See you later."

"Hey! I wasn't kidding."

"Remember the age difference, Gina. I'd hate for you to go to prison."

"So you *are* interested."

"Bye, Gina."

I felt like I'd been on that county fair ride where they strap you in and hang you upside down and twirl you around faster and faster.

* * *

In the business area of town there was water running in a native stone canal and a lot of tall cottonwoods in a city park with a tiny gazebo. I went in every place and said I was willing to do anything as long as it was legal. I met a lot of flirty women who asked nosy stuff, but I stayed non-committal about where I was from and didn't answer most of their personal questions.

For a while, I hung out with a bunch of lively Mexican guys at a feed store. They were waiting to see if they could get hired for day work by one of the big ranches. It seemed like that wasn't going to happen anytime soon, so I went back into the cold.

Casa México was a restaurant on the edge of town. It was closed until eleven, but workers were going in a back door. When I joined them and asked if they were hiring, an older man stepped up and offered his hand. We introduced ourselves.

"I don't do the hiring, but I can tell you we're looking for a dependable dishwasher. You're not in school?"

"No. I graduated already."

He seemed doubtful. "What experience do you have?"

"Most of my experience is in rodeo."

"Oh yeah? Roping?"

"Bull riding."

He didn't believe that, either. "Well then, you must be tough. Have you washed dishes?"

"Only at home."

He laughed. "It'll be easy to learn. What matters is if you show up on time and stay the whole shift."

"I'll work whatever shifts you have. I need to work."

"The boss will be here soon. You should wait."

I got the job and was told to report for work at four that afternoon. I would bus tables, wash dishes, and assist the cooks. The kitchen manager would train me.

I ran back to Sadie's without noticing the cold. She'd left the back door unlocked for me. I used my

phone card to call my mother, but my father answered so I hung up. The last of my minutes were used to call Ron, but the recorder answered. He was probably at work or practicing football. I didn't leave a message because if I said what was on my mind, his parents would have kittens.

* * *

I went to visit Hal and caught him in his stall not paying attention. I didn't want him to feel trapped, so I backed up until I was far enough for him to escape if he wanted to. He watched me from the corner of big brown eyes.

Hal was a well-developed gelding quarter horse, like many working ranch horses. When he didn't bolt, I took a step towards him and stopped, then another. He started getting antsy and reared, flailing his front legs. *I won't hurt you,* I thought towards him. When I made another step, he bolted and ran to the far end of the corral. Once there, he kicked up his hind legs spiritedly.

I ran to a mounting block, leaned onto my arms, and kicked back my legs. Hal did it again. So did I. He began running back and forth from one side of the corral to the other, at an easy, frisky pace. I ran back and forth, too, until I got winded.

I sat on the mounting block and watched him prance. When he tired, he went to the far corner but faced me, watching to see what I was going to do next.

"You're a fine one, aren't you Big Hal?"

He answered with a whinny, and then took a step towards me. I got up slowly, went into the barn, and pulled a rope off the wall. Hal watched as if fascinated. I moved to the center of the corral and twirled the lariat around my head but made no attempt to use it on him. After a while, I lassoed a fence post to show him I knew how, then several more times. He shook his mane as if to say, *bring it on.*

Hal began running circles around me, coming close sometimes. He was daring me to do it. I let the rope land on his back a few times, and he seemed to understand we were playing and never flinched or ran off. When I headed back to the barn, he followed still

keeping his distance, but not like before.

Hal watched while I did the feeding and watering. I held out my hand to him a couple of times but he didn't sniff it, even though I thought he wanted to.

* * *

The kitchen manager was huge. Roger Desmond was his name, but he was called "Tiny." He was the only white guy in the kitchen besides me, and was oily, thick-bodied, and generally unattractive. He had a two or three-day growth of beard the day I met him, which didn't help his looks. A food-and-fry-spotted apron covered a t-shirt with yellow sweat stains under the arms. It hadn't been white in a long while.

Tiny had meaty arms with dark tattoos of death and destruction. I thought some of them referred to white supremacy, but chose not to look at him any more than I had to because I didn't want him to get the wrong idea.

Tiny took a dislike to me, even though I was a fast learner and did what he said. He asked questions and when I answered, his eyes narrowed and he said, "Huh."

"Where you livin' Jed?"

"I rent a room from Sadie."

"Huh. Where you from?"

"Houston."

"Huh. Why ain't you workin' there?"

"Because I moved here."

"Huh."

Later, after he had just about run my legs off, he came up close, towering on legs with thighs the circumference of stumps. "You fucking Sadie?"

I nearly choked with the surprise of it. "No, of course not."

"Is that because she ain't offered or because you prefer boys?"

Damn. The question took my breath. "Sadie's my friend, that's why."

He backed me slowly into a corner. "You like boys, I bet." He was so close I could smell a nauseating mix of sweat, kitchen grease, and discount store cologne.

"What is your problem?"

"Just wondering." He shrugged innocently and started to turn away. Then he came back. "I'm guessin' boys."

"You're wrong."

"Huh."

"You don't know anything about me."

"I know you're purty," he crooned and touched my cheek, "real purty."

I knocked his hand away and went back to the dishes.

"Don't he look girly?" He addressed the kitchen staff at large.

No one answered. They were all Mexican men working to support families, and I suspected some of them weren't legal, not that I cared. It made them quiet—or maybe it was Tiny's meanness that closed their mouths.

He told all the guys not to bend over around me. He thought it was hysterical, but I was relieved he was the only one laughing.

One of the Mexican men, Alberto Ramirez, spoke up. "No Engleesh!" The others laughed.

When Tiny started his purty-girly rant again, I held up my arms and flexed my biceps. "I'm puro hombre." Everyone laughed except Tiny.

It was awful working and trying to ignore him.

* * *

After work, Tiny pulled his old Chevy pick-up alongside me on the highway and offered a ride. When I said I would rather walk, he drove along next to me.

"I'd really like to give you a ride. You worked hard tonight."

"Yes I did." I kept walking.

"See you tomorrow, Jed," he finally said, as if he was normal.

As he left, Gina pulled up. "Get in, Cowboy, and forget arguing about it."

"I wish you'd gotten here earlier."

"Really? You're starting to like me, aren't you?"

I told her Tiny had been harassing me, but not the details.

"Yeah, I heard you're washing dishes at Casa México."

"Word sure gets around."

"You'd better believe it. Half the town already knows I just picked you up, and they're calling the other half as I speak. But listen. Don't worry about Tiny. He can't get along with anybody because he's a miserable jerk."

"Maybe I should find other work."

"He's a big, ugly bully, and if you stand up to him he'll back down. So where do you want to go?"

"Gina, aren't you out awfully late for a school night?"

"I guess so, but my house is so boring. There's nothin' to do there but sleep. We could drive around listenin' to music. You like country? You must. What kind of cowboy wouldn't like it? You remind me of about ten thousand country songs."

"Like what?"

"Oh, *Blue Eyes Crying in the Rain* and *Just to See You Smile,* stuff like that."

"You've never seen me cry in the rain or anywhere else."

"Looking at you makes me want to cry."

"Well don't look at me. Maybe you better take me home."

"I'd love to, but my parents would have a hissy."

"I meant to Sadie's house."

"I know what you meant, but I don't want to take you there yet. We could go to Fort Stockton to a movie or get a burger."

"Let's don't go there."

"Are you wanted by the law?"

"No, but I am hiding out in a way."

She screeched to a stop along the side of the road. "You didn't get some girl pregnant did you? Please don't tell me that's it. It will completely break my heart."

"It's nothin' like that."

"You messed around with somebody's wife?"

I laughed. "Not that, either."

"Oh! I know! You ran away from home because

of—something bad."

"You can't tell anybody."

"Were you being abused?"

"I displeased my parents and they were going to send me away. I decided to take off before they could."

"Aren't you afraid?"

"I was more afraid to stay."

She stuck her bottom lip out. "Oh, my precious cowboy, you're a *stray.* I wonder if my mom would let me keep you. You wouldn't pee on our rugs, would you?"

"No, but I do eat a lot."

"I'm pretty sure it wouldn't be the peeing or eating that'd bother her." She sighed. "Anyway, they'd lock you up and never let me play with you. They're so freaked out that I'm going to have sex with somebody. They probably think that's what I'm doing right now." She gave me a sideways look. "This is where you try to seduce me."

I was speechless.

"Don't look at me like that. I'm just messing with you. Do I make you nervous?"

"A little."

"Don't they have forward women in Fort Stockton?"

"I don't know, Gina. Seems like all I ever did there was school, chores, bull riding practice, and rodeos."

"Hold onto your hat, Cowboy Blue Eyes, 'cause your luck is about to change. Not tonight, though. If I don't get home I'll be grounded until I'm too old to have any fun."

I laughed at that, but I was so relieved she was taking me home I was almost drunk with it.

CHAPTER 7

The next morning I went to play with Hal once the sun was up. When he saw me approach, he began to run and kick up his back legs. I stood at the fence with my arms hanging over it. After a few minutes he came to sniff my hands, then sniffed his way up my arms and finally, my neck. Then I had a big horse face in mine. Without a word, he laid his head on my shoulder and sighed.

I feel the same way about you, Hal. Slowly I brought my hand up until it was near his face. He huffed out a little air but didn't move. My fingers stroked his face. Hal sighed and his warm, oat-scented breath tickled my neck.

I had just climbed into the corral when Gina screeched in on her way to school. She had exchanged the shortest skirt on the planet for the tightest jeans.

She hung on the fence. "How come you didn't call me last night, Cowboy?"

"It was late and I'd already talked to you."

"I stay up late. You should've called. I shouldn't have to tell you *everything.*"

"Don't your parents get mad if people call you all night?"

"I'm not stupid. That number is my cell. What's your number anyway?"

"Same as Sadie's."

"I mean your cell phone."

"I don't have one."

"You're an old-fashioned type of boy, aren't you? I couldn't live without my phone. I was planning to text

you all day and flirt until you're crazy with lust."

"They let you have phones at school?"

"Hell, no; you have to be sneaky." She sighed. "I told the girls about you. What jealous bitches! I'm bringing you to the party, so we need to start those dance lessons soon. What about this afternoon?"

"I have to work at four-thirty."

"We could do it after work."

"Don't your parents care if you're out half the night?"

"You better know it, Cowboy. My daddy already lectured me about having an underage boyfriend."

"Don't you think that's premature?"

"Man, you're so funny." She paused, but not for long. "I really, really like you."

She was wearing no makeup that I could detect and the improvement was one hundred percent. Still.

"I like you too, Gina."

"But?"

"I wasn't going to say but anything."

She sighed. "That's a relief. Sadie says you have a girlfriend."

"Sadie doesn't really know me. I only rent a room from her."

"Okay, well, great! Look, I gotta go. If I'm late again I'll get detention. But I'd stay if you wanted to make out."

"Actually, I'm busy here, Gina."

"Since when is a boy too busy to make out?"

Good question, for which I had no answer I could share.

"Oh! I get it—you're shy. Well, no worries. I'm *so* not shy."

"I hadn't noticed."

She laughed. "That bitch Tanya Keen says you're probably—oh never mind, she's just jealous. You know what Jed? If you got a cell phone I could send you photos of me. You wouldn't know this yet, but I'm practically the only girl at school who doesn't pad her bra." She placed her hands under her breasts and pressed them together. They were impressive. "These puppies are real, Cowboy Blue Eyes."

By the time Gina left, Hal was hiding in the barn, and I wanted to join him.

I got my breath, then the rope, and Hal and I played a while. I let the rope land on his back in a game he seemed to enjoy. I didn't try to ride him. When you want to retrain an animal you have to start at the beginning.

* * *

There was loud knocking that woke me at seven the next morning. I pulled on pants and stumbled to the door.

"I guess you wonder what happened to me yesterday." Gina stepped in without being invited. "I was grounded. I'm *eighteen* and they still ground me. You look like you just woke up. Damn, you're cute. Do you sleep nude? NO! Don't tell me. I do *not* need that image in my head today."

"Good morning, Gina."

She took a deep breath and smiled. "Good morning, Cute Cowboy."

We stood staring at each other. She dared a step closer. "I guess you're wondering why I'm here so early. I don't have my first period class today, so I'm going to teach you to dance. Now don't panic. I see that look. It's just the two-step and maybe a waltz or two if you're as fast a learner as I think."

"I just woke up, Gina."

"Oh, yeah, well I guess you need to wash your face and stuff. I'll just go in the kitchen and see what I can find for breakfast."

"The food is Sadie's, except for a can of peaches and a loaf of whole wheat bread."

When I came back Gina was in the kitchen. She had made a pile of toast, and was opening the peaches. "It's not much. You need to buy some groceries."

"This is fine. Thanks."

"Well? Sit down and eat. Did you miss me yesterday? Tell me the truth. I can tell when men lie."

"I wondered where you were. I thought another man had turned your head."

She slammed herself into a chair across from me. "Let's get one thing straight. I'm not like that. I

don't sleep around from man to man, no matter what these yokels say. I've only had one serious boyfriend. I flit. Like a butterfly. Testing, you know? When I see a flower I especially like, then I check it out. You get it?"

"I think so, but I hope you're not calling me a flower."

She laughed. "It's a metaphor. Don't go all macho bull rider on me."

I couldn't help but like this girl. She was so full of life she was irresistible.

"They keep testing me for ADD," she said, as if reading my mind, "but I'm not hyperactive and I can pay attention to the things that interest me. The thing is, Jed, there's a whole life out there, and I can't wait to try everything, you know? I'm sure not gonna stay in Balmorhea Fucking Texas once I get out of high school. I'm going where the lights are bright and there are things to do and all kinds of people. I love people. I don't care what color they are or what they do for a living or what god they worship or who they love. Can you get that?"

"Yes, I definitely get that."

"These rednecks around here only like white bread. I'm so done with average, Jed. That's why I want to know you. You're so far from that. First of all, it takes some kind of guts to ride bulls. It scares me just to look at them. And you're so good at it you make it look easy. How amazing is that?" She barely took a breath. "And you're so damn beautiful. Man! Look—it's not just that. I'm not that lame. I look into your eyes, and somebody real lives there, you know? You have fabulous eyes and it seems like I can look right into your soul." She grimaced and twisted. "I want to kiss you so bad it's killing me."

"There's a lot you don't know about me, Gina."

"You can't tell me you've done bad things."

"Well, I haven't done bad things, but—"

"Anyhow, I don't care. So whatever it is, keep it for now. Can you do that?"

"Sure. You don't know how easy that is."

"You're not much of a talker, are you? That's okay. It makes us a good pair since I talk enough for

two. You eat. I'm going to my car to get some music."

When she left, it seemed to suck all the air from the room. I ate as much as I could, but I was nervous about dancing. Not because of the sin. I was way past the piddley sin of dancing. It was about being close to her. I wondered what Ron would think of this predicament, and in the next second put him from my mind. Thinking about him was the last thing I needed.

"I hope you like George Strait, 'cause he recorded some of the best two-stepping songs I've ever heard, in every tempo. We'll start out kinda slow and work up. By the way, how can you be sixteen and graduated already?"

"I quit. I didn't graduate."

"I wish I could do that."

"I think you should stay in school. I'd still be there if I had a normal father."

Her hand went to her open mouth. "Oh God, did he sexually abuse you?"

"No, he wasn't that bad."

"Thank God!" She hugged me tightly, but pulled away quickly. "You can tell me about your old man later. Right now, let's dance! We're burnin' daylight, as you cowboys say."

We moved furniture out of the way. *Does Forth Ever Cross Your Mind?* blasted into the room. Gina ripped off her boots and stood toe-to-toe with me. "Doesn't this make you want to move your cute butt?"

I admitted that it did.

"Okay, now watch me. Basically I'm taking two steps then two steps, quick-quick then slow-slow, quick-quick, slow-slow. Start moving. Yeah, that's it. I knew you would get this easy. Now put your hand on my waist and take this hand. That's it. I won't bite you—not today anyway. Now we're going to move together. You start. You're the man and therefore the leader—in dancing. Just go when you're ready."

We went on to *All My Exes Live in Texas* and *Bigger Man Than Me.* She taught me how to twirl her and go sideways and change direction. Then we danced to Alan Jackson, Brooks and Dunn, Tim McGraw, and tunes I didn't know. I took to dancing as if I'd grown up

with parents who let me do it. After the country we danced to pop, shaking and jumping around. It was great.

Eventually Gina taught me to waltz, which was easy. We danced one-two-three, one-two-three all over the room, all over the house. I loved it.

I had never been allowed to be with a girl long enough to know if I even liked them. I liked Gina. In many ways, she wasn't so different from me.

Too soon, she said she had to head to school. She had been uncharacteristically quiet and was really into dancing.

"One more, then I have to go for real. Let's waltz."

We did.

"A lot of guys think waltzing is gay," she said while we were dancing. "They don't like it because they're uncoordinated, but you—I guess it's being an athlete, huh?"

"I guess so."

When the music stopped, she had her arms around my neck. "I swear if you don't kiss me, I'll die right here. How will you explain that to everybody?"

I laughed and then kissed her. I'd be lying if I said it wasn't nice. It didn't make me hot for her or anything, but it was still nice.

"Wow." She seemed stunned. "That's why God made lips."

"You think so?"

"Don't you?"

"Oh, yeah, I think so."

"He shoulda known how much trouble we'd get into. I hope you don't buy all that Adam and Eve original sin stuff 'cause really. Why would God make parts that fit together and then ask us not to put them together?"

CHAPTER 8

The next day, I threw myself across Hal's back and hung over him as he ran around. He didn't buck or try to knock me against the fence. Instead, he kept looking back at me and probably thought I was crazy.

When my stomach tired from bouncing and balancing, I jumped down and brushed him until he shone. He had a corral-full of dirt and dust in his coat. It took a long time to untangle his thick mane, but he stood still while I worked on him.

When the dirt was gone, he was a fine specimen of a blue roan. A horse with a coat of intermixed white and hairs of any other color is called a roan. A blue roan is white mixed with black hairs. The head, tail, and legs are black but the body has a grayish or blue appearance. Hal's age caused him to look more gray than blue but he was a beauty.

The day after that, I saddled him and rode around the corral. When that went smoothly, I rode him the three miles to the convenience store without incident. Sadie burst into tears when she saw me on his back.

I jumped down and put my arms around her. "Don't cry, Sadie. He's come back, that's all. He wanted to all along. I just helped him by reminding him who he is."

"Oh Cowboy, how can I ever thank you?"

"There's no need, Sadie. You've done so much for me already."

* * *

It was an interesting week during which I tried to

keep two women away from me. One was eighteen and the other about double that. I had a come-to-Jesus meeting with Sadie and explained that I wouldn't be having sex with her. She assumed it was because I had met a girl my age and I didn't say different.

Whenever she could, Gina picked me up after work and we rode around, listening to music and laughing. Her friendship helped me endure a job I hated, except she also made me sweat bullets.

She took me to a friend's birthday party-dance. I had never been to any kind of dance, and if I'd realized what I was missing, I'd have run away sooner. Afterward, we were driving around and we ended up in a roadside park talking and listening to music on her Mustang's stereo system.

We were talking about why she didn't want to be a cheerleader—*because it's so lame and those girls are so stuck up*—when she changed channels in the middle of the program. "I want you to touch them, Jed."

I knew exactly what she was talking about because she'd been pushing them at me practically since I met her. I was paralyzed.

"They don't bite," she promised when I said nothing.

The disturbing thing was that I wanted to touch them. Since sixth grade that's all most of the boys I knew talked about: breasts, boobs, bosoms, bazoombas, jugs, titties, tatas, tweeters—to Gina, puppies. The names were endless, along with the talk. Most boys were obsessed. Various friends and I had admired them once or twice—maybe more like a dozen times—in magazines full of naked women. Compared to the others, I had been practically unmoved.

"I need to tell you something." I thought it would be unfair to touch her just because I'd never touched puppies before. Still, it was hard to say.

"Tell me anything," she broke in, "but don't tell me you're gay." She sighed. "That's it, isn't it?"

"Well, what I was going to say—"

"Oh, crap! I just can't believe it."

"Could you let me talk? You asked me a question, but you didn't let me answer."

"That's because I don't want to hear you say it."

I took a deep breath. "I have a boyfriend, Gina." There. It was out. I had come out of the closet, and to a woman. I released the breath in a whoosh. I felt like laughing, dancing, and calling Ron.

Gina looked like she'd lost her best friend. "I knew you were gay."

"Do I look gay?"

"You're so damn crazy. Hell, no, it's not that."

"I want to know how you knew."

"It's more about how you are than how you look. You're such a gentleman and you never want to make out with me, even when I practically throw myself on you. I'm considered very good-looking, but I guess you wouldn't notice that."

"Of course I've noticed, Gina. You're beautiful. I'm gay, not blind."

"How do you know you're gay? You're only sixteen."

"I'm in love with a man, Gina."

"Well, hell, this ruins things." She chewed on her lip. "A lot of the girls told me you're probably gay."

I was horrified. "How would they know?"

"Well, for one thing, you seem immune to girls. And at the dance you were looking at the boys. Also, some of the girls have thrown themselves at you at rodeos. You've never dated a girl, far as anyone knows. The kids in your school talk to the kids in my school at dances and ball games. Anyway, I'm not judging you, Jed. In fact, I think you should try it once with a woman, just to see, and I'd like to be the one."

"If I was going to try it, Gina, you'd be the one."

She chewed a while longer on her lip. "Could you at least touch my breasts and see what you think? It might do something for you."

"I don't think that would be right."

"Why would it be wrong when I want you to?"

"Well—" I didn't know.

She gently put my hand against her right breast, which was covered by a shirt and a sweater. In spite of that, I could feel how cushiony and firm it was because she moved my hand around on it. So this was what the

other boys were so obsessed about. I don't know what I would've said or done if there hadn't been a loud rap on the window.

I jumped, and Gina let out a little cry of alarm. Someone shone a flashlight around in the vehicle, and then into my face, Gina's face, and back to mine. She put the window down. "Get out of here, J.J."

"What are you doing, Gina?" He moved the light, but I was temporarily blind.

"Well nothing, thanks to you, Jerry John."

"You got yourself a new boyfriend?"

"It's none of your business. Get out of here."

He shone the light in my face again. "Who the hell are you?"

"I'm Jed Petersen. Who are you?"

"Oh—you're the bull rider." His attention went back to Gina. "What are you doing, Gina? I know he was touching you."

"This doesn't concern you."

"But I'm pregnant," he wailed, "you can't just walk out on me."

"Have some pride, J. J."

"She's not a respectable girl, Jed Whoever." The light was in my face again. "She's fucked every boy in school and some of the teachers. She'll fuck you if you let her and brag to her friends, and then look for new meat."

Gina put the window up. Jerry John didn't remove his hand until the last minute. She started the car and we roared out of there in a spray of dust and gravel.

We hadn't gone a mile when she burst into tears. "That was all lies."

"I know that, Gina."

"I thought he loved me," she sobbed. "He's the only boy I ever did it with, Jed, I swear. He used me, not the other way around, and he spread rumors and said stuff—well you heard him." She was crying so hard it was difficult to understand her.

"Please stop the car before you put us in the ditch."

"He's ruined everything."

"Gina, please pull over. I think he's a low-life and nothing is ruined."

"But you'll have doubts."

"No I won't. I see who you are, Gina. He looks old enough to know better than to use language like that around a woman."

"You are so old-fashioned," she wailed. Sob. Sob. Sob. "I love that about you."

"That's how I was raised. Please don't cry."

She didn't pull off the road, but she finally quit wailing and sobbing. We flew up and down the Interstate with no regard for the eighty miles-per-hour speed limit. Eventually we laughed about Jerry John and described his bleak, beer-belly-loud-whiny-wife-and-a-dozen-snotty-kids future until we hurt from laughing.

Whatever else I could say about the man, Jerry John had saved me from the puppies.

* * *

Most of the time I was so full of lust for Ron it was awful and, at the same time, wonderful. Nothing held back those desires and it got worse as days passed. I found myself thinking of him, even at work, where I hardly dared think those thoughts.

When it had been two weeks since I last saw him, I couldn't stand it anymore and borrowed Sadie's truck. I waited for him after football practice, and when he began walking home, I followed slowly, enjoying the way he moved.

Finally, I beeped the horn. He turned around, saw me, grinned, and sprinted up to the window.

"Oh God, Jed, I thought it was some pervert following me."

"It is. Get in."

"I didn't expect to see you so soon. You look great! Are you back?"

"I'm living in Balmorhea. Please don't tell anybody. Things are going pretty well, and I don't want my father to come for me."

"Of course I'll never tell anyone. Who would I tell?"

Ron was still dressed in his uniform. In places it

was wet with perspiration, and there was black under his eyes, and sweat drying on his face. He smelled bad and delicious at the same time.

"If I'd known you'd come for me, I would've showered in the locker room."

"We're going to a motel on the Interstate. Can you handle that for a few hours?"

"Well, I have fond memories of that old gas station, but yeah, I could stand a hot shower and a good bed." He grinned. "Oh man, I've never been in a bed with you."

CHAPTER 9

Two weekends later, Gina asked me to a high school dance. I couldn't get out of going without hurting her, and besides, I wanted to go. I had never been to one.

"Wow! You look like a movie star," Gina exclaimed when she came to pick me up.

"I could say the same about you." She was wearing fancy blue jeans with a red silk shirt and soft black sweater, and her hair had been French-braided.

"I wanted you to think I'm a babe."

"You are a babe, Gina."

"But you don't even want to try making out with me."

"Look, Gina—"

"I wish you would wear chaps for me sometime. Chaps are so, so sexy."

"*Chaps?* They're not for dancing, they're for—"

"I know what they're for, for God's sake. Ask any woman what she thinks about chaps on a guy with a nice package."

"I'll take your word for it."

On the way to the dance Gina chattered constantly. One of the things she said was, "I wish you would only dance with me tonight, but other girls will ask."

"I'm going because you invited me. I don't want to dance with other girls."

She smiled and squeezed my hand. "That makes me feel special."

"You are special."

"I didn't wear a bra tonight."

Yes, I had noticed, and it was the reason my palms were sweating.

"I wish we could make out, just once. Maybe you'd like it. How will you know if you never try it?""

"It's something I know, Gina."

She screeched to a halt along the shoulder of the highway. Seatbelts saved us from going head first through the windshield. I stopped speaking because I thought we were getting into a wreck. That was always likely whenever she drove.

She turned to me and laid her fingers against my lips. "I know what you're going to say. I'm asking you not to, not tonight. Okay?"

"Okay, but—"

"I know, Jed. Just forget it for this one night. Can you do that?"

I doubted it. "Sure. Okay, this one night."

So I went to my first-ever high school dance and focused my attention on her and mostly ignored the males, and the DVD player in my head which replayed in vivid detail any moment I had spent sinning with Ron. I was sixteen, always-horny, confused, and out of my element—but the dancing was great. Other girls did invite me to dance, and I refused them with a "thank you but no. I'm with Gina."

"Let's get out of here," she whispered after we'd been there a couple of hours. "Everybody's gossiping about us. Let's go and give them something to talk about."

I took her by the hand and led her outside. It was cold and clear.

She sighed. "I was hoping to dance naked by the lake but I see that's out."

I laughed and opened the passenger door for her.

"You can't drive this car, Jed."

"I'm a better driver than you."

"Who says?"

"Get in and relax. Where do you want to go?"

"How about Cancun?"

"Not tonight. Name another place."

"Let's go honky-tonkin'!"

"But they won't let us in."

"We won't go in. It's a dive anyway, but the music is great. You'll see. Head that way, and I'll tell you where to turn."

I was lost before we got off the pavement. Then there was a long trek down an ungraded road. It was dark as a coal mine except for a house every now and then.

"Are you sure you know where we're going?"

"Just keep driving, Cowboy. Hey, you want a swig of Hot Damn?"

"I don't know what that is, but yeah, if you're having one."

"It's only cinnamon schnapps, but it'll warm us up."

"Pass it over, then."

"You can't get caught driving and drinking. The deputies are assholes. You'll go to jail, and it'll take an act of God or fifty thousand dollars to get you out."

In the distance was a blinking neon sign. "That's it," Gina said.

The place was called The Whiny Fiddle, and I could tell why without rolling down the window. We parked far to the side of the lot and sat in the car for a while, passing the bottle back and forth and listening to music that was so loud we couldn't have missed it. We talked about school and rodeo, and pretty much anything that came to mind. The Hot Damn caused a warming sensation that moved slowly from my lips to my throat, to my gut, and then all the way to my toes. I got more talkative while Gina chattered less and less.

The red neon sign cast colorful shadows around the building, just enough light so as not to kill yourself getting in and out of the place.

Before long, a man dressed in western wear and a woman in a too-tight red dress came out the door together holding hands.

"Well, hello," murmured Gina. "Will you look at that? Those two are married to other people. Huh."

Not long after they left, two men tumbled out the door, swiping and kicking at each other in the neon glow. They each delivered a punch or two, and there

was a lot of cursing and name-calling, but they spent more time rolling in the dirt than fighting. After a while, one of them staggered to his feet and helped the other one up. They shook hands and slapped each other on the back. Gina and I looked at each other and laughed.

"Honky-tonks don't get any more pure Texas redneck than this." Gina took my hand. "Let's dance before we get too drunk."

Fiddles whined while some singer was complaining at high volume, "All you ever do is bring me down, making me a fool all over town." We whirled and twirled and kicked up dust all over that parking lot, fueled by Hot Damn and hormones.

Then the tempo slowed. "You catch on fast," Gina breathed into my ear. She kissed my neck, my ear, took my hand and stuck it under her clothing. "We're moving on to something new now, Cowboy."

Her breast was firm with soft skin, but the nipple was hard and hot and pointy against my palm. Blood pounded in my ears. Gina made a tiny moaning sound that made it worse. I moved my palm slowly over the nipple, then massaged it between my thumb and forefinger, practically as obsessed as any other boy.

"Oh God," she groaned.

I was nervous as hell. This was all new. I hadn't even fanaticized about it.

"Oh…sweet…Jesus," she whimpered.

Somebody began singing "I'm rollin' in my sweet baby's arms, rollin' in my sweet baby's arms." I had her pinned against the back bumper of her Mustang, pressing against her. We were kissing, and I had both hands under her sweater. Then she began to fondle me through my jeans. She got one button undone before I lost it. "Get in the car, Gina."

"We can't get caught doing it here." She unzipped her jeans and put my hand in, sliding it over her stomach, down into her warm wet slickness. She moaned and moved against my hand.

"That's right, Jed. Oh God, that's it, that's it. Jesus, Jed."

I thought I was going to pass out.

"Where can we go?" I croaked.

She pressed her hand firmly against mine then removed it from her pants. "I'm going to want a lot more of that."

"Okay, but where, Gina? Where?" I was nearly whining. For a boy with barely a passing interest in girls, I had certainly risen to the occasion.

"Pull out, go left, and I'll tell you where to go from there." She was wiggling out of her pants. "You're not going to let me down, are you Jed?"

"No, I won't." God, I hoped I wasn't.

"In a minute you'll see a sort of path to the right. Pull in and go slow. It's all mesquite and tamarisk in there, but it'll hide us. There—it's right there."

"Back seat," she commanded the second the car stopped.

I got out, took off my pants, and got in the back. She climbed over the seats. It was close back there, but better than bucket seats. She took my hand and shoved it into panties that were about as substantial as smoke.

"Touch me, Jed, right there. That's it." She chewed and sucked on my neck while one of her hands teased me. "That's it, that's it," she whispered.

"Gina," I gasped.

"You like this, huh Jed?"

"Aawwghhh," was what I said, or something like that.

"Let me get on top of you."

Come on, I thought, but have no idea what I actually said.

She eased herself onto me and my head just about spun around backwards.

"You like this, sweet cowboy?"

"Oh, oh, oh. Don't stop doing that."

"Tell me you like it." She had a hand on each side of my head, which kept it from twisting off. Wisps of her silky hair were stuck to the sweat on my face.

"My God, don't make me talk."

She laughed, which caused a fantastic sensation.

"Can you move a little faster?"

She did, then slowed—it was maddening.

"Gina, please. Let's do this right."

"This...is...right." She grabbed me by the

shoulders. "Oh, Jed—you're hitting my spot! That's it. Oh—oh—oh—oh my God! That's my spot. Jed, Jed, Jed."

We were hitting my spot, too. Every place I had felt like a spot.

* * *

We were still for a few minutes. I tried to recover my breath and watched moisture roll down the windows.

"Is that what you wanted, Gina?"

"Oh. God. Jed. Shut. Up. That was so great. It was Heaven. Better than. I must be dead. Am I dead? I must be."

"Not hardly."

Before long I was back to hitting her spot. We finally exhausted ourselves and fell asleep with her lying on top of me and only my western shirt and a jacket slung over us. It didn't seem like thirty minutes passed before she started shaking me. I could barely force my eyes open. Then I couldn't believe I was waking up with a woman.

"Jed, Jed, please wake up. It's morning. My father is going to kill me. What did you do with my underpants?"

"They might be under me."

"Well get up!"

"I can't move."

"Please, Jed, I'll be grounded until I'm thirty."

"Then let's stay here and sleep. What's to lose?"

I dozed, but she started shaking me again. "Jed, will you take me to breakfast?"

"Now?"

"I always thought it'd be nice to make love all night and then go for breakfast."

"If you make love all night you should sleep through breakfast—at least."

"C'mon, Jed, please do this one thing for me."

"I already did things for you."

"Jeeeddd—"

"Okay, okay. What about being grounded until you're thirty?"

"We'll go to the IHOP at Fort Stockton. Daddy'll

never think to look for me there."

"We can't go to Fort Stockton." Guilt broke out on me like a fever sweat.

"We'll go to Pecos."

"I need to go home."

"But you just said you'd take me."

"I'm sorry, but I need to go."

"Don't tell me you hear your mother calling you."

More like my conscience. "Nah, but I need to sleep."

"Move that cute ass of yours, Cowboy. I'm hungry. Aren't you hungry?"

"I'm too tired to be hungry."

I got dressed, but my clothes were limp and wrinkled. "I can't go like this." I hoped to get out of it.

"Well, I guess you're really gay after all."

"What the hell? My *clothes* are limp and that makes me gay?"

"You know, gay men really care about their clothes."

"Oh, that is such a gross generalization. Now you're pissing me off."

"You're the one crying over clothes."

"Shut up, Gina."

"You do look a little—abused—you poor lil' blue-eyed, bull-ridin' boy." She began laughing and I laughed, too. I couldn't help it.

"You mean I look like I've been rode hard and put up wet?"

That doubled her over.

Then she got serious. "Wanna do it again?"

"And miss out on the rubbery eggs?"

She shrugged. "A person has to have priorities."

"Let's eat and then we'll see."

I rolled down the window to throw out some gum and my conscience went with it. "I want to be on top next time, Gina."

"Ah, the bull rider speaks. I'd be into that."

* * *

On the way to Pecos, she chattered as if she'd slept all night. "Maybe you're not gay, Jed. Maybe you were going through a phase. Boys do that sometimes."

I already knew Gina had it wrong. It was more like she was a phase.

"Unless you're one hell of an actor, you really seemed to enjoy yourself."

"I did."

"Well, explain that."

"I can't, actually. And I wish we didn't have to dissect it."

"All right, but I just want to say one more thing. It's a question."

"Okay."

"Will you let being gay stop you from doing it with me again?"

"I can't answer that right now. It's an unfair question. If you knew I was gay, why did you keep after me?"

"I can't answer that right now. It's an unfair question." She chewed on her lip. "Maybe it's because you ride bulls."

"What does that have to do with anything?"

"Bull riders are macho and so not gay. I don't see how a bull rider could even *be* gay, but whatever."

I took her hand. "Could you drop it?"

"Okay, Jed. I think you're wonderful—gay, straight, or even if you're mixed up about it."

* * *

Later we were eating color-enhanced eggs along with pancakes.

"I hope you're not going to give me hair and fashion advice now," Gina said with a straight face.

"No chance of that."

"Will you paint my nails?"

"Not in this lifetime, Gina."

"Jed, all kidding aside, I want to tell you something else."

"Since when do you ask permission to talk?"

"I feel like I'm getting on your nerves."

"You're not. Well, not much."

"Other guys, well, they're mostly all strut and no waltz. But you, Jed Petersen, are all waltz and hardly any strut."

"That's a very nice thing to say, Gina."

"I mean it."

"Thank you."

"Jed?"

"Yeah?"

"Even if you never do it with me again, it was the best sex I ever had."

* * *

It was after noon when Gina let me off at Sadie's house. Thank God she was at work. I showered, set the alarm for four o'clock, and fell into bed face down.

Gina's father grounded her for six months. She called me the minute he left the house and said she would cooperate with him until she caught up on her sleep. He was furious that she was gone all night with a *sixteen-year-old* boy. "Doesn't he have parents, for Christ's sake? What were you thinking, Gina? You want to go to prison? You want to ruin your life over a *cowboy*? And a *bull rider,* Gina? Bull riders are the worst sort." She did an entertaining impersonation of her dad losing it.

"Jed, even if you get really, really mad at me I hope you won't turn me in."

I laughed at that and swore I never would.

It wasn't long before the new wore off the sex. I know that sounds cold, but I don't know how else to say it. She was fun and I loved her as a friend. When it came to sex, something was missing. We did it enough that I can say for sure.

When I was alone, I thought of Ron. Usually even when I wasn't, I thought of him. With Gina, I felt like I was living someone else's life. I was sixteen and confused, but I knew she deserved better. It took seeing Ron again before I told her.

CHAPTER 10

I worked Christmas and had New Year's weekend off. I called Ron and asked him if I could pick him up, and we would go camping "or something."

"You know it, Cowboy. I'm so ready for that."

Sadie let me borrow her truck again. I didn't contact my parents, but Ron told his we were going camping and fishing down at the Rio Grande, and that was our intention. We barely made it out of Fort Stockton.

"So how's it going, Cowboy?" Ron reached over and began touching me.

"Jesus, Ron." I had to pull the truck off the highway behind an abandoned shack or else wreck it.

The only thing I heard for a while was *Oh Jed, oh God* and a lot of blood rushing in my ears and groaning and breathing and sighing and love talk. We spent the night there even though there was a motel less than three miles away. We couldn't let go of each other long enough to go anywhere, and that was all right with me because we had a lot of lost time to make up. There would be a lot of time to endure before the next time, but I couldn't think about that.

Around dawn, Ron made a little campfire and we sat by it and finally talked some, but then I got to lookin' at his face and that dimple in his chin. My looking made his scar glow pearly white, and he was watching me.

He said, *I love you, Jed* and I said I loved him back, and our clothes went flying, and I thought if I died right there it'd be okay.

We celebrated the New Year in a motel room and never made it to the Rio Grande or even thought about it. The air sparkled even though we didn't have confetti, and we felt drunk half the time even though we didn't drink anything stronger than Pepsi. We didn't talk about going back, and the only thing we said about parting was that we would meet again soon; it was a promise.

* * *

Before I knew it, I was pulling into Balmorhea. I parked Sadie's truck at her house and went looking for Gina on foot. It wasn't long before she passed in a streak of red, turned around on a dime, and came back for me.

"Get in, Cowboy Blue Eyes. I'll take you for a ride."

I got in. "I have to talk to you, Gina.

"Oh, God, it's over, isn't it?" She began to cry.

I nodded. "Please don't cry."

"I knew this day would come, I just hoped it wouldn't be so soon."

"I love you, Gina, but I can't be what you want. I have to be who I am."

She dabbed at her eyes. "I understand that. I wish you were different, but I know we can't change that part of us."

"I'm sorry."

"You have nothing to be sorry for, Jed. You gave me all you could and I loved it. We had some great times, didn't we?"

"Yes, we did."

"If you ever change your mind—"

"I don't think this is something I'll get over like a case of the measles."

She laughed, but I think Gina really got me in a way most didn't. She sighed. "Well, at least now you can say you tried sex with women."

"I doubt if any other women are like you. I hope you'll go out and live the life you dream."

"As soon as they give me that diploma, these white bread rednecks will be choking on my dust."

We smiled at each other a while, and then she

kissed her fingers and touched them to my cheek. When I think of Gina, in the rare moments I do, I remember that sweet gesture more than anything else about her.

Chapter 11

In early March, my mother died in a car accident. My father found out from Ron that I was living in Balmorhea and sent his trusted friend, Marvin Jenkins, to bring me home. Marvin is a gruff man with a thick black beard and a narrow mind. He is known for his opinionated rants about sin, and in particular, homosexual sin.

"I guess you know you shamed your whole family." This was the first thing he said on the way back to Fort Stockton.

"I don't know why they'd be ashamed. I'm working hard and not causing trouble for anybody."

"You know damn well what I'm talking about."

"What I do in my private life is none of your business."

"It's every Christian's business to bring a sinner back into the fold."

"I'm no worse a sinner than anybody else."

Marvin clicked on the radio to the Christian station.

"Don't you ever listen to country or pop?"

"You know, Jed, sometimes boys fall into sinful ways in spite of knowing the difference between right and wrong. They don't mean to, but hormones drive young men to do desperate things."

He went on, but I shut my eyes and let images of my mother come. It was hard to believe I would never see her again. It hadn't really sunk in.

"Are you listening, Jed?"

"No sir. I was thinking about Mom." *She just*

died, you self-righteous asshole.

"Your father is my best friend. I promised him I would talk to you."

"Well, now you have. Thank you for your concern, but I'm living my own life."

"Jed, if you're having sex with boys, you're going to Hell."

Well, it would be totally worth it. "I don't believe that."

"Well, believe it or not, that's the truth. You need to get right with God and beg his forgiveness for whatever you've done. Your father is still willing to pay to send you to the Sunflower Project, but he's tired of fighting you, Jed."

"I'm not going there, so you might as well drop the subject."

"But it's run by good Christian people who have your best interests at heart."

That's one excellent reason not to go.

"You broke your mother's heart when you ran away. I would think you'd be willing to go now out of respect for her."

"Don't talk about my mother. She died."

"I'm talking about honoring her memory."

"My mother loved me as I am."

"That's what you want to believe."

"That's what I know," I answered with so much defiance it silenced Marvin.

Meanwhile, praise music spewed from the radio.

When Marvin spoke again, he still had it wrong. "Christ himself spoke out against homosexuality."

"No he didn't! He never said one word against it. In fact, he didn't speak much against anything. He was always talking about love and how God is love and we should love each other. His messages were positive."

"You need to read the Bible."

"I have read it. In fact, when our preacher spoke about homosexuality practically non-stop, I looked for where Christ talked about it, and he didn't."

"You are sadly ignorant of the Holy Bible, young man."

No I wasn't. He was the ignorant one, but I quit

arguing. Like the preacher, he wanted to believe what he wanted to believe. I didn't care. I just wanted him to leave me alone about it. Instead, he changed the game.

"You're a very beautiful young man; I swear you are."

Okay, that was weird.

"But I wouldn't be too proud of that, if I were you. You're an awful temptation."

His comment made my stomach feel sick. Sometimes your stomach knows something bad is happening before your mind can connect the dots.

"What do you mean?"

"I mean you put sinful thoughts in a person's head."

"I'm not doing anything."

"You don't have to."

My father's best friend, a rigid church elder who railed against homosexuality, reached over and caressed my face. I could barely breathe.

"What are you doing?" It was more out of surprise than anything.

He jerked his hand back. "Nothing."

There was a long, uncomfortable silence then, "We could go to a motel."

"No."

"Come on, nobody has to know."

"Aren't you afraid God will know?"

"Of course God will know, but he's forgiving."

"What about Hell?"

"I'm a fifty-year-old man with a lifetime of right living." He swallowed hard. "God help me."

God help me, I thought, *really.*

"I need to get home." My voice had started to tremble.

"I would never tell your father anything about it."

"Does he know you like men?"

"Of course not. I don't like men in that way—except you put an idea in my head."

"You got the idea all by yourself."

"What's another hard dick to a sinful boy like you?"

"I'm not a sinful boy. I'm a good son, and I want

to go home."

"I guess I must seem old to you."

I stared out the window at the new spring growth on the shrubs along the highway. I wondered what my father would think of his best friend trying to seduce his sixteen-year-old son who had just lost his mother. Would he pin the fault on me? Had he ever done anything like this, I wondered, and then didn't want to know. I was disappointed enough as it was.

"What are you thinking?" Marvin asked.

"You have a wife and children. You have a son older than me. You preach at me about my behavior and then you want to go to a motel with me. I don't understand."

"When I was fifteen, I kissed a boy."

"And you liked it?"

"Oh, yes, I liked it."

"What happened?"

"Nothing. I've just never forgotten it, that's all."

I felt so sad. I wanted to be alone and cry. My mother was gone, and this man that I had known most of my life wasn't who he pretended to be. I wanted to go back to being eight, when it was okay to be small and not understand things, and to look like a girl, and I could sob my heart out against my mother's softness.

Chapter 12

Mourners still crowded our house when I changed into jeans and a denim jacket and snuck away, back over to the cemetery. My mother's grave had been filled in and was piled with flowers. I sat next to it to think, with my knees drawn up to my chest. I wasn't crying but could've been, as heavy as my heart was.

Ron came up silently behind me, pushed the Stetson down over my eyes, and put his big hands on my shoulders. Then he laid his face against my neck and sighed. He didn't say anything, or need to. I listened to his steady breathing and felt his warm breath near my ear. We stayed that way until I began to cry. I couldn't hold back any longer.

"Oh Jed, I'm so sorry about your mom."

I wanted to lay my head on his chest.

"What is it, Jed?"

I blubbered about the sadness I felt over the death of my mother, and admitted to Ron that I'd hurt her, maybe failed her by running away. I never had a chance to explain to her before she was gone.

"Your mom knew you loved her, Jed," he said softly. "And she knew why you ran. I know she was proud of you for being your own man."

I told Ron the story of Marvin Jenkins and his anti-homosexual lecturing followed by his weird request to take me to a motel.

"He's married," I sobbed. "I don't understand."

Ron looked like he was going to throw up. "What a sick old pervert. Did you tell your pop about it?"

"No, he'd just blame me."

"Before the funeral," I added, "my pop told me he loved me."

"Well, that's good, isn't it?"

"He never said that before."

"Maybe he just didn't know how."

"I think adults are more messed up than kids."

"I think so, too." Ron lay down beside me, shielded his eyes, and looked up at me. "I want to hold you, Jed."

I wiped my face on the sleeve of my jacket. "I want you to, but not here."

"Let's get some camping stuff and go where we can be alone." The tiny quarter moon scar on his cheek glowed. He stood, grinned down at me, and offered his hand.

* * *

Ron and I were lying together in two sleeping bags zipped together. We were on top of a butte visited only sporadically by whoever maintained the collection of wind generators that sat up there like rows of corn in a field. We had chosen a spot near the edge, as far from their creaking as possible, but it didn't really bother us. Nothing bothered us, and under the low-slung stars, it seemed like nothing ever would.

"Do you want your hat back, Ron?"

"No, it looks too good on you, Cowboy."

"My pop still thinks I look like a girl."

"Your pop is jealous because you're so handsome and he's not."

"There's a man where I work that shoves me around and says I look like a girl."

"He probably just wants to get in your pants."

"What? I really doubt that. He's a big ol' redneck. He talks about screwing girls non-stop when he's not accusing me of being one."

"He sounds homophobic."

"What's that?"

"It's someone with homosexual tendencies who can't face that about themselves. They respond in an over-the-top way if they get aroused by someone of the same sex. They tend to be the ones that commit violence against homosexuals."

"How do you know all that?"

"Reading." He turned on his side to face me. "You should try it sometime."

"Very funny."

"Want me to come there and hurt him?"

"No. I'll handle it. I'm not afraid of him."

"I could teach him about respect."

"I'll handle it, Ron."

Later, we put on our jackets and sat up, looking out over vast darkness. We could see specks of light from ranches here and there. The faint glow from Ft. Stockton was behind us. There was no moon, so the stars were in-your-face and seemed close enough to touch.

Ron crooked his arm around my neck. "Are you going to keep on with rodeo?"

"I don't know. I don't know what to do."

"You'll be a famous rodeo star if you keep going."

"That's what Pop always hoped."

"Just because your pop wants it doesn't mean it's a bad idea, Jed. You're good at it. I mean really good."

"Yeah, well what choice did I have?"

"What are you going to do about your horse?"

"I don't know. I want him, but I don't know if Pop will let me take him."

"But he's been yours since you were little. You trained him."

"Right, but you know my pop. And anyway, I can't afford to feed him right now. I don't have a place to keep him, either. Maybe I can get him later."

"I hope you can." He nudged me. "So tell me something. Have you done it with a girl? I know they chase you."

I started to lie, but I thought that would make my conscience pain me worse. "I did it a few times."

"And?"

"I don't want to talk about it. If you want to know about sex with a girl, you should have sex with one and see for yourself. There's probably not one girl at school who wouldn't do it with you."

"I don't want to do it with them."

"It's overrated anyhow."

He laughed at that.

"Do people suspect you, Ron?"

"I don't think so. Everyone thinks I bought that abstinence 'til marriage bull crap."

I laughed and leaned against him.

After a while Ron got out his guitar and sang. No matter what he sings, it's beautiful and lands right in your heart. He sang a few songs, but *Are You Lonesome Tonight* was the best. He sang it better than Elvis, better than anybody. His eyes never left mine, and the light from a billion stars was reflected in them.

"I wish we could live together," Ron said.

"I don't see how we could."

"I know; I just wish it, that's all."

"Remember the Wilson brothers."

"Jesus, Jed, please don't talk about them."

The Wilson brothers were not related, not by blood anyhow. They were Randy Wilson and Bobby Hightower and they attended our church, or tried to. They never touched, and rarely looked at each other for the same reason I didn't want to look at Ron around anyone else. There were rumors about them being homosexuals, but Ron and I were ten and eleven and we didn't care or even understand what that meant, except it was a Terrible Sin.

From my current perspective, stark naked on a bluff with Ron's warm body by my side, and both of us glowing as bright as the stars, it seemed like those two "brothers" had been living the good life.

The Wilson brothers and the rest of our congregation were railed at regularly about homosexuality until I wanted to yell to shut up about it already. The reason Ron said *don't talk about them* is because of what happened. First they were asked to repent their lewd lifestyle—something they did not do. The two men neither admitted they were lovers nor claimed not to be. Then somebody told somebody else that they had been seen at the gay nightclub in Odessa, dancing and holding each other—and not like brothers. We kids were stunned to know there was such a thing as a gay nightclub and burned to know about it. And it

was as close as Odessa. We didn't stop talking about it for weeks.

Even as children, Ron and I wondered which of our congregation had been in the gay bar to witness the Wilson brothers so wickedly enjoying themselves. It was a question that never seemed to bother the adults.

The brothers were stylish dressers, and young. They were kind and courteous with everyone, a good reason for Christians to be suspicious.

The adults got together and confronted the Wilson brothers, and as you might guess, they never came back to our narrow-minded church. Men like my father and Marvin Jenkins went to church Sundays and Wednesdays, and served as elders, and thought they had a deal with God where they could do whatever they wanted and be forgiven. When they sinned, they saw it as "boys being boys," while the brothers were true sinners of the worst sort.

The thing Ron didn't want to talk about was that the Wilson Brothers were beaten to death a few months later. Their immaculate home was burned to the ground with their brutalized bodies still inside it. Then our congregation whispered that it was retribution from the Almighty. Even kids knew better than that. Ron thought men from our church had done it, aided by some of the town's other witless rednecks.

"I have a job," I said to get our minds away from the brothers, "but I don't make much and besides, you should finish high school. And where would we live? We wouldn't be accepted anywhere, Ron, and I don't see how—"

"Shh." He rested his fingers against my lips. "Shush. I know all that realistic crap, but I'm still wishing it."

I thought maybe it would be better to live with Ron and struggle every day than to live a lie.

"I wish it on the stars," he said, not sounding like his usual practical self.

"Ron, you should finish high school and go to college like you planned. I can work and save money so we can get a place of our own after you graduate. I can make extra money bull riding."

"You're just trying to shut me up."

"No I'm not. I don't want you to shut up."

Ron dropped the idea of us living together as quickly as he had brought it up. He changed to another subject. "My band is starting to get some good gigs."

"That's great! You'll be famous one day."

"Naw, I won't, but maybe one day I'll be playing at a rodeo where you're riding bulls and winning every prize."

"One day your songs will be played on the radio."

"Oh, Jed, you'd have faith in me even if the rest of the world stepped on my head."

"That's true, Ron, but you're more talented than you realize."

"I don't mean to go all Patsy Cline on you, but I love you, Jed Petersen."

"I love you, too."

"What are we going to do?"

"I don't know, but you better not stop kissing me."

"I wouldn't be able to stop."

Ron begged me to stay, but I didn't think I could go back and live with a father who hit me or who was unable to understand my love for Ron—not to mention the strong physical attraction between us. I didn't want to hear any of his narrow views ever again, or be sent to Kansas to "get over it," or hear his rants about how angry I made his God. I believed in a different God, one that understood how two men could love each other.

CHAPTER 13

Ron drove me back to Balmorhea the next day in his dad's truck.

After a long silence, he blurted, "I have to say something Jed, or I'm gonna explode."

"Well say it, Ron."

"You claim to love me, so why are you screwing around with women?"

It was a fair question, and I really didn't know how to answer.

"It's messed up, Jed, and it hurts."

"Ron, I wouldn't hurt you for anything."

"Well, you're doing it."

"Look; it was just something I tried."

He pulled the truck to the side of the highway and cut the motor. "I know you don't want to be gay. I understand that. Everybody thinks it's wrong. It's hard to accept the negativity when your heart knows it's not wrong. Doesn't something inside you say this is how it's supposed to be and everyone else is missing it?"

"Yes, Ron."

"I think you want it to work with a woman because then you'd be 'normal,' and I don't blame you for that."

"I only did it a few times and I'm not doing it again."

"I've been working through this since I was five. Maybe it came as more of a surprise to you, I don't know. Maybe you're not gay and I turn you on for some reason, but either way, you have to figure it out." He sighed. "Whatever you decide, you need to know that

I'm going to come out."

"You are? What about football?"

"I have to be who I am, Jed. I like football, but I'd rather put all my attention on my music. Anyhow, I can't keep living this lie I'm in." He took my hand across the seat. "I want to bring you with me wherever I go. Will you come?"

"Yes, Ron. Please take me with you."

"Okay, then."

"I'm already out where I live—to a few people."

"You are?"

"It just happened, accidental."

Ron sighed and looked at me with a tender expression. "I love you so much it scares me, Jed."

"Don't let anything scare you, Ron. I love you, too."

* * *

"This place doesn't seem like much," Ron said as we approached Balmorhea. "It looks broke-down."

"That's just this part. It's an okay place."

"I don't know if coming out is a good idea in a redneck place like this."

"Well, I didn't have a choice, and Fort Stockton isn't much different. Anyway, it's too late to worry about it, since I'm out."

"Be careful, Jed."

"I will, Ron. Will you leave me at my work? It's right up here."

"Sure, but I don't want to leave you at all."

We sat together in the lot at the back of the restaurant. To anyone watching I suppose it looked like what it was: two guys having difficulty saying good-bye. We thought we were being discreet, but when people care about each other they might as well wear a sign.

Right before I hopped down from his truck, Ron took my hand and squeezed it tightly. "Don't forget me, Cowboy."

"I won't, Ron. How would I ever forget you?"

* * *

On Saturday night the restaurant was slam-packed. I didn't get out of there until nearly midnight, which made me the last to leave. I locked everything

and turned off all lights, including the one at the back door. Then I stepped into darkness. My eyes needed a second to adjust, so I stood still a moment, entranced by the sky.

I wish it on the stars, Jed.

Loneliness for him was a deep ache, but I didn't know what to do about it. I was so embroiled in love and sex thoughts I didn't notice a large shadow creep up to me until it was there. By then two others were behind me.

Tiny stepped up close enough that I could recognize him. "I saw you with your boyfriend yesterday."

I tried to keep my voice level. "He's a friend from school."

"What about Gina?" He stepped still closer. "I guess you'll fuck anybody. You must be some little stud."

I didn't speak, which angered him, but I didn't know what to say to get his head away from that line of thought.

"If you got nothin' but friends where do you get sex?" That was a different voice.

"His right hand and some of those queer-boy magazines," said a new voice with an ominous tone.

There was laughter while Tiny continued to advance. Looming there in the dark, twisting and yanking at his clothing, he seemed like a person uncomfortable in his own skin. I felt kind of sorry for him, but it was short-lived.

"You're prettier than my girlfriend," said someone, not Tiny.

"That's because she's such a dog." Whoever he was started barking and howling. They thought that was funny.

"I want me some of this purty boy here." Tiny steadily closed in. "Queer boys like it up the ass, don't they?"

"I'm not queer," I claimed, for all the good it did.

I began to lose track of who said what and was drowning in fear.

Tiny shrugged. "Whatever. My friends and I want

you to party with us. We don't care if you're queer. In fact, we think you might be entertaining, don't we guys?"

"Sure we do," agreed a man behind me. "You have the nicest ass—ooh-eee. Ain't that right, guys?"

"Take off your pants so we can 'preciate it."

"Look—I don't want trouble." It's laughable the things you say when pure Hell is staring you down.

They began to talk filthy but I can't repeat it since I had ceased to hear anything but my heart. I have never felt such fear in my life, even when my father beat me, or when I had pulled the number of the meanest bull at the rodeo. Adrenaline coursed through me in a flashflood. It was fight or flight, and I waited for a chance to flee and prayed fervently that I could get away. A small man fighting three bigger men didn't make sense. Chuck Norris I wasn't.

They were slowly closing in when I ducked and ran as hard as I could. They brought me down at the edge of the highway and dragged me back into the shadows of the empty parking lot. Without pretense, they yanked off my jacket and then tore my shirt and undershirt off. I screamed for help while bucking like a bull. When I wouldn't be still, they beat me. They jerked the pants off me, but it took all three of them to do it. I was kicking and fighting with everything I had. They took turns punching and kicking me while they got themselves worked up.

I'm gonna fuck you so good you're gonna beg for more—Hold him, damn it, hold him still—You're gonna suck me, faggot—Hold him tighter—Don't let him get his arms loose again—Hold his legs still.

I was more afraid of the fucking than the beating. I fought so hard one of them brought out a knife. It glinted in the starlight. Then it was held to my face.

"Want us to cut you up?"

"Be still or you'll wish you had."

"We could cut off your dick. How'd ya like that?"

I was still. My body hurt so badly I had nearly quit moving anyway. Then my face was mashed against the ground as I was splayed naked with pebbles biting

into my cheek. Strong hands held my shoulders down, and others, my feet.

I love you so much it scares me, Jed.

A zipper…then shuffling, scrambling…a groan.

"I'm first." Tiny.

No, no, no, no, no.

Someone kneeling…*Oh God…*scrambling groping panting…Tiny… *Oh, Jesus, no.* Fumbling, hands on my ass. *No, no, no.* Stroking, gasping… Wetness on the back of my thigh. *God, no.*

"Shit, man, you didn't even get it in there."

"Shut up."

You have the most beautiful eyes, Cowboy.

"It's my turn."

Are you lonesome tonight?

"Come on, Tiny, it's not our fault you blew your turn."

Do you miss me tonight?

"You show us how it's done, Jocko."

Are you sorry we drifted apart?

"Tiny's ready to go again, aren't cha, Tiny?"

Does your memory stray to a brighter summer day, when I kissed you…

Pain…panting…pain…pushing…pain.

When I kissed you and called you Sweetheart?

Thrusting, thrusting. *You're hurting me!* Welcome to Hell.

"This boy's sweet."

I want to bring you with me, wherever I go. Will you come?

"Look here, it's my turn. You gonna have a smoke or what?"

"Somebody's coming."

"You're the only one coming. For fuck's sake, will you get up from there?"

Let me die. Pease let me die.

"I thought I heard something."

"Yeah, you heard Tiny panting for another go."

Laughter.

Feet shuffled… "You like this, faggot?" Tiny again.

Are you lonesome tonight?

Touching my face, my neck. *DON'T TOUCH ME!* My back. *DON'T!*

"We know you want it."

Different pervert, same pain.

God, God, God help me.

"You did it, now move on." Tiny again. "Now you're gonna get it, sweet ass."

Let me die, oh please, let me die.

"Damn, you're sweet."

Groaning... grunting...pushing...pain.

Are you lonesome tonight?

Do you miss me tonight?

Are you lonesome?

Are you?

Lonesome?

"Let's go before someone sees us."

"Tiny, you going to propose marriage or what? You bring the ring, Tex?"

More laughter.

Tex...Jocko...Tiny...three names.

"Let's leave him over there in the bushes."

"Jesus, look at his face."

"He don't look so purty now, huh?"

"He didn't seem to enjoy it as much as I thought he would."

"Hey—" Toe of a boot in my ribs. "You alive?"

"What if he dies?"

"He ain't gonna die."

"What if he tells?"

"He ain't gonna tell. Faggots don't tell."

"What makes you so sure?"

"Hey guys—I think we really hurt him."

"Come on, I see lights coming."

"Let's go for a beer and some bar-b-que."

"Yeah, I worked up an appetite, and I have to work later."

When I kissed you...

And called you Sweetheart.

I woke up on my back. Not dead. Bleeding, naked, cold, leaking, nauseated. My clothes had been thrown on top of me, along with Ron's Stetson.

Ron.

Oh, Ron.

I shivered uncontrollably, too sad and traumatized to cry. I threw up, then collapsed. Sadie was up the highway, and I knew she would take care of me if I could get to her, but I didn't want her to know what they'd done. I didn't want anyone to know. Nothing is worse than being raped. If there is, I don't know what it would be.

I had turned to my side and was passed out when I heard the crunching of gravel. My heart nearly stopped I was so afraid I would be raped again. I wanted to run but couldn't move. Then a pair of boots stood next to me. Looking to see who wore them was out of the question.

"You alive?" It was one of the perverts, not Tiny. He bent and checked for a pulse in my neck. "We don't want queers here. Are you hearin' me?"

It took everything in me to speak, but I didn't want him to kick me to see if I was still alive. "Heard you," I groaned.

"It'd be stupid to report this. I happen to know the sheriff don't cotton to homos, either." He started to walk away but came back. "Don't force us to kill you."

"I won't."

The second time he bent over me I saw a gun in a holster on a leather belt and an official-looking patch. He walked away, a vehicle started, and the headlights swept over me as he turned it around. Then other lights roared past him, and in a split-second I saw SHERIFF'S OFFICE on the side of the truck. The pervert was a deputy. Or the sheriff.

When dawn barely began to light the eastern sky I made myself sit up. The sun was starting another day, but it would be shining on a different world.

* * *

It took a long time to get myself upright. I limped to Sadie's, going cross-country instead of on the highway. She had gone to work, so I went in and took a bath. The water turned red; I let it out, filled the tub again, red again. When the bleeding stopped, I got out and put on clean clothes. I still felt filthy. The smell of them hadn't left me after all that time in the tub.

When I studied my face in the mirror, one blue eye stared back in defiance. The flesh around it was puffy and bruised, already turning an assortment of colors. The other eye was swollen shut and looked worse. I wondered if my troublesome face would ever be the same, and hoped it wouldn't. It had brought be nothin' but trouble.

My body was one big hurt. I didn't think anything was broken, but I wouldn't have bet money on it. I packed up my things, every movement causing worse pain than the last. I finally dragged my suitcase into the kitchen.

I left Sadie a letter in which I said I had to move on. I hadn't come home last night because of a run-in with some assholes. I asked her to tell Gina I'd be in touch. I said I hoped she knew I'd never forget her or all the kind things she did. I reminded her to ride Hal, or at least touch and talk to him. I signed it: *With love, your favorite cowboy.*

I left twenty dollars on the table because I took one of her knives for protection.

Then I headed out. I stuffed my bloodied, torn clothes into the trash bin out back and went to the barn. When Hal came up and pressed his face against my chest, I wanted to cling to him and cry. I could grimace and groan, but I couldn't cry.

"I love you, Hal. I'll see you again one day. Don't forget what a stud you are, and keep the dirt out of your mane, okay?"

He nuzzled me like he knew it would have to last me a while.

I limped to the highway, fingering the knife in my pocket. I planned to hitchhike, and if the wrong man picked me up, I would kill him.

An elderly rancher-type stopped for me even though my looks might have deterred anyone from doing it. I could barely drag myself into the seat of the truck.

He watched me, grimacing. "Easy does it, young man. Where you headed?"

"Away from here."

"Looks like you ran into trouble."

"Yes sir."

"What happened?"

"Some guys didn't like the looks of my face."

"Guess not. Hope you let them have it right back."

"Well, there were three of them, and only one of me."

"That's unfair fighting."

There was an understatement for you.

"I'm going to Fort Davis, about thirty miles away."

"That's fine."

"You ever been there?"

"No sir."

"Well, it's beautiful country. There are a lot of ranches where I bet you could get work. You might want to think about staying."

I couldn't think about anything.

Chapter 14

My spirits lifted slightly when I saw the mountains. The road turned sharply onto another and there they sat. I had never seen anything like those mountains. They were stunning standing there in the brilliant morning sun.

My rancher friend let me off in Fort Davis at the courthouse, which sat on a large expanse of green lawn. I wanted to lie in the grass but didn't know how they would feel about it. Instead, I went across the street to a hotel called The Limpia and paid for a room. The clerk, a sweet-seeming young woman, looked at me with sad eyes. I couldn't bear it. She assigned me a room on the second floor, and I went to it.

I needed to sleep, but first I thought a long time about Ron. I wondered what he would say about what those men did. It didn't matter because I was never going to see him again. I put Ron Matthews into a compartment in my heart and locked him there. Then I slept.

When I woke, I was so stiff and sore I thought for sure I'd cry, but I didn't. The sadness on me was so heavy it felt like my heart would give way under the terrible weight of it. I wasn't even seventeen yet and I'd worn out my welcome in the world.

I took a hot shower, went onto the street in search of food, and found a dining room attached to the hotel. It was late and the place was nearly empty. My waitress was a cute, friendly blond woman who spoke with a Texas twang. She said her name was Tammy. She couldn't help but stare at my busted-up face, and I

didn't hold it against her. I was looking worse and worse.

"You get hurt rodeoing?"

"Bull riding."

"Man. You're supposed to be ridin' them bulls, not lettin' 'em ride you."

In spite of everything, she made me laugh.

"You need to be careful, Cowboy. Next time you might get your face busted up."

I laughed again. It hurt me everywhere, but laughing felt good to my heart.

She came to refill my iced tea. "Are you in a lot of pain?"

"It only hurts when I'm awake."

She giggled and then entertained me off and on through the meal. I didn't know if she meant to or if it was just her way. Her friendliness reminded me of Gina, and I nearly cried then. Between them, Tammy and Gina turned my head from depravity and violence for a moment, and I felt grateful to them.

* * *

The next morning I ate breakfast in the same dining room and thought about my options. I couldn't see that I had many. I felt as lost as a catfish at a calf roping.

The coffee was strong and hot, and I loaded it with lots of cream and sugar. It felt comforting going down. On my plate was a ham omelet, and big, soft biscuits, but I could barely taste anything and was in awful pain. Meanwhile life was making plans I couldn't have dreamed.

In walked Kathleen Worthington looking like a million dollars and change. The hostess seated her and her friend near me. I couldn't tell you one thing about the friend. Whoever she was, she paled next to the tiny rancher.

Although Ms. Worthington kept looking at me, I thought she was doing it the way people look at a car wreck. I said nothing and didn't expect her to recognize me.

When I stood to leave she spoke. "Excuse me, aren't you the young man who changed a tire for me in

Balmorhea in the rain?"

"Yes ma'am. Jed Petersen." I tipped my hat to her and her friend. They stared at my ruined face.

The rancher stood and offered her hand. "I'm glad to see you again, Jed."

"Likewise, ma'am."

"Please have a seat." She indicated a chair at their table. I didn't think I could bear the scrutiny—or the kindness. I felt seconds away from bawling like a baby.

"I've already eaten, Ms. Worthington. But thank you."

"If I could impose, I'd like to talk to you a moment."

I lowered myself gingerly into a chair.

"Were you hurt in a rodeo?"

"No ma'am. I ran across some bad guys. There was three of them and one of me. Bad odds."

She laughed. "I'll say." Then her look turned serious. "I wonder if you aren't the same Jed Petersen who won the regional bull riding title in Pecos last summer."

"Yes, that was me. Do you follow rodeo?"

"It's a passion of mine. You're very good, and especially for your age."

"Thank you."

"Do you work on a ranch near here?"

"No ma'am."

"Are you looking for work?"

"Well yes, I guess I am."

"Do you know cowboy work, Jed?"

"Yes ma'am. I grew up doing it." I didn't mention that I wasn't especially fond of it, except for riding and working with horses.

"If you came to work at my ranch would you let me sponsor you in rodeo competitions?"

"Well sure."

"How old are you, Jed?"

"I'm almost seventeen."

"I'm going to give you my card. Will you call me this afternoon? I'd like to meet with you in my office at the ranch."

I walked out of there thinking that life had sent me something else and no matter what, it would be better than the last thing that came my way.

Chapter 15

When she discovered I had no wheels, Ms. Worthington said she would send Rick, her head cowboy, to pick me up. Her ranch was too far to walk to in a few hours, she explained. I still had the knife, so I agreed.

Rick was a weather-beaten older man with big, rough hands. He wore a black felt hat much like my gray one, except his was badly faded and stained with sweat. He still wore chaps and spurs, so I thought his boss must have yanked him out of a corral.

"Damn," he said when he saw me. "Whose bad side did you get on?"

"I got in a disagreement."

"Well I reckon you lost."

"Yes, sir." *You have no fucking idea how much, old man.*

"You've got the look." He peered over at me, "but are you an experienced cowboy?"

"I been doin' it all my life."

"Which ain't that long." He sighed and his attention went back to the scenery. "Rodeoin' ain't the same thing as cowboyin'."

"Yes sir, I know that."

"You seem awful young."

"I am young, but I'm willing to learn and I do know the work."

"We don't need some hot shot rodeo cowboy."

"Could you give a guy a chance? I'm not a hot shot. I'm good at bull riding but that's not all I can do. Besides that, I haven't been hired yet."

"I think you're gonna do just fine." He changed directions like the wind. I thought he was probably just messing with me.

The rough bouncing on the potholed road was playing hell with my bruised-up body and especially my backside. I wondered if I would be all right or if permanent damage had been done back there. I thought I should see a doctor but how would I with no truck and no money?

Rick noticed my unease. "You got ants in your pants or what?"

"Yes, I guess so."

"Do you want me to stop?"

"No, I'll be okay."

Enduring that ride was my first indication that I could be as tough as anybody. Well, I guess it was my second.

Rick pointed out mountains by name and told me a few stories about the ranch. It went on for miles and miles in all directions and was the most beautiful piece of land I'd ever seen. He said if I paid attention and worked hard I would get along fine. When he let me out at the office, he shook my hand and wished me luck.

Ms. Worthington welcomed me to her ranch, which was known as Worthington Ranch. The starting pay wasn't much, but I got room and board, most weekends off, and could ride all I wanted in my spare time. She said she even let her hands take a truck to town when they needed one, and that included going to dances as long as nobody drove drunk.

"I'll raise your pay when I see if you're going to work out. And I'll split all rodeo winnings with you fifty-fifty. You keep all the trophies, belt buckles and gear you win. Does that seem fair?"

"Yes, ma'am, that sounds fine."

"In effect, I'll be paying you to train, and I'll pay all your travel expenses and entry fees, too. And anything special you need for any of it. Do you have any questions?"

"Could I bring my horse? I've worked with him since I was a little boy. He's the best working pony

you'll ever see. You could take his feed out of my pay."

"If what you say is true and you use him to work, I'd be glad for you to bring him and feed him with the other horses at no charge. He'll earn his keep."

"Thank you ma'am, I'll make sure he does that."

I agreed to everything regarding pay and living arrangements. I wasn't in a strong position to negotiate a better deal, and anyway I was grateful for the opportunity to get my head away from evil men, and to have my horse with me.

Ms. Worthington, who asked to be called Kitty, sat back in her chair and studied me. "Are you all right, Jed? You seem to be in a great deal of pain."

I stared at her blankly.

"I see it in your one good eye, and the desperate set of your jaw. Also, you're wheezing. I don't think you should be wheezing."

"Well, I was thinking I should see a doctor to make sure nothing is broken."

"I think that's a good idea. I'll take you myself."

"Oh, no ma'am, I couldn't ask you to do that."

"It's no bother. I need to go into town anyway."

When she said 'town,' she meant Alpine, about twenty-four miles from Fort Davis; it was even further from her ranch. She called a doctor she knew and said we had an emergency and were on our way.

I didn't know if I could stand the trip without screaming, but I needed to know the extent of the damage. I didn't need something wrong with me that would keep me from bull riding since it looked like that was going to be my meal ticket. And cowboy work is rigorous. I didn't want the other men to think I was as delicate as a girl.

As we passed through her ranch, Kitty talked about the land she adored. Her eyes shone with joy, and I tried to pay close attention to what she was saying to keep my mind off the pain and dark secrets, but mostly because she was a woman pleasing to watch.

She told me some of the mountains' names, but the only one I remembered longer than a minute was Conrad Peak, named after her late husband, Conrad

Worthington.

There were miles of pasture shining golden with native grasses and in some places, small herds of grazing cattle. There were rugged peaks and stark rock outcroppings. Boulders of all sizes surrounded some of them, as if the mountains were crumbling back to earth.

The thing I liked the most about Kitty was her respect for the animals that made her living. We passed some cowboys working on fence lines and she said she didn't know all their names yet, but she knew every horse. She also said she couldn't abide a man who was cruel to his horse. I agreed and cautiously told her about my gentle system of breaking them.

She was interested and asked intelligent questions, and looked at me in amazement when I answered. She made me feel like an important man, not a boy. Her interest and happiness pushed back the darkness in my head.

"I want to see how you do that," she referred to the taming process, "as soon as we get you well."

"Yes ma'am, I'd be glad to show you, but I feel like I'm going to pass out." The pain made me want to cry, but I couldn't get all Patsy Cline around my new boss.

* * *

The doctor was kind and had me lie down right away. He gently unbuttoned my shirt and sucked in a mouthful of air when he saw the bruises.

"What happened to you? Auto accident?"

I didn't want to say.

"Were you in an accident, young man?"

"I was beaten by three guys—and—and—"

"And?"

"And raped. I was raped." My voice broke, but I had said it and felt better for it.

"You were raped by three men?"

"Yes, sir, and I hurt everywhere. Please help me."

He examined me and said I was going to have to be admitted to the hospital. He called them while still examining me.

"I have a young man in my office that has been

beaten and raped. He has broken ribs, among other problems." He then ordered various tests, including blood work, and told them he would be in after his last patient. "Also, he needs stitches over his eye. Well, you'll see. I'm going to butterfly it for now." He paused a moment to listen and then said, "Yes, you call the Crisis Center, and I'll report it to the law."

"Jed, where are your parents?" he asked after he hung up.

"My parents are dead."

"Do you have a guardian? Who cares for you? Someone has to sign for you at the hospital since you're a minor."

"I'm responsible for myself, sir." Fear crept over me. "I don't want anyone else to know what happened."

"I'm sorry Jed, but a few people will have to know. You need urgent medical attention. What about Ms. Worthington? She'd be your guardian. She's a fine lady and cares about her employees. I assume you work for her?"

"She hired me today."

"I'm going to speak with her."

"Please don't tell her I was raped."

"Jed, it's nothing to be ashamed of. It wasn't your fault, and by law I have to report it. Rape is a violent crime and you're a minor. There's a very competent nurse at the hospital that will do your exam and a counselor from the Family Crisis Center will meet you there."

"I don't want any of that."

He watched me with sad eyes. "I'm sorry, Jed." Before I could say anything else, he left to tell my new boss my secret.

I lay there in agony and prayed to die. After a few minutes Kitty came in and my prayer became more fervent. I couldn't look at her. She took my freezing hand in her warm one and sighed. That was all it took. Tears began to come in a forty-year flood.

"Is there a loved one I should call for you?"

"No."

"You'll be all right, Jed."

"No I won't." I was about to start wailing.

"I'm so sorry this happened to you. You should've told me the truth before, but I understand why you didn't."

I was sobbing in spite of the pain it caused.

"Jed, I'm going to take you to the emergency room." She spoke as she buttoned my shirt. "There, you'll meet people who understand what it's like to be raped and they'll help you get through this. I'll help you, too, if you'll tell me what you need." There was a catch of emotion in her voice. I loved her for that and hated her for knowing my secret. Anyway, it made me cry more.

Then my boss, my new guardian-as-far-as-the-hospital-was-concerned, a woman I would have preferred to impress with my manliness, laid one hand cautiously on my cheek. "Jed, honey, we need to go." With the other hand, she wiped tears from my face. Her voice was as soft as her touch. "Cry as much as you need to. It's okay to cry, but can you sit up so we can go? Doc Cramer is going to think I'm not much use as a guardian."

I struggled to sit up and cried out in pain. She helped me and kept her arm around me until I could stand, and then put her arm around my waist and helped me limp out of the room.

"Jed," Doctor Cramer called from down the hall, "I'll be over after a while to check on you. You let Kitty take care of you, all right? You're going to be fine, young man." The compassion in his voice nearly started me crying again, plus I had a woman wrapped around my waist. There was a gale-force storm of feelings going on in my head. On one hand I didn't want to be touched by anyone; on the other, I craved the comfort of touch the way a little baby does.

On the ride to the hospital I collapsed against the seat, exhausted. Kitty spoke in soothing tones until I fell asleep. I didn't wake up until we screeched into the drive at the emergency room. Two medics met us with a stretcher and lifted me onto it.

"I'm going to park the truck and then I'll find you," Kitty assured me.

A black man was standing like a sentry by the

door. As we went through it he spoke. “I’m Kenneth Morrison, Jed, and I’m here as your advocate.”

He was big, built like a tank, and had a friendly smile. He said he was from the Family Crisis Center. He looked like an Army of One.

“Jed, we’re going to undress you,” one of the men told me. He was a paramedic according to a badge which read TED ANDREWS, PARAMEDIC.

“No,” I said without thinking twice.

“This is hard, Jed.” My advocate had stepped in. “We’re all here to help you. Now just relax and let these men get your clothes off.”

“No. Nobody’s taking my clothes.”

“But we have to assess your injuries,” the paramedic explained.

Then a female chimed in, a nurse who said she was certified to do rape exams, and I didn’t want anyone—not even Ron now—to see me naked. I tried to struggle against them and then Kitty was there. I thought they were going to strip me in front of her, and there was no way that was happening unless they killed me.

“Who are you, ma’am?” the nurse demanded.

“I’m his guardian, Kathleen Worthington,” she said in a six-foot voice. “What are you doing to him?”

I realized she wouldn’t let them hurt me and almost started sobbing again.

“You’re going to have to wait outside, ma’am,” the nurse said. “We’ll call you when you can see him. It’ll be a while because I have to do the rape exam and treat his injuries. A doctor will stitch his face, and any other place that needs it.”

They finally stripped me and did what they wanted to, but I was drugged and didn’t care. It was fine if they called in the whole damn town and showed everybody my stuff.

Chapter 16

I woke up bandaged and clean and tucked into a bed in a bland, sterile room. Kitty was there, speaking softly to Kenneth Morrison, my advocate. My chest was wrapped so tightly I could barely breathe, but I was breathing. Pain was absent for the first time in—how long? I had no clue, and I felt fuzzy and wondered if Kitty had seen everything, and I almost cried again.

She leaned over me and spoke softly. "Hey, Jed, how do you feel?"

I responded with something unintelligible and she took my hand. "Just rest, Jed. You need plenty of rest."

Kenneth Morrison stood on the other side of the bed. He looked ready to keep perverts and national threats at bay single-handedly. "When you feel like it, I'd like to hear your story."

I wasn't about to tell it.

Kitty left to run some errands and said she would bring me a hamburger. Damned if Kenneth didn't work the story out of me while she was gone. It tumbled out in sobs, and I was nearly incoherent. He listened calmly and took notes.

"I'm so sorry, Jed," he said when the tumbling stopped. "I can't imagine how you endured that, but you did. I want to help you move on from here so it doesn't haunt you the rest of your life."

I didn't see how it could ever do anything else.

"I know your first reaction is to not tell anyone what happened. Don't try to keep this in, Jed. Cry and scream if you want to. It's normal to feel a great deal of

grief and outrage. It's also normal to blame yourself or to feel that you did something wrong."

"I didn't do anything!"

"Yes, I believe that. I'm on your side."

"They said I wanted it," I sobbed.

"Nobody wants to be raped. It's common for rapists to blame the victim."

I couldn't hold back the tears. It was awful to cry in front of that big, manly man.

He pressed on. "Are you gay, Jed?"

I stared at him with tears I couldn't stop rolling down my face.

"Jed, listen. You can tell me anything. I want to see that justice is done on your behalf, and I need to know everything."

"I was attacked in the dark and don't know their names. I told you that already."

"That's not what I'm asking."

"I know what you're asking. I don't think it's any of your business."

"I'm trying to help you."

"How will it help me to get hauled in and be outted in court and cause a big scandal in a small place? Who will hire me then?"

"I understand how you feel."

"How could you? Are you gay?"

"No, but I am black and was mostly raised in Alabama and south Texas. I've felt my share of hatred, but nothing as terrible as what happened to you. You're right that you'll be outted. If you haven't come out, that's something we have to consider."

"Look Kenneth, those men thought I was gay."

"Have you ever had a sexual relationship?"

"Why are you so damn nosy?"

"I'm sorry if I seem that way. I want to help you."

"Yes, I've had sexual relationships. One was a man, the other a woman."

"Do you consider yourself gay?"

Not anymore. "Why do you care?"

"I need to know so I can properly represent you."

"I represent myself. What do you mean represent me?"

"Let's talk about the men who assaulted you."

"I don't want to."

"I understand, but how will we prosecute them if you won't say who they are?"

"We won't."

"Then how will you get closure? And what about the other young men they may rape and eventually kill?"

"I can't be responsible for other people."

"Come on, Jed. I can't believe you won't care if you hear that these bigots have done it again."

"Of course I'll care, but I'd also like to live."

"If you turn them in they'll go to jail."

"What if they don't?"

"It's common for rapists to threaten their victims. If you won't come forward with names, then they get away with it. That's their plan."

"I already told you I don't know their names."

"Jed, everything you've just said tells me you know who they are."

I didn't respond.

"This crime has been reported to the sheriff, and you'll be asked for a statement. I need to know how much I can reveal about you and what you know."

"You can't tell the sheriff!" Only pain kept me from lunging out of bed.

"The law says a rape has to be reported."

"He'll kill me!" I groaned and covered my face with a pillow.

"What do you mean, he'll kill you? He's a lawman."

I kept my face covered and said nothing.

"Jed? Please look at me."

"I wish you'd go away."

I slung a pillow at him. He caught it and tossed it back as if we were playing. "I'm here to help you, Jed. I'm on your side."

"Then help me get away from here." I tried to sit.

"Jed, please explain why the sheriff terrifies you."

"Where are my clothes?"

"Jed! Focus."

"You focus. I need clothes."

"Why does the sheriff terrify you?"

"He's going to think I told."

"Who is?"

"The sheriff! Please—my clothes. If you really want to help, get me out of here."

"I can't do that."

"Okay, I'll leave without them."

"I'm on your side, Jed. Please explain what's going on. If you need to be in a safe house after the hospital, I can arrange that."

"Wouldn't the sheriff know where the safe house is?"

"Well, yes, he's the sheriff."

"But the sheriff was one of them."

Kenneth sprang to his feet. "Are you saying a *sheriff* raped you? Our sheriff? I thought you said this happened in Balmorhea." He moved to the side of the bed.

"He'll kill me. And he'll know how to get away with it."

"Please try to be calm. I won't let you be hurt again."

"You won't be able to stop him."

"What makes you think it was the sheriff?"

"There's no way in hell I'm going to testify against him. You would understand if you'd been there."

"I understand your terror, but we're going to keep you safe. Are you telling me it was the Brewster County sheriff or the Reeves County sheriff, and are you sure it was the sheriff, or was it a deputy?"

"Well he didn't introduce himself nice and proper-like when he was fucking me against my will."

"I'm on your side, Jed, and I know this is difficult."

I sighed. "He came back during the night and threatened me, and I saw his gun when he bent down and his badge, and then I saw his truck, just for an instant, when he drove away."

"You never heard any names? What about his nametag? Could you read it?"

"I was dying out there and thought he'd come back to rape me again. I was in a panic you wouldn't

believe, and my eye was swollen shut, and it was pitch-black, so no, I didn't read his name."

"I'm sure the Brewster County sheriff had nothing to do with this. He's a good man that I've known a long time. His name is Billy Lawson."

"Will he make us report it to the other sheriff?"

"No, I don't think so, since somebody in that office is a criminal. Can you describe the men?"

"I want to stop thinking about them."

"We'll take a break. Ms. Worthington is back with your dinner. She was at the door. I'll go get her."

That was when Dr. Cramer walked in. "How are you feeling, Jed?"

Kenneth sat back down.

"I feel better, thank you."

"I have some questions and I want to tell you about your injuries and what we're doing for them. I'd like for Mr. Morrison to stay if that's all right with you."

"He can stay."

"Your eye has ten stitches and all of your injuries have been treated as much as we can treat them. Your ribs are wrapped. We're going to keep you here a couple of days to be sure you're all right. Those men made a big mess of you, but you're young and I believe you'll heal just fine."

He checked my pulse as he spoke. "I've notified Sheriff Lawson, and he'll be here to speak with you any time now and make a report." He took a deep breath. "It will take a while for the results from the rape exam to come back. We're not sure we'll get anything since some time has passed since the rape. Do you know if your attackers used condoms?"

"No." I didn't think so, but I was so beaten and terrorized I wasn't thinking about condoms. "What would you get from the exam?"

"Semen, DNA evidence hopefully."

When he said semen, I realized I knew. "They didn't use condoms." The gruesome details of the hours I was lying in the bushes leaking and bleeding came back in high definition. I felt the muscles in my face begin to twitch and willed tears away. He had the decency not to press me.

"Your blood will be tested for HIV and some other things, but it may take a while for the results to come in. I'll call you if you've been released by then."

I went numb at the thought of AIDS.

"We're administering pain medication and antibiotics through your IV and if your pain worsens, call the nurse. Are you in pain right now, Jed?"

"No sir."

He patted me gently on the arm. "Mr. Morrison is going to give you a lot of good advice over the next few days. I hope you'll listen to him. Do you have any questions about your injuries or treatment?"

"Well, I—" My Army of One was watching us, and I didn't want to say it but I had to know. "Am I permanently damaged in my—back there?"

"No, Jed, you'll be fine. You need a few days of rest, and we'll keep a close watch on you here. It won't be long before you're back to normal. If you have a question at any time, call my office or ask a nurse. There are some male nurses. The same is true if you feel like you aren't healing. Call me. And no question is considered stupid or out of line."

He still had hold of my arm. "Jed, I have some information in my office for young men. It's about staying healthy sexually, and of course that includes condom use. I don't know if you're sexually active, and I don't need to know that right now, but if you are, I hope you're using condoms."

He didn't give me a chance to say anything. "It's a terrible thing that's happened to you. My job is to help you heal of your physical injuries, but the worst won't be the physical. Please do the things Mr. Morrison suggests and accept his wise counseling."

"Yes, Doctor, I will."

"Kitty is waiting in the lounge. I'll speak to her when I go out. I'm leaving now, but she has my cell number if you need it. I'll be back tomorrow morning to check on you, okay?"

Kenneth stood and asked the doc if he could speak with him outside. I flew into a fury. Well, it was as much of one as I could manage. I demanded that my advocate keep what I'd said confidential.

"I will do that," he said calmly. "Your right to privacy is foremost in my mind, but I still need to speak with the doctor."

I slammed myself against the pillows and cried. My plan to keep the rape to myself was unraveling at Gina driving speed and there didn't seem to be a way to stop it. And speaking of her, I wished I could go back and have her hold my head in her soft little hands.

Suddenly Kitty was standing by the bed. "Oh, Jed, are you in a lot of pain?" She turned to set down packages, and then took my hand. "Should I get the doctor?"

"No."

"What do you need?"

I need Ron. I need for my life to be like it was before.

"I don't want to stay here."

"You need to be here, Jed."

"I'm not safe here."

"Of course you are. I'm here, and Kenneth is out there in the hall. He looks like a man who could keep all the demons of Hell at bay."

She was trying to make me laugh, but three evil men had brought Hell to me, and I knew it would take more than one big black man to banish it, no matter how strong and intelligent he was.

The sheriff strode in like he owned the place. The minute he greeted Kitty I knew he wasn't Tex or Jocko. He hugged her, and I felt instantly jealous of him for how casually he put his arms around her tiny waist—and made worse because he was tall and spiffy in a crisp uniform. He looked tanned, wholesome, handsome, a lady-killer if I ever saw one.

He turned and stepped over to me. "Are you Jed Petersen?"

"Yes sir."

He held out his hand and we shook. His eyes were kind, and I couldn't help but like him.

"I apologize for not getting here sooner, but I wanted to come myself instead of sending a deputy because of the seriousness of the crime. When Dr. Cramer called, I was up to my neck in some other

problems."

"That's okay."

"I'm sorry you were so brutalized." He said it with sincerity.

Kenneth came back into the room, shook hands with the sheriff, and then propped himself against the window sill so that Kitty and the sheriff could have the only chairs.

"It looks like you were about to eat," Sheriff Lawson said. "Why don't you eat while the food is hot?"

He motioned to Kenneth and they left together. I would've been upset about that except Kitty was there and she bustled around the room, setting up my food on a tray, and brightening the place with her presence.

"I bought you a pair of pajamas while I was out. I thought they would be more comfortable for you than that gown. Why don't you change while I set up the food?"

I thought pajamas were the best idea I'd heard since I got there and went into the bathroom to change. Kitty helped me maneuver the IV stand, but then she stood there frozen, staring at me with wide eyes.

"Is there any place they didn't hurt you?"

"No ma'am, they got me pretty good every place." I was embarrassed for her to be looking at me the way she was and me barely covered.

When she left and I began to change, I couldn't do it because of the IV. The gown hung up on my left arm. I managed to get the bottoms on and went back to the bed, still wearing the stupid gown.

Kitty looked up from what she was doing. "Oh, we'll tell the nurse. She can disconnect it so you can change."

I crawled back into bed, weak and shaky from the short trek to the bathroom. Kitty said she'd brought cheeseburgers, fries, and cokes. It hurt me to sit up straight because of the binding around my chest, but she arranged pillows around me and behind me until I was comfortable.

Once I bit into the burger I couldn't stop. I didn't understand how I could be so hungry, even though I didn't remember the last thing I'd eaten. Kitty tried to

cheer me by talking about ranching and rodeo. It made me feel normal, except for the IV in my hand. I wasn't about to complain. The drugs killed the pain, and the lack of pain gave me hope, like maybe I would have a chance to be myself again.

* * *

"Kenneth says you don't want to give me the names." The sheriff was back, and he wanted details. He asked Kitty to leave. Before that she had been charming the socks off every man present. Because I was a minor, and she was acting as my guardian, she had a right to be there, but I told her it was all right to go. I wanted to spare her the details. More accurately, I wanted to spare myself the embarrassment of having her hear them.

"I don't know their names."

"Jed, I can't do anything except investigate if you won't give me what I need. I understand how frightened you must be, but I can't rest until I bring those men to justice."

I did not give him names. I made a statement and as I spoke he wrote it out for me. Then I signed it. He had another long talk with Kenneth in the hall, but I couldn't stay awake to worry about it.

When I woke up again, Kenneth was asleep in a chair with his feet in the other one, and Kitty was lying on the other bed, sleeping soundly. They hadn't left me. I couldn't believe it. I turned my face into the pillows and cried myself back to sleep.

CHAPTER 17

Three days later, I was released with a print-out of care instructions, along with pain pills I didn't think I would use. I would be sleeping in a bunkhouse with a lot of other men, and I thought I should stay vigilant until I saw how things went.

Kenneth begged me to give him *just one name,* but I couldn't. I wanted to put it behind me and figure out how to continue living. He made an appointment for me to see him for counseling a week later, but I didn't want to do that, either. I knew he would continue to beg for the names I refused to give to him.

As we turned in at the ranch gate, the last colors of sunset were playing out, making everything a muted golden color.

Kitty sighed. "Isn't this beautiful?"

"Yes ma'am. It's the most beautiful sight I ever saw."

"I'm very blessed to have this land, Jed, and I hope you'll be happy here. I think it'll be a healing place for you."

"Yes, I'm sure it will."

"By the way, the cowboys have been told only that you were badly beaten in an altercation with some ruffians. They don't know where you came from, Jed. I didn't think I should tell them anything about you."

"Thank you."

"They'll ask you a lot of questions, but I thought it should be up to you how much you want to tell them."

"Thank you for not talking about me."

"Listen Jed, it's going to be lonely for you with no one to speak to about this, so I was thinking—I wanted to say—that I'm here if you need someone."

"Thank you."

"Everything you say to me will be kept confidential. My crew knows this about me. I don't like gossip and discourage it when I can. The other thing is that you're going to be living with a bunch of men. I was wondering if you'd be nervous, because if you are, I could find another—"

"I'm not afraid of them, Ms. Worthington."

"Kitty."

"I mean Kitty."

"If you have any problems at all, I want you to come to me."

"Yes Kitty, I will."

She let me off at the bunkhouse. I thanked her, took a deep breath, and went in to see about the rest of my life.

* * *

A week later, five of us were working in a corral near headquarters when the head cowboy, Rick, spotted Kitty walking towards us. He let out a long, low whistle. "Lawd have mercy, Baby's got her blue jeans on," he half-sang.

"How'd she even get them britches on?" wondered Pete.

Harley squatted down. "Here, Kitty, Kitty. Come to daddy."

"I could help her get them britches off," claimed another cowboy called 'Shorty' because he stopped growin' at only six and a half feet.

They gave each other the high-five.

"Keep on dreamin', Shorty ol' boy," laughed Harley. He glanced at me. "Close your mouth, Jed, and try to breathe natural."

I burst out laughing, although laughing and coughing still caused me awful pain.

Nothing more was said as Kitty came closer. We put extra-keen attention on the job at hand. The next time I looked up, she was standing at the corral with her arms hanging over the fence, watching us.

"Good morning, guys."

Everyone greeted her respectfully.

She propped one boot on the fence. "Jed, may I speak with you a moment?"

The other men gaped as if she had offered herself to me. Pete winked. Rick started to laugh and then pretended to have a fit of coughing. Harley put his back to us. All of them were squirming with unspoken wisecracks.

"Sure," I said, cool as you please, and walked over to her.

"Good morning, Jed."

"Good morning, Ms. Worthington."

Her smile was brighter than the sunlight glinting on her hair. "Kitty," she reminded me.

"I meant to say Kitty."

"How are you feeling?"

"I'm a little better every day. Thank you for asking."

"I'm glad to hear it. You're looking better, too. Doc Cramer called and left a message for you."

For a couple of seconds I couldn't breathe.

"He says to tell you that your blood work looks excellent."

I let out a big sigh of relief. *Thank God.*

"He'd like to see you again in two weeks to see how you're doing, okay?"

"Okay."

"Don't forget."

"No ma'am, I won't."

After she was out of earshot, Pete started. "You're looking better too, Jed." He spoke in a falsetto and strutted around, neither looking nor sounding like her. "Doc Cramer says your blood work looks excellent, not to mention the rest of you."

"She'd take off those britches for a blue-eyed heart-wrecker like you, I bet," Harley figured.

"Please. She's old enough to be my mother."

"Yeah, but she ain't. She could teach you things you never even dreamed."

"Oh, he dreams it, all right," said Rick.

"Shut up. She was just bein' nice."

"That's how it always starts," said Pete. "First she's nice. Next thing you know you're ridin' her all night long."

"You make that sound like a bad thing."

"Why do think she sponsors bull riders?" Rick winked. "Endurance is why."

"Yeah, we just hope you can go longer than eight seconds!"

"Hell, yeah, I can go all night."

"Oh yeah? Well, don't wear out your hand, Jed."

They were about to hurt themselves. I laughed, too, and took the ribbing and backslapping, thankful they saw me as one of them. Nobody said anything about me looking like a girl.

That weekend Rick took me to pick up Indio. In spite of thinking of Ron the whole time, I didn't contact him. I couldn't have seen him, didn't want to see him, and yet I felt the draw as if he was standing in front of me. Being so near and not seeing him was almost as painful as the rape.

We came back to Fort Davis through Balmorhea. That wouldn't have been my choice. I would've driven across the country to avoid the place, but it was the route Rick took, and I couldn't think of a manly way to stop him.

I leaned my head against the seat and closed my eyes. I opened them once and saw a sight that lifted my spirits. Sadie was riding Hal through a bright green field at a gallop. They were as beautiful as a picture. I closed my eyes, but held tight to that image.

* * *

I worked hard at the Worthington Ranch and soon gained the respect of the other men. They might have seen me as the little brother of the bunch, but the truth was I worked as hard as any of them, and harder than some. I was also good at the work. I had promised Mom I would finish my high school education, but didn't have time for studying, what with cowboyin' and helping the rodeo team.

Some nights I slept in the barn with Indio, sobbing and whispering my sadness to him. He nuzzled me as if he understood. Other nights, I fell into bed and

mercifully, slept. But when sleep wouldn't come, I thought about Ron. He had escaped the prison in my heart and nothing I did could put him back in. I wondered how his band was doing and if he was all right, but mostly I missed his love, his touch, and the way he looked at me. The lonesomeness nearly made me come unglued.

Sometimes I had dreams: grunting, groping, panting, pushing, painful nightmares of coarse men using me and throwing me into the bushes. It was unbearable, but I never cried out, or if I did, none of the others heard me. I would wake up sweating and with my heart galloping to kingdom come, and then I would lie still and think about Ron and how he had wished on the stars.

Chapter 18

One weekend five weeks after my stay in the hospital, I went with the Worthington Ranch rodeo team to a competition in Pecos, Texas. The world's first rodeo was held there over one hundred and twenty-five years ago, so I knew the name before I had ever been to the town. There's not a rodeo cowboy in Texas who doesn't know about Pecos. I had been there plenty of times.

I hadn't been able to practice because of my injuries, and wouldn't be riding bulls until Dr. Cramer thought my body was ready to take the abuse. I was a team member whether I was competing or not and was expected to go.

The other members treated me with respect because I had a reputation as a serious competitor. They knew my name from other events and last summer's win at the regional rodeo. I had turned seventeen on the second of April and they teased me constantly that I had lost my edge now that I was such an old man.

"Just wait and we'll see," was my response.

The arena was packed, cowboy hats brim-to-brim. The air was as heavy with excitement as it was with dust. Team members from all over the area yelled back and forth, animals jostled each other or rattled their pens, rodeo fans screamed from the stands, and horses whinnied and stomped with impatience. The heady odors of sweat, popcorn, animal manure, and aftershave blended together on the breeze.

We had two other bull riders on our team, Harley

and Pete, and I went with them since it was expected of me. For a while I walked around the bullpens and watched them butt the enclosures and snort with indignation.

I helped our riders ready themselves while we waited out the last of the roping competition, then I wandered around looking for cowboys I knew, but mostly just wandering.

When the bull riding was announced, it was aggravating how excited I was. My blood pressure shot up as if I was about to ride. Harley had pulled the number of a bull named Code Blue, a huge, angry animal that was all but uncontrollable in the chute. It was such a challenge getting Harley onto him that I felt a bald desire to ride him myself. The familiar scene of cowboys, clinking spurs, animals, dust, gawking girls, testosterone crackling in the air—it lifted my spirits. I felt itchy to get my butt back on a bull again.

Code Blue was about as pissed off as I'd ever seen a bull. He resented the weight on his back, and thrashed and reared before the chute opened. Once it did, he leapt out and twirled savagely. He twisted Harley off in three point two seconds. I burned for a turn, literally sweating at the thought.

Look at that Fort Stockton boy ride, buckaroos! He's the cowboy to watch. National circuit, here he comes!

"Damn!" I ripped the TEAM WORTHINGTON cap off my head and slung it into the dirt. "Damn it!" After a second or two I picked it up, slapped the dust out of it against my thigh, said, 'Shit!' a few times and crammed it back on my head.

"Having a problem, Cowboy?" Kitty appeared beside me. Talk about Baby in blue jeans. Wisps of blond hair had escaped a ponytail and curled around her face, framing it. She could have passed for a college girl and damn, she was lovely.

"Well I—it's just that—"

"I know what your problem is." She laughed and nudged me. I froze, but she only said, "You can't wait to get back on those bulls."

"I wanna ride Code Blue. I bet I could go the full

eight seconds."

"Naturally you want to start with the meanest bull and expect the best score."

"Of course, what kind of bull rider would I be otherwise?"

"You're my kind of bull rider." She grinned up at me. "Come on, I'll buy you a beer." I thought maybe she was already drunk.

"I have to wait for Pete's ride, Ms. Worthington. I'm his crew."

"He doesn't ride for at least forty minutes, Mr. Petersen."

"Okay then, I'll have that beer, Kitty."

She laughed and tucked her arm in mine and practically dragged me to the beer booth, talking the whole way. She bought two Lone Star longnecks and we stood at the far end of the arena, against the fence, to drink them. I didn't have a lot of experience, but it didn't take a degree in women to see she was flirting, and she wasn't drunk, and I didn't think I was misreading her.

She made a face. "I don't know why I'm drinking beer. It tastes like piss."

I laughed because I pretty much agreed but didn't admit it. "What do you like to drink?"

"I like whiskey or aged tequila. Margaritas, too, but my favorite drink is sweet iced tea." She turned serious so fast it made me dizzy. "How are you faring, Jed?"

"I'm doing better, feeling pretty good now."

"I'm so glad."

"I'll be ready to start practicing again by next week."

"Not until the doctor releases you and that won't be until those ribs are healed. There's plenty of time."

"Not if I'm going to compete this summer."

"Relax, Jed, there's time, even if you're out for another three weeks."

We talked about the work at the ranch, the bull riders, bulls, and training, but were constantly interrupted by the Kitty Worthington Fan Club. She introduced me to other ranchers, animal handlers,

cowboys, trainers—they were practically standing in line to see her. The time whipped by and soon I had to head back to help Pete.

As I left, Kitty handed me a letter she removed from her vest pocket. "This came for you. I almost forgot." It was from Ron. My heart went into overdrive.

I thanked her, tucked the letter between my shirt and undershirt, and ran towards the bull chutes. A uniformed deputy stepped in front of me. "I need to see your I.D." He spoke gruffly, a man who meant business. "Step over here."

He led me to a wall behind the pens. I thought I was in trouble for drinking and followed him. He looked over my driver's license slowly while I craned to see Pete. My heart sank. He was in the chute, already on the bull. I was failing my team on our first event.

"Jedediah Petersen." The deputy pronounced each syllable carefully. "I remember you well, but I fear you've forgotten me."

In an instant, the shadows in the parking lot returned to my head. Terror came like it had never left. His badge read: "TEX" REARDON.

My heart slam-bammed its way into my throat. When the pervert stepped closer, his hand on his pistol, I ducked and ran as hard as I could towards the chute. If he shot me, so be it. Better dead than raped. I had nothin' to lose.

I flung myself into the fence, gulping at air that didn't seem to make it to my lungs.

"What the hell? Who's chasing *you*?" One of the cowboys standing near the rest of my team stared with his mouth open.

"You okay, Jed?" Pete asked.

"He's got girls after him, I bet," laughed a cowboy standing by the chute.

"Yeah, they swarm him like bees on sweet."

"Or flies on shit."

The bunch of rowdies laughed, oblivious to my suffering.

Pete came up next to me and leaned against the fence. He seemed more concerned than angry. "What happened? You missed my ride."

"I'm—sorry—I—this deputy tried to—"

"You're running from a *deputy*?"

"I had to."

"Christ, buddy."

Harley joined us at the fence. "If he wants you he's going to find you."

"I didn't do anything wrong. Is he following me?"

"No, I don't see anyone, but you're wearing a cap that tells him how to find you if he really wants you. How hard will it be to find the Worthington Ranch?"

I went to the truck and slumped in the seat to watch the crowd. Panic made my heart beat so hard I could no longer hear the rodeo. It felt like Tex was watching and would come for me any second. I had to get the hell out of there.

What I needed was a telephone. After a while I left the guys a note that said I had to leave and would explain later. The truth was I didn't think I'd ever see them again. It hurt me but I didn't see how I could stay. I left my TEAM WORTHINGTON cap on the seat and headed out on foot, back towards the town of Pecos to find a phone. There were probably hundreds of cell phones at the rodeo, but terror kept me from thinking of that. My gut had kicked in and was screaming *run!*

So I ran, constantly checking over my shoulder. They were chasing me, breathing on me, touching, telling me I wanted it and then punishing me in a way I wouldn't ever forget. I could *smell* them. The shoulder of the highway became the parking lot at Casa México and I was running hard and still expecting them to grab me and drag me back to the shadows.

Before long I was sobbing. I only got some control when I noticed a pay phone in front of a Stripes convenience store. I leaned against it, panting, and then pulled Kenneth's tattered card out of my pocket, and called the 800-number of the Crisis Center in Alpine and asked for him.

"Kenneth Morrison," he answered after a few seconds.

I whimpered into the phone when I heard his voice.

"Hello? Who's this?"

"It's Jed."

"Jed, where are you? Are you all right?"

"The safe house—I need it."

"Where are you?"

"I'm at the Stripes store in Pecos."

"I'm coming to get you right now. Is it safe for you to wait there?"

"I think so."

"Do you want me to call the sheriff?"

"No!"

"You'll be all right?"

"Yes."

"I'll be there as fast I can."

He hung up before I could even say thank you. I couldn't believe he was coming for me when I hadn't cooperated with him, had avoided his counseling, and had not returned his phone calls. He barely knew me and he was coming to save me. It made my eyes fill with tears again.

I bought a soda and collapsed against the side of the building in a shadow. For a while I shuddered and held the cold can against my head. After I calmed down a little I took out Ron's letter.

Dear Cowboy,

It took a long time to find you. I've been worried that a demented trucker picked you up on the Interstate. What happened in Balmorhea? A woman there (Sadie) said you left suddenly because of some trouble with assholes.

Then Sadie called. She'd run into an old man she knew who'd given you a ride to Fort Davis. He said three guys had really messed you up. She was worried sick and so am I. So I went to Fort Davis and showed your photo around. My last stop was the Hotel Limpia Dining Room. (Tammy says hey.) On the porch two cowboys stopped me and said that you're working at the Worthington Ranch. I wanted to go to you, Jed, but then I thought if you wanted to see me you'd have called or written. I'm terrified that you have a thing going with a

cowboy, Cowboy.

I keep thinking you'll have a good explanation when I hear from you.

I wrote a song for you. It's called Under the Texas Stars. *My dad (who doesn't have a clue it's about you) thinks I should try to sell it. When you hear it you'll for sure think I've gone totally Patsy, but I want to sing it to you. I want to hold you and love you until you beg for mercy. God, I love you, Jed.*

I got a P.O. Box so you can write to me without anyone seeing the letter but me. Please make a note of the number.

The chorus teacher thinks I should try out for Juilliard. She thinks I'm that good a tenor. What do you think about that? Would you move to New York with me if I got accepted? Will you at least come to my graduation? It's June 5th, 7PM. Big party afterward on the mesa, you + me.

"Cowboys are easy to love and harder to hold"—Willie Nelson.

Love always,
Ron

Eventually I put the paper back into my shirt. I rested my head against the side of the building, shut my eyes, and fingered the letter under the denim.

CHAPTER 19

Kenneth threw the passenger door open and motioned me inside his old Ford truck. "Get in and let's get out of here, then we'll talk."

I jumped into the front seat and engaged the seatbelt while he watched.

"You ready?"

I nodded.

He pulled out in a spray of dust and gravel. When the scrubland of the Reeves County countryside was flying past the window, I began to relax for the first time since Tex Reardon had stopped me.

"Thank you for coming, Kenneth."

"I'm glad you called me. Why are you in Pecos?"

"Rodeo. I'm part of a team, even though I can't ride yet."

His dark eyes moved back and forth from me to the road. "What happened? Why are we going to the safe house?"

"He threatened me—the deputy." I told him the story in fits and starts.

"Are you going to give me his name?"

"It's Tex Reardon."

"Well." He let out a long breath. "That's a start."

I surprised him by saying, "The others are named Tiny and Jocko."

He squirmed excitedly. My Army of One was about to burst out of the chute. "Can we tell the sheriff?"

"Yes, I'd feel better if those guys were in prison."

"I knew you'd change your mind after you

thought about it. I hoped it anyway."

We talked about other things until we got to Alpine. Kenneth never said I was a damned fool for not giving them up before. Nor did he chastise me about not returning his phone calls. Instead he questioned me about life on the ranch, rodeo, and specifically bull riding. He wanted to know how I learned and if I liked it, and seemed interested in what I had to say.

The safe house was empty, which meant I had the run of the place. If a woman was admitted he would move me, but for now this was a more convenient location. The house was cozy, and had a television, radio, CD player, and was stocked with food, CDs, and movies.

Nobody would know where I was. He asked me not to make a phone call unless he approved it, except for 911. In spite of all the food on hand, he said he was going to bring something for dinner.

I asked if he would call Kitty and gave him her cell number. He said he would, except he couldn't tell her where I was. That was okay, I just didn't want her to think I had abandoned the Worthington Ranch without reason. My intention was to call her later and tell her good-bye properly.

Kenneth came back with chicken-fried steak dinners which included baked potatoes, salads, biscuits, and lots of gravy. He got sodas out of the refrigerator and indicated we should sit at the table.

"I called Mrs. Worthington, and she told me to tell you not to worry about anything. She understands why you took off. I didn't give her details, Jed, only that you had been threatened by one of the perpetrators."

"That's good. Thank you."

While we were eating we spoke of more pleasant things, like his activism in the community and especially at the college. He also told me how to get a diploma without finishing high school. I could study, take a test, and get a G.E.D. and he would help me set it up. That sounded good.

After we finished, Kenneth said he wanted to call the sheriff because he would be anxious to pick up Reardon. Sheriff Lawson said he would be right over

and that he had good news about Tex. I couldn't imagine that the deputy had turned himself in, but maybe something else had happened.

While we waited on the sheriff, I tried to understand that I would be safe in the safe house, but my thoughts were dark. I would be alone, and even if I left all the lights on, I didn't know how I would sleep there. I already missed Indio, my cowboy friends, and the familiarity of the ranch.

The sheriff came in all smiles and shook our hands. "I just sent two deputies to arrest Tex Reardon and bring him to the jail here. Sheriff Hoskins already has him in custody."

"That's good." I was amazed but confused.

"Have a seat, Sheriff," said Kenneth.

Sheriff Lawson pulled up a chair and continued speaking. "I have a bit of a story to tell you, Jed. Since you wouldn't give me names, I enlisted the help of the Reeves County sheriff since the crime happened there. We did some investigating."

I happen to know the sheriff don't cotton to homos, either.

Kenneth handed him a soda, and he nodded his thanks but kept talking. "We went to the parking lot of Casa México and found the bushes. There was sure a lot of blood under those bushes, Jed."

I nodded. Didn't he understand that I couldn't keep going back there?

"We scraped up all the bloody ground. Your blood had been there four days at that point, but there had been no rain so I figured if blood evidence was still there, maybe there would be semen evidence, too."

Please don't talk about semen, please don't.

I tried to take in what he was saying and barely could. He didn't slow down and only popped the top of the soda, but didn't drink from it.

"I got the results this afternoon. The crime lab took more than a damn month." He moved the can around on the table. "That dirt held three DNA samples besides yours, Jed. Only one was in the system, Timothy Reardon, because he's in law enforcement. If you'll give me the other names we'll pick them up, too."

"One is called Tiny but his name is Roger Desmond. He works at Casa México or did. They called the other man Jocko. I don't know his last name."

The sheriff made a note. "They're as good as gone."

I put my head down on the table and prayed for it to go away.

* * *

That night while I wasn't sleeping, I answered Ron's letter.

Dear Ron,

I got beat up by some assholes in Balmorhea—nothing for you to worry about. I'm sorry I didn't write before. I'm working and helping the rodeo team, and it takes all my time.

That's great about Juilliard. Yes, you're good enough, and if they don't take you they're stupid.

I'll try to come to graduation.

Your quote is from the song Mamas, Don't Let Your Babies Grow Up to be Cowboys, *made famous by Willie and Waylon. That would be my advice to mamas, too.*

Love,
Jed

* * *

By noon the next day Kenneth came and told me that all three perverts were in jail and were being held on a bond of fifty-thousand dollars each. The bottom line was that if they came up with five thousand they could get themselves bailed out.

I was up and pacing. "When they get out, they'll kill me, Kenneth."

"The sheriff won't let them out, Jed."

"You don't know that."

"This afternoon he's asking the judge to increase the amount of bail. What he really wants is for them to be remanded without bail of any amount."

"Is the judge crazy or stupid?"

"Well, no, but he's being careless. I don't think he has much experience with crime of this magnitude."

"So I have no hope of leaving this house?"

"Jed, calm down. You're jumping to conclusions. You can leave this afternoon. In fact, Ms. Worthington is on her way."

"No, I don't want that. I have to leave town."

"Where will you go? We need you where you can be reached."

"I need to be where I can't be killed or raped again. You don't know what this is like for me."

"I promise you these men are going to stay in jail."

"What if they don't?"

"I would call you if that were to happen, but I don't believe it will." He hesitated and I knew there was something else—something bad.

"What is it?"

"I have to tell you that the men are saying you asked for it."

I threw myself onto the couch.

"They say you exposed yourself and talked about sex all the time. You invited them to have sex with you and when they did, you freaked out and tried to kill them. They say you had a gun."

I couldn't even speak.

"They say you wanted it, that you insulted them and begged them. They just wanted you to leave them alone. They beat you to teach you a lesson. And Tex says he didn't rape you. He says maybe the others did but he didn't, and that you're lying. Of course his semen mixed with your blood at the scene says different."

I still couldn't speak. It was so repulsive I couldn't get my mouth to open.

"He also says he didn't speak to you at the rodeo, that you saw him standing there, panicked, and ran away."

"Okay, I'm done here. I'm getting the hell out of this town and maybe this state. You can't stop me."

"No Jed, don't run."

"That's easy for you to say. Nobody's saying filthy things about you."

"I didn't want to tell you, but you have to know. You're going to hear it from the district attorney."

"No! I'm not, because I won't be here."

"Don't let their lies keep you from pursuing this. The sheriff knows they're liars trying to save themselves from long prison terms."

"What if they get away with it?"

"They won't."

"What if they do?"

"Let's cross that bridge when we come to it."

"No, no, no. I'm not crossing any bridges. I'm leaving."

"Those guys are in a lot of trouble. Of course they're going to try to get out of it. If they were decent men they wouldn't be in this predicament in the first place."

"What else have they said?"

"They say you flaunted being gay."

"I didn't! I was having sex with a woman. You could ask her."

"Whether you admitted you were gay or not, you shouldn't have been raped. Your sexual preference has no bearing."

"Come to think of it, I can't tell you her name."

"Why not?"

"She's older than me and there's that law that says it's illegal."

"It's called statutory rape, but that no longer applies since you're seventeen."

"Well, it's still nobody's business."

"I don't think anyone will need her name."

"I hope not because I'll never give it. What else?"

"The defense attorneys will try to make a big deal out of the gay issue. We might as well face that and prepare for it."

"What do you mean?"

"They'll try to say you're immoral and it might even be worse if they know you were with a woman, too. The district attorney will be able to advise how to handle that. You'll be meeting with him soon. I'll call

you about it."

"So if I was gay that would be immoral and it'd be okay to rape me?"

"Of course not, but that's the idea they want to put into the jury's heads. They want them to think that *maybe* you did invite the guys. All they need is to make them feel a reasonable doubt."

"This is bullshit!"

"I'm on your side, Jed. A lot of people are on your side."

"I don't have a lot of experience, but when you agree to have sex with someone they don't usually beat the shit out of you first."

"Right. We have the photos from the hospital, and the testimony of the doctor and the rape nurse. You have much more on your side than they do."

"So what am I going to do?"

"You're going to go back to the Worthington Ranch and work and try to get on with your life. I'd like to see you once a week for counseling."

"I know you mean well, but I don't want to keep reliving this. It's bad enough I have to go to court and hear them say I was asking for it. You can't expect me to sit still for that. How is talking about it going to help me? I can't keep talking about it, Kenneth. I want to put it behind me. And I'm not sayin' I'm sticking around."

"Counseling will help you put this behind you, not running away."

"Well, if I stay I might try it once, but if I don't like it I won't be back."

"Fair enough."

"I'm not much of a talker as a general rule, and I don't think I can sit around discussing it without going crazy."

"I understand, but you might find it helps. It might surprise you."

I thought that would be a big damn surprise, and I didn't believe it for one second. No way was I going to sit around with another man and talk about how it felt to be beaten and tossed around, or held down like a helpless animal, or how it felt—how it felt in

my heart and soul to take it in the rear from three repulsive creeps who called me sweet and groaned and panted and touched me and said I wanted it and hurt me so bad I couldn't forget. I'd had their semen in me. Sons of bitches! I wouldn't have voluntarily touched any of them in a million years. I just couldn't do what Kenneth wanted. He could understand or not. He had never been raped.

* * *

Kitty seemed to shine while I had a head full of filth. It was awful to have her pick me up and know what had happened to me; for her to *know* that a man who had shoved his penis into me had threatened me at the rodeo, and I had run away instead of beating him to the ground like a man, like a goddamn cowboy. I wanted her to think I was a kick-ass bull rider, not somebody damaged or weak or *used.*

I guess she noticed that I was quiet as road kill. "Do you feel like talking, Jed?"

"Well, not really. It depends on what you want to talk about."

"I guess you've had a rough couple of days."

"You could say that."

"We miss you back at the ranch. The guys are concerned about you. I want to tell them the truth of what happened, but I won't do it without your permission."

"Please don't tell them. I couldn't bear it."

"I think they would be an amazing support system for you."

"I don't want that. I want them to treat me like I'm one of them. I need that more than anything. I want to forget what happened and not think about it all the time."

"Do you think of it all the time?"

"Yes, well no, not if I'm busy. Wouldn't you think about it if...if...?"

"I'm sure I would."

"I want to talk about something else."

"Let's talk about rodeo," she suggested.

Rodeo was a safe subject and something I knew. Since she didn't say anything, and probably expected

me to say something first, I started wondering why she came for me herself and didn't send a cowboy. Did she pity me? Three times I had endured it. Did she believe I wanted it? Did she think I exposed myself to them? My mind took off, conjuring grim answers to dark questions, and I wasn't listening. When she mentioned rodeo, I was back in Pecos with Deputy Reardon leering at me. Then I was running, running, running.

"Jed?"

"Yes?"

"I think you should tell me about taming colts. We'll leave rodeo for another time."

I rubbed my head with both hands. "I'm sorry. I can't think."

"Everything will be all right, Jed."

I had heard that before, but somehow when she said it, I wanted to believe it. She pulled me back from the edge of a dangerous gaping hole in my own head.

After a while, we passed a rancher on a John Deere tractor. She waved to him. "Have you had a lot of ranching experience, Jed?"

"No ma'am. I worked with my dad but we didn't have much land and it wasn't beautiful like yours, but I know roping and riding and milking cows and branding and castrating. I guess I know a little about all of it. I'm a fast learner if you think I don't have enough experience."

"I wasn't faulting you, I was just wondering if you had other ranches to compare with mine."

"Oh no, you must have the best ranch anywhere in Texas."

She laughed. "I meant our operation, not the land, although I agree with you about the land. I just wondered if you thought I was old-fashioned."

"Well, I reckon I wouldn't know that."

"We passed that John Deere and I was thinking that I don't like machinery to do the work if an animal can do it. Animals are what make ranching worth doing. Do you know what I mean?"

"Sure I do. They add magic to a place."

"Exactly! That's what I mean, and especially the horses." She beamed at me and it warmed my heart.

"I couldn't agree more. I love horses, all horses."

"Yes, I do too. If there's work to be done I want cowboys and horses over tractors and other machinery any day. Some say that makes me outdated but I don't care, Jed. It's my ranch, right?"

"Right. You should do it exactly like you want."

"Otherwise what's the point? Why ranch at all?"

"No kidding."

"I mean no offense to you, but men love machinery and gadgets and new things to play with. I know men that will spend forty or fifty thousand dollars on a tractor they are barely going to use. They think I'm crazy for buying a horse for ten or fifteen thousand. But I'll use the horse all the time, and when it's not working I can look at it. I can ride it or play with it. In my mind, horses will never be replaced by tractors, so when I see a man like the one we just passed I just think, you poor ol' idiot."

I laughed in spite of my mood. "Horses are beautiful and each one is different."

"There's no operating manual for horses."

"That's the truth."

After a while I asked her about bulls. Worthington Ranch was famous for its bulls. That got her going, too. "A lot of ranches are buying semen and artificially impregnating their cows. How ridiculous is that? And unfair to the animals! Where's the fun in artificial insemination?" She burst out laughing.

She went on to say that her cows always turned up pregnant when they were exposed to a good bull and she was a big believer in investing money in the best of bulls and thought the cows would vote for that too, if they were asked.

On the way back to headquarters, she took a different route through her ranch. She knew every square inch of it and loved to tell about it.

"I want to show you a special place, Jed."

We passed through a canyon with a spring-fed stream and walls of rippled rock. It was shaded by giant cottonwood trees, and Kitty named other varieties: Emory oaks, gray oaks, pinion pines and juniper trees. She called it Winding Creek Canyon and said it made a

good outing for a cowboy with a day off.

"In late May the cacti will bloom and you should see these walls. They'll be covered with blooms that seem to come right out of the rock. It will amaze you."

I didn't think it could be half as amazing as she was.

We got out of the truck and hiked, looking for what she wanted to show me. We scrambled over boulders, and she pointed out some fossils and a large metate that had been used by Native Americans to pulverize grain or mesquite beans, or both.

"I suppose they used other plants and seeds to make breads, too. I don't really know. Believe it or not, I wasn't here when the natives roamed the area."

That comment made me laugh. She had no idea how beautiful she was.

"Think how gorgeous this place would've been back then." She was as much in awe of it as I was.

We sat on a boulder in a patch of sun and watched birds sweep down out of the trees for water. They were noisy, but the creek barely made a sound, more of a whisper than anything. I thought it would be nice to lie there for the rest of the day, not saying a word or needing to, just being with somebody, not even touching them.

After some quiet time passed, I noticed she was studying her hands and I knew something was coming.

"You're the only one who really has power over your life, Jed. It might not seem like it right now, but that's the most basic truth I know. You can decide how this story is going to end. You can keep your head in a dark place or you can look up and see the sunlight. Only you can decide whether you want to put your attention on the good things about life or the bad." She hesitated, watching me with eyes the color of the sky. "I'm not presuming to give you advice. Those are just some thoughts I have."

"Thank you, ma'am."

"I've had my own hard times, when I didn't think life was worth living, but I made the decision to put my attention on the things I love. That's made all the difference."

I wanted her to lie down next to me on the boulder and tell me everything that had ever bothered her, but no way would I have the nerve to suggest it.

Kitty mentioned that the creek didn't carry much water, but how important that water was for wildlife, and that she didn't let the cattle near it because they would ruin a pristine place like this. There were other special places on the ranch and she would take me to them if I wanted to go.

So just like that she helped me quit thinking of the things I didn't want to remember, the dark, despairing things I couldn't seem to stop thinking about. Kitty helped me put my mind on the natural beauty around me and the good things about living.

It seemed exactly right to me that a woman with such a beautiful heart owned such a spectacular ranch. Some things were fair, and knowing that felt good, and the knowing settled down into my soul and soothed me.

CHAPTER 20

Ron's answer to my letter came right away:

Dear Jed,

Call me Patsy, but I know something is wrong. Did you get hurt by those assholes—I mean permanently? If you're crippled or something, I'll carry you across Texas in my arms. Please, Jed, why are you shutting me out? Cowboys don't work day and night, do they? Don't you ever have a day off?

If you have someone else, will you just tell me so I don't keep making an ass of myself? I told you I'm waiting for you. Don't make me wait if you aren't into it. The least you could do is to send back my heart.

All my love,
Ron

A week later I wrote him back:

Dear Patsy,

I can't be yours now. It's not because I have someone else. Please don't think that.

Find another and forget me. I will miss you, but this is for the best.

Jed

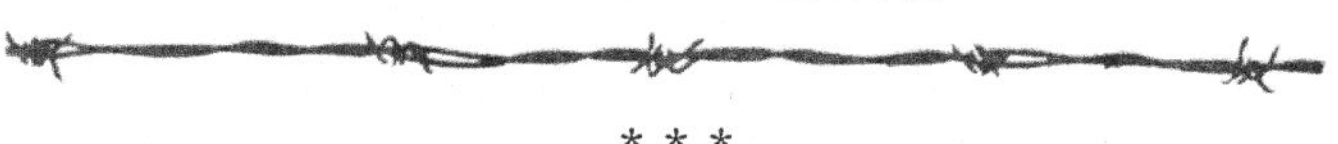

* * *

Once my injuries healed, the team and I practiced whenever we weren't working. Towards the end of June I won my first bull riding competition in the name of the Worthington Ranch. The other guys didn't do as well individually, but the victory belonged to all of us.

When I was riding I was in a comfort zone that most people wouldn't find comfortable. Bull riding was a danger I understood when there wasn't much else I did understand. As I clung onto bulls, the rest of the world slid away. I no longer communicated much with anyone. Oh, I could keep up with the banter of the cowboys and their non-stop bullshit about girls they'd had or were going to have, or whiskey they'd drunk or were about to drink. It was talk about real things I lacked. I didn't know how to get what I needed, and then I turned my heart and head around to where I didn't need anything from anybody.

I didn't attend Ron's graduation. It hurt me and I knew it would hurt him, but I just couldn't go. If I went he would touch me, and I wanted him to, but at the same time I didn't. Before long he wrote that he was tired of making a fool of himself and had met someone else. I cried myself to sleep for many nights. Losing Ron was the most painful thing of all.

During the rest of that summer I competed in local and regional rodeos, and won all of them in the bull riding division. I won nearly fifty thousand dollars in all, which was split with Kitty. I got to keep the trophies, buckles, boots, jackets, saddles, and hats. I saved the money so I could get a place of my own someday.

I spent hours riding over the ranch on Indio; we went up into the mountains I loved and would sometimes spend the night. I wanted to be alone and I was. I would sit on a boulder in a spot I especially liked and survey the land. Most of it was high grassland pasture, but some of it was desert and from the height of the mountains it looked as flat and uninhabited as my heart.

I wasn't gay. I wasn't straight. I was nothing, as

if I had died. Nobody missed me but me. I was so low I thought about throwing myself from a cliff. I still had a rape trial to endure and I dreaded it.

It's hard to explain, and maybe even harder for you to believe, but a problem horse came into my life. In the process of saving him, he saved me.

CHAPTER 21

One day in mid-September, Kitty held me back from going to the nursery pasture with the other cowboys. We were going to check to be sure the new fall calves were thriving, and that all the cows and babies could be accounted for.

When she left word with Rick that I was to stay back, he announced it at breakfast and the others went crazy. They suggested that I was going to be part of a new breeding program—and a lot of other things that would never happen. I thought my skin would burn itself off my face.

As they scrambled out, Rick respectfully removed his hat. "Good luck, young stud. Give it your best. Do us cowboys proud." He saluted me.

I laughed and assured him I would, but I wondered if I was in trouble.

As always, Kitty looked as lovely and fresh as the break of day. "Come in Jed." She smiled brightly and motioned me to a chair. "I want to talk to you about a stallion I have named Midnight."

This was a surprise, as I didn't know she had a stallion.

"I received him a few days ago from a ranching friend as repayment of a debt, but he's—he's not normal."

"How do you mean?"

"I'll introduce you to him. Will you take a ride with me?"

"Sure."

"Could you go saddle Indio and another horse

and bring them here?"

"Of course. Where are we going?"

"He's stabled just a couple of miles from here and it's such a gorgeous day I thought it would be best to ride."

Horses are the best way to go anywhere, gorgeous day or not. We headed across a currently unused pasture that was a sea of ankle-high native grasses and blooming wildflowers. The morning sun was warm on our faces, and Kitty didn't seem to be in a hurry. We ambled along without talking. Birds flitted back and forth among small stands of juniper, or stood on yuccas making announcements about whatever it is that gets birds so worked up.

I mostly watched the mountains. They were more captivating than anything on the ranch, not counting the owner. The sunlight changed them constantly as day progressed. Things in shadow were suddenly exposed, making the same stark cliff look like a different one. Sometimes I could see the layered terrain of the mountains unfolding, like mountains within mountains, and canyons beyond counting. All of it came and went with the passage of the sun through the sky. It was magical, and I wanted to tell Kitty how much I loved her ranch but couldn't find my voice.

She pulled up next to me. "Midnight is already five years old and he's never been ridden, trained, or even tamed. He acts like he's possessed. I would expect for a stallion to be high-spirited and even combative, but this one beats anything I've ever seen. He was delivered a few days ago, and it took four men to do it. He had knocked their trailer to shreds, and he only came from fifty miles away. Do you think you can do anything with him?"

"I won't know for sure until I get to know him. I'll give it my best."

"I don't want you to let him hurt you."

"I'm not afraid of horses, Ms. Worthington. I know how to be careful."

"He had to be sedated so a vet could look him over and also in order to be shod."

"What did the vet say? Did he find injuries?"

"Nothing severe or unusual. He pronounced him healthy. Midnight is a beautiful animal and I want to put him to stud, but I don't see how I can. He would beat a female to death."

"I'm sure I can tame him, but it won't be overnight."

"He's at my private stables. Up over that rise there's another house, one I don't use. I live in the ranch manager's house and its size suits me better. I'm sure the other cowboys have mentioned it."

They hadn't, actually.

"The stables are there." She didn't explain further.

We could hear Midnight before we saw him. He sounded demented and it gave me chills. He was doing the equine equivalent of screaming. I could tell by the sound of his voice that he was also breathless from running. He was being held in a corral with a large metal barn attached. The house where Kitty didn't live was massive too, modern and intimidating. It didn't belong on a ranch in my opinion and especially not the rugged piece of land that was the Worthington Ranch.

The corral and barn were several hundred yards from the house. The place reeked of money and didn't fit with the boss I knew. She seemed more like a female cowboy than a socialite, and her only jewelry was a simple gold wedding band.

Some of the cowhands said she'd murdered her husband because he was old and stood in her way—that she had sordid, burning desires only cowboys could quench. There was some wishful thinking for you. They claimed he had cut off her money when he found out her dirty secret.

They also suggested I make a midnight visit to her in chaps and nothing else since she liked sweet young cowboys with blue eyes better than any. It was more of their non-stop bullshit. A woman who wears her wedding band when her husband has been dead five years sure as hell didn't kill him. She still loves him. It didn't take a genius to figure that out.

"Are you with me, Jed?"

"Sorry. I was just thinking."

"You're thinking the house doesn't fit."

"Does anyone live here?"

"Not anymore. Hammer checks on it a couple of times a week, just doing upkeep work." Hammer was the ranch handyman and could fix anything.

I wanted to ask her why the place was abandoned, but my questions seemed too personal. It was none of my business why she didn't live there, but it probably had something to do with her husband's death. Perhaps it made her sad and besides, it was too big for only one person.

Midnight was totally black and shone almost purple in the sunlight. I had never seen a more beautiful horse, or a more out-of-control one. When he saw us he lifted his front feet high and whinnied and complained so loudly that Kitty and I couldn't hear each other speak. He crashed his big body into the fence, then brought his feet down on it. It was made of heavy gauge cattle wire or he might've already knocked it down. As it was, I wasn't so sure he wouldn't.

"He's trying to get away."

"No ma'am, he's only announcing how miserable he is. He's alone and has no friends. He's been abused and is angry."

Same as you, Jed.

"To him we're enemies who might hurt him. And he's wondering what happened to his herd if he ever had one. This horse is eaten up with fear and anger."

Like you, exactly like you.

"He doesn't want to be alone, but he's afraid of people. He's not possessed, I promise you that."

"You got all that from one look at him?"

"Yes ma'am. He's yelling it."

Kitty said Midnight was a thoroughbred quarter horse bred for racing but had obviously never raced. Rick had looked at him and thought he should be put down or sold to a slaughterhouse. The thought of either thing made my heart ache. I couldn't imagine a horse that wasn't salvageable.

"You can't kill him, Kitty. We have to at least try."

"That's why we're here, Jed."

"Do you know anything about his history?"

"Not a thing, I'm sorry to say."

"That's okay. I'll figure it out."

"How?"

"He'll tell me."

She looked at me as if I had claimed I could fly. "Just for the record, I don't want to put an animal like this down. That's why I brought you. You're my only hope."

"Oh, there're guys much better than me, Ms. Worthington. If I can't do this we could take him to one of them."

"Okay, but first let's see what you can do. What will you need?"

"I don't know yet. I want you to leave me here for a while so I can listen to him."

"And you'll understand?"

"Yes ma'am, I usually can."

"I wish I could watch you work."

"I'm sorry, but you can't. I have to be alone with him at first."

"Is what you do a secret?"

I laughed. "No, it's not that. You might think it's weird, but I don't have any secrets about what I do. I understand the equine language and try to speak it. You could watch but it would be a distraction. I have to establish myself as his partner first, and then his leader. A lot of what I do is boring. I'm doing nothing but being with him. I'll stand quietly and watch and listen to him tell me about his life."

"That's amazing."

"No, it's not really. Since man first started taming horses, he's gotten it wrong. They're easy if you have patience and treat them like you'd want to be treated."

"How did you learn?"

"I don't know. Sometimes I think I was born knowing. I used to watch my father beat and intimidate new colts, and I saw the terror in their eyes. When he'd leave I'd get close and just sit with them."

"So you taught yourself."

"Yes ma'am. I didn't try to touch them unless

they invited me to. Maybe it was because my pop treated me the same way. He wanted to break my spirit, too. Even when I was little I understood how beating and intimidation would never get him anywhere with me or with animals.

"You can get anything you want from a horse, Ms. Worthington, if you just say please so they can understand. Show him some respect and let him know you will never hurt him or abandon him. Horses form an emotional bond with their humans and they can be hurt bad, just like we can. They need regular care, good feed, respect, and consistency, like the rest of us, I guess."

"That's more talking than I've ever heard from you, Jed."

My face went up in flames. "Well, I'm not much of a talker."

"Yeah, I figured that out already. I guess that serves you well when you work with animals, doesn't it?"

"Yes ma'am, I reckon it does."

She showed me a tack room in the barn that had everything I could ever need in the way of gear. There were eight large stalls inside the main part of the barn and they were equipped with an automatic watering system. A door on the right led into a small apartment. As Kitty showed me around, she explained that the fridge was stocked with water, sodas, and juice. In the freezer were frozen pizzas and various dinners, and there were plenty of canned goods. She said she'd bring anything else I thought I would need.

"Do you want me to live here?" I had mixed emotions about it.

Kitty got two sodas and handed me one. "Please sit, Jed. I only want you to stay here if you want to. I'm going to leave that up to you."

"I'd like to be left for now, so I can get to know Midnight. I'll stay a few hours. Then I'll come back and tell you what I think, okay?"

"That's fine. There's a phone on the desk that's an extension of the phone in my office. It also rings in my house. Just pick it up and dial 'one' if you need

anything."

"Please don't let anyone come here until I get back."

I had to practically throw her off her own property. She kept asking questions and was reluctant to leave because she feared Midnight would injure me. I wasn't going to let him. I'd had enough injury to last me forever—but never from a horse.

I watched Kitty ride away, feeling sad to lose her easy company. Midnight watched her, too. He relaxed, thinking he had won his little game of Keep Away. The thing he didn't seem to realize at first was that I had stayed. I knew his game and was sure I could change it, given time.

You're so messed up, how can you help a horse?

I put Indio into the furthest stall from the corral, and shut the doors so Midnight couldn't enter the barn. I got an orange juice from the apartment fridge and went to meet him.

At first I sat up on a fencepost. He didn't like it but didn't know what to do about it. In the wild, horses are prey and are equipped with a well-developed fight-or-flight response. Although Midnight would view me first as a predator, curiosity would get the better of him once I exhibited no predator-like behavior. That's why humans should never strike or yell at a horse. Any type of aggressive behavior is seen as predator behavior and it terrorizes them. Instead, you want to establish that you're part of the herd, and gently demonstrate that you're the leader. Hitting a horse is cruel and counterproductive.

Midnight backed himself into a corner and snorted, watching me, his ears laid back flat against his head. The position of the ears signified anger, but he also pawed at the dirt with a wild look in his eyes. When that got no rise out of me, he tore back and forth from one end of the corral to the other. Sometimes he would stop and claw at the air. He was exhibiting fury, and trying to show me he would defend himself if I meant to harm him. I got it, but he had no way to know that.

When he tired, he stood looking around as if lost,

panting. He did look possessed, but I thought I knew what possessed him. I waited and didn't speak or move much except to drink from the bottle of juice.

Shadows caused by skidding clouds passed over a rugged rock formation at the top of a mountain behind the house. If I had to stay I'd spend some time up there and see how high I could climb.

After an hour, I slipped to the ground and stood. I rested my hat on the fence post so Midnight could see me better. The movement got him going again. Because he was boring me and to show him he was, I did a handstand by the fence and observed him upside down. That stopped him in his tracks. I didn't know it would, but it worked. He started to paw the ground but did a double take. It was comical to watch him study an upside down human. He snorted as if to say *what the hell* and took one tentative step closer. When I didn't move, he took another. His ears had come up into an alert position, and his eyes looked more interested than terrified.

My arms grew tired and all the blood had run to my head, which most likely needed it since blood was always rushing somewhere else. My hair was in the dirt and my shirt slipped down in front of my face so I could no longer see, but I didn't want to move and frighten him away. *What now?*

A huff of warm breath startled me. It rippled the grass, and a big nose began checking me out. Up and down my body he sniffed and snuffled, all of it with curiosity and none with aggression. It was more than I would've hoped. I wanted to laugh and dance and throw my hat in the air, but I was upside down feeling dizzy from all the blood going to my head for a change.

"Hello, Midnight."

He backed away at the sound of my voice, but didn't go far. I came slowly out of the handstand as gracefully as I could. As I straightened into a standing position, Midnight snorted a couple of times, laid his ears back, and pawed at the ground. I rubbed my arms and ignored him.

Before long it was lunchtime. I went inside without looking at the horse and stuck a pizza into the

oven. Midnight was snorting and huffing in the corral, seeking attention. While lunch cooked, I looked around the apartment. It was decorated with western paintings of cowboys doing cowboy work and horses being horses, and of course, cattle.

Stunning photographs of the ranch covered the walls, some of them taken from high in the mountains. Leather was everywhere, in furniture and decorations, and there was cowhide—rugs and wall hangings—as if a cowboy could forget about cows.

Bookshelves were stuffed with Louis L'Amour and other western writers. There were volumes of cowboy poetry, manuals on horsemanship, *Anatomy of a Horse,* and even *The Horse Whisperer.* DVDs and VHS tapes of John Wayne pretending to be a cowboy were represented, and Clint Eastwood's films. I got tired of looking before I saw all of it.

Who in their right mind wants to work with stock all day and then read about it, watch it on TV, and stare at it on the walls 24/7? It was like the apartment was for city people with certain expectations of the old west and swaggering cowboys.

I swaggered back into the kitchen for pizza.

After lunch I did more fence post sitting. Midnight started his old tearing-up-the town routine but tired of it and went to stand in the shade, as far from me as he could get. He wasn't fooling me. At the least he found me weird—maybe interesting—certainly different from other herd members he had known, if he had ever known any.

When I couldn't stand the waiting any longer, I opened the doors to the barn, made sure Midnight had food, re-saddled Indio, and rode away without looking back. Behind me Midnight wailed and stomped his feet like a child. He didn't want to be left. Tomorrow he would be more cooperative. And tomorrow I would stay with him.

CHAPTER 22

Kitty looked up when I walked in and relief spread over her face.

I held my arms out to my sides. “No injuries.”

“Thank God. Please sit, Jed. Tell me what you think.”

“I think he’ll be fine, that’s the honest truth.” I took a deep breath. “I’m guessing he’s been ignored. He was most likely put with bigger animals when he was small and they picked on him. He was a young male with spunk and they kept him in his place by kicking and biting him. In the wild he would’ve gone off with other bachelors until breeding time, but if he was kept in a pen or small pasture, he couldn’t go. And my guess is that there weren’t any other youngsters.”

“How can you tell all that by watching him?”

“It’s easy to see his anger. You saw that. A horse has few reasons to be angry unless he’s been beaten up by humans or other horses. Whoever bred him must have forgotten about him or lost interest. A lot of his behavior is him looking for attention, just like a child will.”

Kitty sighed. “The man that bred him was going through a divorce. I think when Midnight was born he had plans for him, but then put him out to pasture, so to speak.”

“Yes ma’am, I think so, too.”

“You think you can make him normal?”

“He’s going to make himself normal. I’m just going to help him remember what a fine stallion he is.”

“What do you think about staying there?”

"I need to stay, at least for a while. And I want to take a truck instead of a horse, until Midnight can behave better. He doesn't have a right to intimidate our good ranch horses. Also, the horses will distract him from what he needs to be doing."

"And what is that?"

"He needs to get his act together. He's a fine, thoroughbred animal but he's acting like a hoodlum. He has to learn to be a horse again. That means learning to trust."

"How will you teach him that?"

Yeah Jed, how will you teach him to trust?

"I don't mean to be evasive, but I don't know exactly. Every horse is different and needs something different. I have to spend more time with him and then listen to my heart about it. When it's done, I'll tell you what I did if I can."

"What else?"

"That apartment. It's—"

"Over the top?"

"Yes. Can I change it?"

"Of course. Put everything you don't like into a closet. My husband's nephews were coming from New York to spend the summer and help us out. They loved all things western, or thought they did. They were just teenagers and had certain expectations of the old west. We did it as a joke and they loved it until they saw what real ranching was about."

"I like some of the things and I like western stories as well as anybody else, but what I need is a radio and a book about something not western."

"What else?"

"I guess that's all."

She took me from her office into a wood-paneled study with a big stone fireplace and walls of books and green plants everywhere. The furniture was leather and expensive. Huge windows kept the room from being too dark, along with a red sofa that was a bright spot and looked comfortable. I had never seen such a fabulous room.

"Choose any book you want. I have movies, too."

The phone rang in the office and she left me. I

looked out the windows to the rolling pasture and mountains behind that, and wondered what it would be like to sit there and read and know that all that land was mine.

I ran my hands along the sofa. It was as soft as baby skin. I sat for sixty seconds, savoring it, owning it in my heart, and thoughts of Ron came to pester me.

I wish it on the stars, Jed.

Maybe Ron could accept what had happened to me if he knew. *Shut up. Who's going to tell him? Anyhow, he loves someone else now.*

* * *

Kitty insisted I take her XM radio because it was the only way to receive a signal at the Worthington House, the home she had abandoned. Also, she said, cell phones didn't work there. That wasn't news; they worked nowhere on the ranch because it was too far from a tower.

I packed up my bedroll, a change of clothes, and toiletries. I got out before the cowboys came back, although it was tempting to stay to eat with them because the food would be good. It wasn't worth the teasing though. I wasn't in the mood.

As I approached the barn, Midnight went into his don't-mess-with-me-or-I'll-hurt-you routine. I was afraid he'd hurt himself if I couldn't get him to tone that down.

"Yeah, yeah." I went into the apartment to put my things away.

Supper for me would be canned beans and biscuits. I mixed up the biscuits, and when they were in the oven I went into the barn, got a bucket, put a little bit of sweet feed in it and walked slowly into the corral. Midnight reared, whinnied deafeningly, then turned around and kicked at me with his hind legs, but wasn't close enough to harm me.

I set the bucket towards the middle of the corral, walked to the barn doors, and stood right in the middle of them. I crossed my arms and watched him carry on. By the time that stubborn horse moved towards the bucket I could smell the biscuits. He seemed moved by the sweet molasses odor of the feed, but reluctant to

step up and take what he wanted.

Just when I thought Midnight was going to accept my gift, he turned around and kicked that bucket clear out of the corral. Sweet feed sprayed into the air.

"Homerun," I said under my breath, and turned from him, discouraged. The aroma of hot biscuits called me back to the kitchen.

Later I was sitting in the bed of the truck, watching the stars twinkling over the top of the mountain behind the empty house, trying not to think about anything. The XM was aggravating me from the open bedroom window, tuned to Top Country, a mistake I regretted because it made me long for Ron. I should've been listening to Top Twenty. Anyway, it made no difference because when my head decided to mess with me, the music hardly mattered.

* * *

I spent most of the next day watching Midnight and letting him watch me. With my back against the fence, I read *This Side of Brightness* by Colum McCann. I had chosen it because Kitty said it was good, and had nothing to do with cattle or cowboys. It grabbed me from the beginning.

Whenever I entered the corral Midnight went crazy. I did cartwheels back and forth along the fence line until he stopped and stared. I started wondering which of us was crazier. He probably wondered, too. Then, to prove I held that title I stood on my head for as long as I could tolerate it. My arms trembled and my head nearly exploded with all that blood, but he didn't come and sniff me. I thought he was still angry about the offering of oats, a case of too little too late. I went back to reading.

I made pancakes and bacon for lunch, then ate two big cans of pineapple chunks. I could never get full and hoped it was because I was growing.

It was afternoon and the mechanical bull was waiting for me, but damn, he bored me. Bull riding was something I knew. I wanted to learn about something I didn't know, so I went back to the book. It was about the immigrants who built the tunnels under New York

City, working in constant darkness and dank. They were outcasts, mostly black, Irish, and Italian, and many of them barely spoke English. And they were young, low in society, and on their own.

After a while I felt like I was trapped in a dark tunnel, so I pulled on shorts and sneakers and went for a run around the back of the big house and up into the foothills of the mountain I'd been admiring. It was flowers gone wild up there and the air seemed clearer. I thought I might never go back to where the simple humans lived and fucked up everything.

I lay down on a carpet of purple petals and breathed in the subtle fragrance of them. If I looked back I could see a cliff face looming that was much grander than it appeared from below. I jumped up and tried to figure out a way to climb it, but after a few attempts I saw that I was going to kill myself if I kept on, or cripple myself, which would amount to the same thing.

I would carry you across Texas in my arms, Jed.

I followed an animal trail back down, and wondered if Kitty had come up there on horseback to admire the view or the moon or to breathe in the acres and acres of magnificent land. It was all hers. She could sit in her fabulous room and look out at the land and say, *this is mine,* and she wouldn't be kidding herself.

* * *

As I approached Midnight, he started the same ol' scream and stomp routine but didn't seem to have the same heart for it. Or maybe I was getting used to him.

"What are you looking at?" I threw myself over the fence. "Cowboys can wear shorts like anybody else." I stomped off to the barn while he still protested violently to the invasion of his space.

I pulled on socks, boots, and jeans. Then I took a rope off the wall and went to face his demons with him. It was the real beginning of the work I was there to do.

In the wild, when a horse misbehaves or acts inappropriately, he's sent away by the herd. This is serious punishment because a single animal is vulnerable to predators and inclement weather; and of

course there's the feeling of being alone to face the world. When he calms down, he'll be allowed to return. It's a time-out. If he acts up again, he's out. It works for horses and humans. All of us need to belong.

What about you? Where do you belong?

As I walked towards Midnight, he started his hateful behavior and snapped his mouth. The sucker wanted to bite me. I began to swing the rope around and around my head in ever-widening circles. Then I flicked it towards his hindquarters to keep him moving, but I never let it touch him. I was sending him away in language he understood. Even though he wasn't approaching me I was telling him he couldn't.

I realized I needed a round work pen. Midnight tried to take to the corners but I kept at it in spite of the rectangular space. Eventually he was running in a deformed circle around me, as far from me as he could get. What I wanted, and didn't expect to see yet, was for him to make the circle smaller. It would be his way of getting close to the herd, of showing he was ready to behave. Not this horse though; not yet. We both tired and I went inside to shower, put on clean clothes, and think about dinner.

I was sitting on the tailgate of the truck, listening to the radio, and watching the last of the sunset. Midnight was eating in the barn and hadn't kicked anything over yet. Above the sounds of Alan Jackson singing *Pop a Top Again*, I heard a truck motor approaching. I thought it would be cowboys coming to hassle me, but it was Kitty. She was wearing blue jeans, a blue and white checked western shirt, and her fancy boots and matching belt. Kitty the cowgirl dressed up ranch style.

I jumped down off the tailgate, nervous as hell because I hadn't been to practice or even checked in with anyone.

"Hey Jed. I brought you some steaks."

I went to meet her and make excuses, but my mouth wouldn't let me.

"Have you had dinner?"

"No ma'am, not yet. I was lookin' at the sunset."

I took a heavy grocery bag from her and we went

into the apartment. She had brought me more than steaks. There were eggs, apples, oranges, butter, lettuce, tomatoes, and a big bottle of Maker's Mark whiskey.

I was so nervous my hands were shaking. Outside it was getting dark, and I had a female in my space and I was wearing ratty old jeans and a wrinkled blue t-shirt with holes and my beat-to-shit boots and my hair was still wet from showering and was going every which-a-way and my heart was thundering and Clint Black was singing.

"What do you think about us sharing that whiskey?"

I tried to smile. "Well sure, you brought it."

"In that case, I'll pour." She got two glasses out of the cabinet, threw in some ice, poured the bourbon over it, and handed me one.

"Here's to you, Jed." She touched her glass to mine.

"Thank you."

I could barely speak. I'd never tasted bourbon, and I wasn't prepared for the burning strength of it in my throat. I thought I would choke to death, but I held back a fit of coughing because I didn't want her to think I was a pussy. She already knew how I could cry and blubber.

"Jed, why are you so nervous?"

"I'm just—it's that—"

"Why don't you have a seat and tell me about your progress with Midnight?"

I collapsed into a chair.

"Are you having any luck with him?"

"It's early yet, but yes, I'm having some."

And what do you think so far?"

"I think he's been hit in addition to the other things I told you."

I could tell the thought pained her. "What makes you think so?"

"When I hold up my arm, he flinches. I suspect that whenever he became wild someone tried to break him and got frustrated with him. He's been hurt in a lot of ways and it's going to take a while."

"Do you mean weeks or months?"

"I can't say. It depends on him. I'm his way back, but he has to accept me first."

"Jed, are you worried about the trial?" She was so damned direct, and apt to change directions so fast she left me speechless.

I stared at my hands. *Shit! Are you going to cry, little girl? Shit! Think of something else you idiot—think of something, anything. He wanted it, he begged for it. He had a gun. Not that!*

"Jed?"

"Yes, I reckon so." I had a lump the size of her ranch in my throat. "I don't want to go."

God, you're pathetic. You might as well have BOY OF SEVENTEEN *stamped on your forehead—and your throat is on fire, by the way.*

"Jed, you're holding all this in and it isn't good for you. Now I've put you in this situation where you're alone with a crazy horse, and I feel guilty about it. That's why I'm here. Would you like to talk about it?"

"No ma'am, I try not to think of it."

"Are you really an orphan, or are you just estranged from your family?"

"Well, the truth is I still have a father, but he was going to send me away, and I don't want him to know anything about me or what I'm doing."

"Does he live in Texas?"

"Yes ma'am, but you can't make me call him."

"I don't want to make you do anything you don't want to do." She stopped and drank a long drink from her glass. "You indicated that your father beat you like he beat the colts."

"He did. He thought I was willful and sinful; seems like everything is a sin to him. I thought we were going to talk about Midnight."

"Well, we are, but you're more important."

"My father is an angry man. He tried to be a champion bull rider and never was so he expected me to do it. The first time I was on a bull I wasn't quite eight and I was afraid, but nobody can be afraid around Pop because he's like a mean dog. If he smells fear he'll come after you and you'll be sorry. I learned not to be

afraid."

"An eight-year-old isn't physically big enough to ride a bull, Jed."

"You think I don't know that?"

She winced and pulled back from me. "Well, of course you know."

"I didn't mean to jump on you."

"It's okay." She reached out and touched my hand. I didn't intend to, but I pulled away with the surprise of it. I hadn't been touched in so long.

I tried to cover it up by talking. "My legs couldn't stretch enough to cover a bull. By the time I was nine, I had strong legs from hanging on. I would fall off and fall off, and Pop would hit me to make me get back on. It's a wonder I didn't ever break my head open. Did you ever fall off a bull, Ms. Worthington?"

"No. I never tried to ride one, but I imagine it would be terrifying."

I took another sip of bourbon because I didn't know what else to do. It burned but less, and the aftertaste was nice.

"What about your mother, Jed?"

"My mother died. She was sweet and gentle, but she didn't stand up for herself or for me. She was afraid of Pop, like the rest of us."

"So you have siblings?"

"I have two older sisters. They got married and moved away when I was small so I barely know them."

"I think it'd be helpful to have some friends or family at the trial to be there to support you. Would your sisters come?"

"I don't want them to. I'd rather nobody knew what happened. And anyway, I'm used to being alone."

"I don't think that's good, Jed. A young man shouldn't be alone all the time. Don't you miss kids your own age?"

"Not especially. I want to be alone, and now I have Midnight."

"But Midnight is hardly the same as a friend. He's one crazy horse."

"I like him. I guess I'm crazy, too."

"You're not crazy, Jed."

"You don't really know me, Ms. Worthington."

"Would it be so hard for you to call me Kitty?"

"No ma'am, but I was taught respect and you're my boss—"

"Forget all that. Tonight I'm just a friend."

"Well, thank you. I like that."

She laughed and her eyes glistened. "Would you have an objection to us cooking two of those steaks?"

"No, in fact I'm plenty hungry."

She made a salad while I mixed up a batch of my Wonder Biscuits, so named because it's a wonder they ever turn out. Kitty set up the table and poured more drinks, and we laughed and joked around. It felt good to have a friend, and it kept me from thinking about all the things I didn't care to think about. Between her friendliness and the bourbon, I started to relax.

The dinner turned out elegant even though it was only steak, salad, and biscuits eaten off plain white plates in a cramped kitchen at a tiny table with a cowhide-simulated tablecloth. Cowboys and cowhide were aggressively present everywhere but it was elegant because she was there. She was classy—too classy to belong on a ranch or in a simple apartment eating with a simple cowboy, but she was easy to talk to, and her eyes shone when she watched me.

I told her about getting a G.E.D. and the promise to my mother and how much I missed her, and about bull riding, and how I felt about her land, and that I wanted to get a place of my own one day. For a man who never talked much I outdid myself.

We sliced up oranges and apples for desert and shared them from a large plate depicting cowboys branding calves, which would make a person lose their appetite if they thought about it.

We took the bottle and went out to the truck to watch the stars. Midnight jumped up from where he'd been resting and made a fuss. I said *don't look at him, Kitty* and she said *all right, Jed,* so when we ignored him he quit in disgust. We sat on the tailgate and didn't say much, just looked at the sky. It was always a wonder.

"I want to tell you something Jed, and I'd

appreciate it if it was kept between you and me."

"Well, sure."

"Since my husband died his family has tried to get this ranch away from me. You probably don't know this, but the Worthingtons are an old ranching family that has been in this area since before Christ, the way they tell it. I married into the family, and they considered me too young. Also, I was not a Texan. That alone would have made me questionable, even if I'd been the queen of a foreign country. I was the daughter of a Midwestern farmer, and they never quit holding that against me."

"A person can't help where they're born."

"Right, but there are Texas landowners and then there are *others*. They don't believe I have any right to keep land that has belonged to Worthingtons since they stole it from natives, but my husband left it to me. And he made me a Worthington by marrying me, whether they like it or not."

She passed the bottle to me, and I drank from it and passed it back. "See Jed, my husband was forty-eight when I married him and I was only eighteen."

Whoa.

"They think I married him for his money and land, but I didn't care about that. The first time I saw him he was watching me barrel race at a rodeo, and I thought he was so handsome and mature. He was that and more. He looked for me at the dance afterward, and I had no idea he was so old and anyway, it hardly mattered because I fell in love with him."

Her eyes shone so much I felt happy she had been so happy and sad it had ended, and I was drinking too much bourbon but didn't stop.

"At first we only met at rodeos and dances. Then he asked me to dinner and would come to visit me. I was working at a dude ranch summers between college semesters. I thought he was the sweetest man, and he seemed to know what to say while I tripped on words. Oh, how he could ride, Jed. But see, he was a Worthington and of course he could ride. He was probably born on a horse." She paused to drink and seemed thoughtful. "Actually, he was born right here on

this ranch."

"Was he a bull rider?"

"No, he never rode a bull that I'm aware of. Why do you ask?"

"You have a bumpersticker on your Jeep—"

She laughed. "Oh, some bull rider put it on there at a rodeo. Jed, I swear I didn't have a clue that he was rich when I fell for him. I thought he was the ranch manager, and he was, only it was his ranch. I'll never forget the first time he brought me here to ride. It was the most beautiful land I ever laid eyes on. I was just this simple country girl from Kansas. I don't mean to say I was stupid because I wasn't. I was just young and inexperienced. There's no crime in that." She passed the bottle to me. "Drink some of this Jed, because I'm drinking too much and talking too much."

"No you're not. Please keep talking."

"When his family saw how young I was they immediately thought I had seduced him to get his land and I hadn't. He was very proper, and at that point we hadn't done more than kiss. I thought he would want more than that, and I should've realized that he didn't feel the passion I felt. He was looking for a wife because of pressure from his family to produce an heir, but of course they thought I was completely wrong, even for breeding."

My heart, which had felt so happy, sank like a stone in a pond.

"He asked me to marry him, and I was all goofy with a crush that made me weak in the knees. My parents didn't want me to marry so young but I didn't care what they thought—you know how young people are. Anyway, I married him and it didn't take very long for me to realize that he didn't love me."

"How can that be?" I blurted.

"It was awful, Jed, to be so young and to love someone and not be loved in return. I felt like a prostitute and our sex was like that—you know—fast and impersonal. I felt so much passion for him that wasn't returned. Shit, Jed, I shouldn't be telling you this."

"It's okay—I'm not going to tell anyone."

"Have you ever been in love, Jed?"

"Yes, but I messed it up pretty good."

"Don't marry someone who isn't passionate about you."

"No ma'am, I won't."

"I didn't ever get pregnant, and as Conrad got older it seemed less likely I would. So I was a big disappointment in that, too. I wasn't welcome in the family to begin with, and when I didn't produce an heir, I was even less popular. Looking back, I think that was for the best, because if I ever have a child I want it to be with someone who burns for me, you know?"

I nodded mutely.

"But now I'm over forty and oh God, why am I telling you this? Please forgive me. It's inappropriate."

"There's nothin' inappropriate to tell a friend, Kitty. I'm sorry your husband didn't love you. He must have been stupid."

"He was smart and I learned a lot from him about the business of ranching. In fact, I didn't have much else going for me, so I really took to ranching and paid attention. He was willing to teach me what he knew, which was considerable.

"He built that big house for me, and he gave me jewels and cars and other expensive gifts. He tried to love me, but with love you either feel it or you don't. It can't be forced. I don't live in that house because there was never love there. I don't need a place that big—it's not who I am. So it sits there. The Worthingtons can have the house, but not the land.

"Five years ago Conrad died and left me the ranch. I never expected that. I always thought it would go back to his family since we had no children. I think it was his way of saying he was sorry—or maybe it was him thumbing his nose at his stuck-up family. Either way, I got it and I'll never let it go. I've been fighting for it for five years and they aren't going to take it."

"No ma'am, you can't let them."

"Conrad left an airtight will and Texas law is on my side, too. Still, I'll be glad when they go away and leave me alone. Their attorneys have dragged it out and they might think I'll get tired of fighting and give it up,

but I would die fighting for this ranch, Jed. That's how I feel about it."

"I don't blame you. I'd die fighting for it, too."

"First you have to fight for yourself. You can't let those assholes get away with what they did to you. It'll be hard, but I'll be there every day for you."

"I wish you wouldn't come. I don't want you to know the details. I don't want anyone to know. And they're saying it was my fault."

"I know that, Jed. They're filthy liars. They're trying to wiggle out of it but don't let them. You hold your head up and tell the truth and people will hear it. You didn't ask for it, and you didn't do anything to deserve it. They preyed on you and it was three against one. Billy Lawson believes everything you say and the evidence backs it up. He knows you're not a liar and so do I."

"Thank you for that."

"I guess I should go before I make a total ass of myself."

"Kitty, why do you wear a wedding ring from a marriage that wasn't what you wanted it to be?"

"Oh, I'm not interested in another man, and as long as I wear the ring, they assume I'm still in love with my husband. The cowboys talk about it, don't they?"

"You can't blame men for being interested, Kitty."

"I really need to go."

"Don't go. I want to hear more about the ranch."

"I have to go, Jed." She handed me the half-empty bottle and I set it in the bed of the truck.

"I need a round pen," I blurted. *Very smooth, Romeo.* "For working with Midnight."

"How will you get him into it?"

"I'll build it around him—inside the larger pen."

"You really need it?"

"Yes, I really do. I'll explain why when I've had less to drink because right now I just want to lay my head down."

She laughed. "I hear that. I'll call you in the morning."

I helped her out to her truck because she was

weaving and truthfully, because I didn't want to let her go, but I didn't know how to keep her. When I opened the door for her she looked up at me and had this expression like she was going to kiss me and I stepped back, away from what I wanted. Who does that?

Chapter 23

Kitty didn't call me the next morning, which was just as well because I thought I was going to die. In between puking and holding my head, I thought about the kiss I had refused and kicked—tortured—myself with it.

I checked on Midnight but saw him double and the world was spinning. He was unimpressed by my human problems. When he started his demented behavior, I backed off and went back to bed.

I was better by lunchtime and made a few fried egg and cheese sandwiches. I considered calling Kitty to apologize to her for being an idiot, but I didn't know if I should bring her attention to it. Maybe she wouldn't remember. Yeah, right.

That afternoon five cowboys came with fencing panels and we put together a forty foot round pen inside the larger one. Midnight acted hateful the whole time, trying to bite and kick us. He finally retreated to a corner when one of the men screamed at him and threatened him with a stick. That's the way most people react to bad behavior in horses, but I wasn't in the mood to correct a man fifteen years older than me and thirty pounds heavier. I just wanted them to finish and leave.

"Whaddaya think of that big house over there?" Darren asked, but all of them watched me for a reaction. He wore a t-shirt that read: *Half man, half horse—you figure out which half.* "That's where she takes her blue-eyed cowboys, right guys? You been over there yet, Jed?"

“Sure, I been wearin’ her out.” *I couldn’t even kiss her.*

“Good boy!” He slapped me on the back so hard I nearly fell over.

“Where does she take the brown-eyed cowboys?” I asked, making dumb-ass cowhand conversation.

“Shit, she fucks them all over the place, but she gets really heated up over blue eyes—and young ‘uns. She likes them real young and horny.”

That talk continued until they left. By then I wanted to bite them myself. It put me even more out of sorts on a day when I was already losing it, and I still had the problem of getting Midnight into the pen. They said they could force him but I asked them to go on. I would figure out something. There would be no forcing or hitting on my watch. That’s what caused the problem in the first place. I had been on the losing end of hitting and forcing, and it takes the heart out of a person and a horse.

With that thought I sat down in the new round enclosure and cried.

* * *

I moved all of Midnight’s feed into the round space and opened the gate closest to him. He gave me a look that made me laugh. His eyes said he wasn’t going to fall for that old trick, Crybaby Cowboy, but he watched with curiosity. I began to walk around the outside of the circular pen and he had his usual over-the-top reaction to the space invasion. He tore out in front of me, dirt flying, then stopped and reared up to scrape at the air, then continued to run. He looked back to see if I was after him, his eyes wild. It was pitiful.

After about an hour of fun and games, he made a tactical error and accidentally entered the pen. I slammed the gate shut before he could get out. He was so mad I was afraid he would tear the fencing down or injure himself. I walked away calmly towards the barn while he screamed and hammered the new enclosure and then brought it crashing down. That was when my boss drove up. I never wanted to quit anything like I wanted to quit right then.

Because I was at a loss as to what to do, I started picking up the smashed pieces of the short-lived round corral and setting them to the side. I didn't want to face Kitty. Everything was out of control, my skin was burning, I couldn't make myself look at her, and then Midnight went berserk and tried to attack her.

I heard her cry out in alarm and had to turn around. Midnight dashed into the barn and started kicking anything he could find.

"Hi Jed." Kitty was calm, and she reached to pick up her hat. "I guess this is a bad time."

I burst out laughing and couldn't quit. That caused her to start, too. After a while I leaned against the fence and sighed.

Kitty stepped up on the other side, still holding her hat. For a couple of seconds we just looked at each other. The sun was on her face, and I noticed a few freckles across the bridge of her nose I never noticed before. When she replaced the hat they disappeared. It made me think of her ranch's mountains and ridges and canyons that came and went all day long.

"Jed, I came to apologize."

"Don't—"

"I was out of line."

"But Kitty—"

"Please let me finish. I had too much to drink, and I was wrong to bring you liquor in the first place. I don't know what I was thinking. I think of you as being older than seventeen, that's all I can say in defense of my behavior. I hope you will forgive me, and we can still be friends."

"Of course, Kitty."

"I want you to be able to trust me."

"I do trust you. If I didn't trust you I wouldn't be here."

"Oh, thank God." She let out a long breath. "I thought I'd ruined everything."

"No, you didn't. I had fun last night and I like it that you can tell me things that are important to you. I thought I was the one who had messed up."

"No, Jed. I was in the wrong. You didn't do anything."

How ignorant the cowboys were. She was apologizing for getting me drunk and for *almost* kissing me. She hardly seemed the type to be screwing cowboys right and left. It was something they wished, and it passed the time when there was boring work to be done. Plus, she was beautiful and she was the boss, and richer than all of us put together, so that gave her unbearable mystique to a bunch of lowly cowpokes. She could have her pick of men so why would she pick a cowboy?

"I told you I'd call you this morning, but I didn't."

"That's all right. I didn't feel well. I forgot why you were going to call."

"About the round pen."

"Yeah, about that." I glanced at the twisted remains.

Her eyes swept the wreckage. "I sent a crew without calling you because I wanted to speak with you in person and I had to work up the nerve. I guess what I sent wasn't sturdy enough."

"Not for him."

"Will you be able to work without it?"

"I'll have to. I'm thinking Midnight isn't ready to do the work I planned. Somehow I have to reach him, and I don't know how. I have to think about it."

"Jed, you know the state finals are coming up. I think you should practice instead of wasting time here."

"But I'm not wasting time! I told you Midnight would take a while. Somebody damaged him badly and that can't be fixed overnight. What if somebody beat you and made you feel like you were alone in the world? Wouldn't you want somebody to save you, Kitty?"

"Yes," she said softly. Her eyes were so sad. "Yes, I would."

"He's so fine, Kitty. You're not thinking of destroying him, are you?"

"I was going to return him."

"Please don't. You'd be returning him to the hell he came from. I beg you, Kitty. Give me a week, just a week or two."

"Jed—"

"Please, Kitty. I'm in shape for the finals. I can

stay on a bull. I run and work out every day."

"Tomorrow the guys are bringing Death Warrant from his pasture for you to ride."

"Well damn! You want me to die before the competition?"

She laughed. "He's never been ridden, you know." She knew that would make me crazy to ride him.

"Okay. Let's make a bet. If I can stay on for six seconds, you'll let me keep working with Midnight."

"If you can stay on Death Warrant for five seconds you have a deal, because I believe he'd be the biggest, meanest bull at any rodeo. And the fact that he's never been ridden would score extra."

"Okay, five seconds." We shook on it.

"You're one crazy cowboy, Jed Petersen."

"Bull riders are crazy, didn't you know that already?"

"My mother told me to leave them alone."

I laughed at that.

"Okay, I'm leaving so you can work. We'll see you tomorrow afternoon in the practice barn, okay?"

"I'll be there."

"Don't get drunk tonight."

"No, I won't. Don't worry about that."

"See ya, Jed."

"Bye, Kitty." I watched her walk away. Damn.

I went into the barn where Midnight stood in his stall waiting, as if I would serve him dinner on a silver platter. When he saw me he kicked it—hard.

"Haven't you done enough damage for one day?"

He kicked it again.

"Look, we may only have a week and we might not have that long if I get killed tomorrow, so you'd better think about that, buddy."

I went into the apartment, drank water, washed my face, and gave myself a pep talk. It was do or die. I wasn't worried about Death Warrant, but I was sick with worry about Midnight. It had occurred to me that I couldn't help him. I put that thought out of my head and went back to the barn. Midnight had gone into the corral. I followed and took a rope.

He was standing by the feed trough I had moved, and as I approached, he gave it a solid kick. It didn't go far but it made one hell of a clattering noise. Then he kicked it again. I continued to approach slowly.

"All right, Midnight, I get it that you're angry."

Wham.

"I'm angry, too."

Wham.

"I wish I could kill those guys."

Screaming, stamping, and then WHAM and more bellowing.

"God, I'm so furious." I rubbed my head. "Shit. Fuck it. Shit."

He stopped and looked at me.

"What happened isn't your fault." I couldn't believe he was being so quiet. "What happened to me wasn't my fault, either."

His ears had come forward, curious.

"One minute I was looking at the stars and then I was on the ground and men were raping me. Is that messed up enough for you?"

I sat down hard, which left me defenseless if Midnight wanted to attack. "There were three of them. They beat the shit out of me. I know exactly what that feels like, Midnight. When I couldn't fight any more, they raped me. Now they blame me. Is there anything more fucked up than that?"

He blinked and seemed even more curious. "If you can beat that story, then let's hear it. I'm waiting."

He took another step towards me. I held out my hand. He wanted to smell it, I could see he did. "Come on, Midnight, take a chance on me."

The wanting in those big black eyes was clear. A lot of people had looked at me like that, including my boss. *Don't go there, Jed. But I saw it! Don't think about it.*

Midnight's desire was not about love or even sex; it was about acceptance and belonging. After a long moment he turned away from the thing he wanted and put his back to me.

CHAPTER 24

When I got to in the barn, everyone who worked on the ranch was there, even Hammer. Kitty was dressed like her ranch hands, except that they were sweaty and dirty and probably smelled of animals, while she looked like a drink of cool water after a long day in the sun. They applauded when I walked in. I bowed, embarrassed but undaunted.

Death Warrant was behind Kitty, slamming his bulk against the chute, ever suspicious of the humans—for good reason. I was barely aware of him. Kitty stood out from everything else as if the sun was shining on her. It made me feel spun around and backwards, like a ride on a whirly-gig.

"Speech," someone yelled, and I couldn't even say my name.

"I'd like to say something," announced Rick.

"Yo, Rick," they began chanting.

But before Rick gave his speech, Shorty stepped forward. "Try not to hurt this ol' boy, Jed. His testicles are worth about twenty-five thousand dollars apiece, a lot more than yours."

"In whose opinion?" I asked, and they all laughed.

Then Rick took over. "Shut up you rowdy cow wranglers. I wanna talk about Jed. When I picked this boy up for Mrs. W, I thought she was out of her ever-lovin' mind. He was all beat-up and pitiful as a newly-castrated calf." That got laughs and a round of applause. "Then I thought—he's just some ol' rodeo hot shot that won't last a week on a real ranch, but damned if he's not a fine cowboy. Dearly beloved, we're gathered

here today because he's gonna ride Death Warrant. I just wanted to say to ya, Jed, that we're really gonna miss you."

The barn erupted with clapping and laughter. I pulled on chaps and gloves and tried to ignore them. Inside the six-foot deep, coffin-shaped chute, Death Warrant snorted with outrage. I had to focus and mostly, I had to not think about Kitty *(you should go over there naked with only your chaps),* or Midnight and what would happen to him if I lost. *I was going to send him back.*

When I was ready to mount, Rick asked, "Any final words before you get your neck broke?"

I attempted to get comfortable on at least a ton of anxious animal. "I WILL STAY ON THIS BULL!" I screamed and tightened my legs against his bulk.

When I shouted, "Go!" they threw open the chute. Ropes of saliva shot from Death Warrant's mouth. He bucked so hard my teeth rattled and my brain bounced inside my skull. He thrashed and reared, but I hung on.

There was a giant clock on the wall, but I couldn't have seen it even if I'd looked because my eyes were far from focused. I hung on to my good luck Stetson with my left hand and had a death grip on the rope with my right. I was determined to ride for five full seconds if it ripped my arm out of the socket. I had a reputation and a horse to save.

If you've ever ridden a bull then you know how long those seconds are. At times, when your butt hits the dirt it seems like you've been on there a half-hour already, and then the announcer says it was three point four seconds.

Death Warrant finally threw me—and hard—but the cheering was deafening, and I knew I had done it. Two guys helped me up and steadied me. Then they rushed me, congratulating and slapping me on the back and whoopin' and hollerin' the way only cowboys can.

"Seven point two seconds," somebody yelled above the din.

"Now whose balls are biggest?" yelled somebody else.

"No wonder the boy can't hardly walk!"

My eyes were still trying to focus when Kitty parted the cowboys like Moses at the Red Sea. They stepped back, and she stepped up and held out her hand.

"That was amazing." Her eyes glowed.

I took her hand and even through a leather glove I felt the pull of her touch.

"I told you I was ready for the finals." My thoughts were far from that. Bull riding barely interested me anymore. I was torn between a woman I was terrified to love and a horse who was terrified to let me love him.

"Midnight is all yours," she said. "Work with him all you want."

I didn't understand right then that she had given him to me.

CHAPTER 25

The cowboys put me on their shoulders and passed me around along with a bottle of Jack Daniels that wouldn't last fifteen minutes in that crowd. Work was over for the day, for them anyway. Kitty went back to her office, Hammer went off to hammer something, and eventually I went back to Midnight.

He looked up when he heard the truck and continued to watch me. He had begun to think I was interesting—or maybe it wasn't that. At least he had quit trying to tear up Texas when I showed up.

I sat on a fencepost to think about what to do for him, but I thought about Kitty. There was a gap of twenty-five years between her and me. It was like standing on the U.S. side of the Atlantic Ocean and thinking I was close to Europe.

"Besides that," I told Midnight, "I'm probably readin' her wrong. What do I know about women?"

Midnight made a soft sound like a chuckle.

"You're no help. You've never even been laid once. You'd probably kill a female trying to love her, and as for me, I just run away."

I watched him a long time after that, and said nothing more. He watched me, too, and was oddly quiet.

That night I slept outside the fence on top of my bedroll and watched the stars while I listened to Midnight roam. When he thought I was asleep, or dead, he came to the fence and pressed his nose against it to sniff me. I didn't stir or speak, but I ached to touch him.

On the third night of sleeping by the fence, I woke up chilled right before dawn. Midnight was lying against the fence, so close I could feel the warmth radiating off him. I reached out and put two fingers through the wire and touched his side. His skin shivered the way horses do when a fly lands on them, but he knew it wasn't a fly. I moved my fingers slowly.

Midnight started to raise his head but changed his mind. So he knew it was me. I stroked him until my arm tired. It wasn't light yet but it wasn't totally dark either, and in that magic time before daylight drives away night, that horse let me show him some love. It might've been the first time he felt any.

In exploring him with my fingers, I learned of the scars. There were uneven depressions beneath his coat, bites and other injuries I couldn't define with only two fingers and too little light. It made me feel sick.

When my arm tired, I lay there thinking one thought towards him. *I want to love you, Midnight. Let me love you.* I willed him to understand.

Most of September passed like that. We made incremental advances, had good days and bad. He stopped having fits unless a stranger approached. He never kicked anything in the barn again. He never bit me or indicated he wanted to. If I took him a bucket of grain he accepted it. He listened to the radio with me and would lie next to me any time I lay by the fence, day or night.

I tried again and again to approach him on foot but he always shied away. If I pressed him, he raised his front feet in a keep-away stance. We worked with ropes and hand gestures, and I always tried to draw him in instead of sending him away. I started to think he would never trust anyone again. That made two of us, and in many ways we were alike. This understanding did not lift my spirits.

Kitty never returned for an impromptu dinner or anything else. I seldom saw her and was never alone with her. Rick passed her plans and directives to the ranch hands. I hoped she would call me into her office to ask me about Midnight but she didn't. She sent my supplies with Hammer when he came to check on

things, or I picked them up from the bunkhouse kitchen when I went to work with the other cowboys, which I did nearly every day.

My days were busy with cowboying, training for the state bull riding finals, and working with Midnight. Sometimes I would get Indio late at night and ride him bareback across the moon-splattered fields.

I continued to live in the barn apartment and liked being alone, or told myself I did.

* * *

Towards the end of October, Kenneth Morrison called to tell me the trial had been postponed again and a new date hadn't been set yet. That news sent me to a low, low place. Every time I got myself pumped up to face those men it was for nothing. I didn't think I could keep doing it. The trial always hung over my head and worse, the memories.

I dragged myself out to the corral to tell my troubles to Midnight. He had taken to listening to me as if he cared.

"There ain't no justice in this world, fella."

I suppose that was no news to him. He made a soft sound in his throat.

"We have to get past this bullshit, but how?"

I sat in a corner and watched him, and since he said nothing, I kept talking. "Those men don't care what they did to us. You know that, don't you? I'm sick of being lonely, and I don't want to feel so fucked up the rest of my life."

Midnight made one step towards me with his head held high. Then he took two more, waited, and then another. His gait was halting but steady. He was coming to me! I don't think I took a breath the whole time he approached.

I remember exactly how the sun looked glinting off that magnificent animal, the shine of his coat, how it gleamed; his footsteps raised a thin film of dust that hung in the air. He nickered softly, as if to say he understood, and then he tossed his mane with attitude, righteous stallion attitude. Some piece of metal in the corral caught the sunlight and made a glare. I put my hand above my eyes to shade them, and the whole

world looked different.

I jumped to my feet. Midnight stood his ground and I stood mine, and something silent and significant passed between us, one fine stud to another.

That was the first time I ever acknowledged my own fineness with anything other than derision or dread or humiliation—that indefinable thing that some considered handsome—*I love your eyes, Jed* or *You're the best looking cowboy I ever saw*—and too girlish by my pop—*I'll whip that girly out of you, boy*—and alluring, sinful beauty to others—*You are a terrible temptation to a man.* It was loathsome to some—*you wanted it, you pretty little faggot.* To some it was only a joke—*she likes blue-eyed cowboys, Jed, go over there in chaps with those big blue eyes of yours.*

Midnight came to me and put his face in mine and nickered softly, as if to say *here is some love, Cowboy.* In that shining moment, I owned my big blue eyes and my curly black hair and my handsome face.

I raised my arms high above my head. "I'm one fine man," I shouted to the world, and for the first time, felt no shame in it.

A second thought came on top of the first: *I'm going to be all right.*

And then a third: *I have to find Ron.*

* * *

I caught a ride with Shorty; he was headed to Odessa with a prized Worthington bull, sold to a rancher near there. I would figure out how to get back later. All of my attention was focused on talking to Ron. If he couldn't accept what had happened to me, at least I would know and figure out what to do from there.

The closer we got to Fort Stockton, the harder my heart beat. I began to sweat and almost chickened out more than once.

"You sure are quiet," Shorty observed.

"I got things on my mind."

"Are you goin' to visit a woman?"

"Naw, my mean ol' father."

He laughed at that, but he wouldn't have if he'd known my pop.

* * *

"Can I borrow your truck, Pop?"

"You came all this way to borrow my truck?"

"Yes, sir, I need it."

"For how long?"

"Just a couple of hours."

"I guess that'd be okay." Then Pop said, "I'm proud of you, Jed."

I was speechless.

"Watching you ride a bull is like seeing a melody. I never saw anything so smooth in all my life."

"When did you see me?"

"I was there for most of your competitions."

"But you never spoke to me."

"I only wanted to watch. It seems like you don't need any more training from me."

"I'm talking about saying hello to your son."

He didn't seem to get that. "I know I was hard on you, but look how you ride."

"Hard on me? You nearly killed me."

I had never heard my father say I did a thing right. He hit me for jumping down incorrectly, and said if I didn't learn to do it right I would be injured. Meanwhile, he had injured me himself again and again.

The training paid off because when the competition was toughest, and others stayed on the bulls as long as I did, I won more points for what the judges called my "effortless ride and coordinated finish." Effortless, my bull-battered butt.

I would have traded my skill, titles, and all the prizes I had won to have grown up with a father who could show his love.

He took me into the kitchen, which seemed a cold, lifeless place without my mother. He started making coffee. "I guess you heard about Ron Matthews."

My heart rate rose at the sound of the name. "I heard his band is doing well."

"I'm not talking about his band, Son."

"What about him?"

"He caused a big upset by admitting that he's a homosexual. He told his whole class he had a boyfriend and wasn't ashamed of it."

I know Pop expected me to say something, to be appalled, to be repulsed, something. I was unable to speak.

"Shocking, isn't it? I'm sorry, Son. I give thanks that you got over that kid stuff. He was kicked out of church, of course. It's been hard on his parents."

I only wanted to know about the boyfriend.

* * *

I sat in the dark in front of Ron's house a long time, gathering the nerve to find out. I considered not going. It'd be wrong to put myself between Ron and someone else when I had told him to move on, and had written him those emotionless letters. In the end I went anyway and rang the doorbell. That brought Ron's father. He didn't seem at all surprised to see me. He hugged me and invited me in.

"Ron's in Austin, but come on in and talk to me."

"Is he living there?"

"No, he and his band are traveling and looking for gigs."

"I was hoping to see him."

"Will you be here long?"

"Just tonight."

"I guess your father told you about—"

"Yes, he mentioned it."

"Jed, I want to know the truth about something."

"What is that?"

"Was my son in love with you when you lived here?"

"Yes sir and I loved him. I still love him."

"That's good, Jed. He still loves you—not that he's ever said that."

"How I can reach Ron?"

"I'll give you his cell phone number. He might not answer, but you can leave a message and he'll return your call. I know he'll be glad to hear from you."

"What happened about Juilliard?"

"He tried out but then he said he didn't want to go. They don't think much of country music there, and you know how Ron is about it. They wanted to train him as a tenor, but in opera. That isn't what he wants."

"Yeah, he loves country."

"He sold a song, Jed, a really great song. It's called *The Words in My Heart*. Have you heard him sing it?"

"No sir. I'd like to."

"It's beautiful. Somebody big will record it, I imagine."

"Maybe he should record it himself."

"He did record it, but he is still relatively unknown. I guess there's a lot more to breaking into the music business than I ever realized. It's hard to make it nowadays, but he's determined." He smiled at me in a way that reminded me of Ron. "We've been keeping up with your rodeo successes. Ron and I went to the regional finals with your father. You'll make it all the way to State Champion, I'm sure."

"Why didn't you speak to me?"

"We wanted to, but you were overwhelmed with fans and reporters. We could see it was going to be a long wait. Your dad was impatient to get back."

Ron had been there. Maybe I still had a chance.

"Will you please give this to Ron for me? Tell him it's a late graduation present."

"Of course," Mr. Matthews said, and then he saw what it was. "You can't mean to give this away?"

It was a gold belt buckle that read, "Bull Riding, State of Texas, Western Division Champion." It had a raised, engraved center depicting a bucking bull and a rider with his left hand in the air, waving a cowboy hat. It looked like me with Ron's hat, and I hoped Ron would understand what it meant and why I had given it to him.

* * *

A week or so after I looked for him, Ron returned the belt buckle with a note: *I can't accept this, Jed. I want your love not your stuff. You should know that by now. I have another boyfriend, so quit fucking with my feelings. If you ever figure out who you are and what you want, then look me up. Otherwise, quit it.*

I'm trying to make it in country music and it's harder than hell. I know what I want. You have to decide what you want.

Love,

Ron

PS—I sold a song I wrote for you, called The Words in My Heart. *Listen to the radio; someday I'll be singing it on there.*

After a long time, I put the buckle and the letter into a drawer and closed it tightly on that part of my life.

* * *

I turned the love in my heart to Midnight, and he began to accept it graciously and return it. I had made the pen roundish by stacking bales of hay in all the corners. It was more octagonal than round but it served, and we worked long hours sending him away and letting him come back.

Eventually Midnight let me touch him in a horse's most vulnerable places—along the neck where the big cats strike—and on his underbelly where dogs and smaller predators attack first. From there I went to throwing a saddle blanket on him, and eventually a saddle. Each new thing made his eyes wild with fear, but I would jog along next to him as he tore round and round the pen. He would grow calm and try to nuzzle me. Then he would let me hug him.

One day I let him out of the corral. The Worthington House and barn were on a fenced section of land. I had already checked the fence line to be sure it was sturdy everywhere.

For a while, Midnight let me run next to him, but the temptation became too great for him to ignore, and he took off. I lost sight of him after a while, but I knew he was somewhere within that six hundred and forty acres of pasture. I sat in the field and watched the sun work its magic on the mountains.

"Did you lose your horse, Cowboy?" Kitty was suddenly beside me as if she had teleported there. I hadn't heard a truck or a horse, so she must have walked.

"I saw you from the road when you let him out. I hope you don't mind that I followed."

"Well no, this is your ranch, and he's your horse."

"He's yours, Jed. Didn't you hear me say that

the day you rode Death Warrant? I've brought you his papers." She thrust them at me.

"But—"

"You're welcome, Jed. I want you to have him. He'd be dead if it weren't for your patience and love. You are two fine creatures who belong together. I'd like to use him to sire a few colts if you don't object."

"Well no—it would be good for him."

"I would pay you, of course."

"No you won't. He was yours and he's worth a lot of money."

"He wasn't worth fifty cents until you started working with him."

She sat on the grass next to me. "I came to tell you something else, Jed."

"What's that?"

"The trial has been delayed again. Kenneth wants you to call him. And Jed, it's been in the newspaper."

"So the other guys know."

"Yes, but please give them a chance. They adore you and support you all the way. They came to me, stunned that neither of us had told them already. I tried to explain the whys of your hesitation, but eventually you'll have to tell them. They think you don't trust them."

"I didn't want *anybody* to know, Kitty."

"I know that, Jed."

"Now everyone in the world will know."

"I promise you, everything will be all right."

"But how can it keep getting delayed like this?"

"It's legal maneuvering, like what the Worthington lawyers have been doing with me. The defendants' lawyers are trying to keep it from trial as long as possible."

I don't know why, but I looked down at her hands and noticed that her wedding band was gone. I wasn't sure what that meant.

We sat in silence and looked into the distance at land that stretched on a long time, yellow with wildflowers. It looked like a sea of them. There was no sign of the stallion, but he was out there somewhere.

"How are you going to get Midnight to come back?"

"I'm going to wait for him. He'll be back."

Her wedding ring is gone.

I don't know who was commanding my tongue. "I've been waiting for you too, Kitty, but you haven't been back."

She stuttered and stammered and picked at the grass while her face got redder and redder. "That's the real reason I'm here. I want you, Jed. I can't think about anything else. I stare out my office in this direction all day and I feel hot and my heart races. I don't know how you feel and I know you're young—"

I pulled her to me and kissed her. I could never abide so much talking.

She tried a few times to warn me away or to warn herself away from where we were headed. It was the most futile thing I ever witnessed.

"I don't want to do this unless you feel a lot of passion towards me."

I stood and pulled her to her feet. "Come with me, Kitty. I'll show you some passion."

"Oh God, I'm weak in the knees. I don't know if I can walk."

I lifted her onto my shoulder and headed back to the barn apartment.

Chapter 26

"All rise! The honorable Winston D. Forrester is presiding."

Thus began the second worst thing of my life. It was the first week of October, almost exactly a year from when Kitty had come to me in the pasture. It had been eighteen months since I was raped. The wheels of justice turn slowly in West Texas.

The jury had already been selected, but I hadn't had to be there for that. I had to be present for this part, and it was wearing on me, and it was only starting.

The three accused wore suits and were seated at a long table across a narrow aisle from the prosecution's table, where I sat with the District Attorney, Drew Sinclair. I was dressed-up cowboy style with creased blue jeans and a dark blue western shirt. The perverts were wearing suits and were about as convincing as pigs wearing pearls.

The sheriff was seated directly behind us, and behind him, Kitty. I had mixed feelings about her being there. I didn't want her to hear the dirty details but on the other hand I needed her support and, more than that, the love she poured over me. Kitty was like a salve on a searing burn. She was a lot of other things, too, and I'll get to that, but this part is about facing the men who had taken everything from me.

The three were cleaned up and looked around with wide-eyed innocence. Even Tiny looked respectable and had shaved. I hardly dared look. I reminded myself that this morning every one of them had been wearing

orange BREWSTER COUNTY jumpsuits, and they would go back to jail for the night. I would go home with Kitty. As to where we would all be the next day, I didn't know.

The judge gave the jury instructions. I watched them and prayed they would be able to sift through the lies and find their way to the truth that would be presented. It felt like the rest of my life was in their hands.

The charges against the three accused were read and were as follows: first degree sexual assault of a minor, felony kidnapping, terroristic threats, and felony assault with intent to murder. If convicted, these men were most likely looking at life. If they weren't, I thought I was looking at it.

The District Attorney stood to give his opening statement while I tried to reign in my galloping fears. He stated eloquently that he would prove beyond doubt that a minor, Jed Petersen, had been beaten, terrorized, threatened with death, sexually assaulted repeatedly, and left for dead by the three defendants seated in front of them.

The accused looked at their table and at their hands, and sometimes at each other. I wondered if any of them had ever felt remorse over what they did to me.

Three attorneys were working to free the rapists. I thought of them as Hear Some Evil, See Some Evil, and Speak Some Evil. I wondered if they believed their clients or if it was only about money.

The D.A. called the sheriff first. He was sworn in and then repeated his full name and position as he was asked to do.

"Sheriff Lawson, when did you become aware of the sexual assault and other violent crimes perpetrated against the victim, Jed Petersen?"

"It was reported to me by Dr. Cramer of Alpine. He saw Jed in his office because he suffered from a broken rib, internal bruises, and various other injuries. He sent Mr. Petersen to the hospital and that's where I first met him."

"Was Mr. Petersen cooperative?"

"Yes he was, but he was terrified. He said he'd

been threatened with death if he gave the names of his attackers."

"Did he tell you those names?"

"Not at first. He gave them to me later, after he had been threatened again by one of the perpetrators."

"Objection!" See Some Evil popped up. "Alleged perpetrators."

Sheriff Lawson was unperturbed. "He had been physically threatened by one of the alleged perpetrators," he repeated patiently.

"Did you at any time doubt the veracity of Jed Petersen's claim?"

"No sir. He had been viciously attacked. I could see that from looking at him. The hospital confirmed the sexual assault. At no time did I feel Jed was lying except when he said he didn't know the names of his attackers."

"Were you surprised when he wouldn't give you names?"

"No. It's typical of abuse victims to feel unsafe and to believe the threats of violence made by the perpetrators."

"Objection. Hearsay." It was Hear Some Evil. "Stating personal opinion."

"It's well documented by lawmen and crisis intervention centers all over the world," said the sheriff. "I've seen it in my work, but it's not only my experience."

The judge overruled the objection.

There was more from the sheriff, but you know those facts. The defense tried to trip him up, but he was a solid witness and a man who couldn't be intimidated by three monkeys wearing suits.

After Sheriff Lawson was dismissed, Dr. Cramer was called to the stand. He spoke of seeing me in his office and the various damages done to my body, and how he had sent me to the hospital for treatment. His account was painful in its detail, and I tried not to listen, but I heard it anyway. I hoped I would never have to hear it again. It wasn't like I had forgotten any of it, but I didn't sift through those memories for my sanity's sake.

The worst thing about his testimony was that he passed pictures to the jury. The defense had tried hard to get those photographs stricken from the trial as "lurid and sensational" but they had been unsuccessful. They didn't like them because they showed how badly I had been abused by their clients. District Attorney Sinclair made the reasonable argument that the photographs were crucial to the prosecution, and the judge had agreed.

While the jury reviewed my busted-up body, I glanced around at Kitty. She knew how I had dreaded this. Her look was full of love and understanding.

One of the evil monkeys was cross-examining Dr. Cramer with the attitude that he had invented the injuries to make his sainted clients look guilty.

"When Jed Petersen came to you, it was more than twenty-four hours after the alleged sexual abuse and beating, wasn't it?" Hear Some Evil asked.

"Yes, it was."

"How can you be certain the injuries were sustained in that way?"

"Jed Petersen's physical injuries matched his story. I had no reason to doubt what he said because his body backed it up."

"But couldn't his injuries have been sustained in a car wreck or a bar brawl or some other way?"

The doctor looked a combination of angry and amused. "Well, that's true, I suppose, but I've never seen tearing or abrasions of the anus as the result of a car accident or a brawl, Mr. Reeves."

There was a titter in the courtroom. I looked down at my hands on the table and wanted to put my head on top of them.

Drew Sinclair leaned over. "Hold your head up, Jed," he whispered, "the shame in this is not yours."

Holding my head up was harder than it sounds, but I lifted it and watched the witness. Attorney Reeves (Hear Some Evil) droned on, trying to bring doubt about the reasons for my injuries into the minds of the jurors. All he needed to win was reasonable doubt. He suggested that perhaps I had run into rough characters after I left Balmorhea. There was unaccounted-for time.

Why hadn't I sought medical attention immediately if I was so badly injured? Maybe the tearing and abrasions were from rough consensual anal intercourse, which is what his clients claimed. So he'd already brought that into it. Sonofabitch!

"Head up, Jed," Drew whispered, and briefly patted my hand.

Hear Some Evil gave up the witness. He had wandered off so far in his suppositions that the judge stopped him and demanded that he come up with a relevant question for the doctor or dismiss him.

After that, the judge called a lunch recess for one and one-half hours during which the jury would lunch sequestered in the jury room.

* * *

"The prosecution calls Jed Petersen."

I don't know how I made it to the witness stand, but there I was.

"Jed, please state your full name, age, address, and occupation for the record."

"My name is Jed Petersen. I'm eighteen, and I live and work at the Worthington Ranch in Fort Davis, Texas. I work as a cowboy, horse trainer, and bull rider."

Drew Sinclair stated the exact date of the rape then asked, "Will you please tell the court what happened on that date?"

"I was leaving work around midnight. I was the last to leave. I had turned out the lights and stood for a moment to let my eyes adjust. When I did, I was approached by three men who began to harass me. They said I was pretty, but that was just the start. They said a lot of filthy things after that."

"Will you please state some of those things as an example for the court?"

"They said I was queer, but I might be entertaining and that I should take my pants off so they could admire my ass, and that they were going to fuck me. Excuse me, but that's what they said."

"And what did you do?"

"I told them I wasn't queer and tried to run away."

"You feared for your life, didn't you?"

"Yes."

"What happened then?"

"They dragged me back to the parking lot and beat me until I couldn't stand. They ripped off my clothes and when I wouldn't be still, they brought out a knife and threatened me."

"Then what happened?"

"They took turns raping me."

I glanced at Kitty. Her face had crumpled and she pressed a tissue to her eyes. Rick had his arm around her, trying to comfort her. Seeing her almost made me start crying, but I was so nervous, and my face was so tightly controlled that tears were impossible.

"Are the men who assaulted you here today?"

"Yes sir, they're seated right there." I indicated their table with a nod of my head. Three rapists in dark suits glared at me.

"Do you recognize them?"

"Well, I knew Tiny all along, but the others I didn't know."

"By Tiny you mean Roger Desmond?"

"Yes sir."

"What about the others?"

"I only heard their names, Jocko and Tex. It was dark, and I never saw them well enough to recognize them. I would've known their voices."

"Did you have occasion to meet Tex face to face before today?"

"Yes, on the night of the rape he came back alone. I saw him again at a rodeo and he threatened me both times."

"Objection!" One of the monkeys was up, jumping around.

"I'll allow the witness to answer the question," said the judge.

"Tex Reardon returned on the night of the rape to see if I was dead. I saw that he had a gun and an official-looking patch on his sleeve. Then I saw his truck when lights from a passing vehicle hit it, so I knew he was a deputy or a sheriff."

"What did he say to you, Jed?"

"He asked if I was alive and said I should leave town. He said the sheriff didn't cotton to homos, either, and he'd kill me if I told. I don't remember all of it because I was nearly comatose."

"How do you know that the deputy who came back to terrorize you was Deputy Reardon?"

"He stopped me at a rodeo in Pecos to threaten me. I recognized his voice from that night in Balmorhea, and his nametag read 'Tex Reardon'."

"When you say 'that night,' you're referring to the night of the rape?"

"Yes."

"What did you do when he threatened you in Pecos?"

"I ran away from him and called the Family Crisis Center in Alpine, and Kenneth Morrison came for me and took me to a safe house."

"Tex Reardon caused you to fear for your life?"

"Yes sir, they all did, but he was the worst."

"Jed, as you know, all three of the accused have given sworn statements that you teased them repeatedly over a prolonged period of time, and had spoken to them in lewd and suggestive language and eventually invited them to have sex with you on the night in question."

He turned slowly to face the jury, and then back to the courtroom. "They allege that you stripped your clothes off, and when they'd had sex with you, sex which you desired, which you *begged* for, you flew into a rage and attacked them. You pulled a gun and threatened them. They beat you in an effort to subdue you, and they feared for their lives."

He turned back to me dramatically. "Now I remind you that you're under oath, and I ask you Jed, to tell the court which parts of their statements are true."

"None of it is true."

"Not any of it?"

"None of it."

"If what they say isn't true, how would you explain what they did?"

"I can't explain it."

"What did you do to provoke their behavior?"

"If I did anything, I don't know what it was. Tiny accused me of having a boyfriend. He saw me with a man the afternoon before they attacked me."

"Was he your boyfriend?"

D.A. Sinclair's strategy was to bring this into the trial before the defense could, so the jury would get used to the idea.

"He was my friend and lover, but Tiny had no reason to think that. There's no way he could've known."

"Are you homosexual, Jed?"

"No sir."

"But Jed, you just said you had a male lover."

"I was in love with him, yes."

"Well, wouldn't that make you gay?"

"No sir." My face blazed, and everyone in the room gaped at me, just as Kenneth and the D.A. had insisted they would. The defense table was a-buzz.

The judge slammed his gavel and demanded order. It was hard as hell to sit still in that box and be judged by people who didn't know me. Not to mention that some of the ranch hands had come in and joined Kitty. They were my friends, and I wanted them there and didn't.

See Some Evil, whose name was Alan Ridges, came at me like a rattler at a rabbit. It was cross-examination time. Drew had tried to prepare me. *They're going to rip you apart. Hold your head up. Be who you are. The shame is not yours, Jed.* There's no way to prepare for facing the deceit, hatred, the filthy lies that their side brought.

"Mr. Petersen, is it all right to call you Jed?"

"Yes."

"You say you're attracted to women, is that correct?"

"Yes, it is."

"You've also made love to a man?"

"Yes."

"Would it be fair to say that you're attracted to both sexes?"

"I guess so."

"At the same time?"

There was laughter. When the gavel crashed it felt like my head exploded.

"I don't think that's a fair question."

"What's unfair about it?"

"Objection!" Drew stood, fuming. "Judge, that question 'at the same time' is irrelevant and inflammatory."

"I agree," said the judge.

"I withdraw the question. You willingly admit you had a boyfriend when you lived in Balmorhea, is that correct?"

"He wasn't just a boyfriend."

He looked at the jury as if he had just heard the most incredible lie of his life. "What would you call your relationship to him?"

"I was in love with him."

"All right." He smiled his sharp-toothed smile at the jury and then turned back to me. "You loved him. You had sex with him?"

"Well, yes."

"Anal sex?"

"Objection! Again, irrelevant."

"No sir. We never did that," I said above the commotion.

"I'll allow this line of questioning, Mr. Ridges," the judge said, "but tread carefully. You'd better be heading to something relevant."

"I'm trying to establish the credibility of this witness."

Drew Sinclair was on his feet again. "Your honor! What does anal sex have to do with credibility?"

I wondered the same thing but was laid flat by the talk of it.

"I haven't gotten there yet, your honor," Speak Some Evil said.

"Well, get there."

"Jed, you claim you never had anal sex with your lover. Have you ever had sex of that nature?"

"No."

"I believe you're lying. You just said you had sex

with him."

"I'm not lying! There are all kinds of sex. You're a lot older than me. It seems like you would know that."

There was laughter in the courtroom but I failed to see the humor. I was ten seconds from flying out of the stand and taking out a monkey. Kitty stared at her lap. The cowboys were glum and straight-faced. They were probably dumbstruck, and I didn't know how I would ever face them after this or why I'd want to.

Drew was on his feet again. "Your honor, I object to this line of questioning. Mr. Ridges is trying to put my witness on trial for sexual activity that has not one thing to do with what happened to him. Whatever he did with his lover was consensual and between young men. It doesn't have a bearing on the crime."

"But it does Your Honor. My clients say they were seduced by an immoral, sex-crazed teenager."

The judge shot straight up, which sent his chair slamming into the wall. "I want to see both of you in my chambers."

The two men left with the judge, leaving me exposed—worse than buck naked. If the bailiff hadn't been there with his dead-serious look and his firearm, I would've left and never come back. The jury members stared at me like I was a sideshow curiosity, interesting but repulsive. Not one of them looked friendly. Kitty finally glanced up and smiled at me, a sad, sweet smile that pierced my heart.

The judge returned and instructed the jury to disregard the statement made by Mr. Ridges. Did he believe they could?

"Are there more questions for this witness?" Judge Forrester asked.

A different monkey stood, Speak Some Evil, Dwayne Gossett. "Yes sir." His attitude said they had hardly begun.

Bring it on, asshole.

"Mr. Petersen, have you ever had a female lover?"

"Objection! Your honor, please." Drew had popped up again.

"I'll allow the question," the judge said.

"I've had female lovers."

"I see. Would it be correct to say that you prefer men?"

"No sir. That would be incorrect."

Drew Sinclair was objecting as to relevancy.

I turned to the judge. "I'd like to speak about that, sir."

"Go ahead, Mr. Petersen."

I took a deep breath. "I can't explain my relationship to my former lover. It was about my feelings for him, and I was young and confused. You're trying to say that I prefer men because you think that's something weird and dirty. It's not. Anyway, most of my experience is with women. I don't know why it matters one way or the other. Rape is still rape."

Speak Some Evil stared at me with his mouth open. He was considering a new attack; I could see that coming.

"In pre-trial discovery you refused to give the names of any women."

"That's because it's none of your damn business."

More laughter.

"It's because there are no women."

"It's because they were older than me and in this state that's a crime. I don't care what you say I'm not giving you names. I'll never give you or anyone else their names. What does that have to with this, anyway?"

Drew was up, shifting his weight from one foot to the other like a little boy that's about to wet himself. "Your honor, this trial is about a vicious beating and rape. It doesn't matter if Mr. Petersen has had sex with every single man and woman in the state of Texas."

"I've never had sex with him." Mr. Gossett mumbled, but it was loud enough for everyone to hear.

He might have thought that was funny but the judge didn't. His eyes narrowed. "I'm very close to charging you with contempt, Mr. Gossett. One more comment like that one, and you'll be sitting in jail."

"I apologize, Your Honor."

The judge scowled in concentration. "I want you to release this witness or ask a relevant question," he

said at last. “Think about it carefully Mr.Gossett, because I will dismiss this witness if your next question addresses Mr. Petersen’s sexual preference and not the case at hand.”

Gossett looked right at me, goofy as hell. “I sincerely apologize for my earlier comment.” He played the decent man for the jury. I ignored him and did not accept his insincere apology or even acknowledge it.

He looked to the ceiling, as if help would come from above. “Mr. Petersen, isn’t it true that you exposed yourself more than once to Roger Desmond and suggested that he was called ‘Tiny’ because of his large penis?”

I really thought I was going to throw up. “No, that’s a lie.”

“And you rubbed up against him in the kitchen and suggested several times that you would enjoy his company after work?”

“He harassed and intimidated me at work and called me a pretty girl and shoved me around. I hated working with Roger Desmond and found him revolting in all ways.”

“You told Roger that women didn’t excite you and that you wanted him to make love to you.”

“I despised Roger Desmond. Aren’t you listening? He’s filthy and smells bad and he’s—he’s demented. He’s cleaned up today, but that’s not who he is.”

He paused, timing the drop of his bomb. “Your semen was found at the crime scene along with that of the accused. Isn’t it true, Mr. Petersen that you ejaculated during the sex you claim was rape?”

Oh God.

“Well I—”

“Just a yes or no answer.”

“Yes, but—”

“That’s all I have for this witness at this time.”

Damage done.

Chapter 27

I dragged myself back to my chair next to Drew with every eye on me, suspecting and accusing me. I couldn't look at Kitty or the cowboys. I watched the floor and wished for swift death. I had been assured the defense would use this against me, but I was totally unprepared for how that would feel. I was being raped again, and it wouldn't be the last time. This is why victims don't come forward. How many times can a person endure it?

Drew called Kenneth Morrison. He established that he was my advocate, had been with me through the hospital procedures, had suffered along with me, understood my agony, had offered counseling, provided a safe house, and encouraged me to bring my attackers to justice. Kenneth was a strong man with a deep voice steeped with conviction and passion. But who would be listening now?

D.A. Sinclair made his way carefully through a field of land mines, moving towards the lurid fact that had riveted the courtroom.

"Mr. Morrison, isn't it common for the victim of a rape to experience an orgasm during the commission of that crime?"

"Yes, it's a physiological response and does not indicate that the victim is enjoying the rape."

"Will you please explain that in greater detail?"

"Becoming sexually aroused, having an erection, or ejaculating during a sexual assault are normal, involuntary physiological reactions. It does not mean

that the victim wanted to be sexually assaulted, or that the survivor enjoyed the traumatic experience. Sexual arousal does not mean there was consent."

Drew paused to let that sink in. "Thank you. There has been some question about Jed's delay in reporting the assault. Would you address that?"

"It takes a great deal of courage for a rape victim to come forward. There's shame and a feeling of guilt, even though the victim did absolutely nothing to provoke the rape. Also, victims are usually threatened by their attackers, as in Jed's case.

"Rape is an act of power and intimidation. It's not about sex. Men are much less likely to admit they've been raped because of old societal beliefs that a man should be able to protect himself. And the belief that men initiate sex and are not usually victimized by it. Until the mid-1980s, most literature about rape discussed it only from a female's point of view. The lack of tracking of sexual crimes against men and the lack of research about the effects of male rape are indicative of the attitude held by society at large—that while this crime does occur, it is not an acceptable topic for discussion."

I watched the jury. They looked bored and weren't listening. I thought they wanted to hear more about sex with men and ejaculation. They were riveted by the things they considered hot and sinful. I thought Kenneth had already lost them with facts, but he continued undaunted.

"Male victims fear being called homosexual, whether or not they are, and many men are unwilling to come forward for that reason. Male victims seldom receive support from anyone, and are sometimes subjected to unsupportive or cruel statements from their family, friends, and acquaintances. People tend to fault the male victim instead of the rapist."

Yeah, no shit, Kenneth.

My Advocate vouched for me in every possible way. Even he didn't have the names of the women, so when he was asked he couldn't say. He pointed out that Jed Petersen was protecting women he cared about and that fact meant nothing sinister or perverted. But the

defense was bent on putting a different spin on it.

To the horror of the District Attorney, I stood and slammed my hands on the table. "What difference do women make to this? What if there were no women? So what? I was still RAPED!"

The courtroom buzzed. The judge looked speechless.

"Jed, sit," Drew ordered. "Sit right now, Jed."

Judge Forrester found his voice. He slammed the gavel. "Order! Mr. Sinclair, control the complainant, or I will hold him in contempt."

"Jed, sit, please."

I sat, but it was only because I had begun to shake, and I didn't want to fall down in front of Tiny, Jocko, and Tex. After that, the judge dismissed Kenneth and called a five minute recess. Drew tried to calm me.

"This trial is not about women I've slept with, Drew. Get them away from that subject or I'm going to leave."

"You can't leave."

"Want to bet? Get them away from the women, Drew."

"I'm going to call some new witnesses. That should change the direction."

After the recess, he called Gilberto Garcia, one of the kitchen help at Casa México. He testified that Tiny had harassed and touched me, not the other way around.

Then Enrique Guardia said the same thing, then Manuel Solis. One of the workers had returned to Mexico, but it didn't matter because the others were great witnesses, and the defense monkeys couldn't budge them. Enrique said he knew I had dated a woman, and they had teased me because they thought I was too young to have only one girlfriend. The things they said rang true because they were.

Enrique also added that I had spoken of the woman with affection when Tiny was not hovering over me, making all of us nervous. No, they had never seen me with a man. They went so far as to say that Tiny had made it up.

After their testimony came the lunch recess.

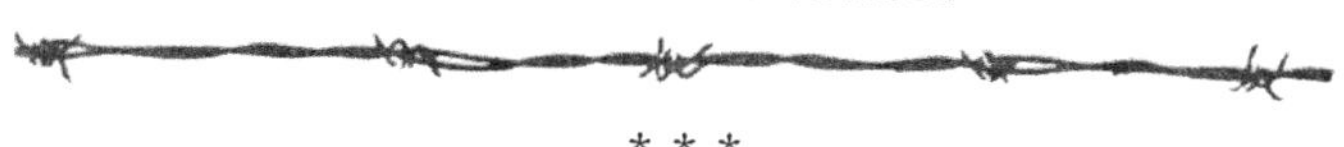

* * *

Early that afternoon, the prosecution rested its case. I couldn't tell about the jury and tried not to think about them.

Nobody holds your life in their hands but you, Jed, Kitty had said. *No matter how it goes, we'll go home and love each other.*

"The defense calls Roger Desmond to the stand."

Tiny stood, tugged at his pants, and lumbered to the witness box. He looked like a gorilla stuffed in a suit, but that was probably just my opinion. It hurt me something awful to look at him. He was clean-shaven and had probably even showered for this occasion. I could still smell the alcohol and meanness on his breath and the greasy, filthy sweat that clung to him like skin. After that came the pushing and panting and groaning. I shook my head to clear it.

I watched the jury watch him, eating him up. He told them the kind of lurid details they were drooling for. They believed him, I realized. No matter what the kitchen staff said, they believed him. He was white. He was married. Christ Almighty, he was *married.* He grew up in Balmorhea. He was a good ol' boy and boys will be boys. In Tiny World it was okay to take what you wanted. That wasn't said, but it was intimated. Unknowingly, I had represented something enticingly different, and he had wanted it, end of story.

I was losing.

I looked around for Kitty and saw the cowboys. Nearly all of them were there. Rick caught my eye, smiled, and nodded as if to say he was hanging in with me.

Tiny said I begged them after work that night. I stripped off my clothes and already had an erection. They decided to take me up on my offer, and when I had later whined and complained, they had meant to teach me a lesson.

My head went somewhere else.

On cross examination, Drew caused most of the onlookers to audibly gasp when he suggested that the three accused were homosexual. Who else would accept such an invitation from a man? If in fact they had been

invited. He persisted in spite of objections from the defense and a heated debate in front of the judge.

It was a good question, but Tiny wiggled out of it. "You know, we just thought we should try something different. It seemed exciting at the time. You know how it is for guys. We got worked up, and he was begging, real sexy-like. And he has those eyes."

* * *

Jocko had been a high school sports star, a small town hero in a small town sadly lacking in heroes. He was roughly Ron's size but had nothing like Ron's good looks or personality. His face was scarred by acne and hard times. His dark brown hair was graying prematurely at the temples.

Jocko's real name was Andrew Sims, and he was twenty-two. The downhill slide from football hero to working as a heavy equipment mechanic in the oilfields around Odessa and Midland had taken its toll on his self-esteem. He spoke in a dull monotone about his life and said he had a live-in girlfriend and a child. The rapist was raising a child.

He testified he only happened to be there that night because he was in Balmorhea visiting his parents. He and Tiny were old friends, and Tiny had said they were gonna have a few beers and "get some strange." Tiny hadn't said anything about fucking a man, but Jocko was up for whatever his friends had going because they were always thinking up new entertainments. Sometimes it was porno movies, or a blow-up doll, or cheap whores Tiny found from someplace, or dirty magazines—you know girls messing around with barnyard animals or each other.

"That Tiny is really a trip."

Jocko didn't have the intelligence of a blow-up doll. At one point Drew muttered, "Jesus Christ." Yeah, it was hard to hear how they had fucked me for fun and then left me for dead—of course neither of them admitted that part. They hadn't realized I was actually *hurt*—why didn't he say something if he felt bad?

Drew did what he could on cross-examination but there wasn't much he could do. Their stories were so different from mine and there were three of them:

manly men against one small, sex-crazed boy who had *those eyes.*

"I'm telling you, he wanted it!"

"We didn't mean to hurt him. He begged for it. He got what he wanted."

"He came, same as us, so what does that tell you?"

* * *

Tex Reardon was called last. He was different, dangerous. He was smarter and the cruelest of the three. Admitting he had wanted to *do it* with a man they thought was queer did not come easy.

He claimed he had been drunk, and the others seemed to be enjoying it plenty, so he gave in to his perverse desire. He said, "The little queer boy wanted it and we gave him what he wanted. It ain't our fault if we were too much for him."

When all the attorneys had given their closing arguments, during which I had to endure a graphic recap of my hedonistic, amoral behavior, and how desperately I had *wanted it,* the trial was over. There was nothing more to be said on either side, and both sides rested.

The judge gave instructions to the jury. I already knew I had lost. Even Drew bitterly whispered that he thought the good ol' boy jury had bought their lies.

I reminded myself that I would go home with Kitty, and to the Worthington Ranch, Indio, the mountains, and Midnight. And other horses that needed me. I had a plan for my life, and I would move on and forget the perverts. Yeah, those are the things I told myself.

* * *

Kitty and I sat in a restaurant looking at each other. No way could we eat. Even talking was strained. Then Kitty's cell phone rang. The jury was back.

I sucked in a deep breath. "This can't be good, they're back too soon." My heart pounded in my ears.

"Breathe," Kitty said, and lifted my hand to her lips and kissed it. "Have faith, Jed. You don't know that this is a negative thing."

We went back into the courthouse and climbed

the steps to the courtroom. People were pouring back in. The jury was already seated.

The foreman brought a paper to the judge. He read it and gave it back. "The defendants will rise," he said. They did. Then he said to the man holding the paper, "Have you reached a verdict?"

"Yes we have, Your Honor."

"What say you?"

"On count one, sexual assault of a minor, we find the defendants not guilty." *How can that be? They raped me!* "On count two, kidnapping, we find the defendants not guilty." *They held me against my will!* "On count three, terroristic threats, we find the defendants not guilty." *We could cut your dick off. Don't force us to kill you.* "On count four, assault with attempt to commit murder, not guilty." *Are you people this stupid?*

I heard but did not believe. They had already taken so much from me, how could it end this way?

Drew shook my hand, but I was like a zombie. "I'm sorry, Jed, I gave it my best. Sometimes juries don't get to the truth no matter what we do." He droned on, but my head wasn't there.

I don't know when the defendants left, but I looked around and they were gone. Kitty came towards me. Behind her was My Advocate.

"You were wrong about everything," I spit at him.

"Jed," Kitty began, but I gave her a look that silenced her.

"You can't ever tell about juries," Kenneth said. "They're always risky."

"Well, it would've been nice if you'd told me that."

"Drew told you that right up front, Jed. I know he did because I was there. You're just disappointed. All of us are so disappointed."

"This is the last time you're gonna tell me how I feel. All of you can go to hell!" I slammed out, took the steps so fast I nearly fell down them, and burst out the front doors of the courthouse onto the lawn. I was too sad to cry, too angry to speak or even think, and I had told people who supported and cared about me to go to hell, including Kitty. Way to go.

I finally calmed down enough to sit on a bench in a covered bandstand. Before long, Kitty joined me. She sat next to me without touching me or speaking, but I knew she was there.

I reached over and took her hand. "I'm sorry, Kitty."

"How can I help you, Jed?"

"Would you take me back to the ranch?"

"Sure. Do you want to get some dinner first?"

"No, I'd just like to go back if you don't mind."

* * *

"I need to be alone a while," I said when we were nearly there, "but I'd like it if you came over later. I'm going to ride Indio, so make it late—if you even want to come."

"I'll call you later on to be sure you're back. Yes, I want to come."

That night I sobbed the whole story to my horse as we galloped through field after field. There was not much moon, but Indio didn't need a lot of light and I trusted him. Later, while he browsed, I lay on my back and watched filmy clouds skip across a sky overcrowded with stars. My outrage and heartbreak backed off enough that the constriction in my chest eased its grip for the first time since I'd heard the words *not guilty*. At least it was over.

When I began to feel the cold seep through my jacket, I remounted Indio, rode him back to the barn, and then walked back to the Worthington House apartment. I checked on Midnight, took a shower, and crawled into bed. By the time Kitty called I was nearly asleep, but told her to come on.

I was unaware of anything else until the next morning, when Midnight began to demand my presence in the corral. Kitty was wrapped around me from behind, supporting me even in her sleep.

* * *

The cowboys never said much about the trial. Each one had a different way of telling me he thought it had been a travesty.

Kitty and I weren't officially living together but were usually together when we weren't working and

nearly every night. She stayed busy with the managerial duties of her ranch. I was preoccupied with work, and training for the upcoming Texas State Bull Riding Championship, to be held in Fort Worth.

I put a lot more attention on training than I normally would have in order to keep my head away from the thoughts making me crazy. I was still grappling with the outcome of the trial, and other feelings I had kept inside since the rape. I never mentioned them to anyone until my carefully constrained life came undone at the competition.

CHAPTER 28

I went ahead of Kitty to Fort Worth in order to practice and check out the arena where I would be riding. She didn't argue because she sensed I needed time alone. The plan was for her to join me for the weekend, when the finals would be held. Harley and Pete hadn't qualified to compete, but since we were a team they went along to assist.

The three of us shared a room, but they stayed up late the first night to drink in the hotel bar and look for women to seduce. The next morning, they were still in bed when I got up with the sun and walked over to the coliseum.

A huge banner hung over the entrance and claimed: *The Toughest Sport on Dirt*. A snorting bull pawed at the ground next to the words of the logo.

Not much was happening, so I stepped back outside to look at the stock. Some of Texas' best bucking bulls would be there, including one born at Worthington Ranch and sired by Death Warrant. Kitty said she had sold him as a young adult to a ranch that specialized in providing bulls to rodeos. His name was Say When and as Kitty put it, "That little outlaw could buck the chaps right off your butt, Cowboy." I took it as a dare and hoped to ride him. So far no one had, which made him a big money winner on the Texas rodeo circuit.

Say When had not arrived, but I leaned against a pen holding another undefeated bull called Texas Twister. He munched hay and looked placid, even bored, but that was deceiving. If a cowboy dared to get

on his back, he would show no mercy. I had seen him humiliate riders before but had never pulled his number. I began to feel a familiar rush of excitement about riding.

I noticed a large, good-looking cowboy hanging around. He went up and down the rows of pens, but every time I looked up, he was watching me. When he caught my eye, he smiled. I felt a rush of warmth, like a shot of whiskey when it hits your gut.

The stranger began to lean on the same pen and pretended to watch the bull. The toe of one of his fancy cowboy boots was jammed into a low part of the fence, and his arms hung over it nonchalantly, hands clasped together. He chewed on a long piece of straw and eyed me from beneath the brim of his hat.

"Are you a bull rider?" he wanted to know.

"Yep. Are you?"

He came around the corner of the enclosure, about halfway to where I stood. He rested his elbow on the fence and took up a sideways leaning stance to study me. His interest was not in the bull.

He pushed the cowboy hat back a little on his head. "You say you're a rider?"

"Yup, that's what I said."

"Are you any good at it?"

"Yes I am."

"What do you think about this bull here?"

"Well, he's called Texas Twister for a reason."

"Which is?"

"He comes out of the chute fast and crazy, twisting this way and that. There's no way for a rider to predict which way he'll go."

"So you've ridden him before?"

"No, but I've seen him ridden a few times. He's hell on riders."

"He seems pretty laid back to me."

"Get on his back and see how laid back he is."

"Could you handle him if you pulled his number?"

"Prob'ly. I'd like to try."

"I'd like to see that, too."

"You never said if you're a rider."

"I hope you aren't wearing those nice boots to ride bulls."

"So now there's fashion police at rodeos?"

He laughed. "Nah, I'm just seein' if you can take some messin' with. I'm not a bull rider. I'm a clown."

"No kidding."

He laughed. "I'm Robby Sheffield, rodeo clown." He came over to me and held out his hand.

I took it. "I'm Jed Petersen."

"Oh. I heard you're the one to watch this year."

"I've heard your name. Your reputation precedes you."

He bowed slightly. "I could say the same thing about yours."

Robby Sheffield was a well-known professional rodeo clown. He was young, no more than twenty-three, and already had the kind of reputation that would leave a mark in rodeo history.

If you don't follow rodeo, you might not know that clowns are serious athletes. They have to think on their feet and do it lightning-fast, and be able to move in the same way. The lives of bull riders are routinely saved by quick-thinking clowns who are able to lure fuming, boxcar-sized animals away from us so we can escape. I had been saved by clowns more times than I could say, but never by one of the stature of Robby Sheffield.

He frowned and made a tut-tut sound. "You're not wearing spurs."

"I'm not riding right now, am I?"

"Well, no."

"Truthfully, I hardly ever wear them," I admitted.

"How come you don't?"

"I've never ridden a bull that needed spurs to get him bucking."

"Aren't you afraid you'll look like a pussy to the other riders?"

"I don't care what they think. When a guy comes bustin' out of the chute, who's watchin' for spurs? Even if they were to think I was a pussy, my ridin' says different."

"So you're a confident man."

"You gotta be confident to ride bulls in the first place."

"Touché—and you gotta be more than a little crazy."

"True. I'm confident and plenty crazy, but I'm no pussy."

"Point taken." He smiled. "Want to get some breakfast? I know a little place."

"Sure."

The little place was several blocks from the coliseum. It was jam-packed with bull riders and rodeo hangers-on. It smelled of bacon and strong coffee. We managed to snag a booth being vacated by a rowdy team from Amarillo.

"Hey Robby, how's it going?" One of the men recognized him and lifted his hat.

"Great, great." Robby lifted his own hat in return greeting. As he slid into the booth, he placed the hat on the seat beside him. Wavy blond hair fell in disarray and curled over his ears slightly. He shoved it back, but it only stayed a second.

"You should try the blueberry waffles," Robby suggested after coffee had been served. "They make the best waffles ever, and I've eaten waffles back and forth across the southwest. Their bacon is good too." He grinned and patted his flat stomach. "I'm a big guy and I have to eat a lot."

"I'm not as big as you, but I still eat a lot."

He laughed. "So tell me about yourself, Jed."

"What do you want to know?"

"How long have you had eyes that blue?"

I opened my mouth but nothing came out.

He acted innocent. "Have you been riding bulls a long time?"

"About ten years. Before that, I practiced on rams and goats or anything my little legs would go around that would buck."

"I started out riding. My father took a dim view when I started clowning instead. But I'm a good clown. I was only a so-so rider because of my size, and mostly because I didn't like it much. But tell me more about you. What do you do when your ass isn't being pounded

by a bull?"

"Cowboy work mostly, and I train horses."

"And for fun?"

"I ride them."

He laughed. "I knew that was coming."

"What's it like being a clown?"

"Aw, it's pretty much like you'd imagine. We're at the same level as the bulls, more or less, which means we get covered with snot and spit and dirt and everything else they kick up or fling at us. We have to be lookin' everywhere at once and stay a step ahead. Once a rider hits the dirt it's Katie-bar-the-door."

"What do you do when you're not clowning?"

"Oh, I'm always clowning—but you probably mean when I'm not working. My father and brothers and I have a ranch in Colorado. Most of the work falls to them when I'm on the circuit, but I'm starting to bring home some pretty good checks so they're getting over it. Where do you live, Jed?"

"I live on a ranch near Fort Davis."

A waitress came and took our orders of blueberry waffles and bacon.

"How old are you?" Robby asked when she left.

"Twenty."

"Stats say you're eighteen."

"If you already know, why'd you ask?"

"To see if you were gonna lie, I guess."

"What are you gonna do about it?"

"Oh, there'll be hell to pay for lyin' to me, I reckon. Do you always lie?"

"Well no, just about my age. Eighteen sounds like a kid."

"Eighteen *is* a kid. But you don't look like one, and you're a damn serious bull rider. Nobody can argue that."

* * *

On the way back to the coliseum, Robby chattered non-stop, a continuation from breakfast. I already knew how he got started clowning, and what drove him to stay with it in spite of getting a football scholarship to a college. *I want to go to college, but I want to go my way and not at the expense of my knees.*

I thought what he was doing would be hard on his knees, too, but I stayed quiet while he jabbered.

His brown eyes shone and every story was entertaining. He admitted that he sometimes rode bulls on his ranch, or aggravated them until they came after him so he could practice ways to avoid them.

I knew he'd been gored twice and where. He showed me the scar on his arm, near the shoulder, and told a hilarious tale about how he got it. He said he couldn't show me the other scar without taking off his pants. It was high on his thigh, near his groin, or as he put it, *that ol' bull nearly took out my reason for living.*

We stood around outside the pavilion, and he got quiet for nearly ten seconds. I don't know about him, but my heart was racing.

"I'm sorry I'm talking so much," Robby apologized. "You make me so nervous. See, I just want to put my hands all over you."

I was speechless, and my reaction to his announcement would've been a clear indicator I was still gay if I'd been thinking about it. The only thing I was thinking about was his hands.

"Damn it! I always say everything that comes into my head, just like a damn clown. You could say something you know, Jed. Don't leave me dangling here, even though I prob'ly deserve it."

As a group of cowboys approached, he moved back a few steps.

"I'm seeing someone," I managed to say.

"Is it serious?"

"I'm in a committed relationship."

"I respect that." He looked sad, which is how I felt, too. Then he brightened a little. "We could still be friends."

"I'd like that."

"Okay, then." Robby took his hands and the rest of him and went on his way. I went on mine, but I felt a sense of loss that picked at my heart.

Just like that, the part of me I had rejected and buried deep had popped to the surface with demands.

CHAPTER 29

The next day I had to put my attention on outscoring other competitors so I could make it to the finals. The purse was two hundred thousand dollars plus prizes offered by companies like Wranglers, Resistol, and Justin Boots. The best thing about winning the state championship would be automatically qualifying for the national competition, which carried larger prize money and more opportunities.

The arena was crawling with cowboys in tight jeans and spur-spangled boots. Fans screamed and stomped, and riders yelled at each other and at their teammates. An announcer bemoaned the poor showing of the rider ahead of me and did it at the top of his lungs.

I looked around for Robby and found him steps ahead of an infuriated bull. He wore red sneakers with red, white, and blue-striped socks, denim high-water pants that were too big and were held up by gold suspenders with multi-colored sparkles. A red bandana encircled his neck, and several blue-checked ones protruded from his pockets. His mouth was an overly-wide, red smile, but that was his only make-up. He looked like a joke, but his business was deadly serious.

Harley and Pete helped me get situated in the chute on an animal that didn't want me situated. Between the bulls and the riders, there was enough testosterone in the air to drown a person. I took a big breath of it and nodded for the chute.

When it clanged open, a huge bull named Maelstrom burst out with me and began a lurching,

jumping, twisting rampage. He constantly bounced me off, but I kept landing on his back. He got more and more irate, and at seven point three seconds, he flung me to the ground. I landed hard on my face and skidded. It hurt and not just my pride. Maelstrom pawed at the dirt, snorting and dripping snot. I knew I had to get out of his way, but the wind had been knocked out of me and I lay there helpless, gasping for breath. Suddenly, two clowns lifted me to my feet and dragged me to the fence while Robby distracted the bull.

My score was ninety-two, not bad for a first rattle out of the chute. I watched Robby search for me when he heard my score announced. I was sitting on the fence being attended by paramedics, and when he located me he smiled, bowed low, and then turned his attention back to the arena.

* * *

There was frantic pounding on the door. When I opened it, a clown burst into the room. He looked bedraggled, and there was a big, painted smile on his face that was more than a little smudged.

Robby wasted no time on hello. "I came to invite you to dinner—no strings—"

Harley banged out of the bathroom toweling his hair.

I spun around. "Robby, this is Harley, one of my teammates. Harley, meet my friend Robby. He's from Colorado."

Harley and Robby shook hands. "I guess you're a clown."

"Aw, man, you got it first try."

Harley reddened. "I mean you're that famous clown, Robby Sheffield."

"I don't know if you should say 'famous,' but I am Robby Sheffield." He turned from Harley to me. "How's your face? It looks painful."

"It is." There was a long, raw scrape along my cheek, a cut in my lip, and my eye was black and getting blacker.

"Pete and me are goin' to have a few beers," Harley announced. "You guys could come with us if you

want."

"Except that I can't."

"I'm always forgettin' you're such a young 'un."

"Ask me again in three years."

"You can be sure I will. Okay, I'm gonna join Pete."

When the door shut behind Harley, Robby asked, "Do your teammates know you're gay?"

"No. And how did you know?"

"I didn't."

"But when you said you wanted to put your hands all over me, how did you know I wouldn't sock you in the face?"

"I didn't know. I've been socked in the face before, plenty of times."

"So that's your plan? You just tell random guys you want to put your hands all over them and hope for the best?"

"Now there you're wrong. You're not a random guy. I studied you intently before I suggested anything."

"So in more or less two hours, you decided I wouldn't clobber you?"

"I didn't know if you would or not. I decided it would be worth it to try."

I sat on the chair at the typical round motel table. "Did you ever have sex with a woman, Robby?"

"Yeah, I tried it in high school. I practically had to, being a football hero and all. A lot of gay men try it, Jed. There's the drive to fit in and curiosity and the 24/7 sexual arousal of teenagers. Oops. No offense."

"None taken. I'm sure you're over that since you left your teens behind."

"Not exactly," he admitted. "Why do you ask about women?"

"Because, well, I'm sleeping with one."

"You're in a committed relationship with a *woman*?"

"Yes and she's wonderful, so don't start talking trash. She gave me love when I was afraid to accept it from anyone else."

"Why is that?"

"I have my reasons, so wipe that smile off your

face, clown man."

"But why were you afraid of love, Jed?"

"I don't know."

"You don't know, or you won't tell me?"

"I was raped, Robby. I was beaten nearly to death and then raped, and I haven't been with a man since that." It felt good to tell someone the truth; it also made me want to throw up.

On top of that, the look on his face made me want to cry. "Oh, Jed, I'm so sorry."

"I pulled away from everything except horses. And this woman—Kitty—kept reaching out to me. She's beautiful and kind, and she loves horses, too."

"You don't have to justify it to me."

"I want you to understand."

"I feel like I'm gonna be sick."

"The worst thing is that there was a trial and—and—they were declared innocent."

"Holy shit. Wait just a minute. I thought you said 'they.'"

"There were three of them."

"You're sayin' you were raped by *three* men?"

"Yes, there were three."

He rubbed his head with both hands. "This just keeps gettin' worse."

"Listen, Robby, I need to talk to Kitty before this ever goes past a friendship. She's been good to me."

"I get it, Cowboy."

"Where are you going?"

"I'm going to go wipe this smile off my face."

CHAPTER 30

Kitty had reserved a separate room for us, next door to the one I had shared with my team. By the time she arrived, I was so worked up I was nearly sick. I wanted to tell her the truth about me first thing and could barely say hello.

Her attention went to my face. "Oh Jed, you've been injured."

I took her hands in mine, but the smooth words I had practiced did not come. She put her arms around me, pressed herself against me, and whispered how much she had missed me. My head demanded that I tell her the truth while my body demanded to press back. I was saved by Kitty's cell phone.

"I should get this." She answered, and after the hellos, "We're here in Fort Worth at the state Bull Riding Championship." A pause. "Well, I just arrived, but Jed's been here since Tuesday evening." She listened for what seemed like a long time. By the look on her face, I thought she was hearing something serious. "I guess you should talk to him."

She covered the mouthpiece. "It's Sheriff Hoskins of Reeves County," she whispered. "He says Roger Desmond was murdered." She was talking about Tiny.

My first thought: *So what? Why call me?*

I took the phone from Kitty. "Jed Petersen here."

"Mr. Petersen, what do you know about the murder of Roger Desmond?"

"Nothing, this is the first I've heard about it."

"Frankly, you're the first suspect to come to mind."

"Suspect? I haven't seen him since the trial."

"I know you were quite perturbed by the outcome of that."

"Yes, but I would never kill anyone."

"That, Mr. Petersen, is what every suspect says. Somebody shot him. I want to know if you've been back to Balmorhea lately."

"No sir, I haven't been there since I was raped. Why would I go back?"

"That's what I want to know from you, sir. Mrs. Desmond says you've been harassing her husband since the trial ended."

"That's a lie!"

"Hm. Where were you on this past Tuesday?"

"I was on the road, on the way to Fort Worth."

"Alone?"

"No, my team was with me."

"Did you come through Balmorhea?"

"No, we did not."

"Balmorhea is the quickest way to the Interstate from Fort Davis."

"Yes, I know, but I would never voluntarily go that way. Roger Desmond and his friends ruined Balmorhea for me, Sheriff. I can't stand the thought of the place."

"Hm." He was quiet for a while, and I heard scratching, like he was writing. "When are you coming back to Fort Davis?"

"Either Sunday or Monday, probably Monday."

"What are you doing in Fort Worth?"

"Riding bulls. Competing in the state championship."

"Hm."

He was starting to irritate me with that 'hm.' "I didn't kill Roger Desmond."

"I didn't say you did. Other than you, do you know who might have wanted him dead?"

Anyone who knew him, I reckon. "No sir."

"I'll be in touch." He hung up without saying good-bye.

* * *

When the stress of being a murder suspect

crashed into the memories of the rape and the awful trial, then the tension of breaking up with Kitty and the pressure of tomorrow's competition and the terror of ever getting naked with a man again, I practically imploded. I argued with Kitty and picked at everything she did. When she tried to love me, I told her I needed to conserve my strength for bull riding.

"Since when?" she wondered reasonably.

Since I remembered who I am.

"I've been riding bulls for three days, Kitty. I just need to rest. Try not to take it personal."

She seemed angry, but after a while she sat next to me on the bed and began lovingly stroking my head. "Surely you aren't worried about that murder?"

"The sheriff thinks I did it."

"I'm sure he doesn't. You won't be a serious suspect. How could you be? You have Harley and Pete as alibis, and before that you were with me at the ranch."

"I'm not sorry he's dead, but I didn't kill him."

"Well of course you didn't. You're not a killer." She stretched out next to me and began rubbing my shoulders. "Until a little while ago you were a lover," she teased.

"Aw, Kitty..."

"It's okay, Jed. Just relax."

We eventually fell asleep with our clothes on. The next morning I couldn't tell by the way I felt if I had dodged a bullet or taken one right in the chest.

* * *

My overall score was high, but not high enough to win without riding again. I pulled the number of Rip Snort, a smallish bull known to be testy. He made up for what he lacked in size with attitude. Harley and Pete set me onto him in the chute and the trouble started. He was so aggravated he would've reached back and knocked me out of the coliseum if he'd had room to maneuver.

When the chute opened, Rip Snort tore out, jumping high and giving a little twist to his rear end that nearly unseated me. The second time he jumped I looked down and saw Robby looking up at me. My

heart, already thundering, sped up. It happened in a split-second, but he smiled and then licked his lips. It made me feel hot and blood rushed in my ears and even my thighs went weak. I didn't feel so hot when I was pitched into the dirt with a force that temporarily knocked me out cold.

When I opened my eyes, Robby was there. "He's up! He's up!" he yelled to the paramedics.

"Your fault," I croaked, but he couldn't hear me and put this ear next to my lips.

"Say that again, Jed."

"It was your fault, Clown Man."

"Sure, blame the guy with the funny face." He made light of it, but his eyes said he knew what he had done. A look passed between us; it was pure longing. Then he was up and running.

* * *

My mistake on Rip Snort cost me point-wise, but I didn't care. I could make it up. I was still high enough in the standing that I would get to ride again. Next time I would avoid looking down. I knew better. I could almost hear my father's voice in my head, and I had worked so hard to get it out of there.

Paramedics checked me over in the staging area, where I was joined by Kitty. They said I'd be okay but if I felt dizzy or nauseated to call them. I knew the symptoms to watch for.

"What happened, Jed?" Kitty wanted to know.

The clown smiled at me. "I don't know. I lost the strength in my thighs."

She looked down at my thighs with a doubtful expression then back to me. "Is something going on with you?"

"I'm just tired."

She hooked her arm in mine and led me away from the other riders. "You're Jed Petersen. You don't make careless mistakes. I sense that something is bothering you."

"Please don't make a big deal of this, Kitty. I'm human. I make mistakes."

"You lost the strength in your thighs? You could bust a basketball between those thighs."

"Let it go, Kit."

"Also, you're always willing to have sex and last night you didn't want to. I'm starting to think you're ill. Is that it?"

"Kit, please."

"I'm going to step out for a little while. Will you be all right?"

"Yes, I'm fine."

"A prospective buyer wants to meet me and talk bulls. It might take as long as an hour—depending on the amount of bullshit we have to wade through."

I laughed at that, gave her a hug, and went back to the staging area. I hung around there listening to the banter, watching other riders prepare themselves and helping when I could, watching them ride; but mostly I was watching Robby. I had to tell Kitty the truth.

* * *

"I want to tell you some things, Kitty."

She was lying on the bed reading and jumped a little at the sound of my voice. "I thought you had something you needed to say."

I sat in an easy chair near her. "I want you to know I came here with every intention of winning, and I wasn't expecting things to happen the way they did."

"I knew something was going on with you, Jed."

"I realized something, and because of it, I've been in too much turmoil to stay on a bull. I lost my concentration. See, I met someone here—someone I was attracted to."

Tears welled in Kitty's eyes, but she didn't say anything.

I felt like shit. "The thing I'm not saying and I have to say is that I'm—it was a man, Kitty. I didn't sleep with him, or even hold his hand, but I wanted to—hold his hand at least. I wanted to get to know him better, but I didn't because it seemed like it would be behind your back. I never want to hurt you."

She took a deep breath. "This is not a surprise, Jed."

How was that possible?

"Sometimes," she continued, "a little bit of a wonderful thing is better than years of something that

is just mediocre. This is how I feel about our time together."

"Thank you, Kitty."

"I knew you would move on, so don't beat yourself up about it. You're eighteen. I'm forty-three. In ten years, you'll still be a young man and I'll be old. It doesn't take a genius to do that math."

"But Kitty, age isn't as important as love."

"I agree, but I saw something in you that made me believe that men excited you more than women. I can't even tell you exactly what, since you showed me so much passion, but I saw it nevertheless. Maybe that's because I saw it before in Conrad. I'm pretty sure he was gay, but he never told me and I never asked. I was going to have this conversation with you—you know how direct I am—but I guess I was riding the wave 'til it hit the shore." She sighed. "Now it has."

Neither of us spoke for a while, and then Kitty laughed. "Just so you know, you weren't fooling me with that *I lost the strength in my thighs* thing. You have to know I know your thighs better than that."

I didn't think I should tell her the reason my thighs had turned to jelly.

"What now, Kitty? Do you want me to leave the ranch?"

"That's up to you, but I'd like for you to stay. You're the best horse trainer I ever saw, and there's rodeo to think about. If you're interested, you could still qualify for the national competition. You don't have to win Texas Bull Rider of the Year to get in, it just makes it easier."

"I think I'd like to try for it, if my thighs will hold up."

She grinned and threw a shoe at me.

* * *

That night the hotel erupted with wild cowboy celebration. Drunken bull riders and rodeo fans wandered up and down the halls, singing and hootin' and hollerin'. You'd think they'd all won the title. I was angry I hadn't and then let it go.

Our room was above the ballroom, where a country band was blasting.

Kitty looked up from the book she was reading. "This is making my teeth rattle." She grinned. "Isn't it great?"

"Yeah, Kitty."

"It sounds like George Strait is down there."

"It's possible; he's a Texan."

"If I thought it was really him, I'd get dolled up and go down there."

"Maybe you should go and see."

"I wonder if I could get somebody to dance with me."

"Jeez, Kitty, they'll line up clear to the Arkansas line to dance with you."

She set the book down. "I think I'll go. Do you want to?"

"You go on."

While she was getting ready, the band announced the arrival of the winner, Seth Reynolds. They yelled "Texas Bull Riding Champion" so loud it probably woke up people in Oklahoma. Then the band started playing cowboy songs like *Night Rider's Lament, Yodeling Cowhand, Cadillac Cowboy,* and it sounded like everybody in the place was singing along.

When Kitty left, she looked more like twenty-three than forty-three. If a hundred guys didn't dance with her I'd have to wonder about the future of straight men.

I went to bed. I was exhausted physically and emotionally.

* * *

There was one queen-sized bed in our room, and Kitty slipped into it next to me. The movement woke me, since I had been half-listening for her when I fell asleep. It had to be late because the band had finally quit playing.

"Are you drunk, Kitty?" I didn't want to tell her what was on my mind if she wasn't going to remember it.

I felt her turn towards me. "No, Jed, I'm just dog tired."

"Did you dance a lot?"

"Yes. My feet are killing me."

"I told you they'd be lined up to dance with you."

"I guess I had my share of admirers."

"You're beautiful, Kitty, and you don't seem to know it."

She sighed. "You're the sweetest man, Jed."

"I forgot to tell you something important earlier. I love you, Kitty. It would be impossible not to love you. I'm sorry it's not exactly the way love between a man and a woman should be, but it's still love. I did my best to show you."

"I know, Jed, and I love you, too. I love you more than you can imagine."

"Could I hold your hand?"

She moved closer and took my hand and held it against her heart. I fell asleep, comforted by her warm, true presence.

CHAPTER 31

Going back to the ranch was surreal. It seemed like nothing had changed, yet for Kitty and me everything had.

After she left me at the barn apartment, I threw my suitcase on the bed and went to see Midnight, who was demanding attention. When he calmed down, he nuzzled me and nickered and pushed at me playfully. He told me in every way he could that he had missed me and loved me. He had come a long, long way, and so had I.

The next morning dawned cold, with a storm front approaching from the north. Since I had a little time to work with Midnight, I took advantage of it. During the lengthy time since I'd first let him out in the pasture, he had never adjusted to the idea of a rider. Time after time, I threw a saddle on him and let him run around with it, hoping he would come to accept the idea. Each time, he threw it off with such attitude it made me hesitate to throw myself up there.

Towards mid-morning I was sitting on a fencepost feeding Midnight carrots. He was in a good mood and had been nuzzling me. I was thinking that the saddle was an inanimate thing with which he had no relationship. I, on the other hand, was his only herd, the crazy crybaby cowboy he had come to love. With little more thought than that, I took a chance and threw myself onto him. I had no real fear of being thrown, having eaten dust since I could remember. What was one more painful spill to the little Fort Stockton

cowboy? *Look at him go, buckaroos, here's the one to watch.*

Yeah, don't miss this.

Midnight reared up and made a snorting sound that was more surprise than anger. Because my arms were around his neck, my mouth wasn't far from his ears.

"Whoa, boy. It's okay, please let me ride."

To my amazement, he settled down after one lightning-fast tear around the corral. He continued making circles, but he slowed, while I laughed and hoped for the best. I clung on while he decided what to do about me. Without gear I had no control of him, but I was at least as stubborn as he was.

About the time I felt like I had been on a demented merry-go-round, he slowed, then stopped and began nosing the ground, picking up wayward bits of interesting things as if I no longer existed. I jumped down.

A truck approached, and at first I assumed it was Rick coming to talk to me about work. I soon realized it was Sheriff Hoskins. He lowered himself from the cab and lumbered towards me, his face about as friendly as an attacking dog. *The Sheriff don't cotton to homos, either.* Yeah, well, I wasn't that scared boy anymore.

He didn't offer his hand, smile, or make a reference to the cold, or even admire Midnight, who usually caused people to stop in their tracks. "Are you Jed Petersen?"

"Yes, I am. Good morning, Sheriff."

"Mr. Petersen, things will go a lot better for you if you tell the truth."

"Yes. I've found that to be true. Would you like to come in out of the cold?"

He hesitated. I wondered if he was afraid of me. He looked towards the apartment, trying to decide. "I could do with some coffee if you have some."

"I do. Come on in that door and I'll meet you inside."

I came in through the barn entrance and opened the door for him since he was standing out there like a

stalled Mack truck. I forgot to mention that the sheriff is over-sized, not in a good way. A flabby belly hangs over his belt and makes his uniform look sloppy. His thick jacket made him look fatter than he was. Sheriff Hoskins was nothing like handsome Sheriff Lawson. The thing they had in common was that they both carried a firearm. On one, it looked like serious business; on the other, it looked like a mistake.

"Come in, Sheriff. Have a seat at the table if you like."

I set a mug of coffee in front of him, and cream and sugar. He looked around like he was afraid of seeing something inappropriate. There were no naked men on my walls. I kept them safely stored in my mind.

There was a knock on the door and Kitty stuck her head inside. "May I come in?"

"Of course, Kitty, come on."

She hugged me and shook the sheriff's hand. "I saw your truck go by," she said, proving that nothing got past her, "and I want to be part of this. This is my ranch. I'm Kathleen Worthington." Kitty was tiny but she had a way of making herself as large as the next man.

"Well, yes ma'am. I didn't intend to go behind your back. I just wanted to get some information from Mr. Petersen."

"Would you like coffee?" I asked her.

For a moment, Kitty stood between me and the sheriff, with her back to him. "Yes I would, thank you." She raised her eyebrow at me and her expression almost caused me to laugh. I was relieved she was there.

"What do you want to know, Sheriff?" I asked. I wanted to get rid of him and back to Midnight—on with my life in other words.

He looked at his notebook, but I didn't think he was reading anything. "Roger Desmond was shot to death last Tuesday, according to the coroner. He was gunned down in the parking lot of Casa México, his place of business. It was late, after he got off work."

Now that was some justice for you. My next thought was that there was something badly wrong

with that parking lot.

"There were no witnesses," he continued, "and his body was discovered the next morning. It had been dragged into the bushes. I believe you know the ones."

"That's not funny, Sheriff," Kitty said heatedly.

"Well I certainly didn't intend it to be."

"I had nothing to do with this. By Tuesday evening, I was in Fort Worth with my team. The rest of the time I was practicing and then competing. So there's no way I could have shot Tiny, even if I'd wanted to which I didn't."

"You're telling me, man to man, that you didn't want to kill a man who you claimed raped and abused you like he did?"

"I didn't just claim it. It really happened the way I said it did. I thought killing was too good for any of those men, but I've been working on letting all that go."

"Have you had success with that?"

"Mostly, yes."

"Mostly. Hm."

I wanted to throw him out on his fat hm-ing ass.

"You look like you were in some sort of row." He referred to my face.

"I was thrown from a bull."

"Looks painful."

"I'm better."

"Hm." He scribbled something in the notebook. "Would it be possible to speak with the rest of your team?"

I looked to Kitty, since I had no idea where they were.

"Yes." She went to the phone, which meant they must be in the barn. There were no phones anywhere else except her house and office.

"Hey, Shorty, I need for Harley and Pete to come to the Worthington House barn apartment." She paused while he spoke. "Yes, right now. Tell Rick to let them use a truck. They won't be gone long." Another pause. "Thank you."

"They're working on tack," she explained to me.

When the weather was bad, we usually repaired tack or fixed things in the barn or got a day off, unless

there was something critical that had to be done outside. In that case, we cowboyed-up and did what we had to.

“While we’re waitin’ on them,” the sheriff said, “I want to ask you about your relationship with Roger Desmond, whom we all know as Tiny.”

“I didn’t have a relationship with him except work. Looking back on it, I think he wanted one with me, but I found him unattractive in every way.”

“Well according to his widow, you pursued him intently all along.”

“That’s a lie, sheriff, as I said already. He made me sick. Maybe someone else was pursuing him, and she thought it was me.”

“I believe it came out in the trial that you had made advances to him, and even exposed yourself to him on occasion.”

“That was a claim made, but like other things claimed at the trial, it’s not true.”

“Why won’t you admit your attraction to him?”

Kitty slammed her fists against the table before I could speak. “What makes you believe that a young, good-looking man like Jed would be attracted to a fat, repulsive, older man like Roger Desmond?”

“He wasn’t old, Ms. Worthington.”

“But Jed was sixteen! Roger was at least thirty or thirty-five. That seems old when you’re only sixteen. That probably still seems old to Jed. For God’s sake, you act like Desmond had the sex appeal of Johnny Depp. Did you ever meet him?”

“Sure, everybody knew ol’ Tiny ‘cause of the restaurant.”

“Did *you* find him attractive?”

Wrong thing to say to this man, Kitty.

“Of course not! I don’t swing that way.”

Kitty got up and began to pace. “So this is all boiling down to how we swing, is it?”

“Well, ma’am, it’s not a secret.”

“What’s not a secret?” Her expression reminded me of bulls I had ridden.

“It’s not a secret Jed swings that way. ‘Course rumor has it he swings both ways.”

"Hey, I'm still here," I interjected. "Stop talking like I'm not."

Thankfully, Pete and Harley knocked on the door before fists started swinging. I yelled for them to come in.

After introductions were made, my team was seated around the table with Sheriff Hoskins. Kitty insisted on standing and stood behind my chair. Pete and Harley were asked to corroborate my statement as to my whereabouts last Tuesday evening, which they did. The sheriff acted like they were lying to protect me. Finally Kitty suggested she could show him gas, food, hotel receipts, and even my registration form for the competition. He put her off, saying he'd get them if he needed them.

Then the sheriff embarrassed the crap out of me by asking Harley and Pete, "What do you know about Jed's relationship with Tiny?"

"We weren't aware of any relationship, only that he disliked him," said Pete.

"He was the ringleader of those perverts who abused Jed," added Harley.

"Do you know of anyone else who had it in for Tiny?"

"No. Except for the trial, he wasn't in our world," said Harley, and Pete agreed.

"You cowboys are a tight-knit group, aren't you?"

"Yes, sir," agreed Harley.

"So if one of your own is in trouble, you stick together."

"What are you trying to say?" Pete asked.

"You'd lie to protect each other, wouldn't you?"

"That's it!" yelled Kitty from behind me. "If you have any more questions for Jed, or any of us, call my attorney, Reva Brooks. She's also Jed, Pete, and Harley's attorney, as well as the rest of my staff. Now get out."

"Next time I have a question," he spit at me, "I'll bring you down to my office. I was trying to make things easy for you by coming here."

Kitty broke in. "You've been notified that Jed has legal counsel so you can question him, but you'd better

not do it without Reva present. Also, Jed has a solid, provable alibi for the time of the murder. Don't you think your time would be well spent to talk to someone other than him? I can understand why he would come to mind, but for the life of me I don't understand why you keep after him."

"Well, I'm sorry you don't understand my methods, Ms. Worthington."

Kitty went to the door and held it open. "Good day, Sheriff Hoskins."

When he was out, she began to rant. "Ooh, that pathetic man! 'I'm sorry you don't understand my methods, Ms. Worthington.' Is his method to have his head up his ass? Does he think I'm an idiot? He doesn't know the first thing about running a murder investigation. Neither do I, but common sense says that if your first theory doesn't hold water you need another."

She turned to me. "Jed, I apologize for barging in like I did. Nobody asked me to, but he has the reputation of being a small-minded bigot. And he had that twisted pervert, Tex Reardon, working for him, so either he's the same way or he's dumber than cow dung." She grabbed her head. "Oh God, that just made me so furious!"

"Calm down, Kitty. He can't prove I did something I didn't do."

"True, but who knows what kind of shit he'll pull. This is small-town West Texas and God knows, there's no justice in these here parts."

I'd already seen how that was true.

"Harley, Pete, don't you talk to him or anyone he might send. Tell them you have an attorney. You go and tell the other guys in case he tries to talk to them."

After Kitty left I dressed warmly and let Midnight take me bareback across the pasture he had once explored on his own while I had explored Kitty. We galloped, trotted, and walked—whatever he wanted to do. He stopped to nibble at brown grass, while I studied the terrain and tried not to think about anything more than that.

CHAPTER 32

The next morning Kitty asked me to come to her office.

"I've been on the phone with the attorney," she said when I got there. "The other two, Tex and Jocko, have been shot to death with the same caliber pistol as Tiny and left in the same bushes. They were discovered this morning. According to Sheriff Hoskins, they weren't killed in the parking lot but were shot somewhere else and dumped in the bushes."

"And he thinks I did it."

"He has no other suspect at this point. And he's adamant that the bushes would have significance to you and not to anyone else."

"That's true, unless someone heard it at the trial. Or it could be coincidence."

"He thinks leaving the bodies in the bushes is a statement, and naturally he thinks you're the one making it."

"So Jocko and Tex are dead?" I hadn't really taken that in all the way. "They're all dead. I guess I should feel happy. Why doesn't it make me happy, Kitty?"

"My guess is that's because it doesn't take away what they did to you. That's why revenge only seems sweet. It's not really, only bittersweet at best, but mostly it's just bitter. You could kill them again and again and it still wouldn't undo what was done."

"But I didn't kill them."

"I was speaking hypothetically."

"I guess the sheriff wants to see me."

"You can bet your sweet spurs, Cowboy. He wants to come arrest you, but Reva pointed out that he has no grounds. It's circumstantial and even weak at that since you have an airtight alibi for the time of Tiny's death. I don't suppose you had somebody with you last night?"

"You know I didn't."

"Well, no problem. You didn't leave the ranch and I would vouch for that."

"Maybe those guys raped somebody else, and he didn't run away like I did."

"Do you know something you aren't saying? Was somebody else raped?"

"No, I don't know that. I was just wondering. I was also thinking about my friend Gina. She called me before the trial to say that if they got away with it, she would kill them and make them suffer first."

"Do you suspect her?"

"No, she would never kill anyone. It was just talk."

"Do you know where she is? Is she still in Balmorhea?"

"Last I knew she was at the University of Texas. That's in Austin, pretty far from here."

"I think you should call her. If she's in Balmorhea, that's a bad sign."

"Kitty, please don't mention this to anyone until I talk to her."

"Well of course I won't. For one thing, I wouldn't lift a finger to help that sheriff. He'll have to figure it out on his own, and I doubt if he can."

"When does he want to see me?"

"He wants you to meet him this afternoon in Balmorhea, at the parking lot of Casa México. Reva will be there, so don't worry."

"He's making me meet him there just to be mean."

"Yes, I know, and Reva is aware of it. Do you want me to go with you?"

"No, I'll be okay."

"Take a ranch truck and look for Gina. Maybe you can find her."

"Even if she did it, I would never turn her in."

* * *

I rode through the little town I had tried so hard to forget, looking for the red Mustang and/or the woman who drove it. I couldn't blame the town for what had happened to me, and in truth, I no longer did. It was just a town, so small as to not even be a dot on most Texas maps.

I went to Gina's house, where I was told by her mother that she was still at the University of Texas unless I knew something she didn't. Her good looks and personality reminded me of Gina. She gave me her daughter's phone number when I explained who I was. If Gina hadn't been there the night before, then she couldn't have killed anyone. Not that it came as a surprise. I didn't need to call her.

I thought of looking for Sadie to say hello but decided against it. I drove by her place hoping to see Hal, but he must have been in the barn. Then I went to the parking lot to wait for the others. I shut my eyes against brutal memories.

Sheriff Hoskins' bulldog face at my window was an unwelcome sight. He made a rolling down motion. I put it down.

"The Texas Rangers are coming and they're gonna figure this thing out."

"That's great." *Thank Goodness.*

"Where's your legal counsel? She gonna show up?" He leaned against the window. "Do you even know Reva Brooks?"

"She's my attorney."

"Yes, but you never seen her, I bet."

"That doesn't stop her from being my attorney."

"You got an answer for everything, dontcha? You're gonna play a different tune when the Texas Rangers get here. They're gonna find somethin' that links you to what you done."

"What makes you so sure I killed those men?"

"Cause-a what they done. I'd kill three men that did it to me." He stopped and scratched his head. "If you did it I can understand, and I don't really blame you, but killin' is still against the law in the great state

of Texas."

"I think it's still against the law in every state." That earned me his angry bulldog scowl.

A Cadillac SUV pulled up, and a Latino in a dark three-piece suit got out. The sheriff gawked at him as if he'd never seen a suit or a Latino. The man walked up to us and shook hands.

"Dustin Villarreal." He shook the sheriff's hand.

He took my hand. "I'm Dustin Villarreal, a partner in Reva Brook's firm. She couldn't be here today, Mr. Petersen, so she asked me to come in her place. She brought me up to speed, so I hope you won't mind if I step in for her."

"I don't mind."

Then he turned to the sheriff with a look that made me think *Holy crap, here it comes.* "It's Reva's understanding you're harassing Mr. Petersen, even though he has an airtight alibi on one of the murders. You said you had questions, but why are we in the parking lot? Don't you have an office? Maybe there's another place where we can meet out of the cold. I'm not going to stand with my client and talk about this in public in a place that must hold terrible memories for him. Why are we here, Sheriff?"

"One of the men was murdered here, and the other two were discarded here after being shot. All three bodies were put into the bushes over there."

"Then there should be a forensics team here, not a suspect and his attorney."

"We're here because my office is in Pecos."

That didn't make any sense, but I stayed quiet.

"But you have a small office here, don't you?" persevered my attorney.

"No."

"I thought you had a deputy here."

"The deputies come through, but the office is in Pecos. We could go into the restaurant. They have a couple of private meeting rooms."

"Is that acceptable to you, Jed?" Villarreal asked.

"Yes, that's okay."

Everything looked pretty much the same as when I worked there, but no one I knew was waiting

tables. That was a relief.

Once we got settled, Villarreal asked, "What questions do you have for my client, Sheriff Hoskins?"

"Where were you last night?"

"I was in my apartment on the Worthington Ranch. I train horses there so sometimes I don't stay in the bunkhouse with the other cowboys."

"Who can verify that you were there?"

"Nobody, except that for me to leave the ranch I'd have to borrow a vehicle, so somebody would have known."

"You could've walked out to the highway and caught a ride."

"It's at least twelve miles to the highway from where I stay."

"A healthy young man like you could do it easy."

"But I didn't."

"So you admit you could've walked out?"

"Yes, and I could have ridden a horse or had someone come for me, or I could've taken a truck without permission, but the point is that I didn't. I was at home alone, except for a horse in the barn next to me."

"What did you do at home alone?"

"I read and listened to the radio. Then I went to bed early because I didn't get much sleep in Fort Worth. I was tired from four days of riding bulls."

"Hm. When was the last time you saw Tex Reardon or 'Jocko' Sims?"

"It was at the trial. I haven't seen them since."

"Are you sure about that, Mr. Petersen?"

"He answered your question," my attorney broke in. "Continuing to ask the same question is harassment."

"Not to mention aggravating," I added.

"Deidra Desmond says you threatened and harassed all the men since the trial, not just her husband."

"Jed has already told you he didn't. Perhaps a review of the phone records of the spouses would show you the truth."

"I didn't say he used the phone."

"Then they should produce letters or photos, whatever they have. Until then, it's Jed's word against theirs. I would like to remind you that Jed works full time on a ranch and has no vehicle of his own. He also participates in bull riding, which takes practice and dedication, and travel to and from rodeo events."

"What the hell is your point?" barked the sheriff.

"Jed doesn't have time to run around harassing people in person."

"So you say."

"Do you have more questions for my client?"

The sheriff produced a photo of a nude man and laid it on the table in front of me. "You sent this photo to each of the men, according to their widows."

"That's my face but it isn't my body, and I think you know that."

"Take a good look."

I wanted to smack the smirk off his face. The man in the photo was hung like a horse. He looked deformed. No way did he seriously think that was me.

"I don't have to study it. I know what I look like naked, and that's not me."

"Okay, well, you must have Photoshopped your face onto another man's body."

"Why would I do that even if I knew how?"

"In order to entice the men to have sex with you, I reckon."

"Sheriff," my attorney interrupted, "anybody could have put Jed's face on that body. This proves nothing and is insulting. Do you have anything real as evidence?"

"This is what I have so far."

"I guess you know that you have nothing, then."

"It seems to me," I said, "since Mrs. Desmond has gone to so much trouble, she might've killed her husband herself and is trying to pin it on me."

"Why would she do that?"

"Don't answer that, Jed. He's asking you to speculate, and it's not your job to solve these murders. I believe we're through here, Sheriff."

After the sheriff left, Villarreal said, "I agree with you about Mrs. Desmond. If she came up with that

photo, it's likely she's the culprit or is covering for someone. It's also possible someone else sent the photo to her. The point here is that you didn't do it. Nor did you kill her husband. I don't think you'll hear any more on this, but if you do, you know our number."

"So I don't need to do anything?"

"No, just get on with your life."

That was my plan.

* * *

A Texas Ranger came by a few days later, accompanied by Mr. Villarreal. He asked politely for permission to take my fingerprints and a swab of my mouth for DNA. He said they were for elimination purposes. He asked a few questions and was gone within fifteen minutes.

When the Ranger left, I went to Kitty and asked if I could have a day off. I needed to think without interruptions. Of course she gave her permission.

I spent that afternoon galloping on Indio. When I arrived at a place I liked to camp, I stopped and let him graze while I made a little campfire in a rock circle I had used before. My camping spot was a protected area at the bottom of the ridge, among giant boulders that had fallen from a stark cliff face millions of years ago. The wind seemed to pick up all over the ranch at night, and those big rocks always sheltered me from the worst of it.

As night came on, I climbed onto a boulder and watched as daylight slowly faded behind the jagged mountain range in the west. Most of the color had drained from sunset's glow and the leftover light looked like the gradual dimming of a bulb. Stars began to pop out, and it was as if one called to another, and then they were all present and accounted for.

I worked things out in my head more quickly than I thought I would. After I ate, I rode Indio home in the dark.

* * *

The next morning I called to make an appointment with Kitty.

"Why so formal?" she asked.

"I have a serious business proposition for you."

"I like the sound of that. Can you come at ten?"

"I'll be there."

I didn't have a suit or I would've worn one. I dressed in my best clothes and thought I looked sharp enough to be taken seriously by a powerful businesswoman.

I knocked on the Worthington Ranch office door at exactly ten o'clock.

Instead of yelling for me to come in, Kitty came to the door and smiled when she saw me. "Come in, Mr. Petersen." She offered her hand.

I took the tiny hand I knew well. "Good morning, ma'am."

"Come in and have a seat. I was pleased to get your call."

"Really?"

"Of course, I'm always interested in business proposals."

I took a deep breath and felt awfully nervous, considering that I knew her so intimately. When you set your dreams out in front of someone who can shoot them down, it makes your stomach twist.

"Is that the proposal you're holding?"

"Yes." I had stayed up most of the night working on it. "First, I'll tell you about it. This ranch has an excellent reputation in the beef industry and is known for its breeding stock, too, but you told me some time ago that your real love is horses."

"Jed, I don't want to breed horses. There's not enough demand for them and it's heartbreaking to sell them to people who won't treat them right, and—"

"Kitty, I don't want to breed them, either. I want to train them and rehabilitate them and make money doing it. I've laid out the costs in my written proposal, and income projections, too. The costs to get started won't amount to much. Basically, you have everything we need, except a round pen. You already know it has to be sturdy, but that'll be the main expense to get started. Also, you'll have to hire another cowboy to take my place, and eventually I'll need somebody I can train to work with me. But to start, I'll do the work myself. I already checked that nobody else in the area trains

horses the gentle way. I can speak to groups and will go from ranch to ranch talking about why gentle training works a million times better than the usual way of breaking horses."

I had Kitty's attention but couldn't tell what she thought, so I kept talking. "We can get the word out that we re-train horses, too. A lot of times, perfectly good horses are shot or sold to slaughterhouses because they've acquired bad habits, or have been injured, either mentally or physically, or both.

"If we do this, Kitty, I want to be your equal partner, not your employee. You have the facilities and a solid gold reputation, so it might not seem fair at first, but think about it. I have the expertise, and the truth is that I have a gift not everybody has. I can use it to help horses and make a good living, too. If we work together, it will be successful for both of us."

Kitty had to stop me or who knows when I'd have stopped myself. "I've never seen you like this, Jed, so excited and confident. It's almost like you're a different man."

"I'm not your average cowboy, Kitty."

"I've known that since day one, Jed. Leave your proposal with me and let me look it over. I'll think about it and get back to you, okay?"

"Do you have any questions?"

"What has happened to you, Jed?"

I could never have explained it then, but even though I barely knew him, my friendship with Robby Sheffield had changed me. He reminded me who I was. I picked up that gift and ran with it.

CHAPTER 33

Later that afternoon, one of the cowboys asked me why I had broken up with Kitty. Right or wrong, I told him the truth.

Two days later I was working out in the weight room in the main barn when Harley and Pete came in and shut the door. Instinctively, I knew trouble was starting.

They greeted me and at first acted like they were only there to work out, too. Then Pete sat down next to me. "We have to talk."

I didn't stop exercising. "Okay. What do you want to talk about?"

"Some of the guys have a few concerns."

"And those are?"

Pete stared at his hands a long time. "Well, damn it, Jed; I don't wanna tell you, but it's about what you told Sammy the other day."

"I don't see how that concerns you."

"It ain't Harley and me that have concerns."

"Who does?"

"Cody and Billy are stirrin' up shit with some of the others."

Those two were new to our outfit. They hadn't arrived together, but it hadn't taken long for them to become friends, based on age (early-twenties) and mutual interests, one of which was bull riding; another was bullying. They signed up for the team and claimed experience but couldn't stay on the mechanical bull for four seconds; and that was on the lowest setting. When I tried to help, they took it wrong. There was already a

rift between us when I left for Fort Worth.

The news had already travelled through the cowboy grapevine, which had probably taken ten minutes. Kitty had mentioned the talk, but when she did I had stormed out, saying it was nobody's business. I still felt that was true.

Harley came into the discussion. "Cody says it's against cowboy code to lie down with another man."

"What about the right to privacy? That's code, too. And I never heard anything about lyin' down with a man being part of the code."

"It's unspoken."

"Bullshit."

"We're just telling you what they're sayin'," said Pete.

"Do you guys want me off the team?"

"Well hell, Jed, without you there ain't no team," said Harley. "It'd be me and Pete with those two-second morons."

"I don't know what you want me to do. Cowboys always talk. If it isn't me it'll be somebody else. The tongues around here got a good workout when I was sleeping with Kitty. It didn't change anything."

"Well it's different now."

"No it isn't. You just think it is because you don't understand."

"You could talk to Kitty," Pete said. "She would help."

"This isn't her problem."

"The hell it ain't. This is her ranch and you're her money-winning cowboy. Plus, she cares for you, Jed. Everybody knows that."

"Maybe you could say you were only kidding," suggested Harley. "That might settle things down."

"That would be a lie."

"Sometimes a lie serves a higher purpose."

"It wouldn't, Harley. If I change to suit other people, then pretty soon I'm not me anymore. I have to be who I am, no matter who gets pissed off about it."

"Have it your way, Jed, but a shit storm is comin'," Pete warned.

"Let it come, then."

"We don't want to see you get hurt."

"Thanks, but I reckon I'll have to face up to whatever they bring."

* * *

I had barely gotten out of the shower when Kitty called. "I'm impressed with your proposal, Jed. It's so thorough and well thought-out."

"Thank you. I tried to think of everything." I had put my heart into it.

"That's evident. I'm leaning towards saying yes."

"Why are you only leaning? Do you need more information from me?"

"How will you support yourself if it takes a while to get this going? If you're not going to be working as a cowboy, you won't be getting pay or meals."

"I have all my bull riding winnings in the bank, and I've saved money from all of my paychecks."

"That's exactly what I wanted to hear!" She sounded excited. "I want a partner who is financially solvent and responsible. Do you have any debt?"

"No, but I also don't have any credit."

"You can get credit later. It's overrated anyhow. Will you continue bull riding?"

"I don't know."

"I realize you may not have time for it once this takes off."

"That doesn't matter. I can't ride bulls forever, Kitty. I need to do what I was meant to do."

"I was thinking of myself; I enjoyed your winning streak. I'm ashamed."

"It's all right, Kitty. And I'm not sayin' no—only that we'll see."

"Of course. Forget bull riding for now."

"I'm still going to work out, and I'll help the others, but when it comes to getting on a bull, I don't know."

"You can see how you feel when spring comes."

"So are we doin' it?"

"What if we give it a trial run, say six months?"

"I think we should do it full out or not do it. If your heart's not in it, then you can say no. I won't hold it against you. I'm going to have to put in a lot of hours

and I don't want to have it hanging over my head that you might pull the plug any day."

"You drive a hard bargain, Jed Petersen."

"Look Kitty, you have this ranch and a thriving cattle business, so I understand if you don't want to take the risk. All I have is my ability to work with horses. If I can't turn that into something for myself, then I won't be able to face the man I see in the mirror. I'll be a highly motivated partner, I promise you."

"Indeed you will. Okay, Jed, let's go for it!"

"Oh, Kitty!"

"Why don't you come here for dinner and we'll celebrate? Better yet, we'll go out. That way we don't have nosy cowboys hanging around."

We agreed she would come for me at seven.

In spite of the cold, I ran out to the barn in boxers to check on Indio and leave feed and hay for him. Midnight was in the corral and I knew he had everything he needed. If I hadn't been so excited I might have heard the truck pull in. I looked up from my chores to see Cody and Billy and a man I didn't know swaggering towards me. They passed a bottle of whiskey back and forth. Everything about the scene said *gay bashing coming.* Or to use Pete's expression, a shit storm.

"Well, well." Cody strutted up. "If it isn't the famous bull rider himself."

"Hey, guys." I sounded amazingly unconcerned.

"We heard you didn't take the championship in Fort Worth like everybody thought you would."

"That's true."

"We figure it was 'cause you was ridin' more than bulls up there."

"You figured wrong."

"And you got ridden plenty, I bet."

"You're talking out your ass."

"That's better'n what you like to do with yours."

I thought it would be better not to say anything and was inching towards the door to my apartment when they moved to block me.

"Where're you goin' so fast?" Cody asked.

"I have things to do."

"We don't want you here, you fag."

That did it. I yelled in Cody's face. "If you wanna fight me, at least do it fair. Just you. Come on."

"Not so fast, gay boy."

I knocked the crap out of him. He flew backwards and fell in the dirt. It felt like my knuckles were smashed flat. The pain was awful. Blood spurted from Cody's nose and it began to swell.

"You broke my nose," he complained in a comically nasal voice.

"You say one more thing and I'll break you in half, asshole."

"Get him," he commanded, and the others came at me.

I spun around and grabbed a shovel from the wall. I had done three against one before; no way was I doing that again. I held the shovel between me and them, ready to do battle for my life.

"Don't be like that," Billy cajoled. "We're just messin' with you a little."

"Then leave. If you don't mean to hurt me, leave and we'll forget this."

"We ain't leavin'." Cody struggled back to his feet. The man without a name gave him a hand up. I could've taken out Billy while he was doing that, but he hadn't done anything to me at that point, and I hesitated too long. So for the second time in my life, I faced three men who meant to harm me.

Billy came closer. "What are you doin' out here nearly naked?"

Cody moved, too. "Are you expecting company?"

"I ran out here to do a few chores. I'd go back in if you'd leave like I asked."

The nameless man got into the act. "We don't like workin' with fairies."

"You don't even work here."

"Cowboys don't like workin' with fairies," he clarified.

"Call me a fairy again and you'll be eatin' this shovel."

"Is that so?" He turned to the others. "Did you hear that? He's a feisty little fairy."

I was raising the shovel when he hit me with a taser. Talk about an unfair fight. That was tongue-biting painful, and it knocked me to the ground. I couldn't move, and for a few moments I didn't even know where I was. The first thing they did was rip the boxers off me. Why do straight men always want to get a gay man naked? Do they think we're anatomically incorrect? That was two of several random thoughts I had while I struggled to make any part of myself work. Terror of being raped just about turned me to Jell-O.

Then I was lifted and Billy whipped off his belt. I was still shaky, and if the other two hadn't been holding me up, I would've dropped to the ground again.

"We're goin' to teach you a lesson."

"What lesson?" My mouth decided to work, but my words sounded like those of a stroke victim. My next thought was *Kitty is coming at seven.* Of course, I had no idea what time it was.

"This is what real men think about working with queers."

"Not one of you can call yourself a real man. You wouldn't know a real man if he broke your nose."

The biting sting of the belt across my bare chest caused me to shut my mouth. It hurt like hell and made my eyes tear up. But out of the corner of my eye I saw Indio begin to move. They laughed at him and passed the bottle of liquid courage around. They said he was a big pussy like his owner. They assumed he was running away in fear, but I knew better. I just didn't want them to hurt him.

The next lash opened my face and the following one, my thigh. Before I was hit again, Indio attacked Cody from behind and bit him hard on the back of the arm, crushing the flesh. He howled in pain and dropped the belt. Then my horse pulled a Bruce Lee, felling two men at once with his kicking legs. He crushed Billy's leg in the excitement, and Nameless Man's arms. All three of my attackers were screaming and crying like—well, like pussies.

Indio came to my side and nuzzled me, sweet as could be.

"Good boy, Indio. Thank you, my friend."

At that point, dressed-up Kitty came through the door from my apartment. "Well what the—" The look on her face was priceless. I was naked and bleeding, standing over three men. It must have looked like I had brought them down myself.

"I'm not ready to go yet." I said calmly.

"Well, why the hell not?" She laughed and then started crying. "I'm going to call for help," she sobbed, and then disappeared into the apartment.

* * *

Kitty and I got to work on our new project. She called all the ranchers she knew, and I called the ones she didn't and explained our new service. By the end of a day, we had three horses coming and many promises to keep us in mind for the future. We followed up our phone calls with letters so they wouldn't forget.

Cody, Billy, and Nameless Man went to the hospital, and then to jail for a few weeks. Then Nameless Man, who turned out to be Hank Richards, was sent back to Wyoming on an outstanding warrant, both arms in casts. The other two disappeared when they were released on bail, and we never heard from them again.

* * *

About three weeks passed, and Dustin Villarreal called to say I could forget about the murders of the three rapists. By then I already had.

"Deidra Desmond, Iris Reardon, and Jocko's girlfriend Yolanda Vargas conspired to kill their partners after they were acquitted of the rape," Dustin said. "The Texas Ranger investigators discovered their dried saliva on the faces of the dead men, which left no doubt. They shot their husbands, spit on them, and then left them to rot."

"I don't know what to say."

"Deidra said she started to frame you but decided that would be unfair, since you had already suffered so much at the hands of her husband," he said. "Let me read to you from her confession, as quoted by the Texas Rangers. 'We knew those sons-a-bitches were guilty as hell, and we thought they should pay for what they did to that young man. And anyway,

who in their right mind wants to live with a man that would do something like that?'"

* * *

Midnight was put to stud, something he took to a whole lot faster than anything I ever tried to teach him. When he wasn't entertaining and impregnating females, he had his own pasture next to one with geldings, so he had a herd but no reason to fight them. He probably pitied them, being the righteous stud he was. There were no more problems caused by him, but nobody could ride him but me. That was fine. He was mine and I liked it like that.

* * *

One day I received a small package in the mail from an 'R. M.' in Nashville. It had to be Ron Matthews. I was afraid to open it and looked at it a long time before I did. It was a copy of a demo CD he and his band had recorded, a song called *Under the Texas Stars.*

A short, handwritten note read:

> *Well, Jed, you were right all those years ago. My songs are being played on the radio, and this one is slowly moving up the charts. I wrote it for you, so I thought you should have it. I keep up with you a little through my father, who hears about you from your father. I guess you've taken Texas rodeo by storm, not that I'm surprised. I'm glad you stayed with it.*
>
> *Love, Ron.*

I read that note again and again, but I didn't think I could listen to the song. I put it into the drawer with the other letters and the gold buckle and tried to forget it.

* * *

There was a lot of talk about the barn incident, and speculation about me, and even about Kitty and me. I spent a lot of time with her, so the cowboys thought whatever they thought, but they didn't bother

me with it.

No matter what was said behind my back, I was treated with respect. There wasn't a man there who could argue about my abilities or my loyalty to the ranch. We went back to honoring the old cowboy code, which includes, among other things, keeping your love life to yourself (nobody talks about it unless you do), and to stand by the other cowboys riding for your brand.

There was no more gay-bashing at the Worthington Ranch.

Chapter 34

About a year later, I was looking for something and opened the drawer that held the CD from Ron. I re-read the note and finally listened to the song. It was beautiful. It brought back memories of our times together when we were so innocent but had loved each other so much. I thought of it as the *wishing on stars* time of my life, and I wished I could get back to that.

Hearing Ron sing such an impassioned song in his incredible voice, and knowing it was written for me, seemed to re-kindle an old flame. I wondered if he was living with somebody, and if he was happy, and if he ever missed me, and on and on. After some thought, I decided to write and ask. I also told him that I thought *Under the Texas Stars* was the most beautiful song I ever heard.

A few weeks later the letter was returned, addressee unknown. I put the CD back in the drawer and tried again to forget it.

* * *

Five more months passed. In fact, it was April and I had turned twenty. Our horse business was a thriving enterprise, so much so that I hadn't gone back to bull riding or even thought much about it. I didn't have time to do everything, and horses interested me more than bulls. We weren't getting rich, but Kitty was already rich. I was making more money than any other person on the ranch besides her, and my income steadily increased.

I wanted my own place so I could live with and love whomever I chose. It would be better not to do it

under a bunch of cowhand noses.

At the time I was working with a horse named RandyRules. He had been burned in a terrible stable fire in which the rest of the Barclay Ranch horses had perished. He belonged to the ranch owner's autistic son, Jake, who loved him dearly. They wanted the animal to live because of the son's deep emotional attachment to him. I was doing it less for the money and more for the sake of the gelding, and an eight-year-old boy who had little to do with anything except for a horse that ruled.

To me, putting an animal down is a last resort but when I went to see RandyRules, I thought that would be the kindest thing. His eyes were so wild and frightened—well, he was the most pitiful creature I had ever seen. He had been kept heavily drugged and as pain-free as possible until the worst of the burns were nearly healed. His body said his ordeal had been horrific, but his eyes told a worse story. Likely the most terrible thing had been surviving a cataclysm in which his buddies had succumbed all around him. That would have put anybody over the edge, and he seemed well over it to me.

I was about to decline working with him, even though it hurt my soul to turn my back on a horse that needed help so much. I'm only human and had other things on my plate.

Before I left, the father came in with his son. When I saw that little boy's face there was no way to turn away from him or his horse. Like the sentimental sap I am, instead of saying *I can't help this horse*, I said, "You'll probably have to sedate him to bring him to me."

"You fix RandyRules!" Jake exclaimed, and he flung his arms around my leg.

"I'll do my best, Jake."

"The only time he speaks is around this horse," said the boy's dad, Johnston Barclay. "We have to save him, Jed. If you can do that, I'll give you anything I have."

"I won't hold you to that. Can you bring him tomorrow around five? Stop at headquarters and the guys will tell you how to find me."

When the animal was delivered, Kitty followed. When the others left, she didn't. She was quiet, hanging on the fence to watch.

"What do you think, Jed?" she asked after a while.

"I can hardly stand to look at him."

"I've never seen a horse scarred like that."

"He should've been put down. But now he's in this place between life and death and he's gonna have to decide which way he's going."

"Well, don't you want him to live?"

"Yes, I do, and that little boy does, but I don't think he much wants to."

She turned away from us. I sat down beside what was left of RandyRules and spoke to him, assuring him he was safe. I recalled a time when I had thought I'd never feel safe again. Now I did, most of the time. I went from wondering if I could help him to knowing I could.

While RandyRules was still sedated, I applied a cream the vet had given me for skin healing from a burn. It kept it moist so it would stretch. Burned skin tends to shrivel and draw up, making it painful to move. All the while I told him heart to heart, not in words, that I was going to help him get better. I told him I understood how it feels to be afraid.

Let me love you, I thought towards him. *Let me love you, RandyRules.*

I turned and saw that Kitty was still there. The sun gleamed off her hair and she squinted as she watched me work; her small boot rested on the fence. It was almost like no time had passed since we'd first become lovers. I still loved her, even though it wasn't by-the-book the way it should be between a man and a woman. I didn't go by anybody else's book anyway.

I walked towards her.

"I know Jed, I should go, but your work fascinates me." She pushed hair back from her eyes with a small, tanned hand I adored.

"Well, Kitty, I could teach you the work if you want. You'd be good at it."

"Could I spend the night with you, Jed?" That

was my direct-as-a-straight-line Kitty.

"Well..." I was still a smooth-talking Don Juan.

"I don't care about sex." She blushed as she lied to me. "I just want you to hold me. I need to hear another heart beat."

"Kitty, if I hold you, there will be sex, you know that." I hadn't held her yet, and I was already thinking about it.

"Truthfully, I just want back in your pants, Cowboy." She cocked her head because the sun was in her eyes. Hers studied mine, and then she smiled. "It's true that I want to hear your heart beat, too."

The sun was setting, making everything magic, and a woman I loved was standing there looking at me with big blue eyes. She had the softest skin I ever felt and a kind, loving heart. She had once brought me back from the dead, and it was all I could do to breathe. All the blood had raced away from my brain, but I could still think well enough to know it wasn't what I longed for, and it could be a mistake, but right then I couldn't reason it out, nor did I want to.

I left feed for RandyRules, and then I hopped the fence and kissed her and took her hand and went inside. We never had dinner or thought about it.

* * *

Where Midnight had been all frantic activity and bursting with stallion hormones, screeching and complaining and destroying things, RandyRules was withdrawn, too quiet. He was a gelding, so no raging hormones, but still his attitude was more like a very old, worn-out horse. His eyes were frightened when approached, but more often dead-looking. He had given up. The only time he reacted was when I tried to get too close to him. I had to sedate him to apply the cream, and I knew sedating him all the time was not helping him come back. My first goal was to touch him without sedating him, but that seemed a long way off.

RandyRules' comeback started with the radio about a week later. Until that point I hadn't made much progress. Kitty spent nearly every evening with me, and as we did on many of them, we were sitting on the tailgate of her pickup, watching the sunset and

listening to an oldies station on the XM. Somebody started clapping and singing,

Lover please, please come back
Don't take a train coming down the track

When it came to the chorus, I started singing along just to mess with Kitty and make her laugh. The point is I was singing loudly.

"Look at that, Jed." Kitty motioned towards the horse. "RandyRules is listening to you."

He did seem more alert than usual. It was the first interest he'd shown in anything. I stood at the fence and sang, and he seemed to like it no matter what it was. I wasn't a good singer, and RandyRules still seemed to like it. I wondered if Jake had sung to him, so the next morning I called to ask.

Johnston Barclay returned my call quickly. "Yes, Jake sang to him," he said in answer to my question. "He was a colt and Jake was only two. It was before the autism took over."

"What did he sing?"

"Oh, bits of nursery rhymes, and stuff he made up, mostly. Why are you asking?"

"Music seems to be the only thing RandyRules responds to. Could you bring Jake over here?"

"Jake quit singing months ago."

"Well, would you bring him anyway? I think it would help."

"Jake worsened after RandyRules was injured. He hasn't been the same boy since. I don't want to make him worse."

"I believe the boy and the horse are good together. I think we should restore that friendship and the quicker the better."

"I don't know. I have to protect my son."

"Please trust me. If Jake has a bad reaction you can remove him. I don't want to hurt Jake, Mr. Barclay. He's the reason I'm doing this."

He thought about it. "Okay, I'll bring him this afternoon. Is three o'clock a good time?"

I said that would work.

When they arrived, the little boy repetitively clenched and unclenched his hands as he followed his

father to the fence. I didn't know what that meant, but when he saw RandyRules he stopped and stared and relaxed his hands.

"I'm glad you came, Jake. Do you remember me? I'm Jed."

"He probably won't respond to you, but keep talking. It's hard to tell how much he hears, but we talk to him all the time."

"RandyRules is your horse and he needs you. I wonder if you would sing to him. He seems to really like singing."

No response from the boy.

"Let's sing." I started. *I can see clearly now, the rain is gone.* Why I chose that, who knows, but I remembered it from somewhere, and it was positive.

As I sang I moved to the rhythm, rocking a little and snapping my fingers. Jake didn't sing but he began to move and snapped his fingers, too. Soon we were doing a coordinated dance. His father watched speechlessly and then he started moving, too.

Gonna be a bright, bright, bright sunshiny day

I sang and we danced. Jake's face was peaceful and happy. He looked like he would burst into laughter but he didn't. After a while, he repeated *bright, bright* when I sang it. He seemed to understand the timing and joined me, but sang nothing else. When I stopped singing and moving, Jake kept going. I stood aside and watched RandyRules. He remembered.

"Let's sing something different, Jake. You pick it."

"Bright, bright, bright, bright," he sang in his high-pitched little-boy voice.

"Don't worry," said his dad. "This is something he does. Just start singing something different and see if he follows. Give him time."

A song Ron had sung came to me; I had once sung it to Sadie's old Hal. It was Carole King's "You've Got a Friend."

Jake was still singing bright, bright, but I kept going.

Johnston Barclay and I were dancing, but his son was grooving on a different wavelength.

RandyRules had come to his feet.

Johnston began singing with me. It wasn't pretty, but it was heartfelt. I know it sounds crazy but sometimes the craziest things work. Most times it's a matter of putting your heart into it.

At one point Jake laughed, either at the dancing or the terrible singing or at something only he knew, but it was such a happy sound that RandyRules took a trembling step towards him. All of us froze in place.

"Touch him, Jake."

"If he hurts him—"

"He won't hurt him."

Jake took a step towards his horse.

"Touch him, Jake." I trusted my gut.

The horse and the boy approached each other in mini-steps. The two were so focused on each other it seemed they were the only living things in each other's world. At last they were close, closing in on the love between them. Jake reached out his hand. RandyR sniffed and sniffed. He didn't seem to trust his nose at first. Then he nuzzled the boy's neck, and finally, sniffed him all over, claiming him, loving him.

I looked over at Johnston. His eyes were full of tears. It had worked. Jake had brought RandyRules back from darkness.

I looked up at the high cliff behind the big house, the rugged one I longed to scale. *Come up here, Jed,* it seemed to say. *Come up here and beat your chest.*

When the Barclays left and promised to return the following afternoon, I pulled on running gear and took off for the cliff. The foothills were crazy with wildflowers again, and I wondered if they ever didn't bloom up there. The afternoon sun was warm, but not hot. Everything was verdant. Bees buzzed, butterflies fluttered, and the breeze that blew was full of sweet scents.

I stopped to drink water from a canteen, and then picked my way through fallen boulders and slip-slide gravel to the back of the mountain that wore the big lopsided rock formation like a funky hat. It was impossible to run. What I needed was long pants and hiking boots.

It took a long time and many false starts just to get to the back of the cliff. I saw a maybe way up, but by then the sun was low in the west and I had to go back. Going down wasn't much easier than going up.

I went straight to RandyRules, who was standing in the corral. His ears perked at my approach. I spoke to him, and then I went inside the apartment, opened the windows, and turned on the radio.

I ate everything I could find in the fridge and cabinets. As long as it didn't have to be cooked, I was into it. Cheese; crackers; Oreos; stale Fig Newtons; three bananas; cold, left-over stew. I wasn't full but I ran out of things to stuff in my mouth. It wasn't laziness as much as dead-on hunger and a driving desire to get back to RandyRules to see if he would come to me like he had the boy.

I went back to the corral. The sun had set but everything had a soft pinkish color, and the distant mountains looked surreal. If I stood there long enough I could believe that they had never really been there.

I made a soft clucking noise and called to RandyRules. "Come here, boy. Come on. Come to me."

He acted like he wanted to, but the only movement he made was to back up a few steps. He was standing, and that was something. Slowly I stepped towards him, singing softly the same songs I had sung with Jake and his dad.

RandyRules watched me with sad eyes. I continued towards him until he backed into the fence and had to stop. After that, he allowed me to approach without protest. That was a sign of better things to come. He seemed to appreciate the burn cream, or at least understood what I was doing. I sang softly all the while. It seemed ironic that my not-so-great singing would have a soothing effect on man or beast.

I continued to think the same thought towards him. *Let me love you.*

I wondered if RandyRules would be able to heal Jake. What I knew about autism was zip, but I felt certain the boy was going to heal the horse. Jake had already brought his beloved RandyRules forward by weeks compared to what I could have done on my own.

He was closer to me than he'd ever been voluntarily. I stretched my hand out slowly but he stepped backwards. Damn.

* * *

"Jed, don't you ever think of finding someone else?" Kitty was lying next to me naked, and my legs were tucked under hers.

"Well Kitty, I've been a little busy with you." I disentangled myself and sat on the edge of the bed.

"I know, Jed, and I feel guilty, because I know you do think of it."

"Don't start. Please. I have a lot of work to do today."

"You work too much for someone your age."

"Would a lazy man make you happier?"

"I don't want you to miss a chance at love because you're with me."

"Here we go."

"Tell me the truth, Jed, or you know I'll never let up."

I sighed. "Yes, Kitty, I want to find a man. But no, I'm not looking for somebody right now."

"Well you should be, Jed. What about that new cowboy, Rowdy something-or-other? He's cute. And I think he's gay. And I know he likes you."

"Hold everything, Kit. I don't want you to find someone for me. Rowdy is cute all right, but he's not gay. Do you want me to get beat up again?"

"Of course not, but I'm pretty sure he's gay."

"Kitty, he's not. Please leave this alone."

"What are you afraid of?"

"I'm afraid of a straight woman who thinks she can pick a gay man for me. Rowdy is not gay. If you think he's cute, make a pass at him and you'll find out. He'll flip head over spurs for you."

"He's too young for me."

"Good God, Kitty. He's older than me by six years—maybe more."

"You're different."

"So rather than go for a good-looking man of twenty-five who's not gay, you'd keep on with a twenty-year-old gay man?"

"I don't want to keep on with you, Jed."

"So that's what this is about? You're breaking up with me."

"It's for your own good."

"So you were just using me to get off for a couple of weeks."

"I didn't hear you complaining about it."

She had a point. "No, you're the one with complaints."

"I don't have complaints, Jed. I love you in a way you don't love me. When I'm with you a while I realize how pathetic I am."

"You're anything but pathetic, Kitty. I need to move on, but so do you. There's a whole world of men out there who'd swoon at a chance to love you."

"And you know this—how?"

"I watch men look at you. One of the most attractive things about you is that you have no idea how beautiful you are. You're the best type of beauty. Kitty, wake up! I'm a gay man, and I'm powerless around you."

"Oh, Jed."

"I don't think Rowdy is good enough for you. He has 'cute' going for him, but he's a drifter with no plan. What about that rancher, Clive Beatty? He's your age. He's very handsome and classy. He speaks to you at every event I've ever been to with you, and he looks at you with longing in his eyes. And they're green."

"Longing in his eyes? Really?"

"Yes. Really."

"You noticed that?"

"Duh, Kit, I look at men."

"So we can break this off and you won't be mad?"

"No. I'm not mad."

* * *

RandyRules went home after five weeks, escorted by a happy little boy. His father offered me cash, a thoroughbred horse, a good used horse trailer. He had already paid the fee so I refused everything. Besides, Jake had brought the magic; I had only provided guidance and a lot of singing and dancing.

"If you ever need anything," Johnston Barclay

said tearfully when he hugged me, "you only have to say the word."

The best thing he could give me was referrals, and he agreed to do that.

* * *

Kitty called about a month later and asked me to come to her office. I was always in her office, but was seldom called in and never in such a timid way. She sounded near tears. Lately she seemed touchy and prone to crying, and I didn't know what she wanted from me.

I went in without knocking. She came around the big oak desk and smiled one of her shame-the-sun smiles. "Would you like something to drink, Jed? Coffee?"

"No Kitty. You asked to see me, and I want to hear what it is you have to say."

She turned red. "I don't know how to tell you."

"Just say it straight out. You know I prefer it that way."

"I'm pregnant, Jed. You're going to be a father."

I sat down hard.

"Well, please say something."

"You took the words out of me. I wasn't expecting anything like that."

"It's hard to get used to the idea, I know."

"It's a surprise is all."

"You're not angry?"

"No. I guess I like the idea better than anything. I never thought about being a father to anybody."

"Look, Jed, I don't expect anything from you in the way of support or being around or anything like that."

"Don't you want me to marry you?" The thought filled me with dread, but as a man, I felt it was an offer expected of me and the right thing to do.

"Oh no, Jed. I wouldn't ask that of you. I'm only telling you because I think it's the fair thing. I'm going to have this baby, even if you didn't want me to. I'm not getting any younger, and I like the idea of a child. I guess I've always wanted one."

"When is the baby due?"

"In January."

"Did you tell anyone else?"

She laughed uneasily. "No, I wanted to tell you first. The others will figure it out soon enough when I begin to look like a blimp."

I didn't say anything, because I was stressing about being a father.

"This is a hell of a thing to do to you, Jed. I know that."

"It's okay, Kitty. My child will have a good mother and that means everything to me."

Her eyes filled with tears, and she came and stood close to me. "He'll have a good father, too, and if you want to be part of his life I'd be proud for that to be the way it goes."

I reached out and pulled her to me and rested my head near the place where my child was growing. She put her hands in my hair and held me there. "I love you, Jed," she whispered after a while.

"I love you too, Kitty, and I'm sorry it's not the way you want me to love you, but it's still love. I hope you know that."

"I do know it."

We held each other a while longer.

"You should go on now, Jed."

I hugged her tightly and released her.

"Come and see me from time to time, okay?"

"I'll be doing that." I kissed her on the cheek, and drove back to the barn apartment in a daze.

I lay on my bed to stare at nothing. I was going to be a father.

* * *

When the cowboys caught on to everything, it was almost unbearable. One day I was working out in the weight room and overheard a typical cowpoke conversation in the barn. I wasn't paying attention until they mentioned a baby.

"Yep, she told Ted Jenkins it was his baby." Ted Jenkins owned a neighboring ranch and was a longtime friend of Kitty's. "And he does take her to all those doctor appointments."

"Well, fuck me!"

"You gotta be kiddin'!"

"He was spendin' all that time over there again. I toldya he was fuckin' her."

"Don't that beat all? I thought he was queer."

"I think he's confused."

"What's to be confused about? There's two clear choices, pussy or dick."

"Maybe he can't choose one over the other."

"What a stud!"

"Ain't nobody safe is what."

"Ain't no figurin' it."

"He must know somethin' we don't know."

"Yeah, you better watch your ass."

"Best not bend over in front of him."

CHAPTER 35

One day when Kitty was about six months pregnant, I took her to another doctor's appointment. Afterward, we went to lunch at a Mexican restaurant in Fort Davis and sat way back in the corner, hoping to avoid nosy people. A scandal was raging for all the reasons you can imagine. Kitty held her head high and said she didn't care what anybody thought. *What's to gossip about? Just because I'm unmarried, filthy rich, and having a gay man's baby, people are going crazy—like it's somethin'.*

"I've been thinking," she said without warning, "that if you're feeling as lonely and horny as I am, we should get a hotel room."

I nearly choked on a swallow of tea. The woman always was direct as a straight line.

"I know you are, Cowboy, both lonely and horny, so I guess what it comes down to is if you want to get it on with a short woman with a fat belly."

I laughed. "You're beautiful, Kitty. I've always thought so, and I still think so. You're more beautiful than ever."

"Is that a yes, Jed, or cowboy bullshit?"

"It's a yes—a big, fat yes. Do you want me to stand on my chair and tell everyone in this room?"

"That won't be necessary. Just a 'yes' is all I wanted."

"If you're through eating we should get moving, Kitty."

"I couldn't eat another bite."

* * *

When it began to get dark I asked if she wanted me to take her back to the ranch.

"Not this week. We're gonna stay here until I get over this desperate need I feel. Just keep it coming."

That was something I could do.

Later I went out for food and brought back cheeseburgers and chocolate shakes. Kitty was asleep, and glowed in a way she never had. I didn't know enough then to know it was from being pregnant. I thought it had to do with being satiated, and maybe it was that, too.

I ate a cheeseburger and watched her. After I had eaten my fill, I turned off the light, stripped, and crawled into bed next to her as gently as possible.

"You've been eating cheeseburgers," she accused groggily.

"Would you like one?"

"That's not what I have in mind right now."

"What do you have in mind?"

"I want to crawl on top of you and see if I can wear you out."

"What's stopping you?"

Nothing stopped her. Eventually I was too weak to. I thought, when I had a coherent thought, about what the waitress had said about me riding the bulls and not letting 'em ride me.

* * *

"You might not know this." Kitty's mouth was full of cheeseburger. "Pregnancy makes a woman extra horny. It's all the hormones."

"Are we going to keep this room until the baby comes?"

"Maybe." She grinned. "Could you handle it?"

"I'll do my best, I promise you. I guess I could call for reinforcements."

"I only want you. I want to love you flat-out, Jed. It would knock your spurs off."

"Then do it, Kitty. I dare you. And marry me. It'll give the baby my name, and you could get rid of that Worthington name. I'd be proud to have you as my wife. I do love you, Kit."

She lay down next to me again. "I want to give

the baby your name anyway. Let's don't talk about marriage. You and I both know that's not a good idea. If you'll just be mine until the baby comes and not leave me, that'll be enough."

"I'll do that, Kitty, but I'm offering you more."

"I know you are and I appreciate what you're willing to give up for me, but I would never ask you to. Marriage to me isn't for you. There's a whole other life biting at your heels. I don't want a husband that might fall in love with a man he meets at a rodeo—or anywhere else."

I understood her point and let the idea rest.

"Let's get some sleep. I believe you've finally worn me out."

I was relieved to hear her say it.

We didn't go back to the ranch until two days later. Kitty called to tell them she was staying in town. She didn't mention me and nobody had the guts to ask her.

* * *

In most ways, the months that followed were good ones. I moved in with Kitty and we quit tiptoeing around about our relationship. I put all my attention on her and working with horses and tried to keep my attention off the life that Kitty said was biting at my heels. I knew it was there but I wouldn't turn around and look at it.

Kitty taught me a lot about managing a ranch. She did a bigger job than I ever realized, and was responsible for the welfare of her employees, the land, and all the animals as well. After a while she turned over a few of her duties to me. One of the things she wanted me to do was to hire a foreman since Rick had moved on.

"You know what we need," she countered when I argued that hiring a foreman was something she should do.

"I don't know where to start."

"First you figure out what you want in a person and how to state it clearly. Then you have to figure out how to advertise for someone. I usually talk to other ranchers I know, see if they know anybody looking for

work."

"I think you should promote one of your cowboys."

"Is there one you'd recommend?"

"Little Mike. He's serious, quiet, and he's done everything as far as ranching work goes. He's been with you for eleven years and knows the work. He's bilingual, too."

She thought about it. "Do you think Little Mike could get their respect? He's a small man and shy. I think they'd run all over him."

"Kitty, it's not about size."

"But look how big Rick was."

"He would've been big even if he'd been a little man. It was his attitude. He commanded respect because of the way he handled himself and because he knew the work. He could brag all day about the things he'd done but he wasn't full of shit. And when he put guys to work, he worked too."

"Why don't I make you the foreman until we find somebody else?"

"No, Kitty, bad idea."

"Why?"

"Aren't you forgetting that I have a job? And anyhow, they don't respect me. I couldn't manage them for ten minutes. In fact, I wouldn't be treated seriously if I only wanted a meeting with them. They would all be knocking against each other and mumbling not to bend over in front of me."

"You're exaggerating."

"You don't know your cowboys very well."

"Do they really say that about not bending over in front of you?"

"Yes Kit and worse. The point is they don't respect me. None of them understand who I am."

"I feel like firing all of them."

"No, don't. It won't be different with new ones. But thank you for the thought."

Kitty seemed deep in thought for a while. Then she changed the subject. "Jed, I feel guilty about something I did. I need to tell you, but it might make you really angry with me."

"Jeez, what is it?"

"I came back to you because I hoped to get pregnant. I know it was wrong to do it without your say, but I was thinking of myself. I wanted to have a child with a man so good-looking and healthy, and you're so kind-hearted. And I guess I wanted to be able to keep a part of you."

I blinked at her. "You were using me as a *stud?*"

"Well, I wouldn't put it quite like that."

"I thought you came back because you miss me and care about me."

"That was part of it, of course."

"So I'm just a penis to you?"

She burst out laughing. "No, of course not."

"Oh yes, that's exactly what this is about." I put my face against her belly. "Hey in there! News flash, kid! Your father is just a penis."

She laughed and told me I was crazy. We continued to bicker, but it was more playful than serious.

I still thought we should marry so we could tell our child in later years that we had been married when he or she was born, but he came before I convinced her. He was early by a nearly a month, but he was ready, even if his parents weren't.

Chapter 36

The day my son was born was one of the happiest of my life and also one of the saddest. I had promised not to leave Kitty, and I never did, but she left me.

I was there when he was born, and it was amazing. I could barely believe my eyes. We named him Jed Andrews Petersen. Andrews was Kitty's maiden name. Our son was laid on Kitty's bare stomach, the most beautiful little human I'd ever seen. When we spoke, he looked towards the sound of our voices, and seemed alert and content.

"He's just like you, Jed, satisfied to lie around naked showing everybody his stuff."

I laughed and said something smart to her but when I bent to kiss her, saw that something was wrong. She went white as a cotton ball and her eyes rolled back in her head. I screamed to the nurses who went into action in a split-second. Kitty's blood was everywhere. It didn't seem like a tiny woman could have so much.

"Jed," Kitty whispered, "don't let them take him from you."

"I won't. You're going to be fine, Kitty. They're working on you now. You hang on, baby, because we need you."

"Go see," she gasped, "Reva...Brooks." I could barely hear her. "She...knows."

"What does she know?"

"Please stand back, sir." A nurse practically shoved me away from her. I grabbed the baby and

wrapped him in my soft flannel shirt. It was cold in that room and no one seemed to think about him or notice that he was missing when I took him.

"I'm going to hold her hand." I shoved my way back in. "I'm here, Kitty. I'm right here."

She didn't speak or open her eyes but when I took her hand, she smiled.

"No one is going to take our son from me, but the point here is that you're going home with us."

"No, Cowboy, not this time."

Oh no, no, no. Please don't take her. Take me, not her.

"I love you so much, Kit." Those would be the last words she would ever hear from me.

"Love you, Cowboy," she whispered. The next second, she was gone.

The hospital is a cold and agonizing place to lose someone you love. They let me spend a few minutes with Kitty, and then they wheeled her away because they needed the room. It was a delivery room, they pointed out. Yes, and nobody healthy should have died there.

A nurse demanded I turn over my son, but said she was only going to clean him up, check him out, and would bring him back. Back to where? I followed her to the nursery and watched through the glass to be damned sure I would get him back. Kitty's words worried me. Who would want to take him?

While I stood at the nursery window, Kitty's doctor came and tried to comfort me. He explained about hemorrhaging, but all I understood was that she was gone. He mentioned that I should sign the birth certificate the nurse would bring. If I decided to give the baby up for adoption, he knew couples that would be happy to take him. He said he was a fine, healthy boy, even though he only weighed five pounds, five ounces. His parents were small, so why wouldn't he be?

"He's my son and I want him." My tone left no doubt.

A nurse came and gave me a bag she said held diaper samples, formula samples, and coupons for various things. Nothing she said registered, and the

whole time she spoke, I had one eye on my baby.

They cleaned him, dressed him, and tried to feed him, but it seemed like he wanted to be left alone to sleep. They exclaimed over how cute he was, the tiny perfection of him, and eventually brought him out dressed in clothes Kitty had brought in her overnight bag. She had known to bring baby clothes and blankets, something that would never have occurred to me. They handed me my son and the bag. I was on my own.

I signed the birth certificate proudly, but it hurt me to see that Kitty's signature would never be on it. For as long as my son lived there would be a big blank spot where his mother was supposed to sign. That would be the least of his worries, though. He was no bigger than a minute and was completely dependent upon a father who didn't know one thing about babies. That was when I cried.

I was leaving the hospital later that afternoon, when all the cowboys from the Worthington Ranch came in. They had heard and come to see what they could do for me. The men that aggravated me no end surrounded me and held me up that day and in the days to come, or I might not have made it.

They took my son and me back to Kitty's house, but I didn't think I could stay there. The only reason I did was because all the baby things were there.

Again, my life had changed so fast it was overwhelming, and would have been so even with Kitty there. I had something too precious to lose, and it was terrifying.

* * *

I sat with my son in the room I called the Fabulous Room because it looked out on ranchlands and the distant mountains. He slept soundly while his dad cried like a baby. I had so many worries my head was pounding.

At first I told myself Kitty would come walking in and say it had been a mistake. They wheeled her away, and afterward she felt better. I knew that wasn't true; I just wanted it to be.

We never married, which made everything seem

worse. Legally I was nobody, and so I worried that I didn't have parental rights to my son—but that had to be wrong. Married or not, I was still his father. But Kitty had said *don't let them take him*. Who? Who would take him?

She had planned to nurse him, and I didn't even know what I would feed him in her absence. I wasn't so ignorant that I didn't know babies drank milk, but what milk? And they needed diapers. The hospital gave me some samples but not enough to last more than a few days once he started drinking. I didn't even know who to call to tell me about a baby.

I knew I should be figuring out how to care for a newborn, but I couldn't move. I was sobbing by the time Little Mike and Pete came in.

"We're so sorry, Jed," Pete said, "and so sad."

Mike sat down next to me. "You don't know the first thing about babies, do you, Jed?" he asked softly. It occurred to me that he was married and had children, which meant he knew babies. The rest of the cowboys were probably as clueless as I was.

I answered Mike's question with a negative shake of my head.

"I don't want to make you mad, but I called my wife to come."

"That's good," I sobbed. Pete handed me a handkerchief and I wiped my face. "I don't know what to do."

"It looks like you have all the things you'll need, Jed," Pete said. "There are diapers and clothes and baby things in the nursery. We checked it out earlier when you were still at the hospital."

"This wasn't supposed to happen," I wailed.

"We know. Our hearts are broken for you."

What could those poor guys say? They stayed with me, quiet, but I knew they were there. And I knew that the others were hovering close by. Kitty was a loss to all of us. She made everyone feel special and she knew how to manage a ranch so that everyone and everything on it prospered. None of us knew who would take over now or if we would still be employed tomorrow.

Little Mike's wife was even tinier than he was. He introduced her as Esperanza. She told me in heavily accented English that she had two children, a boy and a girl, now teenagers. Esperanza means "hope" and she gave me some. She assured me I'd be a great father. She said she would stay with me as long as I wanted. I didn't want her to stay. I just wanted to know what she knew so my son would thrive. She never said the obvious, that he needed his mother.

When my son woke and fussed, she took him from me. "Come with me, Jed."

She showed me how to change his diaper, then how to mix formula and how to warm it just right. She explained about holding him close to feed him and about burping and a lot of other things that seemed important. It was too much to take in since I was still taking it in about Kitty.

He wasn't hungry, and once he was dry and re-wrapped in a blanket, he fell asleep in my arms again. Esperanza offered to take him; she wanted to, and said he was the most precious little baby she had seen since she had her own. She thought he looked *mexicano* because of his black hair but he got that from me. I felt so proud of him and so happy to have him, but I cried most of the first twenty-four hours he spent with me. I was relieved that he slept and didn't have to witness it. I didn't want him to think his father didn't want him. It would be sad enough when he figured out he didn't have a mother.

* * *

The following morning Reva Brooks called and said it was imperative that she speak with me right away. I figured she was going to tell me I couldn't live in Kitty's house any longer.

"I have a new baby," I said since that was the most important thing on my mind. Maybe she would take pity and let me stay a week or two.

"Yes, Mr. Petersen, I know. He's one of the things I need to speak with you about."

"He's my son," I said, daring her to say different.

"Congratulations. I'm sorry we have to meet under the circumstance of Kitty's death, but I must see

you. It's imperative or I wouldn't be calling. Is there someone who could watch your baby a couple of hours so you can come to my office?"

"When do you want to see me?"

"Could you come in around eleven o'clock this morning?"

"I'll be there."

Esperanza made breakfast or I wouldn't have eaten. Cowboys came and went. They asked to see the new baby and spoke encouraging words to me. They reminded me to shower and dress, or I might have gone out looking derelict.

They assured me Reva Brooks was a respectable attorney and didn't want to take my son. She represented the interests of Kitty and the ranch, and Kitty wouldn't have wanted anyone but me to have him.

We had a funeral to plan, but the guys said they had it under control, and I should go to Ms. Brooks and not worry.

I decided to call my son Andy, not Jed or Little Jed. I only let Kitty name him Jed because she wanted to. I had him with me when I went to see the attorney, because I wasn't yet willing to entrust him to anyone else. He slept up against me like his mama had, and it gave me comfort in a way.

"So you're Jed," Reva Brooks said when we had settled in her office. "I've heard so much about you. I'm so sorry about Kitty."

"Thank you, ma'am, my heart is broken."

"I guess you know Kitty loved you very much, Jed."

"Yes, I know."

"What you probably don't know is that she left you everything. I have her signed will here if you'd like to see it."

I couldn't have moved a muscle if the place had been on fire.

"She asked to be buried on the ranch, which I'm sure you would assume," the lawyer continued. "She and I spent a long time drawing up a will that clearly expresses her desire regarding the child should something happen to her. She expects you to raise him

on the ranch, which is now yours, and for it to eventually be his. Since the property is now legally yours, you can do whatever you want with it, but her desire is to see it pass to her son."

I was in a daze. None of it had sunk in.

"She also left you everything else."

"You mean personal things and such?"

"I mean her whole fortune, Jed. Roughly, I'd say you're worth about fifteen million dollars, not counting the ranch, cattle, and land holdings. I have some forms here for you to sign so that you can sign on the bank accounts."

I was more stunned than I had ever been in my life and didn't speak.

"I'm sure this comes as a shock to you."

I tried to speak but couldn't.

"Kitty told me you wanted to marry her and truthfully, she wanted to marry you. She grappled with that a long time. Anyway, we set things up as airtight as we could, but I want you to know that certain members of the Worthington family will fight you for everything. They've been fighting her, as you know. They feel entitled to Conrad's land and won't want to see it go to an outsider. They have an old ranching family sense of entitlement that is legally incorrect and morally indecent.

"Conrad Worthington left everything to Kitty, and she has increased his fortune with good management. Regardless, the land, the cattle, the money, every single thing that was hers is now yours."

"My son is all I really want. They can't take him, can they?"

"No, they can't."

"Right before she died Kitty said, 'don't let them take him.' Who did she mean? Who would want him besides me?"

"Maybe she feared the Worthingtons would try to get him. She has fought them for so long on so many fronts. The law was always on her side, as it will be yours, and I'll help you, Jed. If anyone tries to take your son or your ranch, we won't let them."

"I need to know if you think there's any chance

at all they could take him."

"The only thing they can do is make problems for you."

"Like what?"

"They could report you to Child Protective Services. They could say you're not caring for him properly."

"But I will care for him. I love my son."

"You're twenty-one and capable of raising a child. Kitty sure thought so. You're the boy's father and no court is going to take him away from you unless you mistreat him or can't care for him. So stop worrying about that."

"She left the ranch to me? All of it?"

"Yes, she's left you everything. Out of respect for her, I want you to let me help you keep it, if only for your son. I'm prepared to fight for your rights."

"Thank you. I feel so lost right now."

"I'm sure you do. You loved her, didn't you?"

"Yes ma'am, I did."

"Then this will surely be hard on you. I'm so sorry for your loss, and for your son's loss. I regret that he won't know his mother because she was an amazing woman."

"Yes, she was. I guess I know that better than anyone."

She nodded.

"What do I need to do right now?" I asked.

"You need to sign these papers I've prepared for the bank. Past that, what do you know about managing a ranch?"

"I know a little. Kitty was teaching me."

"She knew what she was doing."

"Yes ma'am."

"If you don't feel capable of managing the ranch yet, I could help you find a good manager."

"I'll think about that."

"Jed, when Conrad died, Kitty was left with everything and she learned by doing. She made some mistakes, but she learned. She must have a great deal of faith in you since she left it to you free and clear and not directly to her child. In other words, she could have

left the place in a trust for him with a manager of her choice, or she could have stipulated that the land be kept for him and all ranching operations cease. There are a lot of ways she could have by-passed you, but she didn't. She was actually quite passionate about you running it if anything ever happened to her. She told me she thought you would make it a horse operation, that you have a special way with horses."

"Did Kitty know she was going to die?"

"I don't think so. When people have a lot of assets, a lot of land and money, they make plans about these things. I don't think Kitty thought any of this would come into play until she was very old. She might have changed her will at some point to leave everything to her son, or children, if she'd had more. Does that make sense?"

Nothing about any of it made sense.

"I don't want this to sound wrong, but would you be willing to take a paternity test so we can prove you're his father? That would eliminate problems along those lines."

"Sure, just tell me where to do it."

"I'll set it up and notify you."

"Did she leave any other instructions about her funeral?"

"No, except she didn't want to be buried with the Worthingtons. She was never one of them, and I guess you already know about the problems she had with Conrad. I was Kitty's friend as well as her attorney, so I knew things an attorney wouldn't necessarily know."

"Yes, she told me about him."

I want a man who burns for me, Jed.

"If I were you, I'd pick a place you know she liked and bury her there."

"I'll do that."

"I'll call you the first of next week to go over a few things with you about the land and cattle. If anyone contacts you or you have any questions, please call me. I'd like to continue to represent the ranch and your personal interests, too."

"Thank you."

"We'll talk about that next week. When you know

about the funeral, will you let me know? I want to attend and I know other friends who will want to be there."

"I'll call you about that later today."

She took my free hand. "Good luck to you, Jed, and congratulations on your new son. He is a fine looking boy."

I looked down at him. Yes, he was, and I was going to make damned sure nobody hurt him because he was.

CHAPTER 37

When I reached the turnoff to the ranch, I stopped the truck, opened the rear door, and took Andy from the car seat. It was cold, but he was bundled and didn't wake up, only whimpered a little at being disturbed. I got back into the driver's seat and held him up to the window.

"This is all yours, every last inch of it, even the animals. The mountains and the canyons and the creeks, they're all yours, Son."

He fussed a little more at being moved and made a tiny frown.

"You'll think differently when you're older. You and I now have the most beautiful piece of land in the whole state of Texas." I still couldn't believe it. It felt like I was reading a part for a play, trying out someone else's lines.

The first thing I did as owner of the Worthington Ranch was to call Little Mike into the office. He was Juan Miguel Estrada and had come from Mexico when he was only fourteen. He had been working as a cowboy since that time, nearly twenty-five years. He had learned English and eventually got his citizenship a few years back with sponsorship by the Worthingtons.

I turned Andy over to Esperanza and shut the office door.

"Please sit, Mike."

I started to sit in Kitty's chair but instead I sat in the other visitors' chair. "She left the ranch to me, Mike, to me and our son. Even the cattle and horses are mine."

"Señor Jed, that's *maravilloso*. You won't have to leave."

"I want to make you the cowboy foreman. Kitty was going to do it but she didn't have the chance."

He looked surprised and didn't speak.

"You're the most qualified man here, and I don't want someone from outside. I know I can trust you because you love this ranch as much as I do."

He nodded at me with tears in his eyes. "Sí. Sí, I do."

"Whatever Kitty was paying Rick, I'll pay you the same to start. Also, you can bring your family and live in that big house near the new barn and corral."

"We can't live there."

"I'll pay all the utilities."

"It's not that, señor. What you offer is very generous, and I want the job, but my family—we can't live in a house like that."

"There's no other place for you to live. Rick's apartment is too small, and I want to live here in Kitty's house, at least for now."

"I'll take his apartment and my family will stay in our house in Fort Davis. My children like it there, and their friends are close. We'll make this work, Señor Jed. I thank you for the opportunity, and I won't let you down."

It occurred to me that I could build him a house on land behind the bunkhouse, near a stand of juniper and ash trees that sat at the base of a boulder-strewn hill. He could be near the ranch hands but not overrun by them. Fifteen million dollars, Reva Brooks had said, not counting the land, cattle, and buildings. I could build any damn thing I wanted.

Oh, Kitty.

* * *

Later that day, I rode out on the ranch, even though a cold north wind was blowing and snow threatened. I wanted to bury Kitty at the place where I loved to camp. Those giant boulders would be there forever and would protect her. Also, there was a good view of the ranch, and I thought she would approve.

I went back and told the cowboys. They wanted

to dig her grave themselves, as is ranching custom. If you keep your body moving, the hurt in your heart backs off a few paces.

It was snowing hard when a large party of cowboys and other people who had loved Kitty started out for the boulders. I was going to join them, but it would have to be later because I was feeding my son for the first time. We were alone in the study I still thought of as the Fabulous Room. There was a fire roaring in the fireplace that gave a false sense of cheerfulness. Snow swirled past the windows, pouring down on Worthington Ranch. Visibility was nil, and I couldn't see as far as the edge of the yard, let alone the pasture or mountains.

My son studied me as he suckled. His eyes were piercing blue, and he never took them off my face. It seemed like he was memorizing every detail and taking stock of me at the same time. I never wanted so much to measure up.

There was a knock on the door. I had left instructions that I wasn't to be disturbed, but maybe I was the only one in the house. I yelled to come in and looked up to see Ron Matthews.

"Jed."

"Ron!"

He shook hands with me. "What can I do to help you?"

"Nothin' I guess. Sit down and talk to me."

"I'm so sorry, Jed." Ron leaned over the back of the sofa to look at Andy. "He's beautiful. He looks just like you."

"He looks like Kitty, too, but he's got my dark hair."

"And your eyes."

He finally sat in a chair across from me. He took a deep breath and let it out slowly. "What are you going to do?"

"I don't know, Ron. She left me this whole place."

I watched that news settle on him.

"It's overwhelming. I have a child with no mother and a ranch worth millions and I can't take any of it in. I have to get through the funeral, and then I'll figure it

out."

Ron was just as handsome as I remembered him only he was a grown man now, and that made him more so. I didn't want to look at him, but I couldn't keep my eyes away. It was hard to believe he had come. Andy was through eating and I sat with the bottle in hand, staring at Ron.

"May I hold him?" Ron stood and held out his arms.

"Yes, but he needs to be burped."

"Yes, I know."

He handled him like it wasn't the first time he had held a baby. He walked around with him, patting his back gently. Eventually he stood by the window and gazed at the snow.

I watched every move he made.

After a few minutes he moved Andy from his shoulder and held him out to look at him. "What did you name him?"

"Jed Andrews Petersen."

"Not Jedediah?"

"No. You know better than that, Ron. I only named him Jed because that was what Kitty wanted."

"Little Jed Petersen," Ron crooned softly. "He's so like you, Jed, only he's just a little bit. Isn't that so, Little Bit? You're a little piece of your old man."

Ron moved back to the chair and sat with my son cradled in his arms. The baby made a small contented noise.

"I have a son, Jed."

Not much about Ron would have surprised me, but that did.

"It's not what you're thinking. I didn't have him with a woman."

"You're not going to tell me you had him with a man are you?"

Ron chuckled. "No. He's not mine the way Little Bit is yours, but he's legally mine and I love him. He's eighteen months old. His name is Luke."

I waited patiently to hear how my oldest, dearest friend had a son without having made one with a woman.

"He's my sister Rhonda's child, Jed. She shamed the family by getting pregnant her senior year, and I brought her to live with me so she wouldn't have to endure that bullshit. I didn't have much of a life to offer her because I was on the road all the time, but I offered her shelter and love and that was what she needed. She named him Luke and made me his legal guardian in case something happened to her."

"Something happened to your sister?"

"She died in a car accident with a member of my band. That was about six months ago."

"I'm so sorry, Ron."

"I was already like a father to Luke. I was there when he was born and had helped care for him, so it seemed natural for me to take him." He laughed a sad laugh. "I'm a better mother than my sister was, it turns out. My parents want me to give him to them. They don't think a gay man should raise a child."

"That's crap!"

"Yes, it is. I've already adopted him legally, so nobody can take him."

I told him about my fear of losing my son. He understood my terror, and I felt better for telling him.

"I have to go, Ron. The cowboys are out digging Kitty's grave, and I need to share that load for my own sake."

"Did you love her, Jed?"

"Yes. I did."

"I'll come with you to dig. I want to do my part."

"Where is your son?"

"He's in Nashville with one of my band members and his family. They're good people and I trust them."

"You're living in Nashville?"

"Not really. I can't live anywhere yet because I have to travel too much, but Frank Porter agreed to join my band about three months ago, and his family is there. He has a wife and two small children. They're watching Luke for me until I get back." He gave me an exasperated look. "You don't know who Frank Porter is, do you?"

"No, I guess I don't."

"He's famous in country music—keyboard

mostly—but he plays anything."

"Do you take Luke on the road with you?"

"Yes, I want him with me all the time."

Esperanza came in to get Andy. We began putting on our jackets.

"How's your music going?"

Ron stopped and stared at me. "Jed—don't you know?"

"You're famous aren't you, Ron?"

"Don't you ever listen to the radio?"

"Not much."

The sadness in his face made me feel ashamed. It made me want to cry but I didn't have any tears left.

"I'm doing well," he said in a reserved way, as if talking to a stranger. I must have seemed like one to him. I figured he was understating his success.

"Ask some of your cowboys if they know who Ron Matthews is."

"I'm sorry, Ron. I should know all about it and I know that. I know how I've let you down and it hurts me. I have a long story to tell you, but not today."

"I sort of thought you did, Jed. I knew you'd come around to telling me in your own time. I want to hear it when you feel ready to tell me."

Man, I loved him for that. With only one small statement from me, my best friend was back, waiting there with his love and support, like always.

Someone had saddled Indio for me and he was huffing with impatience in the barn near the bunkhouse. I started saddling another horse.

"I haven't ridden a horse since—since—you and I got busted by your dad, I guess."

I marveled at that. I would have shriveled up and died without a horse in my life. "Do you want to ride with me?"

He grinned. "Yeah, sure do."

He sat behind and wound his arms around me tightly. It took me back eight or nine years to when everything was simpler, and we were just two boys who loved each other the way best friends do and told each other everything. Life was always good when we were together even if other things were miserable, like being

forced onto bulls, or my pop whooping the girly out of me and shaving my hair off.

Indio ducked his head against the wind and wetness, and I didn't press him to go fast. I wanted to treasure a moment with Ron against my back with his strong arms around me. Nobody could hurt me if he had my back.

In some ways, it took a long time to reach the gravesite; in another way, we arrived too fast. Good progress had been made. I tried to look at it as a hole in the ground and not a place where we were going to put Kitty.

Many shovels and several flasks were being passed around. Ron and I each grabbed a shovel wordlessly and went to work until I was sweating from the exertion. I wiped away sweat, tears, and snow, and kept digging.

"Let me take over, Jed," Shorty insisted after a while.

"No. I need to do this."

"You need to go home and care for your son. You've done your part, now go on. We'll finish this."

I might not have left except for Ron's prodding. "Come on, Jed, let's go."

I didn't introduce him to anyone and never thought of it until after he left to go back to his motel.

CHAPTER 38

Somehow I got through the funeral, though I can't say how and don't remember it much. Hundreds of people came, some of them Worthingtons who were angry that I was burying Kitty in a private place of my choosing and not in their family graveyard. I thought it was hypocritical of people who didn't love or appreciate her to say one word about it, but none of them spoke directly to me. They checked me out plenty and probably the only things I had going for me were that I was a Texan and a bull rider whose name was known.

Conrad Worthington's brother Chad asked to see my son, but I told him no.

They never accepted me. I wasn't a Texan and I even failed them as a breeder.

The Worthingtons weren't related or even people I wanted to know. And I could tell by their attitude that they saw the ranch as something that was still theirs.

At my request, Esperanza took Andy into the nursery and locked the door. He was too new, there were too many strangers, and it was so cold I couldn't bring him out. There was no way any of the Worthingtons were coming in my house. They could all kiss my one hundred percent pure Texan ass.

I took my father in to see my son because I couldn't get out of it gracefully. He was amazed and delighted with his grandson. I had never seen him be so affectionate with anything or anybody, and I wondered if he had ever thought I was tiny and perfect in every way. Had he looked at me with the goofy, loving look he gave my baby?

"Here's the next rodeo champion in our family, Jed." He held him up. If he hadn't been so proud of his grandson I would have knocked him to the ground.

Andy made a little negative snorting sound.

Right, son, only if you want to, I thought. I was glad when his grandfather left.

I wanted to take Andy to the funeral in case Kitty was there and wanted to see him, but it was bitter cold. She would understand.

Ron sang *Amazing Grace, Home on the Range, God must be a Cowboy*, and a beautiful song he wrote called *A Cowboy's Last Good-Bye*. There wasn't a dry eye among us. Even Ron broke down at one point and had to compose himself before he could go on. As the last thing, we all sang *Texas When I Die* so loudly that people in the neighboring county must have heard us.

Right before her coffin was lowered into the ground, I stepped up and told Kitty not to worry. Andy and I were going to do all right, but we would always miss her.

"I'll never forget you, Kitty, and I'll make sure your son knows all about you."

Cowboys descended on Ron when they heard him sing and realized who he was. He cut out gracefully and joined me as I walked away. More accurately, he crooked his arm around my shoulders and held me up. No words were needed between us. When I looked up at him he was crying and not trying to hide it.

* * *

"I have to go now, Jed, but I want to see you sometime. To get reacquainted, you know? No strings attached. What would you think if I called you later?"

"I'd like that, but give me a while. I have to figure out what I'm doing, and I have a newborn that needs me."

"You take care of Little Bit, Jed—and yourself." He hugged me close and for a moment it took me back to when we said goodbye behind the restaurant.

Don't forget me, Jed.

I won't, Ron. How would I?

He paused at the door and turned around. "Listen to the damn radio once in a while, will you?"

"Yes, Ron, I will."

After that I went back to my son and sat with him a long time against my chest, smelling his sweet baby smell. In spite of being numb with grief, I knew what a blessing he was, and I was thankful for him. *Little Bit,* I thought and the nickname stuck.

* * *

In early January I was sued by the Worthington family. They claimed I had seduced Kitty and then moved in with her in order to eventually strip her of her ranch and fortune. They said the baby wasn't mine, but that I claimed him in order to wield power over her. So they still didn't know Kitty, and a person only had to see my son to know he was mine. A paternity test proved what I never doubted. Kitty would never have lied to me.

It hurt to read their claims, but Reva Brooks assured me it was a matter of legal jostling and I needn't worry. In other words, it was going to cost me a fortune. I had one, so it didn't matter. The bottom line for me was having my son and a few acres for horses. Anything past that was icing. I had my own money from bull riding winnings and our horse business, so I didn't need Kitty's, and mostly thought of hers as Little Bit's.

Within a month, construction started on a house for Mike which he helped design. As I had predicted, he was a big man in a small body, and the cowboys took to him as their boss. He was gentle but pounded them with an iron fist when he had to. A few hands quit and new ones were hired, a natural phenomenon with cowboys.

I thought about hiring a general manager but decided to wait. I wanted to try my hand at it. Kitty had taught me a little, and I thought I could get things right if I paid attention and surrounded myself with people smarter than me. I hired an experienced secretary/bookkeeper, which left me free time for working with horses. There were always horses that needed me.

I stripped the barn apartment and decorated it in more of a baby boy theme than a western one. Little Bit and I stayed there sometimes when I had a horse that

needed me, or when I wanted to get away from everyone else. Sometimes the memories were too close and heavy in Kitty's house. On the other hand, the barn apartment often made me crazy with loneliness.

I was mostly getting by one day at a time. Some days were better than others. Little Bit's needs were immediate and were my first priority, and in his innocent way, he saved me from myself more often than not.

Esperanza usually spent the day with me wherever I was, helping me care for him, and on weekends her sixteen-year-old daughter, Claudia, filled in for her.

In April the late afternoons were warm enough to have my son with me in the corral and those were my favorite times. We were alone. If I was working with horses, he watched me from a baby carrier parked in a far corner. If I wasn't working, I took him into the mountains in a carrier on my back. He waved his arms and gurgled at the wonder of it.

Little Bit seemed to thrive on dust and the smell of hay and horses. He smiled and laughed out loud when the animals passed near him or if I held him up to them. He liked singing, too.

William James wrote, "I don't sing because I'm happy. I'm happy because I sing." I made myself sing to injured horses and realized it was helping my own heart.

Little Bit especially liked it when I danced. He had never seen a bigger idiot. At first I couldn't make myself dance, but when I did, it helped even more than singing. Perhaps if you can make your feet act happy, the rest of you will begin to believe you are. I had plenty to feel happy about, and every day he watched me with the bluest eyes you ever saw.

If anyone had come looking, they would have seen a father who took good care of his infant. He was healthy as a little horse and happy. Baby things were strewn all over every place we occupied, but he was clean, the house was clean, and even the barn apartment was clean.

In the last months of her life, Kitty had loved me

flat-out. She knocked my spurs off, just like she predicted. Being loved like that is a hard thing to let go of, but I was gradually healing. The thing I knew for sure was that I wanted to be loved that way again. I would get it right next time.

CHAPTER 39

In June, the cowboys threw a six-month birthday celebration for Little Bit with a cook-out and dance. A lot of people came from neighboring ranches and towns. Where cowboys are there are always a lot of girls, but it was only the males who came that interested me.

Little Bit enjoyed all the fuss and grinned constantly at the crazy people and their beer-fueled antics. He was passed around and danced around until he passed out. I put him to bed and wanted to go myself, but I wandered back out to the party and left Claudia to babysit.

I was twenty-two, too young to feel so old. I wanted to force myself to act my age if only for one night but I wasn't sure how. It seemed like I had been old a long time.

I danced and told myself to be happy, damn it. Several times during the evening the thought occurred that I should take somebody to the barn apartment and give it a new memory to push back the old ones. My body was all for it, but my heart said no way was I going to do that.

* * *

I was privileged to help reclaim poorly trained, abandoned, or mistreated horses during the time that followed. I tamed three wild mustangs for a neighboring ranch. They had been adopted through a special government program meant to save them. Those horses were an icon of the American West and had been the definition of the term *wild and free* until their native lands began to shrink and they became a 'nuisance.'

What a joy they were. *Wild and free* was in their blood, but they were easier to train than horses that had been abused. It was easier to start from scratch than to undo what had already been done to an animal.

Also during that summer, I trained a horse to kneel so that a wheelchair-bound teenager could mount him. It wasn't hard; the horse seemed to catch on from the beginning. It would be fair to say the training was mutual. I learned something new every day and usually more than I taught.

I finally heard Ron on the radio. He was singing a song he wrote, *I Survived Loving You,* which was making its way to number one. Hearing it made me sad. Ron hadn't called, and I suspected he was lost to me. I couldn't even say for sure if that was good or bad and didn't allow myself to think of it.

* * *

In October, a judge ruled that Kathleen Worthington had legally inherited the Worthington Ranch along with all its assets and holdings from her lawful husband, Conrad Worthington. She therefore had the legal right to leave them to anyone of her choosing and had clearly stated her desire in an airtight will. Jed Petersen rightfully owned what had been Kathleen Worthington's. So ended the bitter dispute, and the ranch was truly mine and Little Bit's.

I rode out to tell Kitty the news. That was crazy I know, but speaking with her in that beautiful place where she had been laid to rest was a comfort.

At times I took Little Bit with me and told him about her. He would watch me speak and lift his hands to my face to study me with his fingers as well as his eyes, his message clear: I was the only parent he could know.

One time I was there alone, on my knees, crying and sobbing about how I missed her. The giant boulders watched and listened as they always did, but I thought they must surely be tired of the same ol', same ol'. I don't know if it was them or Kitty who whispered it to me, or if it was just a knowing that came on me quietly, but I had to get on with my life. She would not be coming back.

* * *

At the end of October, Ron called. It had been ten months since I'd seen or heard from him, and I considered telling him no. But it was Ron, and I wanted to see him. He was going to be in El Paso and asked to meet me.

"I want to go someplace where nobody will know me, otherwise we'll be interrupted constantly."

I suggested he come to the ranch because nobody would expect him to be there. After tossing out a few other ideas, he agreed. He said he would come on Sunday and bring his son.

I tried to have no expectations. We hadn't been together in six years, and a lot had happened. He probably lived with someone. He was famous and becoming wealthy in his own right. I searched him on the Internet, but his personal life was carefully guarded. Of course it would be. Gay and country music didn't fit; there are too many narrow minds and too many rednecks.

On Sunday there was only Little Bit and me in the house since Esperanza had the day off. My son was ten months old and crawling everywhere. He could pull himself up on things but hadn't walked yet. He was constantly underfoot as I made meatloaf, mashed potatoes, and green beans for lunch, to be accompanied by a batch of my Wonder Biscuits. Esperanza had left a fudge cake in the fridge for desert. We were ready early.

It's hard to sneak up on a place in West Texas. A plume of dust announces all guests, so I knew the truck was coming long before it arrived.

I went out to meet them, carrying Little Bit on my hip. Ron and I shook hands like men are supposed to. Then he hugged me, embracing my son and me at the same time. His own son squealed from the back seat.

"This is Luke." He began extricating him from the car seat.

"Hey Luke."

"Daddy." Luke smiled at me.

"Luke, this is Jed, and his son Andy."

"Little Bit," I corrected.

Ron grinned over his shoulder and lifted out his son, who demanded to be set down. He was twenty-eight months old, the way I figured it. He not only walked but could also run, and proved it by taking off towards the bunkhouse and the corrals where horses were loitering together in the warm sunshine, taking Sunday off.

He flung his arms into the air. "Hors, hors. Me go hors!"

Ron gave me a look of humorous exasperation and ran after him. I watched him lift his son and show him the horses, patiently telling him about them while Luke continued to yell, "Me go hors."

I walked up beside them. "We can ride later if you want."

"Luke would love that."

Horses were as much a part of Little Bit's life as I was, and he took them in stride. He studied Luke intently though, enthralled by another small person who shared his unbridled excitement about life.

"Da-da!" Little Bit exclaimed happily.

Ron touched his cheek. "Yes, your da-da is nuts for horses, isn't he, Little Bit?" He turned to me. "I suppose he already rides?"

"He rides with me."

"Would you take Luke with you sometime?"

"Sure, but lunch is ready. Let's eat first."

Ron crooked his arm around my neck. "Now that's the Jed I remember so well. Ol' Let's Eat Jed."

I wondered if that was all he remembered about Jed, but I had to laugh at that accurate description. "Yeah, I like to eat so much I had to learn to cook."

"You don't have people to cook for you?" Ron seemed surprised I didn't have servants everywhere.

"I don't like having people around all the time. I want to live a normal life and make a home for Little Bit. Aren't you the man on the run from fans and the people you pay to keep the fans away?"

"Well, yeah, that's me."

"Are you happy, Ron?"

"Sometimes."

"Why only sometimes?"

He didn't look at me. "Could we talk about that after lunch?"

"Okay."

I watched Ron serve his son and then himself. I told him not to worry about the mess Luke made. Little Bit was all over the place when he ate and often wore more food than he ingested and needed a bath afterwards.

Luke looked so much like Ron I thought Ron could have been his father instead of his uncle. The boy had the same large build, blond hair, and bright brown eyes, and the lively, outgoing personality I remembered fondly about my best friend.

After lunch, when the boys were sleeping, Ron and I sat in the Fabulous Room across from each other. In the old days we would have been all over each other, but this wasn't the old days or anywhere close.

"What's it like to be so rich?" Ron wondered.

"I don't know."

"What do you mean you don't know?"

"I mean it hasn't sunk in. I have an impossible amount of money, Ron. I just don't think about it most of the time."

I asked him again why he was only sometimes happy. It seemed to me that he had everything he'd always wanted, with the added bonus of a son he adored.

He watched me a long time before he spoke. "I'm not going to tell you anything about my personal life unless you're willing to tell me why you pushed me away like you did."

I started to speak, but he interrupted me. "I understand you're not gay, Jed, but damn you. You were the best friend I ever had. I needed you. I was in love with you and you said you loved me."

I took a deep breath and said what I had needed to say to my friend for more than six years. "I couldn't tell you this then, but I was raped."

I held up my hands at the look on his face. "No, don't say anything until I get this out. You can't imagine how horrible it was. I responded by withdrawing. I felt filthy and perverted and I questioned

if I'd brought it on myself. I just couldn't let you touch me again even though that was what I wanted more than anything. I took my love for you and put it away where nobody could touch it—not even me."

Ron was silent and his eyes were full of tears as I continued. "I didn't quit loving you, Ron. I guess I never have, but life kept moving and brought me here, to Kitty and the Worthington Ranch."

"Well I stopped loving you. We had something beautiful, or I thought it was. One day you were with me. You promised you wouldn't forget me and then you did—just like that—from one day to the next. You could've told me, Jed. We shared everything. You took all the heart out of me for a long time because I didn't know what had happened to you. I would've died for you, Jed. But I'll tell you one thing. I got a lot of hit songs out of all that misery and heartbreak. I recorded some and sold a lot of them. My songs are hits for other performers. George Strait is going to record one of my songs, Jed. So having my heart broken has made me famous, but your rejection still hurts."

"I'm sorry, Ron. I wish I could re-do it, but I can't. Everything was stolen from me when those men raped me. It's impossible to explain. I was only sixteen; please consider that. I was unprepared for dealing with such violence and hatred. They called me names, and they beat me so bad I had to go the hospital. And after they had nearly killed me, they used me."

"My God." Ron ran his hands through his hair. "You said *they*."

"There were three of them."

"My God, Jed."

"I've put it behind me now, but it's not something a person forgets."

"Three?"

I nodded.

"I'm sorry, Jed. I'm sorry such a terrible thing happened to you. Please tell me those assholes are in prison."

"No, in fact they didn't go to prison. They were declared not guilty in court. But their wives killed them. Nothing will take away what they did, though. I'm only

sane because I turned my attention away from it. I opened my heart again, and first it was only to horses and then, after a time, to a woman. That's how I got my son."

"Oh, Jed."

"Ron, I am gay, just as gay as you, but I was so afraid. For some reason I thought it would be safer to love a woman. I loved Kitty; she was so good to me, but we wouldn't have lasted. Still, it was awful to lose the love she poured over me, and it grieves me that she can't know her son and he can't know her."

"I'm sorry, Jed. I truly am."

"Tell me why you're not happy."

"It's complicated."

"I have all day. Hell, I have all month."

"I live with a man."

"Okay. That's not surprising."

"Well, here's a surprise for you. He's not interested in my son, and he runs around on me, and he threatens to out me to the country music community if I leave him."

"You deserve someone much better than that, Ron."

He stood and paced. "I've been just getting by, same as you. There was a time when I loved him, or thought I did, and he loved me. Rhonda and her pregnancy put a terrible strain on our relationship, but then the baby came and things were better for a while. Then suddenly Luke was mine and Justin changed. He enjoys my money and fame, but I don't think he likes me anymore."

"How is that possible—for him to know you and not like you?" Someone named Justin lived with Ron Matthews and didn't love him. I tried but couldn't get my head around it.

"Now you sound just like my old friend, Jed Petersen."

"I *am* your old friend Jed Petersen."

"I wish I thought that. I wish things could go back like they were."

"We were children, Ron. What I wish is that we could start over as grown men and see what would

happen."

"Do you mean that Jed, or are you just jerking me off?"

"You never used to be so cynical."

"Yeah, well, a man changes. Look at you."

"I really haven't changed much, Ron."

"You're all grown up and taller and—"

"I wasn't talking about how I look. I was referring to how I am. I'm still so sensitive and sweet it would make my father puke. He never managed to beat all the girly out of me. He made me ride bulls and that made me tough, but it didn't change me—not really."

"I always admired that about you, Jed, the sweet and sensitive part. You managed to pull it off and still be masculine. That made me so ho—" Ron quickly changed his comment to, "Are you still riding bulls?"

"No, not any more. It's dangerous, and I had a responsibility to Kitty—and my son. I was lucky to get out with as few injuries as I got."

"That wasn't luck, Jed. You were good."

"Even good riders get hurt and killed, but thank you for the compliment. Yes, I was good, and that was a thrill in a way."

"I shouldn't have come here, Jed."

"Why do you say that?"

"Because I still feel attracted to you, and I'm with someone else, and our sons are here, and you make me feel all twisted around inside and—"

"Twisted around? Is that anything like love—or even lust?"

"Okay, maybe that's a bad choice of words."

"Have you written any songs about being twisted?"

He laughed. "Of course not—well, I have, but not in those words. What's funny is how many songs I've written about you or to you or because of you. I could never mention your name because people would think I was gay."

"What happened to the man who didn't care what other people thought?"

"I don't know, Jed. I could ask you the same question."

"I became cautious. Rape does that to a person."

"Were you raped because of me?"

"No. I was raped because of evil men who thought they could use me as perverse entertainment and throw me away. I was too pretty and sweet and naïve as hell. My father tried so hard to knock all that out of me but he didn't."

"Thank God he didn't."

"I was an innocent boy trying to become a man, and I wasn't hurting anyone and would never have hurt anyone, and especially not you. I was subjected to violent hatred that came out of left field. It was so ugly to be despised and used like that, just because I was different. It made me feel like I was dead, Ron."

Luke appeared in the doorway and called to his father. Ron hopped up and went to him. "Let's go to the bathroom, Son. We'll be right back, Jed."

* * *

Later, Little Bit and Luke were playing together or were at least fascinated by each other.

"What about us, Ron?"

"There is no us, Jed. We can't go back to that juvenile stuff, wishing on stars and making love non-stop, and believing in forever."

I wanted to ask *why not?* but I didn't think I could stand to hear the answer. I knew it was my fault because of how I'd treated him, and it was something that couldn't be changed, as much as I wanted to.

* * *

"We have to go," Ron said before I was ready to part with them.

"I hope you'll stay in touch."

"I will."

I knew he wouldn't.

Little Bit and I watched them drive off. We watched until they had been gone so long the dust settled. Like Kitty, they were really gone.

I went back to rescuing horses and raising my son.

Chapter 40

One day I stood in front of another injured horse. I had been brought to a Kentucky horse farm to work with a former racing champion. I hadn't wanted to go. It meant leaving Little Bit with Esperanza and as much as she loved him, I didn't like leaving him. He was walking, and a whole new world had opened up. I loved seeing it through his eyes. He had just had his first birthday, and Christmas was coming. I didn't want to miss any of it, but I still had my calling and it never let me rest.

After many phone calls, the owner of the horse had won me over. He was stumped by this horse, which he seemed to truly love. Race-the-Wind had won trophies and money, and then had lost his heart and couldn't be ridden, let alone raced. The owner, William Richardson, didn't know if he had employed a cruel groom, a twisted jockey, or if it was something else. He was terrified for his other horses.

He offered me a lot of money to come see his horse. I asked him to donate my fee to the Humane Society of the United States because of their efforts to save wild horses, and I told him I would expect to see a receipt for his donation. Taking me away from Little Bit was going to cost him.

The horse's spirit was injured, not his body, but that's usually worse. He wasn't responding much to anything I did, and I tried a lot of things.

"I'm not going to give up on you." I couldn't give up.

When I told Race-the-Wind I wasn't going to give up on him, I thought of Ron. I thought it *at Ron,* and I

suddenly didn't care if I made an ass of myself. He was Ron, for crying out loud, and I hadn't really tried. I had never been shy around him or held myself back from him until the rape. I hadn't tried hard enough to make him understand. What the hell? I had to leave!

You have to get a grip.

I had to leave right now!

Get a damn grip.

I lay in the fancy bed in Will Richardson's guest house and tried to get a grip. Grown men didn't run off chasing rainbows and wishing on stars. I didn't even know where Ron was. He could be in Europe or Tennessee or Texas, or in any of a thousand places.

I have the money to look for him. I can do anything I want.

You're completely out of your ever-lovin' mind.

I called him in the middle of the night on the cell phone number he had used to call me two months earlier. When he answered, I could barely speak I was so excited.

"Ron, this is Jed."

"Jed! Is everything okay?"

"Well no, Ron, it's not. I'm in Kentucky working with a horse, and I should be wherever you are. You asked me if I'd come with you, and I said *please take me with you.* It was nearly the last thing you ever said to me and before that, you wished on the stars; have you forgotten?"

"Well, no, but—"

"You wished for us to live together, and I said what about the Wilson brothers, and you said *don't talk about that Jed,* and you wished it on the stars anyway. You wished it in spite of what happened to them. You wished it and I took it to heart."

"I was a kid."

"So you didn't mean it?"

"I meant it. I can't talk about this right now, Jed."

"When can you talk about it?"

"I don't know." He hesitated a long time. "I don't know if I want to talk about it. I think we should forget all that, Jed."

"Why? How? You're giving up on me?"

"I gave up on you a long time ago."

"Whoever it is that lives with you and doesn't love you—you have to get away from him. If he outs you to the world, so what? You can't be ashamed of who you are. That's not the Ron I know."

"I'm not that Ron anymore, Jed. Can't you hear? I haven't been that Ron in a long goddamned time."

"Bullshit!"

"I'm not some injured horse you can rescue."

"You don't know the first thing about what I do. Shut up about horses."

"Okay, Jed."

"I make them remember what they are, how fine they are, how perfect."

"Good night, Jed. Don't call me again, I'll call you."

He hung up on me!

Bullshit!

I stomped around. *Bullshit!* I threw things. I couldn't believe Ron Matthews hung up on me. I couldn't sleep or even sit still. I called him back, but he didn't answer.

The next day I went back to work with Race-the-Wind and the day after that and the day after. I was determined to get it done and then find Ron. I was there ten days and Race-the-Wind came back from wherever he had been, but his reason for leaving remained a mystery. William Richardson was thrilled, and the Humane Society of the U.S. got a nice Christmas present in my name.

* * *

In April I would turn twenty-three, and I chose to spend my birthday at a concert where Ron and his band were scheduled to perform. Little Bit and I flew to Atlanta, along with Esperanza and her daughter, Claudia. It was quite a trip, with my son calling everyone 'daddy' and trying to tell them about his horses. He talked a lot and was animated and emotional, not that we understood every word. Trying to keep him in his seat was trickier than I could have imagined. We were flying in an airplane, and to Little

Bit that was right up there with galloping on a horse.

He loved to sit in my lap and explore my face with his eyes and hands. “Daddy,” he would say over and over, trying to tell me something or maybe claiming me as his. He copied everything I did, so I made sure what I did was worth copying.

I left Esperanza, Claudia, and Little Bit in a hotel room in downtown Atlanta. I told them I didn’t know when I would be back; I was going to a friend’s concert.

“You know *Ron Matthews*?” Claudia couldn’t believe it when she saw the ticket.

“I’ve known him since we were little kids.”

“Wow! He’s so hot! Is he all that in person?”

He was all that and more than I dared explain. “I think you would say so.”

* * *

“We’ll be fine,” Claudia insisted when I hesitated to leave.

“Order whatever you want from room service, and if you need anything else, call the concierge.”

“Quit worrying, Mr. Jed. Just go.”

“And call me on the cell phone if there’s any problem.”

“I will.”

I was so nervous I could barely function. I had chosen the final night of the tour, so Ron and I could be together if he wanted that. I didn’t know if he would even agree to talk to me. I had no idea how any of it would work out because technically, we barely knew each other now. I couldn’t move on until I knew. I hadn’t reasoned it all out, and would have denied it, but I was approaching him like I would a horse. I came back and came back, trying different things. I never took no from a horse.

Ron was as irresistible on stage as he was up close. He seemed bigger than life when he walked out, and the audience went nuts. He began to sing and his screaming fans sat, entranced. I had been under that spell since I was a little boy.

About midway through the concert, my cell phone vibrated. I got up and went into the lobby and called Claudia.

"I can't get him to go to sleep until he talks to you. He keeps saying *Daddy, Daddy.*"

"Okay, put him on."

"Daddy."

"What's the matter, Little Bit?"

"Daddy."

"Daddy loves you, Son. Now go to bed, okay?"

"Daddy love." The words were clear. "Daddy love."

"I love you, too, Son. I'll see you tomorrow no matter what happens tonight."

I went back into the concert thinking that the most important thing was that Ron be right for my son, too. I couldn't believe fame would have changed him, but something was wrong. I couldn't bear to think it wasn't going to work.

* * *

I stood backstage with a lot of fans who were pressing to see Ron. Finally I noticed someone who appeared to work for him, or at least looked official, and I pushed my way towards him.

"Can you get me in to see Ron Matthews?"

"It depends on if he wants to see you, sir."

"Will you ask him if he'll see Jed Petersen?"

The man was gone a while, but finally came back and motioned for me to follow him. He left me at a door that I presumed was Ron's dressing room.

I knocked.

"Come in."

There was a man with Ron, and I sensed I had interrupted an argument. I hesitated to pour my heart out in front of a stranger, but I wasn't going to leave.

"I want to talk, Ron."

The man moved towards him as if to establish his claim.

"Justin, this is Jed." Ron introduced us.

So this was Justin, the one hundred percent pure horse's ass.

"He's an old friend," Ron continued to Justin, "and I'd like to speak to him in private."

"He can't just come in here and—"

"Please, Justin, I'm just asking for five minutes."

It was better than nothing.

Justin gave Ron a look. "Five minutes." He held up his five jeweled fingers to emphasize it, but he left us alone.

"Do you love him, Ron?"

"Jed, I want you to leave me alone. I don't know how much clearer I can be. We had something once, but that's over. Shit, Jed, it was over years ago."

"You said you were waiting for me."

"Jesus Christ! That was a long damn time ago."

"Why are you living with a man who doesn't love you?"

"It's a long story. We're trying to make it work. I already told you this. I asked you to leave me alone and I'd think out of respect, you'd do it, if only for old times' sake."

"I still love you, Ron."

"It's too late for that, Jed. I really don't give a damn." He felt around on himself. "Let me see what I can find." He brought his hands up, palms out. "Nope, sorry, I got nothin'. I really don't give a damn."

"I don't know the man you've become."

"You got that right, Buckaroo." He watched me a moment and then his attitude changed, and he seemed sad. "I'm addicted to pills, Jed."

"What pills?"

"Pills to calm down and pills to wake up, pills to keep me working and not slow down, pills to make me happy. You know—*pills*."

"You could quit."

"That's the point—I can't quit them."

"You could, Ron, you just need some help. I know you could quit."

He laughed a derisive laugh. I had never heard anything like that out of him before and it hurt. Maybe it was too late.

"I'm not some pitiful horse you can save."

Let me love you.

"You're settling for a man who doesn't love you. Why?"

"You can't talk to me about settling, Jed. You're the one who was living with a woman and couldn't

admit to being gay."

"Can't you understand that I was young and I was *raped* and terrorized? I didn't think I would even survive it, and for a long time I hadn't."

"I'm sorry, Jed. You want us to become the Matthews Brothers or the Petersen Brothers, but I don't think that will ever happen."

"Oh hell no, Ron. That isn't what I want. We won't be any kind of brothers. If I had my way, people would know the truth. They wouldn't be able to look at us and not know it."

Ron watched me intently and in a way that made me think he still gave a damn, a great big damn.

"We could go somewhere, Ron, just you and me. We could figure out if what's between us is still good. When I look at you, I know it is. You can tell me you're not interested, but your eyes say different."

He looked away. "You always were the stubbornest man I ever knew."

"We used to get our bodies so tangled up I couldn't tell where I ended and you began. I'd just be still, breathing you in, and I'd think that I always wanted it to be like that, smashed up so close to you that we were one person."

"Jesus, Jed." The look in his eyes was soft, the way it used to be when he looked at me.

Ron was moving towards me when Justin came back into the room.

"Your five minutes is up, cowpoke."

Damn, I hated him.

"What makes you think I'm a cowpoke?" I wasn't wearing my Stetson or boots and was dressed like everyone else at the concert.

"You have a big spread somewhere out West, don't you—with cows and bulls? Aren't you a champion bull rider or somethin'? Or was that bull shitter?"

"Shut up, Justin." Ron stood between us. Justin was smaller than Ron but bigger than me. Still, I thought I could take him and was about to try.

"Yipee-ki-yi-yay, get along, little doggies."

Ron ignored him. "Where's Little Bit?"

"He's in a hotel room with a babysitter. What

about Luke?"

"Same deal."

"Let's get going, Ron," Justin interrupted. "They're ready to take you out the back. Say good-night to the blue-eyed cow....*boy.*" He took Ron by the arm and pulled him away from me and back to the pills and a loveless life. I didn't want him to go.

"I'll see you, Jed."

"Soon," I said, but I didn't think I could stomach it.

When the door slammed behind me, I leaned against it for thirty seconds. *Let me love you, Ron,* I thought towards him. But he was not an injured horse. I finally got that and moved on.

* * *

I went home to my big spread in the West, with its cows and bulls. *Home, home on the range.*

Little Bit slept soundly on the way which enabled me to make plans. Before the plane landed in El Paso, I knew the Worthington Ranch was going out of the cattle business. It would now be known as the Kathleen Petersen Horse Sanctuary, no more Worthington name. My Kitty had never been like them and neither would her son. We would train, heal, and re-educate horses, and the people who cared about them.

The Worthington House would be turned into guest rooms for use in conjunction with seminars. It would look different and be different, and I would call it something else as soon I figured out what.

Any cowboys who wanted to stay on would learn what I knew, and together we'd figure out things none of us knew. The ones that didn't like the new plan were free to move on, no hard feelings.

I was giving up the fine Worthington name in beef and bulls, both lucrative enterprises that had run their course on my ranch. There were plenty of other cattle in West Texas. So I was really, finally, completely giving up bulls. No more bullshit.

I met with Little Mike about my plans. He wasn't even surprised and said all of the cowboys had seen this coming for a long time. That part of it wasn't as hard as I had thought it would be. Some of the men left

and some stayed, and I began training them to my way of understanding and working with horses.

We started with taming colts. I wanted to be able to send a couple of my cowboys to neighboring ranches to train their colts free, as an introduction to our methods. If we could get other ranchers to start out on the right foot with their colts, that would be significant progress. Our message was kindness and cooperation instead of intimidation and slavery.

During the year that followed my visit to Ron, I wrote a book. It wasn't a bestseller or anything, and it joined a lot of other books on the subject of gentle horse training, but it was an outlet for me and something to do with my nights. I was about as lonesome as a man can stand, and sometimes I couldn't stand it.

There were times when I rode Midnight all night long, bareback, the way he liked it. Other times I rode Indio, or hiked by moonlight or penlight. The only thing that kept me sane, I think, was my son. Without him I don't know what would have happened to me. Maybe I would've gone back to bull riding and become a bow-legged, skinny-assed, old-before-my-time cowboy, hanging on the fringes and beating my chest about how great I'd been. Well, probably not.

I traveled some, in connection with the book and to hold training seminars. I was enthusiastic about teaching others what I'd learned about horses. Sometimes my travel took me to work with horses whose stories I couldn't resist.

Around every corner I expected to find a man to fall in love with, but I must have been turning the wrong corners.

I couldn't forget how Ron had wished on the stars. It wasn't so much what he'd said, but what had been between us. I tried not to think of it. I willed it away but it wouldn't go. I was Patsy Cline in chaps.

* * *

One day we were working in a corral near Kathleen Petersen headquarters when my secretary came out to get me. "You have to speak with this man about his horse. He's desperate."

I thought if he had gotten past Angie he must

have a good sob-story because she had gotten good at filtering calls. Somebody had to protect me from myself.

I picked up the phone in the office. "Jed Petersen."

"Mr. Petersen, I'm Bob Kensington, the manager of the Rolling Hills Ranch here in the Great Smoky Mountains. We're on the North Carolina side. One of our horses was hit by a semi and injured, but his legs are okay. He belongs to the owner's kids, and he'll pay you anything you ask to come save him."

"I'm not a veterinarian. What does the vet say?"

"He wanted to put him down but that was a while ago. Now his injuries are just about healed, but he's wild and hateful. He appears to have forgotten the kids that love him and won't let anyone near."

"I can't come that far. There are guys much closer to you. A really good one is located in Asheville. If you'll hold I'll get you some names."

"Wait—no, the owner insists that you come. He—uh—read your book and, uh—has a good feeling about you."

I hesitated. This would be a chance to take Little Mike with me and show him what I did for a horse that had been severely injured. Still, it was too far and I had other horses to consider, and my son.

"Money is no object, Mr. Petersen."

I could have said the same thing. My work was not about money and I was fortunate, thanks to Kitty, that I had plenty of it.

"I'll come." I let my heart make the decision before my brain could stop it. "I'll assess the situation and if I think I can help him, I'll want to bring my ranch foreman. Can you put us up?"

"Sure, we have plenty of room. About the money—"

"I can't say what it'll cost until I meet the horse."

"That's fine."

"I'll leave here in a week."

"Just call me so we can have someone meet you at the airport."

"Mr. Kensington, I have a small son. If I think this is going to take a while, I'll want to bring him and

his nanny, too."

"Whatever you wish, Mr. Petersen. We have plenty of room."

He gave me all the details, like which airport and how far it was from the ranch. The place sounded in the middle of nowhere, but it also sounded beautiful, and in a state I had never seen or even thought about.

He gave me a website address and I looked at his ranch. It was different, night and day, from West Texas. There was so much green it was fearsome. The mountains looked hazy and were covered by trees and other green vegetation, and not naked and sticking up in jagged pieces like the mountains at home.

That was okay; I would go anyway.

Chapter 41

Humidity was the first thing I noticed about North Carolina. And it was raining. The second thing was the excessively green countryside, a result of the rain.

The ranch manager, Bob Kensington, came for me himself. On the way to the ranch the rain turned to snow. It was February and we were heading into mountains, so I couldn't hold inclement weather against anyone. Anyway, I was dressed warmly enough.

Kensington asked me to call him Bob. I told him to drop the sir and call me Jed. He was years older than me and calling me sir seemed wrong.

As he drove he told me about the Great Smoky Mountains, that the name came from the natural fog that hangs over the range and looks like smoke plumes from a distance. It was especially noticeable in the mornings and after a rain he said. He spoke fondly of North Carolina, and said he had grown up in the mountains, the son of a national park ranger.

He spoke eloquently about the Rolling Hills Ranch, too. It reminded me of riding through Kitty's ranch with her for the first time.

Bob said the owner and his children were gone and would be back the following day. That was good; I wanted to see how the horse reacted to them. But before that, I would get to know him a little on my own.

It took a long time to get there, and by the time we did it was snowing harder and the ranch was buried in white. It was beautiful, and silent enough to hear your heart beat.

* * *

So I was in another barn in a different state with a different horse. Bob had invited me to get settled first and come for a drink, but I was anxious to get started. The poor horse had already waited too long.

When Bob let me out at the barn he said he would put my suitcase in my room at the house.

"What's his name?" I asked as I got out of the truck.

"Whose?"

"The horse."

"Oh—it's Hope."

"Did the kids name him that?"

"Does it matter?"

"Well, no, I just wondered."

"The owner named him."

There was room for several horses, but there was only one. The barn was well lit once I turned on the lights, but he stood in a shadowy corner with eyes so wide that was all I saw at first. He wasn't in a stall, which I didn't like but couldn't change at that moment. He had backed up as far as he could get when he heard the doors open. I could hear his anxious breathing.

"Okay, Hope, I'm just going to move close enough to see what you look like."

The horse shifted his weight as I approached but didn't go anywhere. He let me come to within a few feet of him. I stopped and sat on some hay bales to observe him. He went back to browsing the floor of the barn but kept a watchful eye on me. He was an old guy. And he wasn't injured, not in the way Bob had described. I pondered that. Where was the horse that had been hit by a semi?

After a while I stood and approached him, speaking softly. "You haven't been hit by a truck, have you, old boy?"

He let me get close, where I could really see him, and he had no injuries. He was on the skinny side, and was probably arthritic, but other than being old, I couldn't see anything wrong. He backed away from me but when I offered my hand he nuzzled it. I definitely had the wrong horse. I felt along his neck, back, legs,

and flanks, and then stroked his face. "Good boy," I whispered. I scratched his head, then along his neck, back, legs, and flanks again, loving him with my hands.

Suddenly there was a voice behind me. "I would give anything—everything I have in this world—if you would do that to me."

I whirled around. "Ron!"

He stood there with snow on his cap, grinning.

I made one step towards my old love. "There's no injured horse, is there?"

"I didn't think you'd come this far except for a horse."

"You didn't even ask. I don't like it that you *sent* for me. I don't want to play games, Ron."

He shrugged his big football player shoulders. "This is no game, Jed."

"What a big idiot you are. You could've picked up the phone and said, 'Jed, I want you to come see me.' You know I could never tell you no."

"I couldn't take that chance, so I made up a story."

"Where did you get this poor ol' fella?"

"I bought him at an auction."

"I thought the story sounded a little like the *Horse Whisperer,* beloved horse hit by a semi, horrific injuries but kept alive for the sake of the child, damaged psyches all over the place. A pathetic animal *and* its sad owners were brought back to life by a handsome blond cowboy. I think that part was played by Robert Redford."

"That's the one."

"You couldn't have come up with something more original?"

"Would you have come if I said I was the one who needed you, Jed?"

"Yes, I would've come."

I didn't move any closer to Ron, though I wanted to. I wanted him to come to me. I was treating him like a damaged horse. I might've laughed about it except it was unconscious and anyway, blood was rushing out of my brain.

"Now that you're here, I don't know what to say."

"Just tell me what's in your heart, Ron." I sat on a bale and patted the space next to me. "Come sit with me."

He swiped snow off his shoulders and shook out his cap. "I never stopped loving you, Jed. I lied about that, and I never stopped waiting for you, either. I didn't want to admit that because you hurt me so bad. I wanted to hate you, but I couldn't."

I waited quietly, wanting to hear everything he had to say on the subject of us.

"I bought this land with money from my first number one hit. I bought it for you. I don't know if you'll believe it, but it's true. The song was about you, so I thought it'd be appropriate. If it hadn't been for you, I would never have written any good songs."

For a second I thought we were going to kiss, but then he spoke again. "I built the house later but I never came here unless I was alone or with Luke. I couldn't think of it as anything but yours. This land would be great for horses, and I thought you'd love it. I didn't know you'd end up owning half of Texas."

He looked down at his hands. "Before, when I was still struggling to make it, I planned to do this kind of movie cowboy thing where I swaggered in to wherever you were and swept you away with me. I thought you'd be totally Patsy Cline about something like that."

I laughed. He really knew me.

"I was going to impress your sweet, romantic side."

"So why didn't you?"

"My music career took off, and you didn't appear to have any interest in me, and then the next thing I knew I was caring for Rhonda and then Luke, and I had this boyfriend around my neck, and my life kept moving out of control." He sighed. "And the pills, the pills happened."

"Did you quit them?"

"Oh yes, I quit them. It was so hard, Jed. I quit Justin, too, but that was easy."

"What happened?"

"I can't believe you! Do you even know what a radio is? What about a TV, or magazines? Don't you

ever read *People?*"

"I guess I stay behind on most things."

"Justin outted me to the country music community and sued me for several million dollars. I don't *have* several million dollars, Jed."

"What happened?"

"He made an ass of himself and got nothing for his efforts. There was a big scandal about me and 'my men.' I was supposedly doing everybody in Nashville who wasn't nailed down—except nobody in Nashville is gay, to hear them tell it. So then they started on men in Hollywood."

He laughed, but it wasn't a happy one. "I didn't have any men unless they were talking about fantasies involving a blue-eyed buckaroo. It died down after a bit, and things moved on. My sales and bookings plummeted, and then I just dropped out and came here to lick my wounds. I got to thinking about you, and here we are."

"Who is Bob Kensington?"

"He's a park ranger over in the Great Smoky Mountains National Park. We met because I hang out there since I got shoved off the country music merry-go-round."

"Where's Luke?"

"He's with his grandparents in Fort Stockton."

"So is anyone else here?"

"We're alone," he said softly, and the quarter moon scar on his cheek rose and glowed. Again, I thought we would kiss. It was so hard to wait, but he wasn't quite finished.

Ron cleared his throat. "I've been selling some songs under the name of Luke Petersen. I hope you don't mind that I use your last name, but it makes me feel happy when I see it."

I took his hand in mine. "I don't mind."

"Wouldn't those macho, tobacco-spitting country singers be amazed to know their hit-making songs come straight from the heart of a gay man?"

"It seems like they would figure it out. You're way past Patsy Cline."

He grinned.

"Maybe someday," I said, "people will understand that it doesn't matter who you love as long as you do."

"I've waited a long damn time to live with you, Jed."

"Me too, Ron."

We watched each other, and I felt the same desperate arousal I'd felt that long-ago day in the lake.

"I can't believe you still wear that old Stetson. Couldn't you afford something a little less beat-to-shit looking?"

"I could, and I have others. I won at least twenty-five of them bull riding, but this one is my favorite."

"Well you sentimental ol' cowboy." He pulled me against him.

"Well," I said into his chest, "now that I'm here, what are you going to do with me?"

He crooked an arm around my neck. "Would you like to see your house?"

About the author:

Elizabeth A. (Beth) Garcia has lived for more than thirty years in the Big Bend country of far west Texas. She has hiked, rafted, explored, and earned a living in this wild desert-mountain land near the Rio Grande, on the border of the United States and Mexico. It was experiencing the deep canyons, creosote-covered bajadas, and stark, jagged mountains; the wide-open spaces and dark, starry nights that eventually brought her to writing.

The Reluctant Cowboy is her third published novel.

One Bloody Shirt at a Time and *The Beautiful Bones* are the first two novels in the Deputy Ricos tales series. Stay in touch for the next volume!

Visit Beth's Facebook page:
http:/www.facebook.com/ElizabethAGarciaAuthor
Website: www.deputyricos.com
e-mail the author: deputyricos@yahoo.com

Made in the USA
Coppell, TX
13 January 2021